Danse de la Folie

Also by Sherwood Smith

RONDO ALLEGRO

Danse de la Folie

Sherwood Smith

First published 2012 by Book View Café Publishing Cooperative
P.O. Box 1624
Cedar Crest, NM 87008-1624
www.bookviewcafe.com

Print edition 2018
ISBN 978-1-61138-740-7

Cover by Scarlett from photo by RuslanOmega
Interior design by Marissa Doyle

Danse de la Folie

One

IT IS SAID THAT the quadrille was first a military exercise performed by pairs of horsemen before the admiring court. Only later did it migrate to France in the form of a lively dance performed by two couples in squares.

The more stately quadrille that came to England was still a few years off when my story begins; imagine the opening strains playing a sprightly air in celebration of the hunting season in the first year of the new nineteenth century, deep in the county of Hampshire.

My first heroine, the Honorable Miss Clarissa Harlowe, smiled to discover with the morning post the new edition of Wordsworth's *Lyrical Poems*. She looked forward to taking advantage of the last gasp of summery weather by reading in the garden, but before she could excuse herself, the butler entered the ladies' breakfast room with a summons from his lordship for his eldest daughter.

Lord Chadwick seldom interfered in the lives of his offspring. Clarissa's step-mother and her half-siblings looked surprised—everyone exhibited surprise except Aunt Sophia, who made a business of folding her napkin, with enough smugness in her countenance to serve as warning.

Clarissa went straight to the library, a room only used for interviews. Her father stood before the fire, a tall, fair-haired, hawk-nosed man dressed by preference in riding clothes. Not ordinarily given to any pursuits that, as he put it, "rattled his brain," he eyed his eldest daughter with brow-wrinkled bafflement.

"Here, girl," he greeted her, "that's a fine gown."

Clarissa smiled a little at the spurious compliment, and curtseyed. "Thank you, Papa. You sent for me?"

"Now, girl — Clarissa — you're deuced — ah, very modest, which is what everyone wants in a girl, and you've prodigiously shining parts."

To hear herself thus complimented for precisely those intellectual qualities she'd been scolded for by her aunt might have inspired another smile, except Clarissa now suspected she was not going to like the intent of this interview.

"Shining parts, reading, and the like," Lord Chadwick added, with a vague wave of his riding whip toward the undisturbed books resting on the shelves around them.

He eyed his daughter's inquiring expression, harrumphed, and took refuge in defense. "Your mother was always buried in a book. Which is why I let your grandmother the duchess pick your governesses, though monstrous interfering I found it, and as for that sour-faced French one, hey day! What a fright that woman put me in every time she poked her nose into a room. As if your stepmama couldn't have found a better... well! What's past is past, and I don't mean to be criticizing her grace."

For a moment an expression akin to fear furrowed his features, as if the redoubtable dowager were listening through the keyhole, and he hastened on. "But here I thought it settled that you would make a match with the Wilburfolde boy. Good thing on all sides. Doubtless your grandmother thinks so as well, if only we knew," he added somewhat hastily.

Ordinarily Clarissa would have been diverted. She alone of her family was very fond of her awe-inspiring grandmother, but now with her future at stake she turned the subject back, asking quietly, "Has Lord Wilburfolde called on you to that end, Papa?"

Lord Chadwick took a couple of hasty strides across the room, then paused to kick at a log in the fireplace with the tip of a glossy boot. "Yes, with his Mama. Yesterday, while you and the girls was at the vicar's. Made his offer, with prodigious punctilio. I said I'd speak to you, and send your answer over this afternoon."

"Did you inform him that I have stated that I have no present wish to marry, Papa?"

"I did. Lady Wilburfolde put that down to modesty. Said she likes that in a lady. Wouldn't want anyone at The Castle who was not *bien élevée,* and you were the finest young lady in the parish, and there was a lot more on that order. Here, you don't mean to refuse, do you?" At Clarissa's nod, he frowned. "I can't write that! Devil take it, what a monstrous position to put me in."

"Papa," Clarissa said softly, "when I was small you promised I should not be made to marry anyone I did not favor."

"Aye, and so I promised all you girls." He flung his riding whip on a side table and ran his fingers through his thinning blond locks. "But you know, you've got to marry *someone,* and out of all my pack of brats I thought you was the least headstrong and had the most sense. What's against young Wilburfolde?"

"Nothing at all," Clarissa said, though she was thinking of Lady Wilburfolde. But it seemed indelicate as well as impolite to refuse a gentleman because one had taken a strong dislike to his mother. "We've scarcely met above twice. But I was serious when I said that I do not wish to marry."

Her father eyed her with baffled exasperation; the truth was, of all his pack of brats she caused him the least trouble. She wasn't a Diamond like the rest, so one would have thought she'd be glad to find a leg-shackle ready to hand. "Every girl says that," he replied. "Until she's asked. The females are all agreed it's a good match."

Clarissa suppressed the urge to retort that *they* could marry him. She apologized, temporized, and endured the short-lived storm of her father's temper, for she knew that it arose out of vexation, not real anger. Her Papa was too fond of his family (and too indolent) to remain angry long.

Clarissa was dismissed to resume her breakfast while Lord Chadwick went out to ride his temper into cheer again. As expected, her aunt scolded with all the fretful vehemence of the person whose cherished project has been smashed. Aunt Sophia's tangled sentences about gratitude, expectations, and the care older and wiser heads took for heedless youth showed no sign of coming to a natural end, moving Clarissa's pretty step-mother, who cherished peace even more than Papa, to murmur, "Clarissa, dear, did I not understand that you were agreed on this marriage?"

"Not I, Mama," Clarissa replied firmly.

Lady Chadwick blinked, then turned to look at Aunt Sophia. "Well! Odd, how one gets these impressions... wasn't it you, Mrs. Latchmore, who said so?"

Clarissa kept quiet. She knew that her aunt had been busy on her behalf, and while she sympathized with her aunt—no one could wish to end up an indigent widow, living on her younger brother's charity—she was not willing to sacrifice her life so that her aunt might make herself out to be a matchmaker, a person of interest in county society.

Aunt Sophia raised her voice to the pitch of righteous anger. "What, pray, is amiss with Lord Wilburfolde, that you should be so *nice* in your tastes *at your age?*"

Clarissa was caught. She could not, especially before the wide eyes of her young half-sisters, declare that she had yet to meet a gentleman with whom she wished to share anything more intimate than a book.

"I do not wish to be married," was all she said.

Two months later, Clarissa reflected on how she ought to have foreseen that a young lady setting herself up in opposition to her betters would cause her aunt to ring such a peal that Papa would take steps to restore order to his house.

Aunt Sophia ought to have foreseen that her brother would remove *all* the causes of contention.

Clarissa had always wanted to travel, but the difficulties in France had made that impossible. Papa told Clarissa that she could visit her maternal aunt while peace was talked of, and told his sister that she would be delighted to accompany her niece.

So here they were ensconced on her Papa's yacht in the middle of winter weather.

Aunt Sophia put her cup down with a clatter.

"Clarissa!" Her voice sounded like the last, quivering gasp of a dying Christian Martyr. "My love," she added, clasping her hands fervently to her impressive, lace-ruched bosom.

The drama of this gesture was missed by Clarissa, who was gazing out the broad stern windows at the last of the harbor, diminishing behind them.

"Clar-issa!"

The thrilling moan on the first syllable once again evoked arenas and raging lions, but the pettish rise of *issa* made Clarissa think of a shed full of squabbling hens.

The older woman lay back on the cushions, assuming the look of patient suffering that she had demonstrated before her mirror when her vexatious brother insisted she must go on this horrid jaunt.

But Clarissa saw only that her aunt's claim of faintness accorded a trifle oddly with the rich crimson of her plump cheeks. "Your pardon, Aunt?"

"Oh, Clarissa," Aunt Sophia moaned.

"I'm sorry, Aunt Sophia. I am looking forward to traveling, and seeing a little of the world."

"In *winter*, with French revolutionaries hiding in every bush? I just pray we do not end up on the guillotine!"

"I do not believe that the French would use the guillotine against English ladies." Clarissa leaned forward earnestly. "Since peace is all but declared, this is the only opportunity to travel that has come my way, I am grateful that Papa furnished this opportunity. If you are ill, dear aunt, you could return home. I really believe that my father's steward, my maids, and the men who sail the yacht, will see me safely across the Channel into Holland, and Aunt Beaumarchais' hands."

Aunt Sophia gave a loud, comprehensive sniff, which effectively expressed her disdain for this host of nominal persons. "I would be Failing in my Duty if I did not see you safely there." The capital letters were clearly enunciated. "No, I do *not* wish to go, but no sacrifice is too large for my family! *I* was taught that a true lady always performs her duty. Just as I did when my sainted Papa made a match for me with my sainted Latchmore, though I hardly knew him—had not met him above twice, and that in company."

Clarissa looked down at her gloved hands. "Yes, aunt."

Snapping her fan out, Aunt Sophia flapped irritably at her purple cheeks. "Many a female at your age would feel grateful for any offer, much less one to be so highly desired."

Clarissa said, "I would feel grateful if I was wishful to marry. But I am not."

"So say you now. But trust me, when you are my age, or even the age of poor Miss Frease, obliged to accept Sir Pericles Denby, and who is to say that he will be any better on his third marriage? She will be forced to turn a deaf eye to his... his tendencies toward unmarital felicity. There is nothing humorous in this."

Clarissa tried to smother her guilty laughter. "I beg your pardon, aunt. I agree about Sir Pericles, it was just Miss Frease's unhearing eyes that—"

Aunt Sophia said impatiently, "I have always sincerely pitied Olivia Frease, though she is *not* biddable, and indeed has said she never *wished* to be married. But when the old baronet died, there she was, a burden that her brother's wife declared they would do well without. So there she was."

There she was without the means to set up her own establishment, Clarissa thought. But it would be indelicate to remind her aunt that this was not her own case; though she did not know precisely the extent of the fortune she was to inherit, she did know that to mention it would vex Aunt Sophia, whose widowhood had found her left with nothing.

Aunt Sophia was already vexed. "You are nearly five-and-twenty, and you do *not* have the looks of your sweet sisters. It was no mistake that Hetty went off in her first year last spring, and it shall be the same for Amelia this year. And when you stand by her, even the immensity of your dowry, which I always told your Papa the amount of which would only cause you to set yourself up unbecomingly, and it is just as I foretold..." Aunt Sophia paused, trying in vain to recover the thread of her discourse. "Well," she finished with a twitch of her shoulders. "I have *done* with you. I believe I'd be better employed trying to compose myself a little before we are sunk, or attacked by howling Thermidorians."

"Then I shall remove myself, and permit you to rest in comfort."

Clarissa smiled gently on her fuming aunt, and slipped into

the smaller cabin outside the large one. Her maids, waiting there, were sorry to observe the familiar faint line between their mistress's brows, but when Clarissa turned their way, it was with her ready smile.

"Mr. Bede says we'll sail at once, Miss," Rosina said. "Becky has your wrap right here, should you be wishful to take a turn in the air." Rosina indicated the deck.

Clarissa smiled gratefully. "That is exactly what I was about to do, and I didn't think of a wrap. Thank you."

In comparison to her four half-sisters' beauty, no one but her fondest relatives could find anything to compliment outside of her classic nose and forehead, and her elegant posture. Her eyes were well spaced, but not cornflower blue, and as for her hair, her grandmother had stated firmly that tresses a quiet shade of chestnut were not as *showy* as her sisters' guinea-colored curls, one of many hints that her grace did not find Lord Chadwick's second wife as highly-bred as his first.

Clarissa, very aware that her step-mother's pedigree was perfectly respectable, had grown up regarding these matters with a sense of humor. How else could one regard such absurdities? It was either that or descend into a fretful and futile temper against the vagaries of fate, as demonstrated (for instance) by her aunt.

It was also true that Clarissa took little interest in her own appearance—there were days when she did not glance into the pier glass once from the moment she woke up until she was ready for bed.

It galled Rosina, once her mother's maid and now hers, that to keep the peace Clarissa permitted her aunt to have the ordering of her clothes. The dresses that Aunt Sophia chose were meant to make Clarissa look as young as her sisters, but the whites and pinks that looked well on the younger girls turned Clarissa sallow, and aged her unmercifully.

Clarissa peered into the clouded glass, which did not hide the limpness of the short side-curls dangling next to her long face. She sighed and went out, watched by her silent maids.

Her heart full, Rosina muttered to Becky, the young lady's maid in training, "It breaks my heart, it does, to see her head dressed so ill-suited."

Becky agreed. *Dressing mutton for lamb just makes the ewe look the older next or nigh a real lamb*, Becky's mother had stated bluntly, as she gave the butter churn a hard wring.

"At least this blue kerseymere looks well, and not a word could the old tabby gainsay, when the lengths were sent by her grace the Duchess-grandma herself," Rosina said with satisfaction to Becky, who—the perfect assistant—always agreed with her senior.

Clarissa stood on the deck, watching the last of Folkestone Harbour vanish. She loved the swell and sinking of the billows, the salty bite of brine, the ever-changing patterns of the sea in motion. So this was why men left their warm homes for the sea! She turned around once, looking up in admiration at the complication of ropes and spars and curving sails. How glorious!

Mr. Bede, Lord Chadwick's steward, saw her looking about, and recognized in his lord's quiet daughter one who had fallen instantly in love with the sea. No stranger to this spectacle (Mr. Bede's brother had run away from a print shop at fourteen, and was even now a master aboard a tea wagon on the far side of the world), he pointed out several sights to her and chatted genially about travels he'd made before the French ruined such jaunts, until the weather turned foul. As the swell began to increase, he recommended she step back into the cabin.

Clarissa found her aunt breathing in stertorous sleep. Grateful for the respite, she cast aside her bonnet and muff, and picked up the new edition of Wordsworth's *Lyrical Ballads*. She read and dreamed over the poetry until the light began to fade. *How I wish it were possible for a lady to own and sail a ship*, she thought wistfully.

The sun was setting, and wisps of fog drifted across the dark grey water, bringing the enclosing gloom of gray sky meeting grey sea even closer. The prospect of two months of travel cheered her immensely, in spite of the fact that Aunt Beaumarchais's letters had made plain her old-fashioned respect for fathers ordaining suitable marriages for their daughters.

But as the fog thickened and the sun set somewhere behind

them, she tucked herself up more firmly, finally nodding off over the book.

She woke abruptly when she heard a loud cry from somewhere outside the cabin.

"HO! LIGHTS AHEAD, LIGHTS—"

The shouter was interrupted as the yacht lurched, viciously in a terrible sound of splintering wood and groaning metal. Aunt Sophia woke screaming. Clarissa, trying to stand, was entangled in blankets and shawls and lost her balance. As the ship rolled, she pitched forward toward the door, hit her head on a low bulkhead, and slid into darkness.

Two

SHE WOKE TO THE scent of strong cologne, which made her head throb. Opening her eyes, she looked up into a stranger's face.

"Just lie still," the stranger whispered. "You've had a knock on the head. At first we did not see you, as someone had flung blankets over you where you lay on the decking. But the older woman sent us back to look for you."

Clarissa's gaze traveled over the face, noticing in a detached way that its features were beautiful. Large hazel eyes reflected a wavering light with a kindly expression. Long fringed dark lashes framed these eyes, with winged dark brows above, and below, a fine nose and a mouth beautifully curved. These features graced a heart-shaped face that came to a smallish but well-defined chin, determinedly set. Yes, it was a beautiful face.

Clarissa then noticed that tendrils of black hair were escaping from a battered cap, and that a worn and outmoded great-coat covered the rest of her rescuer. He was a boy, no, a young gentleman. His small hands, as he gently wiped Clarissa's brow with the damp handkerchief, were smooth and light in their touch.

"No doubt you have sisters," Clarissa said in a faint but conversational voice.

Instant laughter quirked the hazel eyes. "If you wish," the soft voice soothed.

Clarissa glanced beyond the boy to a lantern set on a shelf. Her host said, "The fog was very thick, and your yacht ran into our cutter. No one was hurt, though your yacht I fear is too badly damaged. We will take you to Tarval Hall."

"Tarval Hall?"

"Our house. It is—"

"Kit!" The cabin door opened with some force. Clarissa winced as a voice said in a strangled whisper, "You were *supposed* to lie low. Now he'll ride rusty, and no mistake."

Her companion looked up apologetically. "Oh, Ned, I *couldn't* let her wake up, and not know what happened."

"Hey day! Come help me with the—the trim. We still have to bring her in, and the wind is up something fierce."

Kit got to his feet with a swift and apologetic smile, and left.

Clarissa tried to move her aching head as little as possible while taking in her surroundings. Her gown had been thoughtfully smoothed about her ankles, and a pillow put beneath her head. Where were Mr. Bede, Rosina, Aunt Sophia and the others?

Presently the door was opened again with a clatter, and this time two men entered. A lantern swinging in one's hand played light crazily over his grizzled features as he said, "Come, missy, and pull your cloak about ye."

As Clarissa got slowly to her feet the second figure sprang into the room to offer an arm. The light of the lantern on the shelf showed Kit's concerned face. The ship under her feet was rolling unmercifully, and Clarissa fought for balance.

As soon as they stepped up on deck the cold air turned into a strong, icy wind. Sleet ripped at her clothes, and yanked her hair free of its loosened pins. Clarissa squinted about her, and Kit shouted, "This way! The rowboat is waiting."

"My aunt," Clarissa replied, but the wind shredded her feeble voice at her lips.

"Please! You must come away!" Kit shouted.

"My aunt—my father's steward." Clarissa lifted her voice.

"They're in the other boat," a new voice spoke at her elbow. She looked up as lightning flickered, meeting a searching gaze, grayish green, the color of the sea. This gentleman was older than Kit. "I'm desolately sorry for the accident but the yacht is sinking, and we must get you to safety," he shouted in the accents of a gentleman.

The grizzled man took her arm, and guided her to the side of the yacht. There was only a rope ladder, which swung as the ship rolled and tossed. Sprays of water splashed up to sting her face. "Can you manage?" Kit called, his voice high.

Clarissa gripped her skirts firmly at the knee with one hand, too frightened to reply. With her other hand she grasped the rail and eased one foot over the side, feeling for the swaying rope. The older man took a strong grip on one of her arms as she felt her way down, rung by rung. The wind pulled at her, and the movement of the ship made it seem she would fall into the darkly boiling water below, and be lost forever.

But then someone yelled, "Hi there! Drop now!" as arms clasped around her middle. She was lowered to a wooden bench in a pitching rowboat. Other figures were dim lumps about her; there was a high, thin sound, like a kitten in a closet, which she recognized as Aunt Sophia's wailing voice.

The rowboat was pushed from the side of the cutter, and it seemed that the wind redoubled its fury. Clarissa could not discern any division between the high sea-waves and the low and thunderous clouds.

Aunt Sophia sat as rigid as a stone, and so Clarissa took hold of her, using her own weight to try to get her aunt to move with the movement of the boat.

Clarissa was frightened, more than she had ever been in her life, but even as the boat was tossed and huge spumes of winter-cold water splashed across their faces she was aware of a feeling of exhilaration.

Two men rowed mightily, often ruddering the little craft as the storm flung them toward the shore. Then the men jumped over the sides, and held tightly to the boat so that the fast breakers would not push it to crash on the strand.

The rowboat beached itself with a swift motion, jarring them from their benches. Aunt Sophia fell, shrieking, and would not get up. Clarissa tried but could not budge the heavy, rain-soaked woman. Bulky-coated sailors came to Clarissa's aid, and she gestured wordlessly toward her aunt. Supported by the two men, the older woman was lifted to her feet.

Clarissa followed, joined by three bent figures: she barely recognized Rosina and Bardle, Aunt Sophia's maid, Becky behind them. They stepped carefully; their thin half-boots did not protect their feet from sharp stones.

When they stopped, Clarissa made out the welcome sight of two carriages, and horses stamping and shaking their heads. Weak yellow light flickered in several storm lamps.

One of the carriage doors was pulled open, and a lamp set on its floor. Aunt Sophia was handed in first, where she collapsed at full length across one of the seats, moaning piteously. When one of their rescuers held out a carriage rug for the women to put across their laps, Aunt Sophia snatched it, and wrapped it securely about herself.

"Aunt Sophia, you will have to make room for another," Clarissa said breathlessly as she stepped in and took the seat opposite her aunt. "It will be warmer, so." Clarissa motioned Bardle to take the place next to her aunt, and beckoned her own maids to crowd in beside her.

The lantern light shifted wildly as the man who had helped her began to shut the door. His face was obscured by a high, thick muffler and a hat pulled low over his forehead and ears. All she saw were two sea-hued eyes looking back at her appraisingly.

"I apologize for the inconvenience, ladies," the man said. It was that same gentleman. She had to admit, if only to herself, that she felt a degree of easement in this fact, though she was very well aware that persons of high degree could be as untrustworthy as anyone else.

As she studied him, he studied her.

Braced as he was for vapors and hysteria, instead he found the last of the rescued females calm, with a faint air of question in an intelligent face. She seemed unaware of her sodden clothing and hair half-tumbled down her back.

He half-stretched out a hand. "The steward said the yacht belongs to a Lord Chadwick."

"My father," Clarissa said.

"Whither were you bound?"

"To Holland," she said, her lips bluish, and the lantern light creating dancing light motes in her eyes.

"Then you were very much off course," he said, recollecting himself. "I am afraid that your luggage was lost as well as the yacht. But your Mr. Bede informs me that all persons are accounted for."

"I am truly grateful to hear that." Clarissa spoke with feeling, shivering in the cold air coming inside the coach. "May I know who is our benefactor?"

"Hardly that, in the circumstances." The man bowed with a rueful air. "I am St. Tarval, and I assure you — little as we look it — we are indeed civilized. With your permission, I will take you to my home, Tarval Hall, where my sister, Lady Catherine — " His voice betrayed a tremor of laughter. " — will look after you."

St. Tarval? Had she not heard that name before? Clarissa's head hurt too much to think past the conviction that she had not met anyone of that name. She thanked him, then before any further words could be exchanged, a man yelled incomprehensibly from somewhere outside the coach.

The gentleman touched his hat courteously, and pulled the door shut.

After a couple jerking false starts, the carriage began to move.

"Might we share that rug more evenly?" Clarissa asked her aunt. "Becky here is quite chilled."

"And leave me to die of the cold?" Aunt Sophia pulled the rug closer to her chin.

Clarissa stretched out the second rug between the rest of them, each taking a corner. She suppressed the desire to take more than her share when icy water trickled inside her sleeve, and dripped from her hair down the back of her neck.

Clarissa said, "Rosina? Becky? Are you injured?"

Even in her distress, Aunt Sophia made a soft noise of disgust. She had stated so many times that it was inappropriate to use Christian names with maids, that they would take advantage, and that it would give them airs above their station. But Clarissa had known both all her life, and refused to change now.

Rosina said, "We did not come away with the vinaigrette, but I did find your trinket box." There was a wet slap as she struck her bosom.

Clarissa smiled in the darkness. "Thank you, Rosina. Such loyalty can only be repaid in kind. You may take your pick of anything in that box, when next we are in comfort."

Rosina's shivering words of thanks were cut short by a sniff of disgust from Mrs. Latchmore, who pulled the rug over her head. Silence settled over the coach's occupants, each of whom was endeavoring unsuccessfully to stay warm.

The horses were splashing along at a good pace in spite of the wind, when they slowed, then stopped, the coach rocking. Clarissa leaned forward, listening to men's voices shouting. She could not hear the words; the door was violently pulled open, and the boy named Kit stood, clutching his lantern with one hand, the other raised to his mouth. His eyes were round with terror.

"What—" began Clarissa.

"'Tis the horrid Riding Officer," Kit said, his voice high and very near tears.

"Riding Officer?" Clarissa repeated, wondering if she ought to revise her estimation of Kit's age lower.

Kit glanced over a hunched shoulder, his under lip caught between small white teeth then he turned large, sooty-lashed eyes Clarissa's way.

"It—he knows me," he whispered, tears barely held in check, and with a sense of shock, Clarissa saw past the old coat and the breeches: Kit was a female.

Three

JUST AS CLARISSA HAD no notion of herself as heroine, she had no idea that she had just met her fellow heroine. The dance had not begun; the prelude still played. For my just-met heroines, the dark, wintry night was fraught with new dangers.

Clarissa was only thinking, a female dressed in male attire? She had never heard of such a thing, outside of the sort of plays of a hundred years previous that her governess would not permit her to read. Riding Officers, females dressed as... were they fallen in amongst thieves? Riding Officers were employed to investigate practitioners of the smuggling trade, or worse.

A single glance at Kit's terrified face, and Clarissa instinctively felt that she could dismiss the 'worse.'

The instincts of a kind heart prompted her to stretch out a hand, and grasp Kit's wet sleeve. "You must come in with us. Put off that hat," she whispered, glancing at her aunt, who still had the rug pulled about her head.

"Where should I..." Kit looked about wildly.

"Sit upon it."

Kit did as told, while Clarissa tore at the clasp of her sodden, woefully inadequate cloak.

She flung the cloak around Kit. "Tug it close," she whispered, and motioned for Becky squeeze in beside Bardle on the bench opposite. Kit sank into Becky's place next to Rosina, casting

Clarissa a grateful look before Clarissa snatched the lantern and blew out the light. She set the lantern at her feet, and pulled a fold of Rosina's cloak across her lap and over the lantern.

No one spoke. Not many minutes later, tramping feet approached, and the carriage door was opened again. A big lantern was held up, casting its light over the occupants of the carriage. A weathered man glanced inside, his eyes narrowing when he recognized Kit.

"Ho, Lady Catherine," he exclaimed.

Clarissa did not like his tone. "And who might you be?"

"My name is Talkerton, and I am on Official King's Business. And who might you be, Miss?"

"I am Miss Harlowe, daughter of Viscount Chadwick. My aunt, Mrs. Latchmore, as you see, is quite ill. Our yacht foundered. These people were kind enough to rescue us."

"That's what *he* says, or much the same, and there ain't nobbut in t'other rattler, neither."

Aunt Sophia moaned loudly again, and her head emerged from the rug. Talkerton gazed at her, and when she moaned in rising shrillness that he should help her, save her, that she was about to expire from cold, he shut the coach door rather hastily. Soon the carriage began to roll.

The women sat for a long time in silence. Presently there was the sound of wet cloth moving, and a cold hand reached across Rosina, found Clarissa's equally cold and sodden gloved one, and squeezed it. "Thank you," Kit whispered.

Clarissa said nothing, but sat back tiredly to think over the startling events of a night that seemed destined to go on forever.

The ride was long. Clarissa's headache returned, and she could not contain the chills shuddering through her body.

The carriage rolled directly to a huge door in an impressive old-fashioned columned façade. The house was lit welcomingly, and as soon as the ladies were assisted out of the carriage, they were bustled indoors and straight to the state apartments which, they were informed, were "all they had for visitors," by a fat, pleasant-faced housekeeper.

Clarissa scarcely noticed the others being escorted in different directions by unfamiliar figures. The throbbing in her head had increased. She was vaguely aware of a grand hall very much in the old style, and beyond that an antechamber with a fine vaulted, carved ceiling. She was escorted to a huge state bedchamber complete with thirty foot canopy above the bed, and a railing around. On the other side of the room stood a massive marble fireplace with a copper tub set up before it. A kitchen maid poured steaming water into the tub.

The housekeeper led her beyond to a smaller cabinet-bedchamber, with the fireplace also lit, and a more accessible bed.

"I am obliged to say, ma'am, that we are somewhat short-handed here, and I am to convey the marquess's apologies."

"I understand. Please see to my aunt, and I shall be fine lying next to this fire," Clarissa said, for she had been trained to respect her elders, and she was also disinclined to move.

She gazed into the fire, finding it helped calm some of the pounding in her head. She was vaguely aware of voices somewhere in the vast room behind her, but did not turn; Kit, shivering in her wet shirt, waistcoat, and breeches, grasped the housekeeper's plump, warm wrist. "Mrs. Finn, see to the young lady Miss Harlowe, as soon as you may. She took a nasty knock on the head, and the old one is just vaporish. Perhaps..." She gave a breathless laugh. "Perhaps you should give her brandy, and say it is cordial."

Mrs. Finn glanced into the next room, where the older woman was moaning and complaining while her sodden, shivering maid was busy chafing her hands. "You leave me to handle her, Lady Kitty," Mrs. Finn said. "Did my lord get the cargo in?"

"Yes. That is, I think so. He and Edward went back with Scott and the men to make certain. Talkerton stopped us..."

"That I know, and you may be sure I am going to speak to your brother, lord or no lord, about your taking part, dressed in that heathenish way. No good can come of it, or him either, smuggling, I make no mind what your Papa did in his day. And so I will tell him before he is much older. Now get you into some dry clothes. I directed Alice to wait upon you."

Kit fled upstairs.

Clarissa still gazed into the fire, mildly soothed by the low voices of the two women. But rouse she must, for there was a rustle and a step, and a very young housemaid bobbed a curtsy. "Miss, I am to help you, and will have a hot bath directly. And Lady Kitty, that is, Lady Catherine, she invites you to have a late supper and tea. Right here, if you wish. *And* Martha is bringing chocolate if you are wishful for some."

Clarissa must stir, and must find the words to thank this girl. It took all her strength, but her reward within the hour was to be warm and dry, wearing a borrowed gown, and swathed in a robe of softest wool.

"Are you feeling better?"

Clarissa recognized Kit, who was dressed more like a Lady Catherine—or a Lady Kitty— should be, in an old-fashioned round gown. She clutched around her shoulders a knitted shawl of wool. Her thick profusion of black curls was tied back with a ribbon, framing a heart-shaped face of such loveliness that Clarissa wondered how she ever could have mistaken her for a boy.

Kitty clasped her hands, her head tilted a little to one side, reminding Clarissa of a kitten hopeful of milk. "Did you say your name is *Clarissa* Harlowe?"

"My mother, unfortunately, was very romantical," Clarissa admitted, blushing. "By rights, one of my sisters should have been named for Mr. Richardson's interesting heroine."

Kitty said, "Mrs. Finn shall soon bring a supper on a tray, so you need not stir from the fire. She believes we should eat before retiring, as it will give us strength to resist whatever illnesses are lurking in the night air."

"Thank you," Clarissa said with real gratitude.

"I also wished to thank you for speaking up for me as you did before Mr. Talkerton. I am persuaded, that is, I know that this is not what you are used to, and I wish to explain."

Clarissa looked down at the fire. "My father has had converse with the 'Gentleman' as I believe the free traders style themselves. As for..." Her gaze flickered toward Kitty's gown and then away.

Kitty hurried into speech. "I was dressed as I was to aid my brother. I have only done so at night, when they are short-handed, for I would not dare in the light of day. It has been my job to hold the horses, but this time, I needed to go aboard to tend the helm."

Clarissa thought it ought not to be done at all, but forbore commenting. Several years of Aunt Sophia's remonstrations had engendered in her a profound dislike of expatiations from the moral summit.

Kitty, encouraged by her silence, went on. "My younger brother, Ned, says that it is horrid luck that Carlisle inherited along with an exalted title equally exalted debts. And I'm sure you must know his betrothed, that is Carlisle's, not Edward's, for Ned is not betrothed, what I mean is, you must know her in London. And so I wish to beg of you, that no word of my... Of me, or, or any of us smuggling might reach her ears." Kitty tipped her head again, looking anxious.

Clarissa hastened to assure Kitty. The urge to laugh bubbled inside her at the notion of introducing the topic of smuggling into any London conversation. But she hid it, afraid to injure Kitty's sensibilities. "To whom is your brother betrothed, pray?" she asked.

"Miss Lucretia Bouldeston." Kitty sat in the chair opposite Clarissa, observing her face.

"I think we might once have been introduced," Clarissa said slowly. "But I was not aware of a betrothal."

"Nothing has been inserted into the papers." Kitty's gaze shifted around the room. "It is more in the nature of an Understanding."

Mrs. Finn entered at that moment, leading a train of three servants.

A massive table with lion claw legs and impressive inlay was soon hidden by a damask tablecloth, and set with enough food for five men. Clarissa forced herself to eat, and discovered soon that the effort repaid her with a considerable lessening of her headache. That and Kitty's consideration (for after a reflective, wide-eyed gaze, she kept quiet) contributed to a diminishment of illness.

<hr />

Clarissa woke to the sound of Aunt Sophia's complaining voice. The side of her head ached abominably, and she did not want to get up.

But it was impossible to go back to sleep, so she opened her eyes, and discovered herself lying in a high-ceilinged chamber, with two tall windows in one wall. On another wall hung a tapestry, green with age, the figures wearing long pointed shoes and caps. She noted the dull and mossy curtains over the windows. The brocade must have been beautiful a century earlier. In fact, everything in the room not made of marble or wood seemed sadly aged and even shabby in the merciless light of a winter morning, however splendid these things once had been.

With that light came memory, and she recollected the occasion of her having heard the name St. Tarval.

It was the year previous, when the family sat at breakfast. "The old marquess is dead, St. Tarval that is," her father had said. "Quite run off his legs. He was a blade, old Theo. Wild as the devil from a boy—sent down from Eton, packed off to Europe, fought duels all across the continent, returned and who does his eye fix on, but Carlisle's black-haired daughter. She was the toast that year, wouldn't powder. She nearly started a fashion, but he ran off with her in the teeth of the Duke of Firth, who was the favorite in the betting."

Her father had laughed and wiped his eyes as Clarissa's sisters gasped and begged for more details. For them, an abduction was romantical... if the abductor had the courtesy to be handsome. "Old Carlisle *and* the duke chased 'em, you know. Never caught up till the knot had been tied two days. No turning back then. What a husband Theo must have made! But she was as wild as he was. Had the infernal impudence to name the oldest child Carlisle, after her father, who'd disowned her. They retired to his place in Kent, you know, and would be there now, for all we know, if she hadn't got herself thrown from a horse and broke her neck. He went to the devil then, so I heard, bringing home his—"

An alarming cough from Aunt Sophia had caused him to recollect his audience.

Clarissa blinked away the memory. So she was somewhere in Kent, at the estate of the marquess of St. Tarval, whose father had been a wastrel, and who now was a smuggler. And he had apparently dragged his sister into it. Her gratitude for the rescue was mixed with apprehension.

The door opened and Alice came in, bearing a tray. "Good

morning, Miss. Lady Kitty sent some tea, and I should say that she is glad to lend you a gown and anything else you might need. And she invites you to breakfast in the morning room, that I am to bring it to you if you are wishful."

"Pray convey my thanks to Lady Catherine, and inform her I shall join her as soon as possible."

Rosina entered, wearing an ill-fitting servant's gown. She laid an armload of fabric before Clarissa, saying, "Mrs. Finn, that's the housekeeper, is ever so kind. And Lady Kitty sent these for you, until your traveling gown can be cleaned and mended."

"Lady Kitty?" Clarissa asked.

Rosina blushed. "She bade me call her that herself."

"Then all is as it should be." Clarissa turned her attention to a gown of good muslin, though, like everything else in this house, it was worn.

It was also somewhat too wide, and the flounces at the hem ended closer to her ankles that to the tops of her feet. Rosina tied the sash under the bosom. When Clarissa glanced in a spotted mirror at her reflection, she observed the puckers and folds, reflecting that Lady Catherine had not seemed any larger than she, though she was certainly shorter. Then she looked closer at the striped poplin, and saw that it had been remade, probably from a *robe volante*, which meant it might not have been originally Lady Catherine's, either. Her gaze transferred to the side of her head, and then away from the purple bruise.

Alice had departed, so that Rosina could help Clarissa dress, but she reappeared and dropped a hasty curtsy, then unspooled a carefully coached message. "I am to say that his lordship sends his respects. He must needs go away on business, and he joins his sister to invite you to remain as long as you need, *but* the coach can be ordered put to if you are wishful for to leave at once."

Clarissa thanked her and sat down, her head swimming sickeningly. At no time was she comfortable closed in a coach. Now the thought was unbearable. Surely Aunt Sophia would wish to rest a day or so, as Lady Kitty's guests?

She did not. Aunt Sophia insisted upon leaving at once, a prospect that left Clarissa looking so obviously ill that Aunt Sophia hit upon the notion of traveling back into Hampshire, and sending their own carriage, plus Clarissa's clothing, back for her. No Sacrifice was considered to be Too Large, she insisted several times as Clarissa thankfully accepted this amendment.

Lady Kitty repeated her brother's invitation, with the result that, four hours later, Clarissa clasped her aunt's gloved hand as she sincerely wished her farewell.

The St. Tarval servants had labored long that night to restore her clothing to a semblance of normal, but Aunt Sophia did not appear grateful for this or for the pillow-lined, ancient berlin waiting below in the court, with Becky and Bardle already seated inside, a packed hamper between them.

"...A more tumbledown barrack I have never seen," Aunt Sophia said agitatedly. "Clarissa, it is my duty to express my misgivings at leaving you here in this dreadful house. There was something not quite right about things last night. Ill as I was, I could not but observe some irregularities." When Clarissa dismissed these, Aunt Sophia clasped her hands with the air of one offering an unassailable argument, "And what must people *think,* your staying in the home of a man of the old marquess's reputation?"

For the first time in five years, Clarissa was thankful for the fact that her aunt considered her on the shelf. "No one will think anything of an aging spinster staying as the guest of the *present* marquess's sister. With her maid. Until you can send Mr. Bede to return for me. The marquess in question is dead, and unless you are afraid of licentious ghosts..."

Aunt Sophia began to protest, but gave up her expostulations when Kitty joined them. She was dressed in a simple gown of exquisite white *linon mouchette*, a fabric that Clarissa had once seen in the trunk containing her own mother's clothes. So Lady Kitty *was* wearing her mother's gowns, adapted by a clever needlewoman. Over her gown she had pulled a thick knitted shawl.

Mrs. Latchmore scowled at the gown, and Clarissa knew she recognized an old one when she saw it.

Kitty stood by, intensely aware of that scowling stare. She knew very well what it meant. She could only be glad when Miss Harlowe spoke a hasty farewell and joined Kitty, who led the way back inside, her gladness divided between the imminent departure of the terrible woman, and the fact that the pleasant one was staying. She was so lonely—company would be so wonderful, even for a day or two!

She and Clarissa watched from the morning room above as the well-muffled driver cracked his whip over his leaders' heads, and the coach rumbled over the slushy ground until it was hidden by the thick copse of winter-bare trees of the Park.

Kitty said with somewhat forced cheer, "Sadly outmoded it may be, but that old berlin *is* comfortable."

As Clarissa followed her hostess away from the window, Kitty had been squaring herself to the question she had been dreading all morning. "Did your aunt guess?"

Clarissa tried to summon a reassuring smile. "She did not. That is," she corrected herself scrupulously, suspecting how her aunt's conversation would go when she reached Oakwood, "she questioned the significance of our accident, but I also know that my family is used to her...flights. My step-mother will be grateful that I am well taken care of."

"Step-mother! You have a step-mother. I hope she is not wicked?"

"Not at all. It would be difficult to find a more tender-hearted parent," Clarissa said loyally, not adding that it would also be difficult to find one more absent.

Kitty sighed. "I used to half-wish that I would get a step-mother. It would have been more agreeable than..." She gave her head a little shake, then said, "But I was afraid that she might be wicked. Did your mother take a fall from a horse, too?"

Clarissa looked away. "No. She was ill after a difficult birth," she said. "My brother died with her."

Kitty begged pardon for being inquisitive, and returned to the subject that worried her. "You might think I am demented to... dress as I have, and to join with my brothers in such a venture."

Clarissa said, "No, not demented." She made a quick gesture. "Please do not think I am passing judgment, but you appear to be

25

concerned with the consequences should you be caught at it. Yet you went ahead?"

"I know," Kitty said, her head drooping as she led the way down a long hall full of old pictures and heavy Tudor furnishings. "My brother Carlisle does not like me by. But I *wanted* to help, and they needed me, and Ned made it sound so much like a lark, and romantic, to go on board the yacht, when usually I just hold the horses until they arrive. I do so *love* romantical things. And my life has been so...so unromantical," she burst out, then recovered, saying in a stiff, small voice, "I know I ought to be grateful for what I have. My grandmother, before she died, made me copy out Mrs. Lennox's book *three times*, to cure me of romance."

Clarissa had read *The Female Quixote* once. She sincerely pitied anyone having to write out the pages of earnest sermonizing at the close of that novel.

"Here we are," Kitty said, as they traversed a gloomy hall into another part of the house, this wing much older. Though the house was primarily made of dark wood in the style of Queen Bess, this portion was well-cared for, the parquet under their feet shining with polish, the gilt-edged frames dusted. It had only been the state bedchambers that had been left to molder; Clarissa wondered if they had been shut up for at least a generation.

They passed an enormous staircase broad enough to accommodate a royal coach-and-six, and entered the westmost wing. Here the light was more subdued. "In summer, it is wonderful," Kitty said, opening the door to her sitting room, which was hung with peach-colored paper, beautiful arabesque and acanthi moldings under the ceiling. The cabriole-legged chairs in green and peach striped satin showed signs of careful repair.

In the winter light the room looked shabby, but Clarissa tried to imagine it filled with summer light, with greenery outside the four windows, for this was a corner room. When she observed her hostess's expectant air, she pronounced herself comfortable.

"Alice will bring us something warm," Kitty said. "But I wanted to say, it's Ned who is determined to carry on with the smuggling trade as my father had established it, for he is a favorite with the older men of the house, all of them devoted to my father. Ned heard their stories—for they talked only of success—and he was very proud of himself, hitting on something that would help the estate."

Clarissa remembered the grizzled oldsters, some of whom had sounded like sailors.

"He likes adventure, but we cannot afford to buy Ned a commission, and anyway, everyone says that peace is being declared with France at this very moment. They say that General Bonaparte will surely become the First Consul, if he does not declare himself the new king of France. If there are no more wars, I confess I am glad. I should not like to think of Ned in one."

Clarissa hesitated, not wanting to ask if the elder brother had no influence with the younger. But Kitty, who had been watching carefully, hastened to say, "Carlisle would not suffer Ned to risk danger without he must be there as well, and as he was made lieutenant before Papa died and he had to come home, he knows better than any how to command a sea vessel..." She frowned. "You do not look at all the thing, and here I am, my tongue on wheels, as Papa used to say. Please go and lie down! We dine at five in winter, but you may sleep as long as you like, and command a meal when you wish."

Clarissa thanked Kitty gratefully, and retired.

Four

THE PRELUDE TO THE *danse* is nearly complete. Our heroines have met. It remains only for them to meet their partners, and the quadrille can begin.

When Clarissa woke at half-past four, she felt somewhat recovered. The side of her head remained tender to the touch, but the ache within had lessened to such an extent that she was determined to regard it as negligible.

Rosina had her traveling gown laid out. As Clarissa changed, Rosina set a very old-fashioned curling iron on the hearth. "Alice found this for me, Miss Clarissa," she said.

"Pray do not trouble with it, Rosina," Clarissa said. "I shall be ridiculous anyway, sitting down to dinner in a traveling gown, but I believe that Lady Catherine cares nothing for the modes. So my hair can be arranged as it is for home."

Rosina pursed her lips, thinking that Lady Kitty would care very much for the modes, if she could, but she kept that to herself. She thought Lady Kitty, as everyone in the household called her, quite the most beautiful thing she'd ever seen — at least as beautiful as the Golden Guineas, as Lady Clarissa's sisters were known in the neighborhood around Oakwood.

Clarissa mourned the beautiful India-shawls now no doubt at the bottom of the ocean, but there was no help for it. At least Rosina had made her look presentable, she thought as she walked through the enormous stateroom to the head of the stairs, and down to where a tall, gloom-faced old butler waited in stately dignity to lead her to a side chamber off the main hall.

He announced her in a portentous voice, and Clarissa looked around in wonder. There were two suits of armor stationed at either side of that entry hall, under old shields. Those and the formidably magnificent French Renaissance cabinets with carved front panels gave the house an old-world air.

The chamber overlooked the low spiky trimmed canes of what would probably be a splendid rose garden. The space was covered with a smooth carpet of snow, framed by a handsome window embrasure. To catch the light, Kitty sat nearby at a delicate scriptoire, busy with pen and ink. She dropped her pen and rose. "Good evening, Miss Harlowe! How is your head?"

"Much improved, thank you, Lady Catherine."

Kitty flushed, for she had unpleasant memories attached to hearing her full name like that. But she was afraid of disgusting this quiet, elegant guest with an unwanted familiarity, so she gestured toward a fine walnut table, which, to Clarissa's surprise, had been set for dinner. "I'm afraid this is our dining room in winter. None of the formal rooms, which our ancestors *would* put on the north side of the house, are bearable this time of year."

"I think myself very comfortably placed where there is a good fire, and a pleasant garden view," Clarissa said.

Kitty smiled, commenting ruefully, "I suppose you must say that, but for my part, I find winter tedious to the infinite degree. There is so little to do, and you must know, you are my very first visitor outside of neighbors. I mean, a lady, for my brother's friends do not count, as I had to stay upstairs, and as for my Papa's..." Kitty shook her head so that her curls bounced. "Oh, *those* days are gone! But I shall say only this: if one *must* live out one's life in an old house, why could it not be enlivened by a ghost?"

"Would it seem churlish, or merely poor-spirited, to admit that I would very much rather not meet a ghost?"

"Oh, but..." Kitty reminded herself that this lady was very fashionable, and dismissed her words with a flick of her hand and an apologetic smile. "Please sit down," she said, remembering the duties of a hostess. "We may as well make ourselves comfortable, for I have no notion when my brothers might—"

She was interrupted by a crack behind them as the door was thrust open by a careless hand. In strode a young man in a carefully mended, old-fashioned coat that in their grandfathers' dashing days was called a *roquelaure*. Clarissa recognized his round, genial face and unruly black curls escaping from under a battered tricorne, which was quickly pulled off his head.

"Ned," Kitty cried.

"Hi, Kit. Jupiter, what a ride. I could eat a table!"

Kitty jumped up. "Ned, where are your manners?"

"Servant, ma'am," he exclaimed, blushing mightily, as Kitty said self-consciously, "Miss Harlowe, may I beg to present my brother Edward, that is, Lord Decourcey?"

Edward executed a correct bow, then said with his sister's lack of formality, "None of us have quite got used to my wearing my brother's title, which of course he passed off to me on Papa's death. I wasn't long enough at Eton to get used to it—we couldn't afford it," he said with his sister's same cheerful insouciance. "And as soon as Carl gets himself a son, off the title goes again, and I'm back to Mr. Decourcey."

Clarissa looked her confusion, and Kitty laughed. "The family name and the Viscount title are one and the same, due to some very tangled history, which starts on the continent, as you may imagine, marquesses not often being found in England."

"And nary a bit of land goes with *my* airy title," Edward said, as the servants' door opened, and in came the butler and a footman bearing heavy silver trays. "Much less money. All gobbled up in St. Tarval long ago. But as I said, it sounded fine at Eton—" He had unbuttoned the heavy roquelaure as he spoke, then looked down in dismay. "Hey day! My boots! I'd better change or Mrs. Finn will..." He bit off what he was going to say, and vanished precipitously, chased by Kitty, whose voice could be heard, "Oh Ned, I did so want to show Miss Harlowe that we are not completely uncivilized..."

Clarissa was left sitting at a table alone, with two servants standing by, holding heavy trays, as another door opened, and a gentleman entered, tall and mild of manner, his hazel gaze and curly black hair instantly familiar. Here was the gentleman who had rescued them.

The marquess bowed to Clarissa. "I trust you are recovered, Miss Harlowe? Now, where have my brother and sister gone off to? Here, Clemens, go ahead and serve. They are sure to appear before things get cold."

As he spoke, he sat at the head of the table, and kept up a mild commentary to his servants as they set out the meal, which gave Clarissa time to recover from this abrupt introduction; it could have been awkward, but somehow he made it easy.

His siblings reappeared as the servants departed, Kitty saying happily, "Oh, there you are, Carlisle. Have you two become acquainted? I hope so, for I do not want to perform another introduction, not without practice."

"We've all met," Edward said breezily, sitting down in a more fashionable coat that was slightly too short, making Clarissa wonder if she was seeing the last of Lord Decourcey's Eton wardrobe.

As the Decourcey family settled to the meal, Clarissa took the opportunity to covertly study her host. She was aware of extreme ambivalence as well as interest: this man, though polite, and her rescuer, had taken his brother and his sister out on the water as smugglers. And though she knew she owed him her life, she wondered if he had inherited those qualities that had earned his father a troubling reputation.

He certainly looked the gentleman. He might not have the perfect Grecian profile of her cousin Devereaux, who was the target of many young ladies in London, but his mouth was well-shaped, and his countenance pleasing; the Bedford crop was particularly flattering to the shape of his head, for he did not wear his hair unfashionably long, nor too short.

When he happened to glance her way and their eyes met, she became aware that she was staring, and hastily confined her gaze to her plate.

The food was plentiful and excellent, the conversation easy, without any reference to smuggling or Riding Officers.

At the end of the meal, after a couple of meaningful glances from the marquess (in so kindly a manner that Clarissa found her estimation of him improving decidedly), Kitty sat up. "Oh!" She blushed as she invited Clarissa to withdraw, which they did with correct punctilio.

The two ladies settled in the small paneled chamber next door, where a good fire crackled merrily, not quite subduing the odor of mildew. Chairs had been brought from under Holland covers and polished.

Having established Clarissa by the fire, Kitty excused herself to change her shawl, an excuse that was patently false when her voice rose plainly through the connecting door: "Ned! I will expire if you do not tell if me you successfully delivered the cargo."

Edward's voice was even clearer than his sister's. "What we could save of it. Deuce take that yacht captain—what was he at, so far off course? How are we going to repair the damage?"

"It's all the fault of that evil Talkerton," Kitty declared.

The marquess's quiet voice came clearly: "No, the fog was at fault—that and the fact that the wind died, setting the yacht adrift. And Talkerton is not evil. He's merely a man employed by the government to what he considers an honest end, though it's one I do not envy. And he knows quite well what our father was at, and that the older men in the countryside were in league with him. The evil, if any exists, I think lies with that innkeeper Dobbs, who I suspect is lying. He knows well there isn't anyone we can complain to."

"If Father were alive, that villain Dobbs wouldn't be whispering about thin markets, and the rest of it, so he can cheat us," Edward declared in a ringing tone.

Clarissa looked around in despair. The room was too small for any corner to be safe from eavesdropping. There was another door, but if she were to go through it, what would be the result except further embarrassment? Ah, but in the sideboard in the corner, there were books. She pulled out a random volume of Rollins.

The marquess said, "Kit, did you visit the tenants this afternoon?"

"As soon as Mrs. Latchmore and Mr. Bede were gone. Everyone was snug. One of the outbuildings at Highgate Farm was damaged in the storm, that was all."

"Cottage Row?"

"Sound, all sound. Old Widow Iverson said to convey her thanks for the rethatching, and she will put up supernumerary mint jelly for us. Little profit, then? Mrs. Finn read me *such* a lecture for going out."

"She nabbed me on my way downstairs," Edward said.

"And I, on my way in from the stable," the marquess stated. "If there is money to be made in free trading, I am not convinced we have the way of it. I mislike having to deal with that rascal Dobbs, but Father's old connections seem to have vanished, and as I told you before, I would hate to meet the *Amelia* in the Channel. Proby and I served together aboard the *Tarleton*, and he would be sick if he caught us."

"You'd think he'd look the other way," Ned said. "No, no, don't say a word on it. I know that you don't put a friend to such a choice, but dash it, Carl, winter's not over, there's yet a couple of new moons before the days get longer, and we did promise the Cowman—"

"Cowman," Kitty interrupted. "You would think your mysterious organizer, and I do not think much of his abilities, would have the wit to think of a better *nom de guerre*."

"Egad, Kit, left up to you he'd be Lord L'Inconnu or Comte de Sinistro, or some rubbishing name—"

His voice had risen, until the marquess broke in dulcetly. "Or the Count de Treasure."

The other two broke into laughter, and Kitty said, "I should return to our guest, before she wonders if I am knitting a new wrap."

"Oh! I nearly forgot Miss Harlowe," Edward said. "A guest in this house, do you know what this means?"

"I am afraid to ask," the marquess responded.

"That we now have a fourth for whist," his brother said triumphantly.

"I hope she doesn't play," was the retort from his sister.

By the time Kitty reappeared, Clarissa had been able to make a fair attempt at her book, so that she could look up naturally.

"We shall have tea brought in a moment," Kitty said, and then tilted her head. "How do you feel? Are you quite fagged? The bruise looks very tender still."

"I am well enough," Clarissa replied.

"Should you like to play a rubber or two of whist with us?"

There was, of course, no answer to be made but an affirmative. Clarissa was used to such games, and prepared to be sadly bored. Much to her surprise, she wasn't: the marquess and his brother and sister did not quarrel over the cards as her brother and her eldest half-sister so frequently had at home, for one thing, and for another, they were excellent players.

As Ned said cheerfully, when totting up points after the first game, "When you have little to do and many hours to do it in, you become a thumping Captain Sharp. Shall we play for our old stakes?"

Kitty said to Clarissa, "What we do is play a hundred guineas a point. It's quite fun to win and lose enormous sums, and at the end of the evening, we throw the papers into the fire."

"Do not feel yourself obliged, Miss Harlowe," the marquess said to their guest, who when sodden and half-frozen had seemed self-possessed, and now sat there with calm poise.

But then she laughed, and it transformed her face.

The marquess was unaware of his entry into the *danse* as hero; in that moment he was unaware of his brother or sister, or the cards he still held in his hand.

And Clarissa was only aware of the fact that she'd never heard of such a thing. But if one took a moment to consider, was it not more sensible than the particulars of gaming as generally accepted? "I quite understand," she said. "And I confess I consider it perfectly sensible."

"Here, Carl, give me those. Unless you intend to play that as your next hand?" Ned looked inquiringly at his brother, who apologized and relinquished the playing cards.

He made an effort, recollected himself, and Ned dealt.

And so it was that by the end of the evening, Clarissa had won fifty thousand pounds, but had lost nearly two hundred thousand, and she had never known an evening to pass so fast in her life.

The bell had chimed midnight before they broke up the party, Edward pitching their scribbled IOUs into the fire. "And there goes my coronet, a string of racers, and a phaeton," he said cheerfully, as the marquess handed the ladies their candles to light their way upstairs.

⸺⬥⬥⬥⬥⬥⬥⸺

The next morning, Clarissa woke to stormy weather. The ache in her head had faded. She felt a dull pang only if she touched the bruise. One glance out at the low gray sky and the ghostly branches nearly hidden in the whirl of white, and she knew that few would be traveling this day.

While she sipped at the tea that Rosina brought her, downstairs, the brothers met, the younger surprised to find the elder in the dining room rather than the kitchen, as was his wont. He thought nothing of it beyond a reflection on how they must remember their manners, now that Miss Harlowe was among them.

The marquess's reflections were more troubling. Nature had fashioned an energetic young man whose sense of fun led him to enjoy being outdoors in all weathers, but circumstances had made him serious before young men customarily settle down. He found himself responsible for the languishing estate before he inherited it, with the inevitable result: he worked very hard, and spent a great deal of time contriving ways to deal with disasters and to brace for the next.

He did not regard Miss Harlowe as a disaster, but he had woken aware that the previous evening's pastime had been the most enjoyable ever, and that was in large part due to their guest. It wasn't that Miss Harlowe was exceptionally witty, or indeed, that she had claimed more than her share of conversation. It was the way she had appeared to enjoy her company, an attribute that in the cold light of morning he had to attribute to excellent manners.

A well-bred young lady used to the ways of London could scarcely be expected to be entertained by a family party round an old table in a tumbledown barrack of a house. He must not think anything beyond that. It was a firm decision—and yet when he found himself twice looking expectantly at the door, he outlined a day's worth of labor that would fully occupy him and his brother.

36

Ned whistled as they departed, wondering if the weather was what got a burr under Carl's saddle.

Kitty and Clarissa came down soon after they left. Clarissa had waited until she heard Kitty's step creaking on the wooden floor outside her door. She did not wish to go down alone and perhaps cause an awkward encounter with anyone else in the family.

Kitty had woken up remembering a certain humiliating encounter when she had tried to go into company once before. Knowing that she had no social experience, during breakfast she scrupulously adopted what she had been told was the proper demeanor of a young lady of Society.

The result? At the end of the meal, Clarissa rose, and said softly and apologetically, "Forgive me, please, for the imposition of my presence. There is no need to abjure the order of your day in my favor."

"Oh," Kitty exclaimed, so dismayed she forgot her careful formality of manner. "Of course, if you wish to be alone, I quite comprehend."

Clarissa regarded her gravely. "I do not wish to trespass on your time as I have in your home, Lady Catherine."

Kitty clasped her hands. How to answer?

"I wish you would call me Kitty," she said tentatively. "*Lady Catherine* is what my grandmother insisted upon, and I know it is proper, but it makes me feel that I am being scolded."

Clarissa's puzzlement vanished; she recognized in the substantive change in manner that her hostess had been acting a part, one perhaps that she thought was expected. "I, too, have a brother," she ventured. "He *will* forget what is due to visitors and family, and my sisters are lively. So we are informal among ourselves. If you would not consider it pushing, do call me Clarissa."

Kitty's face transformed. "Well, if that is the case, then, pray come to my parlor. You may speak when you like, or not, as you please."

They ascended to Kitty's private chamber, which was warm and snug. Kitty moved at once to the little *secretaire*, with a furtive look. She sat down with a bit of unnecessary bustle, moving her chair, resettling her skirts, and then restacking a quire of papers, all with occasional glances Clarissa's way.

Clarissa perused the small shelf of books. She had read them all, for none were more recent than twenty years, and the greater number were improving works. A schoolboy edition of *Rollins' Ancient History* – battered from much rereading, unlike the leather-bound Rollins downstairs, which Clarissa suspected had never been opened – rested on the top shelf, along with tomes of an instructive nature by Wilberforce, Macaulay, and Hannah More.

Below those, far more well-worn, the works of novelists. She selected *The Fortunate Foundlings*, which her grandmother had once said was her mother's favorite.

For a time there was only the rustle of pages and the scratch of Kitty's pen on her foolscap.

Then the scritch-scratch ceased, and when Clarissa looked up, she discovered her hostess regarding her with a curious demeanor.

"I see you are reading a novel," Kitty ventured. "I gather you are not an enemy of novels?"

"I read them with great pleasure."

Kitty made a deprecating gesture. "I know those are all horridly old-fashioned. Though *Cecelia* is one of my favorites." She said in a rush, "And you know, it is one of the very few that carried beyond the marriage, and so I –" Kitty resolutely controlled the impulse to confide her most cherished secret.

But then she dared to raise her eyes, and found only sympathetic interest in her guest, and so the words came tumbling out. "The truth is, pray do not – that is, I trust, I *hope*, you will not be offended, but the truth is, I am minded to help my brother by commencing author." And at Clarissa's look of surprise, "Situated as I am, it is unlikely I will make a great marriage. Or any marriage at all. But Carlisle is in desperate need of..." Aware that she was compounding her error by vulgar reference to money, Kitty twisted her fingers together and mutely regarded her guest.

"It is a laudable plan," Clarissa said. "Can one prosper by the pen?"

"It stands to reason," Kitty said eagerly. "Does it not? If everyone in England has heard of Dr. Johnson, and buys his books, would not that add up to an immense sum? And from what I have heard, novels are more popular, are they not?"

"People certainly do talk about them at least as much as they talk about plays or music."

Kitty went on, "It seems to me that one must write a story that pleases everyone, so that each household will want their copy. We have talked about this a great deal. Ned said he would visit the booksellers on my behalf, if I just get it finished and copied out fair."

"How do you go about pleasing everyone?" Clarissa asked.

"Why, you have elements to please all. There must be romantic and tender thoughts for the ladies, and fashion as well. There must be danger and striving for the gentlemen. Perhaps some great thoughts for those older, and instruction for those younger, though Ned says that they yawn over that in school, and what you really want when young is something humorous. But the young don't buy their books, do they? Do not their guardians buy them, always looking out something instructive?"

"Your elder brother. What says he to this laudable plan?"

"Oh, Carlisle says I may do what I wish. He engages only for a different story than the usual moldering castle and abductions by Greek banditti. He thinks if I were to write a romance entirely modern, it would do well through being something new, especially if it might be witty."

Clarissa could not help but agree.

Kitty had been observing her closely, and tipped her head. "Yes, I see you think so, too. And I would agree! But how can I write about modern manners when I am never to go into society? At least with Greek banditti, no one in England has seen them, so they cannot scoff and point out how I got it wrong. And," she finished, waving her quill in triumph, "I am ahead in that I can have them converse in their own tongue. I never thought I would get any use out of helping Ned get up his Thucydides during the holidays, for he isn't bookish."

"Except...forgive me, but would banditti converse in the classical mode of Thucydides?" Clarissa asked.

"Carlisle asked that, too," Kitty said. "But I said, since we haven't any examples of banditti speech, why should they not?" And when her guest smiled, making a gesture of acceptance, Kitty confided further, "As for Greek banditti and the like, one must write about *something*. I know what a moldering castle feels like, as I live in one. That is, a moldering house. I know it's not a castle, and really, I'd as lief not live in one if it's all to be stone, with a noisome donjon and moat. But that is beside my point." She determinedly wrenched herself back to her topic, "I know nothing of what goes on in society, as someone hinted once." Kitty looked down, her face red. "So I might just as well add in some exciting chapters about banditti, because at least I've read about them. This is another reason why I wished to go aboard the cutter, so I could add some chapters about smugglers from my own witness. Only I thought I might make them over into pirates."

Clarissa wondered who would be so mean-spirited as to hint about ignorance of society and not offer to amend her hostess's knowledge, but she forbore questioning, and so the two returned to reading and writing respectively, in perfect charity with one another.

By the time they were called to a nuncheon, they had reached that stage of acquaintanceship that can ripen into friendship, as each gave her opinions on things, instead of supplying the answer that polite company is supposed to wish to hear.

"I can sympathize with a wish to see the world," Clarissa was saying as they sat down to sliced turkey, bread, and butter. "But I must confess, I would be happiest at home. I am not a romantical being."

Kitty's eyes rounded, their color a vivid green in the warm light of the fireplace. "And yet we found you crossing the Channel in the dead of winter, with the peace not yet signed!"

Clarissa smothered a laugh. "My Aunt Beaumarchais, as staid as one may find, would never have invited me to come had she not been convinced that peace is to reign at last, and she assured my Papa that Holland is quiet."

"Holland," Kitty repeated. "I do wish I could travel. I long for adventure."

Clarissa could not suppress a smile. "You wish to be abducted by a set of Greek banditti?"

"If their leader was handsome, and a gentleman, why not?" Kitty answered, and gestured quickly with her butter knife. "Yes, I know handsome, gently-born banditti must be scarce, but surely sometimes there are missing heirs, and mysterious political factions, and suchlike. They cannot be entirely made up, or why should there be so many of them in books?"

Clarissa gave a thoughtful nod, vouchsafing only one comment, "I should think such a life would be disagreeable, not romantic, but perhaps I may be mistaken."

Kitty put down her knife. "Why is it, given the peace not yet signed, this aunt could not wait for spring to invite you?"

Clarissa hesitated. She was in the habit of keeping her own counsel. But her hostess had been so kind, and had shared her own thoughts, and so Clarissa admitted, "It was to get away for a time, for I refused a perfectly good marriage."

Kitty's lips parted, and her eyes took on an intent look that Clarissa, by now, had little difficulty in interpreting.

"This eligible connection is not a villain! He is regarded highly in our parish for his sobriety, learning, and filial respect. It is merely, I have no wish to be wed. I am comfortable enough at home."

At that moment, the door opened and the butler entered. "Miss Bouldeston, my lady."

Clarissa gazed as a vaguely familiar young lady paused on the threshold, one mittened hand going to the bonnet that charmingly framed her round face. Honey colored curls escaped from its lacy frame, half hidden by the pink silk bow with which it was tied. Her rosy cheeks dimpled as she smiled, and light blue eyes crinkled as she smoothed her hands down her frilly pink dress.

That was chiefly how Clarissa remembered Miss Bouldeston, by her preference for all the variations of the color rose. Her gown was like a doll's dress, right down to the layered lace flounces of the hem.

Lucretia crossed the room in little steps toward Kitty, her movements arch and fluttering.

"Dearest Catherine," she exclaimed in a high, fluting voice. "This weather, it has cast us all down. I promised myself, as soon as we gain the merest peep of a blue sky, I would call upon my dearest—"

At that moment, Lucretia seemed to catch sight of Clarissa in her chair. She gave a little start, her fingertips rising to her rounded mouth, and her eyes widening in affected surprise. "Can it be? Why, I did not expect...Miss *Harlowe*? We were introduced at Almack's, I believe."

Clarissa had risen. She bowed as she returned the young lady's greeting.

"You must have heard about the accident to her yacht, Lucretia," Kitty said. "Ned says the news is all over the countryside."

Lucretia abandoned the affect of surprise, and turned to Kitty. "I must say, what a great piece of luck for *you*, Catherine."

"Me?" Kitty asked, bewildered.

"That your dear brother chanced to rescue instead of some horrid fisherman a person who travels in the *highest* circles."

"I would not call it luck," Kitty said.

"You would not?" Lucretia posed her fingers on either side of her chin. "Surely you would not wish for Miss Harlowe to find herself wrecked on the shore, to put it no worse?"

Kitty waved her hands in agitation. "Oh, no, no, no, no. I did not mean that. I quite meant that —"

"May I sit down?"

Kitty blushed scarlet, hands out. "Oh! Please. Everyone, do sit down."

Lucretia sat on the edge of the hassock, toes together, just peeping under the edge of her hem, her hands hidden in her muff on her knees. She turned to Clarissa. "I suppose you have been entertaining our dear Catherine with tales of the doings of our mutual acquaintance in town?"

"Lady Catherine has shown more interest in literature than in the particulars of current events," Clarissa said, then caught sight of Kitty's stricken look.

A new thought darted into Clarissa's mind. Though the two young ladies appeared to know one another well enough to use Christian names, it seemed that Lucretia might not be aware of Kitty's novel.

Lucretia certainly did not refer to it, as she said, "Well, my dear Catherine, I had intended to entertain you with news of our preparations for moving to Town, but I can see you have far more entertaining company that my poor self. For you must know, Miss

Harlowe," she added, turning to Clarissa, "we are neighbors. Riverside Abbey, my home, is just across the river. We have known the Decourceys *forever.*"

Lucretia rose, as did Kitty, who said with better manners than conviction, "Oh do not rush away, Lucretia. Pray stay, and drink some tea with us."

Lucretia bridled, casting her eyes down in a rather affected semblance of modesty. "I do not wish you and your guest to find me *de trop,* as we say in Town."

Clarissa was surprised that Miss Bouldeston would find it necessary to add that little rider after a French expression that had been trite in her grandmother's day. "Not at all," she said politely.

"Then perhaps just half an hour, mind. Mama will expect me before too long. There is much to be done if we are to be ready to go Tuesday week. My sister Lucasta is to make her come out this year, you know, Miss Harlowe. You may imagine the to-do."

Alice brought in the tea things, her manner stiff and correct. Kitty served the tea and handed around the fresh-baked macaroons as Lucretia proceeded to talk exclusively to Clarissa about London. Except for the appendage "my sweetest" in front of the word Catherine, she seemed to have nothing to say to her hostess.

Clarissa found herself closely questioned about whom she might be seeing on her arrival in London. Also, what entertainments Clarissa's family considered giving, as Lucretia seem to know, without Clarissa telling her, that another of her sisters also was to come out.

At the end of her half hour, Lucretia made a little business of examining the clock on the mantel, but when she did not receive an invitation to stay, she said airily, "Mama will be looking for me. I must hurry myself away."

She was thinking, silly Catherine, trying to keep Miss Harlowe to herself! Lucretia advanced two steps toward the door, and then turned as if struck by a new thought.

The other two saw her pose, her fingers touching her chin in a gesture of sudden inspiration. "Where are my wits? I was just put in mind of a question. My father would think me shamefully remiss if I did not ask how does your cousin Mr. Devereaux? We were introduced at the Castlereaghs' ball, and I have heard Papa say time out of mind that they belong to the same club."

Clarissa said, "I believe he is quite well, thank you."

Lucretia gave Clarissa a dimpled smile. "Pray convey my mother's compliments, of course. That would be only proper. It has been most diverting to meet you *here*, Miss Harlowe." Lucretia turned to Kitty. "My dear, I know I may rely on you to convey my best to your brothers." Miss Bouldeston curtseyed and departed, leaving a trace of pleasant French scent, and a sense of general constraint.

Five

"How many duels are fought in a year?"

During luncheon, the weather cleared, giving the young ladies a desire to take an airing in the garden. Both were well wrapped up, Clarissa wearing a bonnet that had probably belonged to Kitty's mother.

The question came as such a surprise that Clarissa almost laughed. She recollected the novel that Kitty was writing and turned her head to hide any trace of smile. "None, I am afraid. That is, if there are, news of such things would not reach my ears."

"But if there *had* been, I suppose your brother must have told you?" Kitty sighed. "I am afraid that modern times are dull. How exciting it must have been in our grandmothers' day!"

"Exciting, perhaps. Uncomfortable, if half the stories are true," Clarissa said. "I for one should have hated wearing a wig quite as large as a chair upon my head, and a skirt wider than a doorway. And as for duels, how very distressing to see one's brother carried home with a sword-wound, following a foolish quarrel over cards or some such trifle."

Kitty's enthusiastic expression showed how thoroughly she disagreed. "How affecting it would have been, your lover brought to your door dead from the dueling field. You would swear to seek vengeance, even if it took twenty years, and you would die an old maid, brokenhearted."

"I do not think that young men were brought anywhere but to their homes."

This caveat was dismissed with a wave of Kitty's hand. "One's husband, then. Or better, a cold and loathsome duke whom your family forced you to marry." Kitty gazed across the snow-stippled, truncated rose bushes, to the white-rimmed low slate wall bordering the far side of the garden. Her expression was rapt. "Cruel... Sinister... Though, of course, impeccable in taste and quite handsome in appearance..." She tipped her head, the old-fashioned bonnet framing her lovely face. "So his death would set one free. Only one might not wish to avenge him, if he was so cruel and cold. And here's another thing. Seeking vengeance might be very well in its way, but I think upon reflection it would be better to forgo it then to be honor-bound to spend the rest of one's days as an old maid. No, as a widow."

Clarissa made a polite noise, not quite agreement, which Kitty—wrapped in romantic imaginings—took as enthusiastic corroboration.

She heaved a great sigh. "But unless the Squire's son alters a great deal, or some wealthy and mysterious nobleman chooses this area to rusticate in total anonymity, while looking for a bride, I am not likely to meet with much in the way of romance. But *you* cannot escape it, in London." She turned to Clarissa. "The balls, parties, everything one needs to aid one falling violently, *hopelessly*, in love."

"I do not see the appeal in hopelessness." Clarissa said apologetically. "I am afraid one sees more of vanity and ambition and calculation, and boredom, than love."

"Is that true? How horrid!"

"Perhaps I may be mistaken," Clarissa hastened to say. "Perhaps one only hears more of those things. Gossip, I have discovered, is seldom spread about people who find happiness or contentment."

"Then I shall imagine romance for my book," Kitty said. "One wants a story full of love, if it is difficult to find in the way of life. Which I can corroborate," she added in a low voice, almost under her breath. "In my circumstances."

Clarissa looked away, over the bare tree tops beyond the wall.

"Laying aside the disagreeable topic of fortune hunters of either sex, as far as I am able to determine, a hopeless passion would make one miserable. As well as every creature around one. And a violent attachment must be doubly tiresome to everyone else."

"Tiresome!" Kitty exclaimed, aghast. "Forgive me, Clarissa, but you sound as if you are an enemy to romance. Is this true?"

Clarissa had, from her first introduction into society, observed the feminine wiles cast out to attach her cousin, and last year the desperate ruses young gentlemen employed to catch the eye of her eldest half-sister, Hetty. She had also been the sympathetic auditor of her half-sister uttering threadbare phrases about eternal passions and tragical despair, but until now nobody had ever asked what she thought.

She had a horror of sounding impertinent, or snubbing, which would be worse. "That is not precisely what I meant. But if one has expectations, or scruples, and the gentlemen to whom one is introduced do not meet those expectations, for whatever good reasons they might have, one might slowly come to believe that the single life is not so very bad a thing."

"Then you are not an enemy to romance?" Kitty swung around to face her.

"Seeking romance appears to be another term for hankering after the impossible. For example, in my situation, the offers—and there were only three—that I have turned down were not because the gentlemen did not resemble the hero of a novel, but because upon consideration I thought I might be happier at home."

Kitty nibbled on the tip of her gloved finger.

Remembering Hetty's episodes of high drama the year previous, before she was at last successfully married, Clarissa could not help but add, "Would you wish to share a parlor with one of those heroines when she is prating and prosing forever about love, fainting over every couch in sight, and exclaiming in loud accents that she is about to expire?"

"There is but one answer to be made to that. One *must* be the heroine," Kitty stated triumphantly.

"Then you must tell me about your heroine," Clarissa said, smiling.

Kitty's eyelids flashed up with pleasure, her eyes glowing an arresting greenish shade in the weak wintry sunlight. "It is difficult to know how to begin. It is about a beautiful orphan named Andromeda, who it turns out in the end, is quite high-born. In the beginning, when she is but an infant, she is deposited in a basket by a mysterious woman veiled in black, but with fragile hands and a great diamond on her ring finger, and when an orphan meets a mysterious Duke—"

To Clarissa's consternation, Kitty went on to describe a plot that sounded very like *Evelina*, mixed up a little with *Sir Charles Grandison*.

Before they'd proceeded to volume two, there came a welcome interruption. "Kit!" Edward hailed across the garden.

"Bother," Kitty whispered, without heat. "Ned? We are here."

Edward pushed impatiently through the shrubbery, his round face beaming with a broad smile. "Mrs. Finn said I should find you here."

He crossed the garden at a lope, marring the clean white snow with footprints. The marquess appeared a few steps behind his brother, and joined the group in motion toward the house.

"Ned, Carl, how did you do? Anything?" Kitty clapped her hands.

"Ah," Edward exclaimed. "Found ourselves run aground." And at his sister's start, "Ah, so to speak. Talkerton was out nosing about the cutter, and clap me up for a fool if we didn't have to lie up in a dashed snowdrift for an hour until he finally stopped poking about. I thought I would catch my death for certain."

Kitty turned wonderingly from one brother to the other as they approached the doors. The marquess's eyes narrowed, his mouth pressed in a line. "If that fellow had not had the happy thought of seeking employment as a tidesman, he'd have done well to go to London and work in Bow Street. I am come to the conclusion that we would be wise to put an end to our careers in free trading."

Edward crowed with laughter. "Listen to old sobersides. That isn't what you said when we left this morning."

The marquess looked away as he gave a soft, embarrassed laugh. "I was angry then. I must admit I would gain an inordinate amount of satisfaction were we to land a thumping great cargo. But the man should not be faulted for doing a better job at catching smugglers then we are doing at being smugglers." He opened the door to let the ladies passed inside.

Edward stripped off his muffler and roquelaure, then flung his cumbersome load of winter gear onto a chair. "I still think, if we both confront that rascally Dobbs..."

"I think we had better give it up." The marquess laid his great-coat over the back of a chair and stretched his hands out to the fire.

"But Carl—"

At this point the marquess glanced significantly at their guest, who had moved to the window to stare silently out, as if she heard no part of a conversation she knew did not include her.

The marquess dropped his voice. "We will come about, Ned, but there is no need to bore our guest with our affairs."

Kitty danced forward. "Oh, Clarissa is discreet," she said blithely. "Besides, my novel may take, you know."

"I have it," Edward cried. "I will go to London with Kit, and look out an heiress. Miss Harlowe, you know Town, are you acquainted with any beautiful heiresses?"

"Pray do not be absurd, Ned," Kitty declared in disgust. "As if any papa would permit his daughter to marry a nineteen-year-old boy who did not also come with a fortune. And how should *I* come to London anyway? Sooner the moon."

Edward turned in surprise to face his brother. "You didn't tell her?"

"When, pray, have I had time?" St. Tarval demanded in exasperation. "Kit, we were coming up the River Road just past the Abbey, when we encountered Lucretia. She said she had called. But she did not speak to you?"

Kitty said somewhat stiffly, "She told us about her plans for the Season, and also said she was to leave soon."

The marquess said, "I do not claim to understand the ins and outs of female etiquette, so perhaps Lady Bouldeston required her to speak the invitation through me. The long and the short of it is that Sir Henry and Lady Bouldeston have kindly invited you to ride to town with them, to spend the two weeks before Easter with Lucretia in Mount Street."

Kitty's cheeks reddened, and not from approbation, Clarissa saw.

Clarissa gazed in consternation. No doubt Miss Bouldeston had meant her gesture kindly; from the expectation in the St. Tarval brothers' countenances, it was clear that they regarded the invitation as a generous one. But Lord Edward had clearly never been to London during the Season, and Clarissa suspected that if the marquess had, it was not for very long. Being invited for the two weeks before the Season would be very like being invited to watch a family get ready to host a dinner. There would be the bustle of getting dressed, and looking at the finely set dinner table...and then? Just as the door was to be opened to the first guest, one would be expected to return home.

But *Kitty* knew it.

Clarissa heard her own voice before she was aware of speaking. "Alas, as it happens, your sister has already accepted my invitation to accompany me to London as my guest."

Six

THE BRILLIANT LOOK OF gratitude Kitty cast Clarissa must be her reward, for as soon as the words were out, Clarissa felt the inevitable reaction of dismay engendered by a reflection on what her family might say.

St. Tarval did not miss Kitty's look, Clarissa was certain, but he only bowed and said politely, "Then no more must be said, beyond you should send an answer to the Bouldestons, and thank them for their kindness."

Kitty exclaimed, "So I shall, and you may be certain that I'll say everything that is proper." She bit her lip, then turned to Clarissa. "Perhaps we should leave my brothers to their luncheon. Should you like to step up to my bedchamber with me?"

Clarissa bowed slightly to the gentleman and passed through the door, wondering at her own motivation. She, who so rarely gave in to impulse! And this was no small thing. For a short time she wished she could take the words back as she considered what her aunt would say, but then Kitty shut the door, and turned to Clarissa, gripping her fingers tightly.

"I thank you for speaking up as you did," she began in a low voice, for she'd seen the contraction of Clarissa's brows, the flicker of dismay hard on the astonishing invitation. "They did not understand how horrid it would be...well, it's of no consequence. But of course you did not mean it, and we can forget it. I can tell my brother something—"

Clarissa understood a part of her motivation. She had wished to see surprise, even gratification in the marquess's face. But instead, she'd seen it in Kitty's.

She must not fail Kitty now.

"I should have liked to invite you anyway," Clarissa spoke as soon as Kitty paused to draw breath. She smiled. "It is little enough return for your kind rescue. My father loves order, and I should have wished to write home first. But truly, after a small bustle, there will be no difficulty. My step-mother is kindness herself, and you will adore my sisters. Everybody does."

"Oh!" Kitty clapped in excitement, and her eyes filled with tears. "Oh, thank you." She dashed her hand impatiently at the tears. "I have never been anywhere, other than a single disastrous visit to Tunbridge Wells. *This* time, I intend to be properly prepared. If you would be so good as to come up with me, and help me go through my mother's gowns, and choose out what is suitable to be made over?"

Remembering that Kitty's mother had died many years ago, Clarissa was dubious, but she said, "I am happy to be of service."

Soon they were kneeling on the cold floor of Kitty's dressing room. The bedchamber was large, with two south-facing windows. New hangings and a fire would've made it very cheerful. Clarissa pulled her shawl around her tightly, marveling how Kitty did not seem to heed the bitter chill.

As Kitty flung open one of the three large, battered trunks at least a century old, she said without a trace of self-pity, "My Papa was quite odd, and very selfish. He had no interest in ordering clothes for me until I should—*some*how—attract an eligible husband, so I have been wearing my mother's clothes since I first put up my hair. With great good luck, he had enjoyed seeing her in the very best, so I have had much to choose from. I have discovered that many of the fabrics are dreadfully outmoded. My brothers have fared rather better, as Papa never stinted for himself, either, and he only died a little over a year ago."

A powerful aroma of lavender pervaded the room as, with careful hands, Kitty spread one gown after another over the other trunks. "When I first sorted through her things, I saved out what I thought might be turned. Most were those great, stiff-bosomed things with the wide skirts. And the tall wigs she preserved, oh how they would make you laugh. She, with the most beautiful hair."

Kitty fingered the folds of a heavy silk sacque embroidered over with rosebuds as Clarissa asked, "Are there any more?"

"Oh yes. Here are the ball dresses."

Kitty opened a second trunk, and pulled forth glorious lengths of laced and embroidered taffeta, velvet, and silk. Some still retained their beauty, others were faded or spotted. All were quite hopelessly outmoded.

"You can imagine many of these were my models for Andromeda, on her adventures," Kitty said shyly as she smoothed the heavy lace on a sky-blue caraco jacket. "She is wearing this, for instance, when the Duke spies her through the window of the house where she is imprisoned. And this one," she breathed with reverence as she unfolded silver paper.

From the nest of paper she lifted out a magnificent ball dress of white satin with seed pearls and tiny diamonds sewn down the front of the bodice and across the over skirt, and bunches of velvet ribbons on the underskirt and at the richly lace trimmed sleeves. "Andromeda wears this gown at the masquerade she attends under an assumed name, and the Duke dances with her. But before they can discover one another's true names, the villainous Count Scorbini abducts her."

"From the ballroom floor?" Clarissa blinked in surprise.

"Why, yes." Kitty sat up, smiling brightly.

"And no one comes to her aid?"

"Well, they don't know who she is. She doesn't struggle, for he puts a potion in her glass of orgeat, and she feels faint, so he says he will carry her to a sofa, but instead takes her out to his carriage."

With careful hands, Kitty folded the gown back into its protective silver paper and laid it in the trunk. "Ned thinks it a preposterous dress, but all he cares about is sporting, and war, that is, if the French were to start it up again. Carl has been much too busy to go into society, but when I showed him this gown, he said if I ever wore it anywhere, he would go just to see me beat the other young ladies all to flinders. Not that I should wish to go to go just to shine down others, but oh, to catch the eye of a duke! Or it doesn't have to be a duke. I know there are not all that many of them, and it is highly unlikely that I would be put in a place to meet one, if there were. But some gentlemen who is highly romantic, and ever so handsome, and rich enough to help Carlisle out of his straits, who would see me across the ballroom floor, and love would instantly dart into his heart. And mine, too, of course."

She looked up at Clarissa, appeal in her gaze.

"A romantical vision, and I hope it comes to pass," Clarissa said, shifting uncomfortably on the chilly floor. "What is in the third trunk?"

"Three velvet riding habits, a couple of redingotes, shoes with great paste buckles, and accoutrements like lace caps, and sashes, fans and the like. The preposterous headdresses and so forth are up in the attic still." Kitty's excitement dimmed a little, and she cocked her head to one side. "What is amiss? Are they none of them suitable?"

"Are there any other day dresses aside from this white gauze?"

"I have been using them these seven or eight years. So Mama's things are hopeless, then?"

"The gauze could be turned. I suppose. Though I do not see how, as its neck is so wide and the waist so low. The remainder... The ones closer to the modes of today are the materials customarily worn by married ladies."

"That I learned to my cost once," Kitty said grimly, and turned her face away as she busied herself with weighing the old finery back in the trunks.

Clarissa took a deep breath, wanting somehow to help this generous, kind-hearted, romantical girl. "I think... Yes. I do believe I have a way to resolve the difficulty."

Kitty's head turned, as she hastily daubed at the revealing tears on her eyelids. "What? How?"

Clarissa betrayed a blush as she gazed upward. Then her lips pressed as though she wish to hide a smile. "You shall see, I promise. Soon."

Kitty clasped her hands. "You would not be playing a trick on me?"

"Never." Clarissa shook her head emphatically.

"Oh, thank you. How kind you are. Not only for myself, as of course I shall enjoy myself beyond anything, but in London, I might be able to help Carl. I am now determined that I shall find and marry a rich man. London must be full of *them*, however few dukes there may be, for I must not be thinking solely of myself. If he is rich, nothing else matters, save that he is not cruel."

Clarissa, thinking of Lord Wilburfolde, reflected that there was a vast range of possibilities betwixt handsome and cruel. Ordinary men without the villainous proclivities of a Count Scorbini could be just as vexing in a thousand small ways from which there might be little escape.

At the end of that evening, Clarissa could see the tiredness and preoccupation in her hosts' faces, though they strove for politeness. Being conscientious, she rose far earlier than she might have, and professed herself ready to retire.

Edward promptly rose with her, yawning behind his hand. "Lord! I trust you will forgive me, Miss Harlowe, but I am asleep on my feet. We were up and riding long before the sun chose to rouse itself. Here, I will light the way for you."

He picked up a waiting branch of candles and led the way out.

Kitty was not tired, either, but she had a great deal to think about. She could see it her elder brother's countenance that he wished to talk to her. "Are you going upstairs, Kit?"

"Not immediately."

"I had hoped to find a chance to talk to you."

She puckered her brow. "Oh, Carl, I do *hope* and trust that you are not going to tell me I cannot go, for some horrid reason."

St. Tarval did not speak immediately. Kitty's consternation altered to surprise as her brother took a turn about the room, then stopped at the fireplace to stare down into the flames. His profile was pensive as he said, "I take it, then, you wish to accompany Miss Harlowe to London?"

"Above anything."

He remained silent for a time, his long fingers so much like

Papa's absently toying with the fire tongs. Seeing his profile bent so seriously, his gaze distant from the employment of his hands, Kitty said quickly, "You are thinking perhaps it will not answer, my going to stay with someone so recently a stranger to us. But recollect Clarissa and I spent all this time solely in one another's company, and I know she feels grateful for the rescue. And oh, she is so easy to talk to, and though she is ever so well read, she is kind."

"Miss Harlowe's manners are particularly good," he said, still staring down at the fire.

Kitty's eyes widened. "You do not think she only pretends to like me?"

"No, Kitty. That is, not precisely. But she does not know you, and you cannot say you know her after so short an acquaintance."

"But I have formed a very good impression of her. What inspires your doubt, Carl? Do you think her invitation insincere? Surely you do not believe she is the sort of heartless fashionable that you despised in London on your one visit?"

"I do not. Yet we know so little about her or her family, beyond the title, the family name, and that they live in Hampshire. We do not know what kind of welcome you might meet."

"Though I have never been to London, please credit me with some sense," Kitty exclaimed indignantly. "Do you think I would wish to go if I thought they were all like that horrid aunt?"

"I think there is very little you would not tolerate if you thought you were to go to London." He smiled.

Kitty pressed her lips on a retort that a *kind* invitation would have been for the two weeks following Easter, one would think.

Aloud, she said only, "Clarissa has spoken a little of her family. I do not believe that I will find unwelcome there. Except perhaps from Mrs. Latchmore. The *things* she said to Alice and Mrs. Finn! But that is neither here nor there."

"Why is she not married?"

"Who? Mrs. Latchmore? She is a widow."

"No. Miss Harlowe," he said, walking to the window. He stood thus, looking out, though the darkness must have precluded his seeing much.

Kitty gazed at him in astonishment. "I can scarcely ask her

that, not unless we had known one another for ages. Though I own, it seems odd to me, too." Kitty's eyes narrowed reflectively. Her interest in people caused her to consider her guest. "She did mention offers, but delicacy forbids me to ask more. Perhaps she has no wish to marry. Why these questions, and the long face? Do you mislike Clarissa?"

"I have scarcely exchanged a hundred words with your guest. I cannot claim to be any more than acquainted."

"Then," Kitty waved her hands, "you must sit down with her and converse. She is as well read as you are. You shall find her interesting, I vow and declare." She peered into her brother's face. His expression was somber, and so she said in a very different tone, "Carl? Do you really fear that my going to London is a mistake?"

He dropped into his chair and forced a smile. "Not at all. Merely, I wish circumstances were such that *I* might be taking you to London. I am failing you in that I am not."

She flew up out of her chair and gave him a quick embrace. "Absurd creature! As if it were duty to waste time and money on such a thing. I regard Clarissa's invitation as an unlooked-for treat, a reward for our good offices when their yacht strayed so horribly into our path. Let us hear no more of duty. And," she said earnestly, her cheeks red, her gaze determined, "I would be less than honest if I did not assure you that there are things I would as lief give the go-bye, even to get to London."

He looked up sharply, and she took a deep breath. "I did not wish to go with Lucretia. And not just because I knew I would be sitting in their house listening to them plan balls, and talk of their invitations, or watching Lucretia and Lucasta while they are visiting milliners and dressmakers. The truth is, I always feel so countrified in her company. I did not become aware of it until I spent this time with Clarissa, with whom I never felt it, not for a moment."

St. Tarval looked uneasy. "Lucretia has said countless times that she feels for your lack of a mother or a sister, and I know she looks out ways to help you to the mode with her suggestions."

Kitty sensed the question underlying these words, and she knew that delicacy forbade her from entering into a discussion from which either of them might not be able to extricate themselves creditably. "It is very kind in her, I am sure," Kitty said in a subdued manner, and bade her brother a good night.

Seven

AFTER BREAKFAST THE NEXT morning, unprecedented noise reverberated through the windows.

Clarissa and Kitty rose to look out , witnessing an impressive cavalcade of three carriages bumping up the drive to vanish beyond the hedgerow dividing the house from the stable yard, the horses in snow up to their fetlocks.

Leading the way was the ancient berline belonging to the Decourcey family. The second bore the Chadwick arms, and all three were piled high with luggage.

Kitty said, "Perhaps we should go to the drawing room?"

The young ladies were standing in the chilly room, in which a housemaid was just laying a fire, when the butler announced Lord Chadwick's steward. Mr. Bede greeted Miss Harlowe, and then handed her a sealed letter.

Clarissa had assumed as soon as she saw the mountain of baggage that her aunt had equated Tarval Hall with the Antipodes. The letter and the huge sum of money it said had been entrusted to Mr. Bede confirmed her speculations.

Mr. Bede said, "If you are wishful to set out today, Miss, if I may be permitted to say, it's coming on gray. We'd be best to start out as soon as may be, but I smell snow on the wind."

Clarissa glanced from him to Kitty's pale face, then said firmly, "We will depart on the morrow, for Lady Catherine will accompany us. Did you bring Oliver along, Mr. Bede?"

"Yes ma'am."

"Then we shall send him on ahead with a letter to Lady Chadwick. Will you see to it that he has something to eat, while I pen this letter? Thank you, Mr. Bede."

As soon as the steward had left the room, Kitty danced around the cold room, far too ecstatic for mere words.

Oliver the footman departed just after midday, under lowering steel-gray clouds. Having been issued a generous sum to see him back into Hampshire, he left in sanguine spirits. If the weather forced him to halt, it would mean a snug night at an inn.

Up in the house, Clarissa watched him go, her spirits uncertain. She moved about the room, absently picking up and setting down a little China shepherdess. The truth was, she was ambivalent about quitting Tarval Hall. She knew why she was ambivalent, which meant she must depart as soon as they were ready.

She had begun her stay disapproving of a man in St. Tarval's position indulging in unlawful acts such as smuggling, but from little things she had overheard, she had gained a better understanding of the burden of debt that the marquess had inherited, with little prospect of getting his neglected, heavily mortgaged lands in good heart once again. She could understand his following a course of action his father had once established.

"Pray, is something amiss, Clarissa?" Kitty's voice broke into her thoughts.

Clarissa set down the shepherdess, her face warming. "I beg your pardon. I was woolgathering. By now they should have carried those trunks to my bedchamber. Might I beg you to step upstairs with me? I wish to show you something."

The two were crossing the great, marble-floored front hall, when the door opened, and they were met by the marquess. Snowflakes dotted his glossy black curls, the shoulders of his greatcoat and his riding boots.

After he greeted the young ladies, he smiled at Kitty. "Forgive me for casting a damper on your quite understandable desire to flee your home, but it looks as if is coming on to blow."

"I have already spoken to Mr. Bede," Clarissa said. "I have only to apologize for saddling you with all these extra people to house."

"I think we can manage for a night," the marquess said, making an airy gesture upward. "We've only to open a few rooms, light some fires, and perhaps air things as best we can."

He smiled, his voice was light, but there was that at the corner of his eye and in the quality of his smile, and in the very airiness of his gesture, that prompted Clarissa to say, "This is a beautiful home. If I did not fear I might freeze, which could happen anywhere, I would beg to be conducted over it and be told its history."

The marquess flushed. "Thank you," he said. "No doubt every man in the country would say much the same about his ancestral home, whether castle or cottage, but I believe some of our stories are diverting enough. Kitty knows them all." He turned to his sister. "How long a visit are you making? You will need to give your orders to Mrs. Finn."

Kitty turned to Clarissa, her lips parted.

Once again Clarissa, customarily so careful, spoke recklessly, "I had hoped she might wish to enjoy the Season."

"Ah!" Kitty uttered a small shriek, causing the others to turn to her.

The marquess laughed, then said to Clarissa, his color high, "I trust you know just how much we are in your debt."

"On the contrary. The debt is mine, for you preserved our lives."

"Oh, thank you, *thank* you," Kitty cried, taking Clarissa's hand. "Let us go look at your things," she cried, and flitted away down the passage to the stairs, leaving Clarissa to make a more appropriate curtsy of departure.

The marquess said, "I'm afraid my bailiff is waiting upon me in two minutes. I must go. May I speak to you later?"

"Certainly, sir."

He bowed, and walked on. Clarissa followed after Kitty. As a shortcut, they passed through Kitty's own bedchamber to the suite allotted to Clarissa.

Kitty's bedchamber was frigid. Kitty seemed accustomed to the cold as she walked through to the significantly warmer guest bedchamber. In the walnut-paneled dressing room, they found two large and well-built trunks set against one wall. Clarissa had to smile. "As I thought. Between my aunt and my step-mother, they must have sent me enough gowns to last me a month at the least."

Clarissa flung open one of the trunks, and began pulling out gowns. She shook them out, and cast them over the nearby chair. Sucking in her breath at such cavalier treatment, Kitty reached out to pick up a cerise-striped spencer with reverent fingers.

Clarissa said, "All of these things make me look vile, which is why I did not want to take them to Holland."

"But these look quite new," Kitty exclaimed as she fingered a knot of yellow ribbon at the neck of the Indian mull walking dress that Clarissa had just thrown over the chair.

"Many of these my aunt insisted upon ordering, as they are her favorite colors. In her defense, I must say, I do not think she sees how badly they look on me. She is accustomed to my sisters, who can wear any color." She held up another gown, this one made of beautiful, heavy linen figured with classical geometric shapes in a shade of yellow that was unfortunate for Clarissa's complexion. "Do you see? Hideous the first time I put them on, and I refused to wear them."

Kitty saw the justice of this remark but, out of sympathy, said nothing.

Clarissa picked up this armload of fabrics, and held them out to Kitty. "But you would look charmingly in these shades. If you would do me an immense favor and take them, they will be put to good use, and my aunt cannot claim that I was wasteful." As Kitty gaped, lost in euphoria, Clarissa's cheeks reddened, and she bent hastily over the trunk again. "Here is another. The accents in this craped muslin would match your eyes." She laid the dress over Kitty's unresisting arm. "And this pink morning gown. I once came down to breakfast in it, and my father asked if I were ill."

"What will you do for gowns?"

"Why, order some more, as soon as we reach London. And if you accompany me, then my aunt will be free to see to my sister Amelia."

Finally Kitty could speak. "I never thought I should be thankful for a shipwreck."

They laughed.

Rosina, Clarissa's maid, entered with Becky shortly after. They were delighted to be taken into their mistress's confidence, and once they learned that these gowns (which Rosina had long deplored) were to be made over for Lady Kitty, they closeted themselves with Alice, who had her mistress's pattern.

Alice, given to understand that she would be promoted to lady's maid and taken to London, received this news as one stunned by a thunderbolt; as she went down to Mrs. Finn to retrieve sewing supplies from the linen closet, she dreamed of herself in Lady Kitty's old blue wool gown at church, and wouldn't *that* just go to show those encroaching Riverside Abbey servants!

Clarissa and Kitty met the brothers at the midday meal. Kitty could scarcely contain her joy. But, where once she would have blurted out her good fortune, there had been that odd moment with Carlisle, that note in his voice that she could not define, the glance of his eye, when he'd said that he should have contrived her visit to Town. Perhaps it might be better not to mention the gowns—women's topics—probably not suitable for the table—she must accustom herself to Town manners.

She sensed a similar constraint at table, and she longed for Carl to know how generous Clarissa had been. Perhaps if they all spent a little more time together, the news might slip out.

And so she was on the watch for an opportunity. It came at the end of the meal when Edward sat back, heaving a sigh as he tossed his napkin away. "Lord! What shall we do? We could propose a whist table, but I've been sitting too long."

Kitty said, "I suggest we all take our guest over the house. You shall help me with the family history."

"Ah!" Edward jumped to his feet. "The gallery! Or, as Papa used to call it, the Rogues' Roost."

Clarissa readily assented, and so Kitty linked arms with her guest, in charity with the world as they walked through the cold halls to the vault-ceilinged gallery. The marquess had intended to get to the many tasks awaiting his attention, but he permitted himself to be drawn along. It was polite—Kitty expected it—but the truth was, he wished to see a little more of Miss Harlowe. Perhaps she would find herself sadly bored. He did not know if he wanted her to be bored, or dreaded it.

Framed pictures crowded the walls, some protected by layers of cloth. Edward dashed about, pulling down these shrouds to reveal some splendid portraits, many by famous artists.

As he pointed out ancestors, Edward began giving an irreverent history of the family. In this, he was joined by Kitty as the two exchanged laughing commentary on their ancestors.

The marquess hung a little back, for the first time in his life discovering a sense of unease. He had never considered this gallery full of his ancestors private or secret, and yet he could not rid himself of the sensation of intrusion. No, that was not it. Miss Harlowe was not the least intrusive. He was being a fool. Merely he was unused to entertaining, and those rare times were confined to the drawing rooms.

Clarissa did not hide her genuine interest as Ned and Kitty explained that the family was ancient but the title was not, the first marquess having gained his title on the continent in aid of one of the bewildering series of alliances that Charles Stuart made before he returned to England as King Charles II.

Though strictly speaking, it was a continental title, on the boat ride over before Charles's triumphant landing, the happy, generous young king had assured the marquess that equivalent lands would be found in England. A suitable holding, which had once been the monastery (to which Riverside Abbey was a mere annex), had changed hands rather frequently under the Tudors, only to be granted a grim new owner in a Puritan commander.

"This," Edward explained with a suitably airy gesture that took in the entire estate, "was bestowed upon the marquess after the Restoration, who promptly pulled down the Puritan's grim old barrack, and put up the new wings."

Kitty pointed out the gentleman's gold-framed portrait. "He wrote a vast number of pompous epistles about his progress to his wife."

"Our tutor once made us copy out some of them to improve our handwriting," Edward put in. "You cannot conceive the outlandish language, half in French."

Kitty said, "The letters lie in the family treasure room, in cedar boxes. No one has wanted to burn them."

Clarissa observed the arrogant gentleman, and next to him, his plump, close-mouthed wife wearing gem-encrusted court dress in the Louis XIV style. "Why did he write to his wife? Was she not here?"

"She did not come to England until she was ever so old," Kitty explained. "He had to visit her in France, where all her children were born, for she was convinced that the Puritans were merely biding their time before springing upon Charles II to decapitate him as well."

Edward took over, explaining that it was the second marquess who increased the family fortune by investing in ships with which he imported tea. This fortune came down more or less intact, in spite of some wild ventures and even wilder excesses, to the present marquess's father, whose single talent, Edward said with a laugh, "was fiendishly inventive ways of spending." Ned shrugged, hands outstretched. "He was known through society for being *point-de-vice* in matters of dress, and...well, if I tell you that he was friends with Fox, you will probably understand how it could come to pass that by the time he took himself off to the afterlife, he'd left behind nothing but—"

He was interrupted by St. Tarval, who regretted his younger brother's openness. The marquess indicated a painting near at hand. "That was painted when he reached his thirtieth birthday. He sat to an artist he'd met in Florence. When the fellow came to London, Papa hired him at once."

They looked up at the handsome gentleman in his heavily laced blue satin coat, the glint of a gorgeous brocaded waistcoat under it, the long beringed hands carelessly disposed. The heavily lidded eyes gazed with secret amusement out at the viewer.

Next to him, in an equally heavy frame worked with real gold, was his wife in portrait. She was decorously seated on a bench in a Sylvan setting, and wore an elaborate feathered hat that obscured half the sky, set over a profusion of magnificent blue-black curls.

As Ned talked on, Clarissa discovered that the marchioness owed the golden tints of her skin to ancestors from southern France, and the bright green of her eyes was the legacy of her Irish grandmother, a famous beauty in her day.

"I don't recall her ever sitting still like that," Edward observed. "She was always a goer, Mama, clear to the end."

Clarissa observed the deep dimple beside her enchanting mouth, and the secret smile, as Kitty said, "Mrs. Finn once told me that they watched one another while those portraits were painted, and they wouldn't stop joking. How I wish I had known her."

St. Tarval reached out to flick one of the long black curls lying on Kitty's shoulder. "You have her laugh, Kit."

Kitty shrugged, not knowing what her laugh sounded like. Her mind was running on other things. "When I was little I could not believe she made a runaway match. She looked so decorous in this portrait. Did you not tell me that your mother died young, too, Clarissa?"

"My mother was not precisely young. That is, she was nine-and-twenty when she married my father, but she did not live long after I was born, which was a year after her marriage. She had always been sickly, I was told," Clarissa said. "She was soon in child again, and though my grandmother insists that she would have recovered her health had not my father brought what she called London quacks to physic her, she died and my brother was stillborn."

The Decourceys hastened to say what was polite, the marquess with regret, and Kitty with her ready sympathy. Then Edward opened his hand toward the gallery. "Have you as sound an array of rakes and wastrels behind you?"

Clarissa had been dividing her interest between the portraits, the stories, and the marquess when his profile was turned her way as he gazed reflectively up at his ancestors. What could he be thinking?

Clarissa was thinking, *What a handsome set of ancestors*. But she was curiously loath to say so. "The Harlowes do have a few black sheep," she said slowly, "but until recent generations our picture gallery is a most unprepossessing display. In fact," she said with a glance at Edward's expectant face, "my brother said once he has never seen such a set of hum-drums and lobcocks in his life."

At that they laughed, and as the room was icy cold, they descended in search of refreshment.

Kitty ran off to speak to Mrs. Finn—and also to check on Alice's progress on the enchanting prospective wardrobe—and Edward dashed away on some errand of his own, leaving St. Tarval to open the door to the drawing room for Clarissa.

For the first time, they were alone together. He had not meant for this to happen. He'd intended to be the first away, but his heedless siblings had decamped, and good manners required him to stay. Besides, he knew he ought to put some questions to Miss Harlowe.

Clarissa took a chair and occupied herself with stretching her hands to the fire. It had been a very long time since she had felt so self-conscious. It was unsettling, like being a girl of eighteen again.

She was attempting to scold her thoughts into order when he spoke.

"Miss Harlowe, I hardly know how to begin, or really what to say. But for my sister's sake, I feel duty-bound to make the attempt. You have been living in the first circles, I know, and I believe you are aware that my sister has never been introduced into society outside the occasional parish gathering. She has, in fact, only once gone into company outside our parish. It was not successful for reasons I still do not precisely understand, for I was not present."

He walked toward the fire, standing a little apart, his profile lit as he stared down into the flames. Clarissa waited, for he seemed to be choosing his words. "My grandmother had her in charge, but she refused in later years to come downstairs. We had just left off mourning after her death when my father died." He made a quick gesture, his fingers open, almost in appeal. "I trust you will forgive me for boring on so about our affairs," he began.

It was that gesture more than the words which prompted Clarissa to say, "If I may be permitted a guess, your brother and sister have largely fallen to your charge. And while you may introduce a brother into parish society, it is difficult to do so for a sister."

His brows lifted. "That is it exactly. And so, I entreat your understanding when I ask, will it really do, for Kitty to go with you to London?"

"Do?"

"Yes. Clothes, fans, you know the things one must have. Manners. Despite all her talk of writing novels, in spite of her reading — perhaps because of it — she is not at all conversant with how to go on, and I hardly know the right way of bringing her to it. In the last years, the reason our grandmother kept Kit upstairs was because my father sometimes brought..." St. Tarval turned away and shook his head. "I beg your pardon. Perhaps this is not a topic for the drawing room."

"If you will forgive me, I must disagree," Clarissa said earnestly. "Your sister has been nothing but kindness and generosity. I could not begin to repay her, except in this small way."

"But it is not small," he returned gently. "Were a season in London small, I should have contrived it somehow, four years ago, when Kitty turned eighteen."

He took a turn around the room. Clarissa could see that he was disturbed; she sensed his inward struggle, but was helpless to identify the cause. She only knew she wanted to help if she could.

He stopped by the fireplace and spoke while looking down into the flames. "I had thought that under Lady Bouldeston's eye, and for only two weeks, I could feel confident that she might see something of the city, but not make the sort of unhappy mistake that occurred on her single venture into company unknown outside our parish. As for what she needs, circumstances are such that I can only put the sum of fifty pounds into her hands. I do know that that will not cover a portion of what she will need."

Clarissa said, "We are already far along in solving that difficulty, for all your mother's fine things are well preserved. I believe we shall contrive very well. And I will promise you this. If she is at all unhappy I will see to it that she returns safely to her home. It is the least I can do in trade for the preservation of our lives."

"So you have said," he rejoined, "but we both know the truth. If my cutter had not been there on illegal pursuits, you would be in Holland now."

"All the more reason for gratitude," Clarissa retorted, thinking of Aunt Sophia's lachrymose hatred of travel. Then she blushed.

"Ah, pray overlook that, if you please." She transferred her gaze to an ornamental grouping of flirting shepherds and merry shepherdesses on the mantelpiece. "The truth is, I am a selfish being. Your sister's presence in town will be diverting in what would otherwise be another sadly boring year."

There was no answer to be made to that. He suspected her claim of selfishness masked a kind heart, but he recognized that his wish to believe the best of her was putting them both in danger. And so he must surrender to the demands of good manners. "Thank you. You have relieved my mind greatly." He bowed, and left the room.

She watched the door close, aware of an almost overwhelming desire to go after, to call out some new subject so that he might linger. She scolded herself for that, waited until she knew he would be safely away, then went upstairs to her bedchamber.

———⟨≻⋅⋅⟩———

To spare the family the expense in firewood, Clarissa had given a considerably surprised Rosina orders not to light her fire.

Waking up and dressing in a frigid room gave Clarissa a new understanding of what Kitty's life must be like. But understanding only goes so far. She went down early to the little drawing room outside the breakfast chamber to wait for the others.

Rather than dwell on their imminent departure, Clarissa let herself enjoy the absolute quiet of a country-house parlor on a winter's day. The room really was handsome, even if the furnishings had been new around the time of the first George. Though the things were thus worn, they were not neglected. Careful hands had done they could to preserve threadbare cushions and carpets.

She entertained herself with imagining the room fitted up with new hangings and new furnishings in an elegant classical style. She had finished the room, and was busy replanting the garden outside the window when the door opened, and St. Tarval entered.

She felt a momentary confusion, but his quiet and pleasant "Good morning, Miss Harlowe," set her at ease. He was dressed in riding clothes, his worn boots shining from a good polishing, and his outdated blue coat setting off his shoulders admirably.

She looked away quickly when *that* thought formed. "I am come with what I fear might be disappointing news," he said. "I have just met with Mr. Bede, who agrees that it might be safer to delay your departure one day, as we cannot trust the main roads."

She was surprised by the bright leap of warmth — of hope — inside her. "I quite understand." And because she could not hide the warmth in her cheeks, she picked up the book lying on the table next to her chair, and opened it, noting with relief that he had several letters in hand.

She pretended to read, though her eyes did not see the printed text on the page. The marquess did not demand her attention, or intrude upon her notice. He quietly read his letters.

And so, in spite of the previous evening's conversation, which had troubled her for half the night, this morning, it seemed, all they needed was the thin light of winter — and the respectable intrusion of letters of business — to establish a congenial atmosphere. Clarissa kept to her book (it was a book of hymns), aware of every rustle of his papers, the shift of cloth as he moved, and she felt curiously suspended in time.

She recognized the cause, for hers was a reflective nature. It was so simple to pretend that this was her own parlor, and that wintry garden outside was hers to order when spring's thaw began. And this man sitting so close by, with the substantial table between them, what would it be like to have his company each day? And at day's end, as the servants brought the bed candles, to walk on his arm up the stairs to...

She must stop herself there. This gentleman was not hers to imagine such things about. He seemed to have formed an understanding with another lady, so delicacy forbade trespass even within the safety of her own mind. That could not lead to any happy conclusion.

The maid brought in the tea, and because Kitty was not yet downstairs, Clarissa bestirred herself. The tea must be poured, which in turn required a little bustle, and a little talking, but that, too, was accomplished with a minimum of words.

The marquess had only meant to see that their guest was well occupied, since Kit was so late in coming down. But he found himself enjoying the quiet fireside with Clarissa. Hers was such a calm presence, and as she was safely absorbed in her reading, he could permit himself a glance or two—she would be gone on the morrow—and observe the curve of her throat, the unconscious grace with which she sat. The softness of her lips, as she gazed fixedly at that old book of hymns. Did she really read such? No, her eyes did not move across the page. What could she be thinking about? Or did she merely wish to avoid speech with him?

For the first time he began to regret his situation. He had never permitted himself the luxury of looking for love, aware he had nothing to offer a lady but this barrack of a house, lands mortgaged to the hilt, and an all-but-empty title. Lucretia was the daughter of a neighbor upon whose goodwill the marquess depended; Sir Henry Bouldeston knew exactly what St. Tarval was worth, for he held some of those notes of hand.

Lucretia had been pretty and persistent at sixteen—it had seemed natural to kiss—and Sir Henry had only smiled, said, that youth would be youth, but sixteen was too young to think of marriage immediately, and so nothing had been said past Understanding.

Since then, St. Tarval had considered himself bound, whenever Lucretia wished to speak. As the Bouldestons were not wealthy, his only thought about the matter had been a modest expectation that she would bring as dowry a forgiving of some of his father's debt to the baronet.

But here was Miss Harlowe pouring tea, and there was the quiet smile again, as she held out a cup and saucer. The marquess reached out his hand, aware of a tremble in his fingers, and his heartbeat quick in his ears. The room had never seemed so cozy, and he sustained a fancy, as sudden as it was fervent, that he would see her there tomorrow, and the next day, too.

He took the saucer, and the brief contact of their fingers was so sweet, so dangerous, he had to turn away, and sit at a distance where the fire was not so warm. He forced his mind to the matters at hand. "If you will forgive my vexatious return to the topic of my sister, Mrs. Finn has told me the secret of the gowns. I will not trespass further upon your good nature beyond my wish to thank you yet again."

Clarissa blushed. "It is nothing. So easily done. Your sister's delight already dispels the fatigues of early spring in anticipation of the move to London."

"Kitty will never be able to effect a fashionable ennui, I fear."

Her hand flew up in protest. "Do I sound jaded? It is not that. But... The need to be continually in the mode... The round of parties in spaces too small for the company, frequently stuffy and overheated, and people saying the same things endlessly repeated... The truth is, I prefer our life in the country. I am a bit like my mother, in being an enemy to the hurly-burly of city life."

St. Tarval laughed. "Will I sound demented if I admit that sometimes I agree, and other times I wish to revisit the foreign cities I only caught a glimpse of, when I was an impecunious lieutenant?"

He was interrupted by the appearance of Clemens, who announced that there was a message from the abbey that required an instant answer. The marquess found himself annoyed with his butler, an unsettling reaction that warned him he had already trespassed into dangerous territory.

So he set down his untouched tea and excused himself.

Clarissa watched him go, aware of a sharp sense of disappointment. They had finally got themselves past the tedium of polite gratitude and were embarking on a real conversation, so rare in her life! Then he was gone.

It was better that way—she must depart. She welcomed the opportunity to be left alone, for she had to restore order to spirits.

Kitty entered the salon at last.

After hearing out the messenger, the marquess had waited beyond until his sister finally appeared. He followed her in order to say to them both, "I am the bearer of an invitation. It seems the main road is entirely snowed under, but the Bouldestons are having River Road cleared at this moment. You and Miss Harlowe are invited to spend the afternoon with the ladies."

Kitty had been looking forward to another day of conversation about her novel, clothes, and London. Her expression changed from happiness to dismay.

The marquess looked uncomfortable. "Kit, you know I'm not cognizant of the ins and outs of female niceties, but it seems to me that after having turned down their generous offer, it might seem rude give them the go-by today. Especially as they must have old Tom Garrow and half their men out in the road now, clearing it."

"Yes, I agree," Kitty said quickly. "It is very kind and generous in them."

The marquess's expression eased. "Young Tom is in the kitchen now, drinking some hot coffee. I'll give him the message." He vanished.

Clarissa was silent, aware of her own disappointment, but she was also curious to know more about this young lady to whom St. Tarval was attached. First impressions could be deceptive, and she must not judge too hastily.

Kitty turned a troubled gaze her way. "I think...I think this invitation is in your honor," she said tentatively.

Clarissa said the proper nothings, and a few hours later, found herself welcomed by Lady Bouldeston herself, a round woman dressed very stylishly, with a quantity of curling light brown hair done up in a youthful style under her lace cap.

She conducted Clarissa to the best chair in a pleasing salon, where the sideboard was loaded with good things to eat. Then Lady Bouldeston brought forward her second daughter, Lucasta, to introduce to Clarissa.

Lucretia poured out the tea, and Lucasta — who looked very much like her sister but with darker hair and a higher voice — said, "Oh Miss Harlowe, you cannot conceive how excited I am to enter society at last, and yet my trepidations. You will laugh at me, I know, when you see how shy I am. Everyone teases me about it." Her head drooped forward, but not far enough to hide how assiduously her eyes darted about to see the effect her words were having.

"Another cream cake?" Lady Bouldeston said, gesturing impatiently at the neat maidservant. "Pray, bring Miss Harlowe another cake."

"No thank you," Clarissa said.

"You must know that my cook is French. Escaped the guillotine, just barely, though the rest of the family did not. They were *noblesse présentée,* of course. Sir Henry is quite particular that way. It is said that these almond cakes were favored by Queen

Marie Antoinette herself, but the receipt was not for sale."

Lucasta had been waiting impatiently for her mother to finish speaking. "Oh, Miss Harlowe, surely you have a French cook. You must be accustomed to everything of the best, situated as you are with respect to the Devereaux family, and her grace of Norcaster, your grandmother."

Lucretia interpolated a remark here. "Lucasta, you ought not to trouble Miss Harlowe with such questions. She told me herself, upon our introduction, that she seldom sees any of her Devereaux connections, except in town."

Clarissa was surprised that Lucretia should remember so threadbare a politeness. She had become accustomed to young ladies offering a kind of mendacious friendship in order to obtain an introduction to Clarissa's handsome cousin, the Honorable Philip Devereaux, or failing an invitation, at least to insinuate through questions news of where he might be expected next.

Clarissa had become skillful in deflecting such ruses, though not without sympathy. It was the business of young ladies to marry as well as they could, and Cousin Philip was not only eligible, he was very rich, third in line to a dukedom, and she had grown up hearing everyone praise his handsome countenance.

"It is true," Clarissa said, feeling safe enough in that.

Lady Bouldeston pressed more refreshments on Clarissa, who refused politely while noticing that none of the Bouldeston ladies bestirred themselves so assiduously on Kitty's behalf.

But by now she suspected the cause behind this invitation and the fulsome treatment. It was a passport to claim acquaintance in London.

It was no more than so many others did. She should not be angry, but she could not prevent the thought that this was another reason why she detested the London Season, as Lady Bouldeston leaned toward her and said with a rehearsed air, "Perhaps we may amuse ourselves with a little music. Lucasta? Pray entertain us with that German air you have learnt."

Lucasta protested, hiding her face. "Oh, pray, Mama! Miss Harlowe is sure to have such exquisite taste, hearing London performers!"

Lady Bouldeston lifted her hands. "Miss Harlowe is certain to be charmed, Lucasta, and as for Lady Catherine, we quite count her as one of the family, old friends as we are."

Clarissa's middle sister, who alone of the family had a lovely voice, commonly made just such protestations, so Clarissa offered polite assurances.

Even so, Lucasta displayed a tendency to dramatize her reluctance until her elder sister said in a sweet tone, "If you cannot overcome your apprehensions, Sister, I shall offer an air of my own."

Lucasta tossed her head. "I would not wish to disoblige Mama." She moved with alacrity to the pianoforte on the other side of the room.

Lucretia sat down to play, and Lucasta took up a stance, eyes soulfully turned toward Heaven, and began to sing Schiller's "The Song of the Bell."

Lucasta's voice was nothing remarkable. In point of fact, she did not always hit each note true, but seemed to feel that adding embellishments such as trills, and striking affecting poses, masked these shortcomings. If she was even aware of such shortcomings, for her mother exhibited every evidence of enjoyment.

When Lucretia joined her on a French ballad, the two sisters dragged one another off the note entirely. They sang the louder, or perhaps that was the effect, while their Mama beat the time on her knee, and as she turned her smiling face to Clarissa, it was clear from her countenance that she believed she had offered her guests a rare treat.

"As you can see, my girls have had the benefit of superior training," Lady Bouldeston said at the end, and leaned forward with an air of confidence. "I understand that it is not always the thing to mention Lady Hamilton, and yet she was once received everywhere—her entertainments were *tres jolie*, as I am certain you are aware, Miss Harlowe, therefore you will not mind when I confide to you that Lady Hamilton was present at a little gathering when Lucasta was still very much a schoolgirl. So she did not go out into company. But Lady Hamilton positively begged to hear my girls sing, and afterward, pronounced them quite *distinguée*— agreed that had they not had the disadvantage of being ladies of birth, they might have performed anywhere on the European stage, even before kings."

This call for compliments was too loud to be ignored, and perforce Clarissa must provide the expected praise, which Lady Bouldeston and her daughters took as a request for further entertainment.

Kitty largely remained silent throughout, betraying a faint wince during a high note, which Clarissa secretly found reassuring. She was not being too *nice* in her tastes. Still, when at last the visit drew to its close and there must be a bustle of further compliments and thanks, and assurances of seeing one another in town, as hats, gloves, and coats were putting on, Clarissa wondered if her own mother might have boasted in like manner of Clarissa's modest talents, had she lived?

Eight

LADY BOULDESTON HAD LOATHED the marchioness of St. Tarval for her beauty and her instant popularity in the parish after her disgraceful marriage. It was (she had assured anyone who listened) a disinterested dislike, as she was a just woman, and as such, equally faulted the marquess for jilting her elder sister in order to make this runaway match. She had put a mourning band to her hat when the wretched woman had killed herself riding a half-tamed horse, but as she had observed to Sir Henry on the way to the funeral, "It can only be regarded as an act of Providence."

Sir Henry, who had very much admired the dashing marchioness, had wisely kept silent.

Providence had certainly been dilatory in administering justice. By the time Lady Catherine reached the age of ten, it had been obvious to all that she had inherited her mother's beauty. Lady Bouldeston had done what she could to aid Providence by talking everywhere of the girl as a "sad romp" when the present marquess had permitted his sister to gallop around the countryside, and lamented Lady Catherine's brazen lack of humility when she came to church in her mother's turned gowns.

She had instructed Lucretia, being the same age, that it was her Christian duty to administer hints at Lady Catherine's sad lack of social grace. Lucretia, who inherited much of her mother's nature, was an apt as well as enthusiastic pupil to her mother's teachings.

Kitty was only aware that this visit had gone much better than most of her visits to Riverside Abbey. She was certain she had Clarissa to thank. She had never seen Lady Bouldeston more cordial than when, on their departure, she had said, "It is a pleasure to observe that we will all see one another in London quite soon."

So her spirits were high as they returned to the quiet of Tarval Hall, where they found the marquess in the warm study. Kitty had pulled off her hat, and, swinging it by its ribbon, she said, "Do find Ned, Carl. I propose an evening of whist—I feel as if I shall win thousands!"

At the marquess's behest the cook had put forward the salt pork in keeping for Sunday; his intention was to offer their departing guest a fine meal, after which he would keep himself occupied in another part of the house. But he could not forebear to glance at Miss Harlowe—he saw her smile—and he thought, *It's only an evening*. Why should he not enjoy it, as it would be the last?

Clarissa's thoughts ran along the same path, and so, entirely due to Kitty's and Ned's wish for untrammeled wild play, Clarissa and St. Tarval found themselves partnered for the game.

The poets would never laud the words spoken that evening, any more than the wits of London would hail the speakers. There was no flattery, no clever references to Cupid's shafts or slain hearts or the powers of the cruel fair—the sort of flirtatious talk that Clarissa hated most. Praise of the excellent dinner led to the weather, and thence to roads, subjects so mundane they could be tedious, and yet weren't. The marquess would occasionally interpolate mild observations, such as his comparison to the roads of Sicily, which adventure the marquess described so well that Clarissa forgot that it was her turn to play, and kept the Decourceys waiting until she recollected herself.

She would have been glad to hear more, but Edward interrupted his brother, saying, "We've heard all that times out of mind. Who cares about places we shall never see? Your trick, Kit, I believe."

St. Tarval might have been justified in expressing affront, or even irritation at being so summarily interrupted, but he only said, "Quite right, Ned. I do not have license to bore my auditors about my travels until I have passed fifty. Did you say clubs are trumps?"

There could be no intimacy in such a gathering, and yet in Clarissa's eyes, a gentleman who took evident pleasure in a family party was more interesting than the best dancer or whip she had ever heard extolled. She found herself distracted by the humor in his voice, by the glimmer of firelight in his eyes, by the fine shape of his hands.

Soon—too soon—there would be a Lady St. Tarval sitting in this very chair. Clarissa could envision Lucretia Bouldeston in her place, a thought that hurt so much she almost missed a trick, and had to scold herself into self-control.

She ought to have known better, she thought when—too soon—the evening came to an end, and Kitty lit the way to their bedchambers. There, Clarissa found a candelabra lit, a generous gesture that only hurt the more. When she blew the candles out, she resolved that she would keep to her room until it was time to depart.

After she climbed into bed, she lay staring up at the blurred shapes of angels and tried to banish the images of the evening, unexceptionable as they were.

It was strange that her Cousin Philip—well established in town as the handsomest of men—stirred no such emotions in her. She valued him, she liked him, but she had never listened for his voice, or wished to sit close enough to catch the firelight glowing golden along the edges of his eyelashes.

What did the term 'handsome' even mean? The marquess's eyes were not nearly the deep green of his sister's, or his smile the flashing, dimpled grin displayed by his younger brother. She had met many men with black hair, both curly and straight, and hazel eyes were to be found by the dozen, as were firm chins, high brows, and good limbs.

His coat was well-brushed, very near to being shabby. Why should the sum of ordinary parts add to an extraordinary whole from whom the awareness of parting caused a regret sharp enough to term pain? She was only aware that he was the dearest man she had ever met.

But he was promised to someone else.

After a sleepless night, St. Tarval rose with the sun and stayed busy until Ned came to find him. "Hey day, Carl, I've searched all over for you! Kit was looking for you — wants to bid you adieu."

The marquess said, "Tell her I will be there directly. I must wash my hands."

He was there to hand the ladies into the coach. He smiled, they smiled — though Kitty's smile was teary — everybody smiled until the coach door was shut, and the driver nodded to the boy at the leader's head to let go.

As the coach rolled away, the marquess was seized by a sharp sense of regret. But he was accustomed to regret. It was a part of life. As he followed Ned back inside, he told himself that things were better this way; now he could school himself to duty.

Inside the coach, Clarissa gripped her hands, controlling the impulse to press her nose to the glass for one last glimpse.

After a time, Kitty's soft voice broke the silence. "Are you unwell, Clarissa?"

"I must confess that being confined in a closed coach can sometimes bring on the headache, but it is winter, and there can be no open carriage. Pay me no mind, I beg."

Kitty did her best to sympathize, and settled back, thoroughly enjoying the deep squabs of the cushions, and the hot brick on the sheepskin-covered floor.

After a time the newness wore off a little, and as they passed through the familiar countryside, she began to nod. The night before, she'd scarcely slept a wink for excitement.

For a time the sight of unfamiliar country was interesting, but after all it was much the same as the parish she knew: hills, trees, the snow-topped roofs. Clarissa's eyes were closed. Kitty snuggled down deeper in the carriage rug, her eyelids drifted shut, and the next thing she knew, she woke when the carriage had ceased to move.

Men's voices shouted unintelligible words outside, amid laughter from one. Kitty looked around, startled awake, to discover Clarissa gathering the folds of her traveling cloak about her.

"Have we reached your home?" Kitty asked.

"Oh, no, we have a long way to go yet," Clarissa replied.

"It will be dark very soon. Where are we?"

"I believe I recognized that bridge, which means we must be arriving at the posting house in Thames Ditton. I know my father keeps horses there. Mr. Bede—"

The carriage door opened to a burst of cold air. Mr. Bede appeared, his nose red with cold, ready to hand them out.

The carriage steps had been let down. Mr. Bede and Oliver—who had arrived the night before—were there at either side to make sure the young ladies did not slip and fall as they stepped to the slippery, slushy yard.

Kitty followed Clarissa to the door, where the landlord stood bowing and smiling in a gratifying way. Clarissa did not seem to notice the bustle to make them welcome, but Kitty did, and enjoyed every moment as they were conducted to a parlor pleasantly warmed by a substantial fire.

Clarissa sat down and pulled her gloves off.

Kitty said, "Do you still have the headache? Shall we ask for a tisane?"

Clarissa said, "It is nothing—it will soon pass off, thank you."

Kitty said everything that was polite, though she could see in the way Clarissa's eyes narrowed that the headache was real.

When Rosina appeared, and said that the bedchamber was ready, Clarissa excused herself to lie down for an hour, promising that she would be better company once she had rested her head.

The parlor had been equipped with several back numbers of *La Belle Assemblée*. Kitty picked up the most recent of these, and began leafing through the fashion plates. She was much entertained by imagining herself in this or that mode, mentally subtracting various embellishments which the artist had seen fit to cumber the doll-like ladies depicted.

She was startled to hear a female voice in the hall before the door was opened by an impatient hand.

Kitty beheld a young lady in the muslin gown, mittens, and severe bonnet of a schoolgirl. This girl caught her breath on the sob and dashed the back of her hand across her eyes. "Oh! *Pray* excuse me, that is, I did not know..."

With ready sympathy, Kitty said, "I assure you, it is of no

consequence. Do you need help?"

The girl, thus encouraged, stepped in, shut the door behind her, and burst into a noisy tears. "I wish you could," she cried. "That hateful wretch. I hate him!"

Kitty stared in amazement, then exclaimed, "Are you being abducted?" The moment the words were out she was embarrassed both by their unlikelihood and by the small surge of excitement that she felt.

If the lady was discomposed by Kitty's hopeful tones, she evidenced no sign. Her tear-drenched honey-brown eyes regarded Kitty in wide question, then narrowed in intent. "Yes," she said briskly, the tears gone, the tremble vanished from her small mouth. "Do you perchance have a carriage? Are you about to depart? If I could escape this very instant, all Might Not Be Lost."

Kitty heard the capital letters, and her sympathies kindled. "We do have a carriage, that is, it is not mine, but I know my friend would be happy to help—"

The door opened again. This time the entrant was a tall, powerfully built gentleman in a many-caped driving coat. He looked exactly like a Greek god. An angry one.

And here at last is the fourth dancer, who was deeply chagrinned to open the door and find a strange young lady within. "I beg your pardon—" he began.

"Oh, *no!*" the schoolgirl cried.

Kitty looked from one to the other, her mind leaping to the obvious conclusion—that this was the Evil Abductor.

She heroically placed herself between the Innocent and the Ravisher, and turned to the former. "Is this your hateful wretch?"

"Yes," the girl cried, and once again burst into a storm of tears.

"Bess—" the man attempted to speak again.

This time he was interrupted by Kitty. "Wretch indeed! Why, you might almost be her father."

The man looked completely thunderstruck. Then color flooded his well-chiseled cheeks as he drew up in hauteur. "Ma'am, if you would kindly accord us a moment of privacy—"

Though Kitty craved romance, she had never dreamed that she would attain the exalted heights of actually assisting in foiling a real abduction. If only the man wasn't so handsome—but then *handsome is as handsome does*, as Kitty's grandmother used to say rather too often.

"If you intend to drag this child off, you must go through me," Kitty stated head held high. And to the young lady, "What little protection I can offer you, make sure I shall."

"Beast!" Bess declared, peering past the protection of Kitty's shoulder.

"Coxcomb," Kitty added. "Rake!"

"Bess, what did you tell this lady?" the gentleman asked in a tone of extreme vexation.

"Monster!" The young lady popped up on Kitty's other side long enough to retort.

Though Kitty knew little about romance, she had enough experience with brothers to recognize a taunting tone. That was puzzling. If she were being abducted, why did Miss Bess sound like she was gloating?

Kitty was about to frame a question when the door opened again, and Clarissa entered, saying, "I thought I heard a familiar voice — *Philip?*"

"Oh, my," Kitty breathed.

"Bess?" Clarissa went on. "I thought I recognized the carriage in the yard, but I couldn't be certain. How come you two here?"

"Elizabeth!" the young lady declared, emerging with arms crossed.

"I beg pardon, Cousin Elizabeth," Clarissa said, with no evidence of surprise.

A profound silence ensued, during which Kitty's entire body flamed with painful prickles of embarrassment.

Bess was the first to speak. "At least *one* of my relations is kind enough to call me *Elizabeth*, and *not* address me like I am a *mere child*," she muttered.

"Good day, Cousin Clarissa," the gentleman said. "We are just arrived this moment." He turned an exasperated glance Kitty's way, but good manners constrained him from speaking until they were introduced.

"Jupiter," Kitty exclaimed, and blushed the more, thoroughly vexed with herself for permitting one of her brothers' expressions to escape her lips. She turned a reproachful look on Bess. "It is quite wicked to tell untruths, particularly to strangers who are trying to help you."

Bess stamped her foot. "It *is* true. He *has* abducted me."

"Bess," the gentleman said, in no tone of approbation.

"I do not *wish* to go back to Bath," Bess stated, and dissolved into tears.

Clarissa advanced into the room, suppressing the urge to laugh. In her best company manner, she said, "may I make you all known to one another? Kitty, my cousins Devereaux. Cousin Bess—"

"Elizabeth!"

"I beg pardon. Cousin Elizabeth and Cousin Philip, may I present Lady Catherine Decourcey, who is accompanying me to Oakwood."

Mr. Devereaux made a stiff bow in response to Kitty's equally stiff curtsy, then said in a low undervoice to Clarissa, "I must thank you. Your entrance interrupted the third farcical tragedy I have had to endure this day."

Kitty had been determined to remember her company manners, but that resolve was overwhelmed by a tide of embarrassment. With the freedom she used when talking to her brothers, "I daresay if you had not stepped in here looking *just* like a villain, without so much as a knock..."

"Ma'am," the gentleman responded, in accents of extreme chagrin. "I was referring to my unfortunate sibling, but in any case, I beg your pardon."

Clarissa interposed herself. "Perhaps, Kitty, if you would take Bess to wash her face and hands..."

"I hate him," Bess declared, sobbing loudly.

Kitty was all too happy to get herself out of the room. She indicated the door to the angry girl, who said over her shoulder, "If you feel the need to send for the Bow Street Runners to guard the room, *pray* do so." And seeing that this shot had not the effect that she had anticipated, Bess added, "No doubt if I were to die on the spot, you would be cast into high glee."

Kitty pulled the door shut, and drew the sniffling girl farther down the passage to her bedchamber, where Bess flung her bonnet to the floor, and flounced to the only chair.

Kitty picked up the bonnet, saying sympathetically, "Can you tell me what happened?"

"Oh, the *stupidest* thing." Bess scowled. "I was sent down from Miss Battersea's Academy for Young Gentlewomen, because that cat Arabella Campbell peached on me. And it was the worst lie in the universe, for I was *not* going to run off with M. Bonneau."

"Who?"

"M. Bonneau, the French master. Several of us got up the silliest flirtation with him, all in fun, you know, for it made the lessons so much less tedious. But Arabella is jealous because the younger girls all like me better, and was so horrid that I had to act, after which she said it was her duty to tell Miss Battersea, and so I was to keep my room in disgrace until I had copied out *all* of the *Sermons to Young Women*."

Bess paused to wipe her eyes on her sleeve. "But then I thought, I am *nearly*, almost *sixteen*, so why should I have to stay, and so I sneaked out after the post was delivered, and used my pocket money, and took the mail coach to my friend Margaret in London, and it was enormous fun, you cannot conceive, except for the old lady with the basket who kept poking me, and the man who ate onions, but I pretended to be an orphan, and then a French immigrant, escaped from the guillotine, and Margaret was in transports to see me, for she was sent down last winter, but then her horrid mother wrote to mine, and so my *horrid* brother came to get me, and..."

Kitty stared with interest at Bess, who could not be five feet tall. She had tiny hands and feet, and wide, expressive light brown eyes. She reminded Kitty of a flower.

"And all I can say is, in a better day, sixteen was quite old enough to be presented," Bess finished.

"Do you wish to be married so soon?"

"Oh, no, I have no idea of being *married*. At least, not until I've had seasons and *seasons* of balls, and parties, and all the fun I *should* have. But mama declared that I must go back for at least two more years, and ordered Philip to take me back to school, and he would not so much as listen to any of my ideas."

"Such as?"

"He could take me to Paris. If they want me to be expert in

French, what could be better, now that everyone says there is to be peace at last? And I should like very much to see Madame Bonaparte, who everyone in the world says is the most beautiful of women. After a season there, I would be willing to go back to Miss Battersea's, for then I should have something that is quite as good as Arabella's horrid golden hair: a wardrobe of French clothes."

"What was the cause of the disgrace, may I ask?" Kitty asked.

Bess eyed her, but saw only sympathy—that and the fact that this unknown "Lady Catherine" was far, *far* lovelier than Arabella Campbell could ever hope to be.

"I vowed, if Arabella made one more fling at my brown hair, or called me *Bess* in that monstrous tone, I would put a toad in her bed, and she did, both! So I put a brace of toads in her bed. Nice, moist, fat ones."

Kitty hid her laughter, saying only, "I quite sympathize. But it does not put your brother at fault, if he is executing your mother's wishes."

She scowled. "He could as *easily* take me to *Paris*. I overheard him saying he might go to Italy, now that there was peace on the continent, and Paris is quite on the way. And expense is no matter, so why should he not?"

Kitty made a sympathetic noise, which Bess found encouragement to go on. "But he refused! *Then* he said if I keep prosing on about despising the name 'Bess,' people would lose sympathy, and I said it was unfair, just because there has always been a 'Bess' in our family, ever since that horrid queen who cut off the head of the beautiful Mary Stuart, and I did not *ask* to be inflicted with it. The name, I should say, not the head. And so Philip knows, and that is why I have, well, I have tried different names, but only a very, very few! When I was young and silly I insisted they call me Clothilde, and last year I wanted to be Rosamunda. Is that not the most romantical name? Ross-ah-mooon-da."

"Indeed, it's very—"

"You *cannot* be dowdy if you are a Rosamunda, but Miss Battersea said I must use my given name, and then Philip had the audacity to say he quite understood—that he never liked being saddled with Philip, but I probably would not like the formality of

Elizabeth after a time—and I said it is *quite different* for men, and that he knows *nothing about* it, but however least he could lend me the money to go alone, for I would pay it back when I am five-and-twenty, which is when I will gain my fortune. Either then or if I marry, which, you know, is horridly unfair, because then it will just go into the hands of my husband, and I will not touch a cent of it. And if Mother didn't keep me on the most beggarly allowance for pin-money, as if we had to ride in the poor-basket!"

Kitty could not help glancing at Bess's well-made traveling clothes, to the costly kid boots that she was scuffing on the floor, but she said only, "Is his appearance at your friend's one of the tragedies to which he referred?"

Bess fixed her gaze on a point somewhere over Kitty's head. "No, well, yes, the first one. The second came after, when I jumped out of the carriage, for I thought it would be more fun to run off again. So I did. But the snow was so wet, and so cold, and it began snowing harder, and I had quite forgotten that I hadn't a penny in my pocket, that I decided I might as well go back, only he'd gone in the wrong direction to look for me, thinking I was running back toward London, and so, by the time we found one another again, it was late, and he felt obliged to put up here for the night, as we often have done when visiting my cousins in Surrey. And I could not *bear* the idea that he might ring a peal over me." She eyed Kitty, her lip trembling. "You think I am hateful—spoilt. Do you?"

"I allow that the provocation must have been extreme, Miss Elizabeth," Kitty said diplomatically.

"Oh, *thank* you for calling me Elizabeth."

Though she did not have sisters, Kitty had experienced Lucasta's expertise in employing tears, and detected the signs that Bess might be inclined in the same direction. She hastened to say, "In any case, we shall assuredly join parties, as you are connections with Clarissa, so there will be no opportunity for lectures. Clarissa is far too kind for that."

"Very true," Bess stated, sitting up a little straighter. "Philip has often said that he prefers Cousin Clarissa to most females, but then everyone says he dislikes most females, because they *will* chase after him, though I cannot imagine why."

Bess rose with alacrity, washed her hands and face, employed

Kitty's comb to tame her thick brown hair, and then smiled with sunny anticipation as they walked back to the parlor.

While Bess had been employed in restoring her appearance to civility, Kitty had time to reflect on her *faux pas*. And before she had even set foot in London! At least, she told herself as she followed Bess into the room, the gentleman was soon off to Italy. Maybe he would go straight there from Bath, and Kitty would never have to see him again.

The conversation was thus constrained as the four whiled away the last hour before parting again to dress for dinner. Clarissa still had the headache; her cousin Philip had retreated behind extreme reserve; Kitty behaved like an effigy of herself, responding with such careful politeness that Clarissa would have suspected her of satire had she not seen the troubled pucker in Kitty's brow. Only Bess chattered on, apparently unaware, or maybe she wished to prevent a recurrence of the earlier vexations.

In any case, it was a relief when the innkeeper came to inform them that dinner would be served in half an hour.

They parted to dress. Kitty bolstered her faltering courage with the sight of Clarissa's yellow muslin newly made into an evening dress, with tiny pearl buttons (removed from one of her mother's ball gowns) sewn down the front of the bodice, and the simple yellow ribbon at the sleeves and waist.

She smoothed her hands down the skirt and turned to observe herself in the long pier glass. At least no fault could be found with her appearance, she thought as she scratched at Clarissa's door.

Bade to enter, she observed Rosina trying to coax side curls to fall at either side of Clarissa's ears

Kitty said, "Clarissa, would you forgive me for observing that the other style is more flattering?"

"Which?"

Kitty gestured with her hands, indicating the smooth crown of hair on top of Clarissa's head.

Clarissa blinked in surprise. "That is how I wear it at home. It is not at all modish."

"Perhaps not the mode, but it is *a* mode. What's more, it is attractive."

"I wonder..." Clarissa saw the quick twitch of approval in

Rosina's lips, and nodded. "That is what I shall do, then."

Rosina cast a grateful glance at Kitty, then began brushing out Clarissa's hair anew. As she did, Kitty explained what Bess had told her, figuring that the maid had to have heard most of it—along with the rest of the occupants of the inn.

At the end, Clarissa said, "You must know that Bess—Elizabeth—has been much indulged. Her father was very old and her birth was most unexpected, which is why there are a dozen years between her and Philip. After her father died, her mother treated her like a pet. It was actually Philip's idea to send her to school, for she must learn how to go on in Society. Her hoyden's tricks were smiled on at home, but a young lady cannot indulge in pranks or distempered freaks when her will is crossed."

Clarissa saw comprehension in Kitty's expressive countenance. She'd requested Kitty to take Bess out so that both might have a chance to recover countenance. She and Cousin Philip had chatted of travel, and he asked about the details of the shipwreck, expressing real concern, for he was partial to sailing.

She was surprised to discover, when the two parties rejoined, that he had exchanged his riding dress for the fine coat and satin knee breeches of proper evening wear. She was used to him relaxing social strictures such as this when away from London.

Kitty, whose brothers had invariably worn riding dress, found his formal appearance intimidating, perhaps even a rebuke. She confined her attention strictly to her plate.

A glass of wine and some food chased away the last of Clarissa's headache. This was fortunate, as she felt obliged to take the lead in conversation. Her initial forays, however, resulted in only the most polite of nothing-talk. Bess was resigned, Kitty subdued. These reactions she understood. But Cousin Philip was unaccountably quiet, even when she introduced the topic of literature, on which they shared many tastes. He must still be aggrieved with his sister—or maybe he was apprehensive of her indulging her moods again?

His reflections had nothing to do with his sister.

Beautiful girls he had seen aplenty in his years on the Town. Beautiful girls unconscious of their effect—whose faces changed with quick wit—were rarer. But hard on that appreciation was the hideous prospect of a young lady who shared Bess's most unfortunate characteristics. He braced for another outburst, permitting himself to relax only when it became apparent that this unknown Lady Catherine very plainly regretted their unfortunate first encounter. Her manners had become so stilted they were nearly wooden.

He felt a strong impulse to coax her out of her stiffness, but squashed it. Far too often what he regarded as the most disinterested kindness seemed to engender expectations. And so he confined his conversation to polite necessity.

Clarissa, despairing of the prospect of an evening with three silent people, turned to her younger cousin. "Have you received a letter from my sister Eliza?"

"Not since Christmas, Cousin Clarissa," Bess replied, very politely.

"Then you will be hearing from her soon, I am certain. You know that Amelia is to make her bow to society this year, and as a consolation, Mama is going to invite several of Eliza's and Tildy's particular friends for a week. I heard your name mentioned."

"At Oakwood or in Brook Street?"

"In Brook Street, to be sure."

"I shall write to her *at once*, as soon as I reach Bath," Bess responded, her mood visibly brightening.

That was the highlight of the conversation, in spite of Clarissa's best efforts. She was relieved when they all parted for the night, and moreso to rise the next morning to the news that that the Devereaux party had just departed.

Nine

MR. BEDE HAD ALL IN readiness once the ladies had broken their fast. They departed under leaden skies. By noon, Clarissa had succumbed to another headache, made worse by the rocking of the coach as a cold wind rose.

Kitty, face pressed anxiously to the glass, feared being stranded in a blizzard when the carriage rolled onto a well-graveled road between beautifully tended hedges. The first flakes were falling as they climbed out of the carriage, and were led into a hall.

A stout, red-faced butler had just shut the front door behind them when two young ladies skimmed down the broad stairway, their slippers whispering on the checkerboard marble floor.

"Clarissa! You're home! Clarissa!" they clamored, trying to be heard over one another.

"Were you really attacked by French agents?"

"Is this Lady Catherine?"

"Mama says we are to go to Brook Street early to order gowns!"

Clarissa kissed them both, responding in a gentle voice that caused the two to lower their own tones. She introduced Kitty, who found herself regarded by two pairs of celestial blue eyes wide-set in round faces framed by curling fair hair. She couldn't help but think that Cendrillon had been turned about, for the stepsisters were very beautiful — much more so than Clarissa — but it was also apparent that Clarissa was much beloved.

The girls dropped neat curtseys and promptly resumed their questions. Kitty had the leisure to observe that Amelia was a trifle taller than Eliza, and that the latter's hair was more golden, whereas Amelia's would probably be ash in five years. Though nothing would mar her astonishing beauty.

"Where is Mama?"

"In the Red Saloon, to escape Tildy's noise. She's trying to learn off that horrid Haydn sonata. You cannot *conceive* the false notes."

Eliza added from the other side of her sister as they started up the stairs, "Papa fears Tildy is just as unmusical as Hetty."

"Oh, Lizzy, give over boring on about the pianoforte. Clarissa, you do not know the best. Papa says I am to have my very own riding hack for Town. But he says I cannot ride without a groom, like you, until I am one-and-twenty, if I should stay unmarried that long." She ended on a decidedly peevish note.

Eliza added in a low, indignant whisper, "Aunt Sophia told Papa that young ladies who ride without a groom are considered fast, even though we all saw Amabel Whitlew riding with her twin sister, last year, and neither of them above eighteen, and that horrid old stick Miss Kiddermore rides alone, and James said, if *she's* fast, then — "

Amelia cut in, "For my part, I think Aunt Sophia says it because she does not like horses. Whatever anyone does that she mislikes, she always says it's fast."

Eliza tugged Clarissa's arm. "What, precisely, *is* fast, anyway, Clarissa? Amelia doesn't know anything, James just teases, and Hetty won't talk to me at all, though before she was married she promised to tell me *everything*."

"Perhaps you should ask Aunt Sophia," Clarissa suggested.

"And be scolded into writing out my Collect ten times? I think not," Eliza declared, marched across the landing, and flung open the gilded door to a charming saloon newly done in the Athenian style. "Mama, they are *here*."

"My dear, do not bounce so," a faint, drawling voice was heard from within.

Kitty entered to discover a vision in blue gauze rising from an elegant reclining sofa. "Clarissa, dear." The vision kissed Clarissa, then turned Kitty's way. "And here is Lady Catherine? Oh, you have such a look of your mother. She was pointed out as the diamond of diamonds, when I was in the schoolroom. I still remember her appearance at Vauxhall, in a gown of—but never mind that. Clarissa, your trip was dreadful, of course?"

"I will be quite recovered as soon as I drink some tea," Clarissa said.

Lady Chadwick gestured for the girls to be seated. Kitty perched on the edge of a lyre-backed chair cushioned in red satin, and regarded her hostess, who, in spite of five children, had managed to retain her figure. She dressed to make the most of it. Her ashy blond hair was youthfully arranged under its frivolous lacy cap, and her pretty face had been delicately enhanced by an artistic hand.

Lady Chadwick put a few questions to Clarissa, then dismissed her younger daughters, who were whispering on the other side of the fireplace.

They obediently retired, but their raised voices echoed off the marble as they walked away: "Well for my part I find her beautiful, and I cannot see that she is dressed at all peculiar."

"No, indeed. Aunt Sophia must have windmills in her head."

Then the two voices fell suddenly silent. Kitty blushed, her cheeks hot, but Lady Chadwick was so unmoved it was clear that she paid no heed to the girls' prattle as she said, "I rang for tea as soon as I heard you were arrived. Pray sit down, my dears."

On her last word, the reason for the girls' sudden silence entered the room in the person of Mrs. Latchmore, who was fanning herself agitatedly with several pieces of paper. "My dear Lady Chadwick, I've just received three applications for the post, and, oh, Clarissa, I see you are returned at last. And safe, thank Providence, which is more than I expected, though of course devoutly to be hoped for. Lady Wilburfolde has been asking every day. And Lady Catherine! Why, what a lovely traveling gown, and I do hope—travel. What was it I was about to say?"

The moment she walked in, a new and hideous worry had crowded out the old in Kitty's head: what if Mrs. Latchmore recognized Clarissa's made-over gowns? But the quick glance, the slight brow-lift of approval and the general air of indifference reassured her as Mrs. Latchmore turned back to Lady Chadwick, and began talking over her business as if the girls were not in the room.

Clarissa touched Kitty's wrist. "We will drink our tea elsewhere. Permit me to show you the house."

Kitty followed Clarissa, relieved to have avoided another hideous scrape. She shivered as she followed Clarissa out onto the landing and across to the other side, where the sounds of determined fingers working skillfully at a Haydn sonata could be heard, strongly marking the time. But as the two proceeded along the landing, the music halted abruptly.

A leggy schoolgirl appeared, and flashed a happy smile as Clarissa and Kitty approached. Kitty smiled back, thinking that this child would easily be the most beautiful of all Clarissa's astonishing sisters.

As soon as Clarissa had performed the introductions, Matilda clasped her hands and declared, "Oh, Clarissa, were you truly in a shipwreck?"

"Yes, Tildy."

"Oh, if only I had known you would have such an adventure, I would have been *wild* to go. Was it the French, or pirates?"

"Neither," Clarissa said. "Are you quite finished with your lesson? I am afraid that Miss Gill will be disappointed in me if I interrupt."

Miss Matilda Harlowe lifted an impatient shoulder. "Just as I thought. It was only Aunt Sophia making things up again. And I know that Lady Catherine does not wear her maid's cast-off clothes, either. I never believed that, but I did hope about the French or the pirates. Now that we know that you survived," Matilda added hastily.

Kitty's cheeks warmed unpleasantly as Clarissa said, "I believe Miss Gill is waiting, Tildy."

Matilda cast a heart-felt sigh. "If the Prodigy Mozart had any notion how much torment he might cause people who had done no harm to him, he surely would have confined himself to stickball with his friends."

"I believe that particular piece was written by Mr. Haydn," Clarissa said, as Matilda started away with lagging steps.

"It is all one," Matilda replied. "Horrid! But I shall conquer, see if I don't!"

Kitty was given a charming room with hangings of rose and gold in the very latest Athenian style. The beautiful room quite oppressed her, as did her reflections on the day. She fell asleep wondering if it might be best to go home after all.

But she woke to such a beautiful morning that her courage soon returned. Alice appeared with the hot water, full of praise for everything that she had seen so far. She and Clarissa's maids had become fast friends, and Alice was learning very quickly how to go on.

Kitty was just putting her feet into her slippers, and Alice bent to tie the ribbon, when she added that Lord Chadwick and his son had arrived during the night, and Kitty would find them at breakfast.

Kitty knew it was silly to imagine falling in love with Clarissa's brother, but she could not help thinking of it as she went downstairs. She entered the breakfast room in a little flutter of trepidation, and took her place at the noisy, lively family table.

Clarissa's brother James was certainly handsome, but within a very short time he reminded Kitty so much of her brother Ned that she began to enjoy herself, the fancy quite forgotten.

Instead, she looked with interest at her host. She detected a faint resemblance to Clarissa in Lord Chadwick's long face, though there it ended. Lord Chadwick, like his son, was dressed in riding clothes.

The voices rose, Mrs. Latchmore's above them all as she tried to scold the younger girls into silence. Lord Chadwick took no notice as he addressed himself to his breakfast.

When that was done, he looked up, and Kitty was startled to find him eyeing her. He gave her a genial node, and said, "St. Tarval's daughter? Lord, you've a strong look of your mother. She was a reigning Toast, you know."

Kitty thanked him demurely, hiding the urge to laugh. She could not but help think of the warnings she had grown up with while her grandmother lived, that she must not do this, or think that, lest she become as notorious as her mother, which would spell instant social ruin.

The ease with which Clarissa's family accepted Kitty reassured her, and she had begun to relax when Matilda, who had been writhing with increasing impatience under her aunt's continued scolding, cried out, "Papa! What did you bring us?"

Amelia had been talking to her brother across the table. She broke off to say triumphantly, "Nothing but my London hack."

"It is not a long-tail gray," Eliza stated.

Lord Chadwick had risen. Paying no attention to his younger offspring, he said to Clarissa, "I'm off to my study. Want to speak to you."

Kitty's enjoyment had vanished like the sun behind the clouds now gathering outside the bow windows. Eliza and Amelia glared at one another in a way that called the Bouldeston sisters to mind. Too often when Lucretia and Lucasta argued, Lady Bouldeston would admonish them in a low, cruel drawl, "What will people say about you?"

'People' meant Kitty, usually, for seldom was anyone else present. To be regarded as 'people' made Kitty feel like an interloper, someone whose presence required a false front.

It did not help that as soon as Lady Bouldeston was away from the room, the sisters would turn angry glances her way, though she never once said anything to anybody. Not after Lucretia had observed in a sweetly horrid voice a couple of years before, "I suppose you are going to run to Carlisle. I cannot stop you from saying horrid things about us, but it is just a little disagreement like anyone may have."

Kitty hated the thought of being a tale-bearer. She also knew that she did not understand the rules of society, as Lucretia often reminded Kitty, adding the rider that her motive was enlightenment, and charity.

No one likes charity, Kitty thought as she sat there mute and miserable, intensely aware of being in a strange house, with sisters glaring at one another across the table. She braced herself, waiting for Lady Chadwick to admonish them in a way that would make Kitty feel like a stranger. But Lady Chadwick was reading her letters as if no one else was in the room.

Then Clarissa rose, touching Amelia on the shoulder. She did not say anything. Her smile was small, her gaze steady. Amelia met that gaze and the anger died out of her face. She blushed a little, then said to Eliza, "No, quite right. But she is beautiful, even so. Come out to the stable and see her. Perhaps you would like to ride her when you come down to Town."

Eliza's mutinous expression vanished. "Oh! May I? Oh, please?"

Clarissa whispered to Kitty, "I will join you presently." And she walked out, leaving Kitty feeling puzzled to understand what had taken place.

Ten

WHEN CLARISSA REACHED HER father's study, he tossed aside the newspaper. "What is this I hear about French agents? More of Sophie's turning dust into mountains?"

"There were no French agents, Papa," Clarissa said.

"Thought not. Had a stay with old Theo St. Tarval's boy and girl? That was a good notion, to bring her back with you, if you girls have taken to one another. She is a diamond, like her mother, though I hope she isn't as wild a piece. Dark, too, so Amelia won't get into a pucker."

"Yes, Papa."

"The Wilburfoldes have called, the both of them, since news of the mishap was noised round the parish." As he spoke, he eyed his eldest daughter. She was always calm, but her eyes had a way of smiling, as her mother's had once done. At the mention of the Wilburfoldes, she did not pout or flounce or wail, like his other girls were wont to do. But every hint of smile vanished as quick as if he'd pinched a candle.

He sighed. "What do you want, girl? Here is a respectable offer, no, better. Money, title, a family known in the parish as they live close by. Here is your chance to become your ladyship, and have your own establishment instead of hanging on James some-day. You know he'll marry sooner or later, and the chances are good his wife won't want another woman in the house."

This aspect of the matter had never struck Clarissa quite so hard. Until recently, she'd always assumed that any woman James married would be like their sisters, but men were unaccountable in their tastes. What if James brought home someone like Lucretia Bouldeston?

There was no villain here. Her father thought he was doing his best by her according to the rules of society.

Now, everything was different. No, everything was exactly the same as before, excepting only this: she had discovered what all the poetry and the music was about. But the man was as out of her reach as any German Archduke or Greek prince of the most dramatic and unlikely tales.

Her father said, "I know you girls like to fix your affections, but you have not done so in six years on the Town. Ten to one at your age, you never will. And you are old enough not to turn missish if I remind you that, so long as you give that muffin-face an heir, at least he would never notice..."

Clarissa made a quick, inadvertent gesture of revulsion, and Lord Chadwick abandoned that line of discourse, and thrust his hand through his hair before patting her hand. "There, now, let us say no more for today. I'd be a devilish unnatural father if I did not wish to see my girls creditably placed. We can talk again when we come home after your season. You go and give St. Tarval's girl a good time. And if it's true she's wearing her mother's gowns — and I remember hearing something or other about old Theo run off his legs — then fix her up like Amelia, and hang the expense."

"Thank you, Papa," Clarissa said, dropping a curtsy, then kissing him on the cheek.

Lady Chadwick bestirred herself long enough to invite their guest to join her in the red salon. Here, she indicated a stack of new books lying about, and said, "I do not know if you like to read, but we have a number of novels."

"Oh, thank you," Kitty exclaimed. "I like them very much."

"Clarissa reads them, and so do the girls, from time to time. I confess I cannot understand the interest in reading about a set of

DANSE DE LA FOLIE

persons one does not know. Unless it is one like *The Sylph*, where everyone rushes to see if they have been hit off in it. Or their friends," she added. "But that was long before your time," she observed calmly. "I was very young, too, when all the big girls were whispering about it. The Duchess of Devonshire introduced *all* the fashions in those days. The hats! You cannot conceive how monstrous, though we thought them *le dernier cri*, at the time."

Greatly entertained, Kitty hoped that Lady Chadwick would talk some more about the famous duchess, who, she knew, had been a great friend of her mother's. But her grandmother had refused to have the duchess's name is spoken in Tarval Hall, and of course there was no copy of the novel that the duchess might or might not have written.

Lady Chadwick was distracted when the footman brought in a silver tray stacked with letters. She interrupted herself without a thought, and picked up the first letter.

Kitty was thinking that she might as well choose one of the books when Mrs. Latchmore entered and sat down, making a business of setting out fabric, thread, and sisters from her huswife. Taking in Kitty, she muttered about the luck some had to sit about like ladies of leisure with no fine work to do.

Kitty was ready to turn her hand to anything Mrs. Latchmore might need done, but the lady never gave her a chance to speak. Instead, she went on about a great many subjects, from Matilda's torn petticoat (which apparently no one in the household was capable of mending properly) to how uncomfortable it was to be a widow in straightened circumstances, whose sacrifices went unnoticed by all. Kitty began to suspect that what Mrs. Latchmore wanted was an audience in preference to another needlewoman.

Kitty was certainly the only listener, as Lady Chadwick peaceably read her letters, even when the younger girls ran in and out on their own pursuits. Kitty was secretly diverted by her observation of the lady's method for dealing with a noisy family.

Mrs. Latchmore had not run out of words when the stately butler appeared at the door.

"What is it, Pobrick?" Lady Chadwick asked.

"Lord Wilburfolde," the butler announced portentously.

A little sigh escaped Lady Chadwick, and she laid aside a letter and rose to greet the gentleman who entered with a heavy tread and approached her with a deliberate air. Kitty had also risen, and while she waited to be introduced had leisure to observe this gentleman as he bent over Lady Chadwick's hand. He was somewhat shorter than Kitty's brother Edward, solidly built, and impeccably dressed in a sober shade of brown. At first Kitty assumed he was older, for there was a hint of jowl at either side of his chin, emphasized by the pursed line of his lips. His hair was a shade of black similar to her own, clipped very close to his head, which made his face seem rounder than it really was.

"Dear Lady Chadwick," he said. His voice was as heavy and deliberate as his tread, each word carefully picked out. "I know that I see you well, for you are handsome as always. My mother requested me to carry to you her compliments. Mrs. Latchmore, I trust I see you well. If my mother had known you would be present during my call, I feel certain that she would have encouraged me to proffer her compliments, as well."

He paused as the ladies responded politely, then turned Kitty's way, as Lady Chadwick performed the introduction.

Kitty held out her hand, which he gave a ponderous shake, up and down twice, so careful and so precise a motion that she wondered if he was counting under his breath.

At Lady Chadwick's invitation for all to sit Lord Wilburfolde settled carefully into a chair, and after Mrs. Latchmore made a polite inquiry about his mother, with the same care and deliberation that he had exhibited so far, he commenced giving the ladies a long and exact description of the history of Lady Wilburfolde's medical complaint.

Mrs. Latchmore entered into a comparison of symptoms as experienced by her late spouse, and she and Lord Wilburfolde were deep in a discussion of the respective cases when Clarissa entered the room.

Mrs. Latchmore interrupted herself to say, "Clarissa, dear, look who has ridden out in this filthy weather, just to inquire after you. We have been happy to give him the news that you are returned safely, but alas, Lady Wilburfolde is unwell."

Clarissa entered with her customary calm demeanor, but Kitty thought she detected the shadow of a pucker in her forehead.

Lord Wilburfolde rose to his feet, and with the same ponderous deliberation, bowed over Clarissa's fingers.

No sooner had everyone sat down again and exchanged another round of polite nothings when Mrs. Latchmore surprised Kitty by snatching up her stitchwork and saying, "My dear Lady Chadwick, I just bethought myself that we must speak to Mrs. Bith about the supper. It is already late."

Lady Chadwick looked from her aunt-by-marriage to Lord Wilburfolde, then blinked and murmured something unintelligible before following Mrs. Latchmore out. Lord Wilburfolde stood once again, bowing to both ladies until the door shut behind them.

He then began to inquire into the accident to Clarissa's vessel. Kitty looked round-eyed from one to the other, trying to comprehend why the gentleman's questions were so lengthy, yet the lady's answers were wondrous short.

This had gone on for some time when the door opened a little way, but instead of Pobrick, it was Mrs. Latchmore.

"Do not let me intrude, pray," Mrs. Latchmore said. "I just wish to request Lady Catherine to help me find my needle, for I dropped it on the landing, and I require a pair of young eyes to find it."

Of course Kitty must rise. As soon as the door was shut behind her, though, she discovered Mrs. Latchmore already at the other end of the landing, whispering to Lady Chadwick, "I told you that this would be the Occasion. You'll see that I am right."

Lady Chadwick cast a look toward the salon. She seemed uncertain, and Kitty wondered if she were waiting for Clarissa to appear, or some other sign or signal. But the door remained closed, Mrs. Latchmore was insistent, and so the ladies vanished into the breakfast room, leaving Kitty standing uncertainly on the landing outside the salon.

Kitty had glanced at Clarissa while passing. How to interpret the look that she had seen in Clarissa's eyes? Did she wish to be alone with this caller? Then she remembered something curious that Clarissa had said when they first met, and prompted by instinct, she eased the door opened slowly.

She did not intend to eavesdrop, but Lord Wilburfolde's voice was not a quiet one. "... And I addressed your esteemed father, who was flattering enough to encourage my suit. If you would name the date that will make me the happiest of men, I will thus be able to carry the news back to my good mother, who I feel certain would rejoice enough to rise from her bed of discomfort."

Kitty was then astonished to hear Clarissa say in a soft voice, "After the summer season, it shall be as you wish, Lord Wilburfolde."

Eleven

CLARISSA CAST HER TEAR-SODDEN handkerchief aside and sat down at her dressing table, where she gazed resolutely at her red nose and swollen eyes. No one would ever call her beautiful or fall in love with her. That was life. She could count up all her blessings — she knew she ought to — except that would not make her feel better.

She turned away as fresh tears burned her eyes. Married to Lord Wilburfolde, she would be the lady of her own establishment, and therefore no burden on James's future wife. Why had she never looked at Aunt Sophia and considered her position? Because she'd grown up with it.

I will not be Aunt Sophia to my future nieces and nephews — that must be a consolation, she thought resolutely. Another consolation would be her own children, eventually, and until then, she would dedicate her life to being useful to others. That must be her chief pleasure.

She thought of Kitty and the guest chamber and the urge to confide in her was nearly overwhelming. Kitty's amazement had been more difficult to endure then Mrs. Latchmore's triumph and the careless congratulations of her family. She had expected her father's relief and her step-mother's benevolent indifference. She had expected her sisters' gleeful expressions about weddings, bride clothes, and fuss. She had not expected the mute question in

Kitty's countenance. There was true concern! There was unselfish sympathy!

Clarissa was also certain of Kitty's heartfelt sympathy if she were to confide her feelings. But that was the very reason she must say nothing. She already sensed that Kitty was not fond of her sister-to-be. Confessing the incipient sensibilities, or fancies (for she would not dignify a three days' acquaintance with the term *regard*) she had developed toward the marquess could only be a burden for Kitty. *She* could do nothing. However irregular the engagement with Lucretia Bouldeston might be, it existed. Kitty had told Clarissa. Her brother had hinted at it. He had enough feeling for the young lady to wish to make her his wife, and Clarissa would keep honor with her sex by not even permitting herself to think of the gentleman.

She did not go down to dinner when Rosina came in to help her dress. The maidservant, who knew her quiet mistress best, withdrew to inform the family that Clarissa was laid down with the headache.

Kitty woke late the next morning. When she thrust back the curtain around her bed, she gave a contented glance around the lovely bedchamber. She never tired of admiring the smart, fresh hangings on the wall, the matching Sevres vases on the mantel-shelf, the leaping fire in the fireplace.

This is truly the way to live, she thought as Alice shouldered her way through the door, carefully carrying a loaded tray.

"I thought you might be waking, Lady Kitty," Alice said as she set the tray down. "Lawks! The household is turned a-bedlam."

In other circumstances Kitty might have found herself diverted by Alice's evident pleasure at the stir and noise of 'bedlam' had she not suspected the cause.

Kitty recollected all the hints that Clarissa had let drop about not wishing to be married. What could make her change her mind? Little as was her experience of the world, Kitty was very certain she had not seen any signs of love in that woeful countenance.

The only way to solve the mystery was to get out of bed. And indeed, Clarissa was the subject when she joined the family for breakfast.

The first voice Kitty heard was Mrs. Latchmore's. Apparently she had not got enough praise for her efforts in matchmaking, for she was going on above the noise of the younger girls trying to get out of having to pay a call on Lady Wilburfolde. "So affecting! Clarissa will always be in reach, and as Lady Wilburfolde, she may entertain in London, which will be to Eliza's and Matilda's benefit."

"Not she," James put in. "The old dragon won't let Clarissa spend a groat. She'll go right on spending their fortune quacking herself. You watch."

Kitty was interested to see Lord Chadwick give an actual shudder at the words 'old dragon.'

There was a pause, then Tildy stated, "And that is why I do not wish to go calling. I am not being married. It is horrid enough when Lady Wilburfolde calls, smelling of evil medicines, and all she talks of are her symptoms."

Lady Chadwick murmured, "You will go because it is the civilized thing to do. But we will only stay fifteen minutes, for no more is required when someone is unwell."

Tildy gave a loud sigh, but spoke no more.

As Kitty had not yet been introduced to Lady Wilburfolde, she was not expected to join the Harlowe ladies and Mrs. Latchmore in paying this call. She was more relieved than curious, especially when she saw Clarissa looking, as she thought, very much like Marie Antoinette entering the tumbril as she climbed into the carriage with the others.

Sorry as Kitty was for her friend, she could do nothing in her aid. Meanwhile, Clarissa's woeful profile inspired Kitty to fly to her room and dig her novel from the bottom of her trunk. Paper, ink, and pens were a-plenty on the pretty desk, and so the morning sped by as Andromeda's adventures included a forced betrothal—her features taking on a semblance of Clarissa Harlowe's.

On the ladies' return, once again Clarissa retired with the headache, after a softly murmured apology, and so Kitty joined the younger girls at their invitation, as Amelia described, in detail, the wardrobe she was accumulating for her launching into Society.

Kitty's curiosity about the mysterious Lady Wilburfolde was assuaged the next day, when they were all gathered in the morning room after breakfast. Clarissa had said that she must write some letters, then she would devote her day to Kitty. The latter said she would be happy to occupy herself with a book, as the younger girls ran in and out, and Mrs. Latchmore busied herself with mending a fire screen, speaking at least ten words to a single stitch.

That was when Pobrick came to the door. His voice, Kitty thought, was even lower than normal when he announced, "Lady Wilburfolde."

Everyone rose, Lady Chadwick as quickly as the schoolgirls.

Lady Wilburfolde walked in, a tall woman of formidable mien, who much resembled her son, except her hair was iron-gray. She let Lady Chadwick advance to her to shake hands, and introduce her to Kitty, who detected the faintest sniff on the words 'St. Tarval' as this lady looked Kitty over from hair to toes, then bowed from the collarbones.

Lady Chadwick invited the caller to sit, whereupon with stately assurance, Lady Wilburfolde took the best chair. Lady Chadwick sat on the sofa beside the girls.

"I count nothing, least of all, my own health, when it comes to a question of what is due to our positions in life," Lady Wilburfolde stated in what Kitty suspected was a well-rehearsed speech. "Edmund, as you may suppose, is quite pleased."

"The girls have been in transports," Lady Chadwick answered, sounding like a girl herself.

Aunt Sophia started in eagerly, "Oh dear, oh my, yes, just as I've always said —"

"It seems odd to me, then, Mrs. Latchmore," Lady Wilburfolde interrupted, frowning, "that this business could have been conducted with a bit more firmness and celerity. I might have had an heir growing under my instruction by now. But Providence has granted me this much time, so I intend to put it to good use before I am reunited with my sainted Wilburfolde."

Kitty sustained a sudden, horrid picture of this formidable lady supervising a marriage bed, an image that caused her to take her lip firmly between her teeth. She was relieved as the tea things appeared, and a bustle and fuss must be made over that.

The lady then went on. "We spoke yesterday of the Hymeneal arrangements. Edmund and I conversed upon this head last night, and he agrees with me that a new house is an unnecessary expense. It is not only economical for the marital couple to live in The Castle, where there is so much space, but we desire the Wilburfolde heir to grow up in his ancestral home."

Nobody said anything. Clarissa looked startled.

Before she could speak, Lady Wilburfolde turned her way. "That does not mean that the young people ought not to have their treat. I have no objection to Edmund and Clarissa going up to London for a week or two each spring. Edmund tells me he finds the metropolis improving, but of course he is always glad to return home from the noise, stink, and frivolousness of London ways."

Again, no one had anything to say to that, except to make polite noises. Kitty's mood shifted to indignation. It was very clear that this household was about to embark on a lengthy stay in London, so that speech could only be understood as a kind of rebuke.

Lady Wilburfolde eyed her untouched tea and macaroons as if they were spiders, then said, "The question was also raised yesterday regarding the nuptials themselves. I wish to settle this question while I have the health to deal with such matters." She then turned toward Clarissa with stately deliberation. "I believe it is traditional for older and wiser heads to come to decisions, but I feel that a bride, when she has shown that she has earned so marked a tribute, ought to be consulted. Therefore, Clarissa, I desire you to make your wishes known."

Clarissa lifted her head. "Perhaps next spring?"

Mrs. Latchmore gasped, for she had been speaking of a June wedding.

Lady Wilburfolde nodded minutely. "I quite agree that persons of our order must not display an unseemly haste in nuptial arrangements. But may I remind you that you are no longer a girl. Five-and-twenty is not a youth of eighteen, and the Wilburfoldes historically do not breed like persons of the lower orders."

Mrs. Latchmore gasped. The girls giggled, hilarity instantly quenched when the imperious eye turned their way. Amelia turned her laughter into a cough, and begged pardon.

Lady Wilburfolde ignored her. "It was quite fifteen years before Providence enabled me to present to my sainted Wilburfolde the fruit of our affections. If my health permits, I would be inclined toward a September wedding, as is traditional in the Wilburfolde family. It is a respectable half-year from now."

Clarissa looked around her, like (Kitty thought compassionately) a bird in a gilded cage. "Oh, but my sister Amelia—if she should—"

The dark brows rose. "I should hope, Lady Chadwick, that you would not repeat the harum-scarum haste of your eldest daughter's marriage last year. Weddings in summer. Extraordinary! And in any case, I believe that you must have precedence over a mere girl, Clarissa." Lady Wilburfolde then trained her guns on Amelia. "If you are as pretty-behaved as your eldest sister, there is no reason why you should not contract an equally eligible situation. And there is something to be said for a Christmas wedding."

Amelia made polite noises, looking very much as if she had received a threat.

Since no one vouchsafed an answer, Lady Wilburfolde rose in her stately manner. "Very well, then, it is all settled. Clarissa, you and I will closet ourselves upon your return from the metropolis, which I trust will be soon. I have only one last piece of business: the dress-party, before you leave. Would the week of the fourteenth be acceptable?"

Lady Chadwick said, "Thank you, Lady Wilburfolde. The very thing."

"The fourteenth, then, if the weather is clement. I have not been in the way of entertaining since my widowhood, but I believe we may expect our neighbors of position to attend such an event at The Castle." She added in Amelia's direction. "Since you are to make your bow to Society, we will expect you among the guests."

Since all had risen, Amelia dropped a curtsey, then said with a scared look, "Should I go when I am not yet Out?"

Lady Wilburfolde paused in her tread, and gave her a decided look of approval. "You are much less flighty than your sister Hortensia, it seems. A family party is quite acceptable for a girl in your situation. As for dancing, of course there will be no such thing. I believe my thoughts on dancing are quite well known, and as the season is Lent, there is no question." She then turned her dragon gaze on Kitty. "As you are a guest in this house, we would be honored to extend the invitation to include you, Lady Catherine."

Kitty dropped a curtsey, as Lady Wilburfolde went on, "You must know that I am very well acquainted with both your grandmothers. Lady St. Tarval, your paternal grandmother, was an excellent woman. And I hold Lady Carlisle, and the Stithwalds, in high esteem, in spite of unfortunate events that it is better to pass over."

Kitty was forced to say, "I am unacquainted with that side of my family."

"A pity," Lady Wilburfolde said, rather (Kitty thought later) as if someone had dropped a dead mouse in her lap.

She took her departure. Lady Chadwick and her daughters all saw her out. Kitty stared at the door, her sympathies for Clarissa having intensified to vexation.

Carlisle had always said, if something vexes you that you cannot fix, there is nothing left but to find the humor in it. Kitty was trying to find something amusing in that woman's tyrannical statements, not to mention the unsubtle slight against her father, mother, and brothers, when she saw James approaching from the other end of the hall.

As always, he was dressed in riding clothes. Kitty could not understand why a young man in fine riding boots would steal along as if he were walking on eggs. When James saw Kitty he gave a start, and his wide blue eyes rounded with alarm.

"Is she gone yet?"

"Who?"

"The old Puritan. Eh, Lady Wilburfolde, that is."

Here at last was the humor. Kitty tried to suppress the urge to laugh as she said, "Your family is walking her to her carriage, I believe."

"To make certain she gets into it," James commented. "I never thought Clarissa would get leg-shackled to Wilburfolde. Females are unaccountable." With this piece of wisdom, he strode away, now confident that no dragons lay in wait.

Twelve

"THEY WHAT ON THE fourteenth?"

Lord Chadwick's voice echoed up the stairwell. "No one told me that. By God, we're off to London on the day after, then. We'll not be tied up with them before September, when there is no help for it. At least then I'll be up north, safe out of reach."

The news was welcomed with general relief by the entire family, saving only Mrs. Latchmore, denied of her chance to triumph over the neighborhood in having brought about the match. She had planned a series of select parties meant to show off the newly affianced couple before the journey to London. Kitty was secretly amused at Lord Chadwick's selfishness, but grateful for its beneficent effect.

She hid her reaction as well as her growing concern over Clarissa's somber gaze when she thought nobody was looking. Delicacy forbade teasing hints or coy remarks or penetrating questions. Kitty had learned as much from observing Lucretia tormenting other girls in the parish with such teasing.

But at the same time, she reasoned, it was not acting the part of a friend to pretend not to notice how unhappy Clarissa was. Her own family seemed unconcerned, or perhaps only unaware.

Kitty determined she must do something about it. But what? She had no experience outside of novels on which to draw. And she knew there would be no convenient deathbed confessions,

Greek banditti, or rakehell German dukes to intervene on Clarissa's behalf.

An unexpected opportunity occurred the day after Lord Chadwick's announcement. As the servants threw themselves into readying the family's things for the shift to London, Clarissa asked Kitty if she knew how to ride, and on being assured on this point, invited her to join her in an airing before breakfast.

Kitty was given a pretty bay who was obviously friends with the young, prancing gray gelding Clarissa rode. Kitty was surprised to see Clarissa riding so spirited a horse, but a swift gallop across the fields behind the garden and down a shady lane made it clear that Clarissa was an excellent horsewoman.

When they reined up, Clarissa's wan cheeks had gained color, and there was a brighter look to her gaze as she looked about appreciatively at the copse of ancient ash, the craggy branches — dotted with green buds — overreaching the stream swollen with snow melt. The only sounds were their own, the rush and chuckle of the stream, and a few distant birds.

"I do love to rise early, before anybody. It is so peaceful," Clarissa said.

"This is a very beautiful place," Kitty said.

"I was used to come here often when I was a child," Clarissa admitted. "I could read without interruption. I still sometimes come here, as far into autumn as the weather cooperates."

Her smile vanished as she looked about, and Kitty thought, *You are remembering you must move away.* Greatly daring, she ventured a question. "If you will pardon my intrusion, you do not look happy, and I might guess why."

Clarissa's expression went remote, then she smiled. "I suppose every woman has been apprehensive about entering the married state."

"Apprehensive if it was not their choice," Kitty said.

"It was my choice." Clarissa sighed. "It is as good an offer as I am likely to get, and the Wilburfoldes are neighbors. Though I do not really know Lord Wilburfolde, for he suffered delicate health when we were all young, and so was seldom from home, I am certain he is all he ought to be. I count myself luckier than most."

In the distance some children shouted, joined by barking dogs.

The mood of confidence had broken. Kitty sensed it, and remembering how uncomfortable it could be to be pestered by questions by those who professed to have one's best interests at heart, firmly closed her lips against the host of questions and exclamations she might have offered.

Dear Carlisle:

We have been in London these three Days. I am actually here! You can have no Idea. So many people in so small a space, carts, horses, carriages. The Noise at night is nearly as much as daylight.

But I do not complain. Clarissa and I have already been twice to Bond Street, and we have visited too many shops to count. But you will not care for that, I know. Let me continue where I left off in my last, before Lady Wilburfolde's Dress Party.

We were Welcomed in Great State by Lady W. in their Large, Overheated house, which, though called The Castle, is nothing so interesting, but merely a very large brick house. I think it quite undistinguished, and its situation horrid, squatting in a valley, where it is certain never to catch a breeze, not that any stray air is permitted inside. It was amazingly Stuffy, as Lady W. feels that open doors and windows are more dangerous than French grenadiers, and the place smelled of Medicine.

A Toast of Watered Wine was offered in honor of the happy couple, after a long Speech. It is a shame that Ladies cannot run for Parliamentary seats, James said to me, after Lady W. had gone on for what seemed a thousand Ages. The toast was all the wine the gentlemen were to get, Lady W. feeling that spirits are prejudicial to the health. So everyone must drink Lemonade, and I wish I could have drawn a picture of Lord C. drinking this down.

Lady W. had assembled everyone in an old-fashioned Circle, like our grandmother's time. I was seated between a Squire, who was soon nodding in his Chair, and the Vicar, who was very kind, having (as he informed me) five Daughters of his own.

But there was no Time for more than that, as Lady W. then took charge of the Conversation, and, as Lord C. said on the way home, Told us what we Thought about the Nuptials to come—and about the Weather, and the State of the Commonwealth. I was very relieved when she told us we were all Tired and sent us home.

There is little to be said about the journey to London, which is very Large and old and Dirty, except for the Genteel section, in which there is a vast deal of Planning and Building going on.

At first I tried to look for Grosvenor Street, where you said our old House is Located, but the streets are so many, and I am afraid to find myself Lost. When I asked Clarissa, she said it was only two streets from Brook Street, on the other side of Grosvenor Square. But then she said that her cousins the Devereaux family live in Grosvenor Street, so I was very glad I did not walk there. With my Luck I would run smack into Mr. Devereaux, though I still say it was Not my Fault that his sister told me she was being Abducted.
I have a very pretty room with Blue hangings and Embroidered bolsters. Alice is very happy.

We have had to leave off our warm Pelisses, as Clarissa says that nothing is as dowdy as being seen with a Warm Wrap. Oh, that puts me in mind. There are so many ways to get into a Scrape. We cannot walk into St. James's Street, though it is quite open. Nor can we visit Bond Street when it is not Daylight.

I conveyed your Thanks to Clarissa, who Colored up, and

proclaimed it Naught. But requested me to send her greetings. So I do. Or, to be clever, Adieux.

Your Kitty.

Post Script. Everyone in the family calls me Lady Kitty, excepting Clarissa, who calls me Kitty, and Mrs. Latchmore, who persists in that dreadful Lady Catherine, but I must become accustomed, for that is what I shall hear in company. Yet I quite Sympathize with Miss Elizabeth Clothilde Rosamunda Devereaux with her plain Bess.

Edward put the letter down, and looked up in query at his brother. Carlisle had been restive these past few days. Edward was puzzled. He thought he knew all his brother's moods, but this was a new one. One would think they had traded places, for he had always been scolded by their grandmother for not sitting still, whereas Carlisle had been the quiet one, happy with his books until he understood their father's situation. After that discovery he had conceived the idea of joining the Navy in hopes of prize money.

Carlisle prowled around the dining room, pausing frequently at the window. What could he possibly see in the garden?

"Carl?" Edward asked.

St. Tarval struck his hand lightly across the back of a chair. "We will try it," he said.

"Try what?"

"One more load. Cowman says he quite understands—he would not gainsay—but he said that the cutter is so fast, he had pinned his hopes on me. This is the biggest yet, but we are agreed it shall be the last."

"What about Dobbs?"

Carlisle dropped into the chair. "This time, I shall take Dobbs aside and remind him that I still have influence in this area, and I might just have to invite Talkerton to set up an office in the village, the better to have access to the coast, if he doesn't cooperate."

Edward laughed. "Oho!"

Carlisle's smile was wry, bringing their father unexpectedly to mind. "Let us see if that causes him to reflect on the wisdom of cheating us. Of course he will attempt to do us an ill turn afterward, and I shall permit him to think we will go on smuggling so that he may look forward to confounding us. But once we get rid of those barrels, we are done. Dobbs may put as many spies around the yacht as he wishes. In truth, I hope he may, for it will keep those loutish nephews of his well occupied until some enterprising lieutenant comes along and impresses them into the service."

"You may count upon me." Edward handed Kitty's letter back. "Are you going to tell Kit when you write back?"

"No. I will not worry her. When I write, it is all home news, nothing to spoil her visit, or worse, cause her to come posting back to Tarval Hall, thinking she is duty bound to aid us. She will never get this chance again. Let it be unmarred from our end."

"Well, she certainly seems to be in high glee." Edward flicked the pages. "Jupiter, if she doesn't publish her novel after all! This one is longer than the last." As Carlisle took the letter, Edward said, "At least it isn't Tunbridge Wells all over again."

"No. I do not believe that Miss Harlowe would permit Kitty to make a guy of herself." He stopped there.

Edward eyed his brother. "You think there was something in it, the way the Bouldestons foisted themselves onto Miss Harlowe, after Kit got her invitation?"

"I did think of that," Carlisle admitted.

"Won't that give them a claim on her in town?"

"I believe it will." Carlisle stared down into the fire.

Edward discovered a new idea, and gazed at him in amazement. "It's Miss Harlowe. Isn't it?"

Carlisle glanced his way. "What matter if it was?"

Edward grimaced. "Seems vastly unfair to me that Lucretia holds all the cards, but we've been over this ground before."

"So we have."

But Edward was going to go over it anyway. "You prate of honor, but how honorable is it for her to keep you dangling on a leash you two affixed six years ago, but she won't have it announced? It's because she's up in town looking out something better. Tell me why that's honorable."

"It may not be honorable, but it's acceptable," Carlisle responded. "If she fixes her interest with someone else, well and good."

"But if Lucretia is looking for someone else, then that means she don't want you any more than you want her. Why don't she break it off?"

"I think she likes the idea of being married to a marquess, if nothing better comes along."

"And that makes it acceptable? I still say you should pick a quarrel with her. Lord knows she's got a nasty temper."

Carlisle shook his head. "I can't do anything dishonorable, not with Sir Henry being so generous. He could have called in Father's debt any time these past ten years, but he hasn't. And he could be forgiven having called it in, considering Father's actions toward the family."

Edward sighed, remembering the ancient history their grandmother had had a tendency to bore on about. The old baronet and Grandfather St. Tarval had betrothed Philomena Bouldeston to their father when the two were in their cradles, and everyone had expected them to marry.

But a month before he was to wed the elder Miss Bouldeston, their father had run off with their mother. Philomena had finally been married off to a William Kittredge, younger brother to a baronet. On old Sir Harold's death, Riverside Abbey had fallen to a second cousin, Henry Bouldeston, who had married the younger sister, the present Lady Bouldeston, thus keeping what fortune there was in the family.

Edward kicked at a log in the fireplace, sending a shower of sparks spiraling up the chimney. Philomena Bouldeston had often been held up as a pattern for female behavior to Kit by their grandmother, who had very much wanted the marriage. Edward had met Mrs. Kittredge one summer, when she'd come with her children to the Abbey. Edward said, with feeling, "I have to say, I am glad Papa never married Philomena Bouldeston that was. If I were her son, I'd hate myself."

He was surprised when Carlisle burst into laughter.

Thirteen

"IT IS AMAZING," CLARISSA said with gratitude, "how quickly you have learnt to discern what is flattering, and what is not. I never can see it until it is too late. You were correct about the gold braid. It looks very well. Ruffles make me into a dowd, no matter how expensive the fabric was in the shop."

"You are not a dowd," Kitty said. "You have excessively pretty sisters, but I do not think they move in a room as well as you do. Ruffles do not suit someone with a graceful carriage like yours, that is all. And your hair also looks elegant in this simple Grecian style, with the flowers set at the back."

The days were getting longer but it was still early in the spring, and the rays of the sun slanted across the streets and through the budding trees, giving the world a golden cast. Kitty loved going out, the streets so clean-swept, everyone so finely dressed.

Even so, her first visit to Hyde Park caused her to look about with a troubled air.

Clarissa said, "Is something amiss? I assure you, Kitty, you look very fine."

"Oh, I am happy enough, truly. It's just that I had envisioned the park so differently. More wild. These trees are placed so far apart." Her voice lowered. "The ruffians who pounce upon Andromeda and bear her away in the middle of the promenade could never do it here. But how else am I to get her to the dungeon of Castle Fearmore?"

"A blow," Clarissa acknowledged. "Perhaps if you were to send Andromeda on a picnic to Hampstead? There are portions of it that might suit your needs."

"A very good notion," Kitty said, and studied the ground with the eye of an author, quite unaware of the effect her appearance was having on passing gentlemen.

Clarissa noticed, however, enjoying the admiration of two fellows riding down the Row—both distant acquaintances with whom she'd gone through the motions of dancing last year, when they were inspired to try wrangling an introduction to her sister Hetty. She had never felt this enjoyment when Hetty was introduced to society, though she was fond of her sisters. And she'd been proud of Hetty's success. But she was thoroughly enjoying the admiring looks following Kitty, the more that Kitty seemed to be completely unaware of them as she looked about with that faint pucker between her brows. No doubt she was concocting more absurd adventures for the hapless Andromeda, who, it seemed to Clarissa, would have truly earned her wealthy duke by the time her third volume was completed.

Perhaps the general wisdom is correct, Clarissa thought, laughing to herself, that we only value that which comes the least easily.

"Oh, pray, look," Kitty exclaimed. "What a handsome carriage. And those horses!"

Clarissa glanced up at the high-perch phaeton drawn by its nervous matching chestnuts. A gentleman was driving, the lady beside him self-consciously twirling her sunshade.

"That is Sir Joseph Gates," Clarissa said.

"And the lady?"

"His bride, Miss Plumley that was. He was quite the despair of the drawing rooms these three years. A desperate flirt. And he ended up marrying his cousin, whom he has known all his life."

"She is not at all beautiful," Kitty observed as the phaeton rolled by. "But she has a friendly smile."

"She is very friendly. I expect she will be an excellent hostess when she has found her feet," Clarissa said.

"I hope they are very happy, for I—Oh!"

A cavalcade of gentlemen on horseback rode by, many in scarlet coats, their buff facings indicating one of the infantry regiments. Clarissa took Kitty's arm and they turned down a side path. "They will quiz you if they see you staring," Clarissa explained.

"Oh, I did not think of that." Kitty colored. "I was only noting the details of their uniforms."

"For Andromeda?"

"Yes! I was just thinking of those fellows serving as models for the rescue party when she is nearly overpowered by French agents, and—oh, here is another handsome carriage. Is that a tilbury? I saw one once. But I shall not stare."

"Good. For that is Mr. Brummel, being tooled about by Lord Alvanley. If *they* are here, it means the season has begun."

"I do hope he may not dislike me," Kitty said, stealing a quick look backward once the gentlemen were safely past.

Clarissa smiled. "The only persons he takes notice of outside of his particular set, and is quite unkind to, are the very rich, the very prominent, and the very vulgar."

Kitty's lips parted. "But..."

"But?" Clarissa prompted.

Kitty colored, remembering Lucretia's much-repeated anecdote about Mr. Brummel's compliment. Clearly there were exceptions. She said, "It might be better to have him meet Andromeda, as Mr. B—, it is much *safer*. Tell me more about the officers. I know so little of the army, my brother having been a naval lieutenant."

A hail from behind caused them to turn. "Hi Clarissa, Lady Kitty! On the toddle, eh?"

It was James Harlowe, walking with two friends. All three young men were dressed in the tight coats and pantaloons of the dandy, golden watch fobs dangling at their glorious waistcoats. One was James's age, perhaps a year out of Eton. The other was somewhat older, a tall, thin gentleman with a long face that resembled a hound dog. This gentleman raised a quizzing glass to his eyes, and interrupted James, who was in the middle of describing to Clarissa and Kitty a capital turnout a mutual friend had recently purchased.

"My dear Harlowe," this gentleman drawled. "If you do not stop chattering and introduce us, I shall be forced to employ extreme measures."

"Devil take it," James exclaimed. "I forgot you were not known to one another. Lady Kitty, may I present to you Mr. Thomas Canby, and Sir Blakely Sheffield? Oh, I should rightly have got that the other way around. Gentlemen, Lady Catherine Decourcey."

Mr. Canby, the tall gentleman with the quizzing glass, blushed when he met Kitty's friendly gaze. She regarded them unselfconsciously, for in her mind, James's friends fit that same mental slot as did James: brother.

Sir Blakely was far too shy to actually address Kitty himself, but by nudges and meaningful glances, he encouraged James to change the direction of their walk, and so the young ladies found themselves in the center of a group.

James asked Kitty what she thought of London so far. She expressed her delight with that same unselfconscious charm, turning to each gentleman in turn to ask their opinions. Clarissa walked along quietly, reflecting on the fact that she had never before been in the center of such a group. Kitty was fascinating without artifice, and Clarissa was able to see how it worked, for Kitty clearly found her auditors as interesting as she found the city.

Clarissa laughed to herself. Human nature was so odd. Beauty rendered the most commonplace words fascinating, and charm compounded itself when Beauty found others as interesting as they found her.

James directed their walk alongside the Row so that the gentleman might quiz the passersby the easier. Here they were interrupted by a female voice.

"*Catherine*, is that you?" Lucretia approached them, her sister by her side. Lucretia managed to cover the ground swiftly in spite of her tittuping steps. She was dressed in her favorite pink, her gown formed of layers and layers of ruffles. Her bonnet was decorated with bunches of pink ribbons and silken roses.

She rushed up to Kitty, greeted her with an effusion of

"dearest" and "so vastly surprised" ending with, "You were dressed so beautifully that I did not at all recognize you."

She then turned to Mr. Canby. "Dear Mr. Canby, was that not a dreadful squeeze last night? Oh, is that Mr. Harlowe? *Catherine*, do introduce us."

Yes, Clarissa thought, there was definitely an emphasis on that 'Catherine' without the honorific 'Lady' preceding it. Here was Miss Bouldeston making a parade of her intimacy with Kitty, and yet she had never seen fit to invite the latter for a visit to town? That seemed so odd.

Kitty performed the requested introduction, and then Lucretia inserted herself into the center of the group. She turned to Clarissa. "So, Miss Harlowe, were you vastly diverted by your stay at Tarval Hall? It must've been quite a change for *you*."

"What is that, Miss Bouldeston, you know Lady Catherine's home?" Mr. Canby asked, quizzing glass raised.

"Why, yes, Mr. Canby. I thought the entire world knew that we were neighbors, and that Lady Catherine's brother, the marquess, has been my oldest admirer."

Kitty gazed at Lucretia, not knowing what to say. She understood that Carlisle's and Lucretia's engagement was not to be widely known as yet, but she had always assumed that that was for reasons of delicacy. Yet it did not seem delicate at all to be hinting that Carlisle was the pursuer instead of the pursued.

But then, she did not know Town ways. She must not judge.

Lucretia went on to present her sister, then she took Mr. Canby's arm, saying, "I must and will know what you said to Lady Sopwith last night, at Lady Hertford's ball. From all the laughter, I know that it must be quite witty. Do, pray, tell me, for above all things I love witty sayings. You were talking about Miss Beccles, now, *weren't* you? And you men say that *we* gossip."

James dropped back, having no interest in balls, especially one he had not attended. Sir Blakely showed signs of wanting to follow, but Lucretia chanced to look his way, and smile, beckoning with her free hand. "I make it a rule to always defend my sex. Come, help me uphold Miss Beccles' sad reputation, Sir Blakely, for I once heard it said that you had an interest in that direction?"

Sir Blakely perforce joined Lucretia on the other side, losing himself in a morass of painful words as he tried to explain himself.

James took his place, exclaiming, "My word! The season is starting up already. Just as we entered the park we walked into Charlie, who was trying to get away from some duchess, and that stiff old Lady Pembroke."

"Are you so surprised?" Kitty asked, smiling.

James kicked at a rock in the gravel forming the path. "It is just that I hate balls. Mama will be expecting me to squire Amelia around in stuffy rooms, if you two are not going."

At that point Sir Blakely, who had been glancing back, found his moment to rejoin James. Mr. Canby also turned, saying, "There you are."

Lucretia exclaimed, "So slow. How did we become separated? Usually it is I who is scolded for being behind. I feel the veriest infant around all you tall ladies! Dearest Catherine, I shall call in Brook Street now that I know you are here, for we have a thousand things to talk about, and I can warn you off our most dangerous flirts, like Mr. Canby, here."

Lucretia took two steps away, but then turned back, making a pretense of dropping her fan and picking it up as she peeped coyly up sideways.

A lone horseman was riding along the Row, a few paces away. The sun was directly behind him, creating a tall silhouette of a man in a beautifully fitted riding coat. Then he moved and golden light limned fine dark hair. He reined in a well behaved dappled gray, and gave a slight bow. "Cousin Clarissa," he began his greetings, but Lucretia moved forward and interrupted.

"Mr. Devereaux, are you arrived in town? Then the season must truly have begun."

Mr. Devereaux bowed acknowledgment, then his gaze moved on. "Lady Catherine, I believe? How do you do?"

He was about to greet the gentlemen, but again, Lucretia interrupted, after giving a start of surprise. "Dearest Catherine," she exclaimed. "Have the two of you met? How can that be, when you are just arrived in Town?"

Kitty looked down at her gloved hands, wishing she could sink into the ground.

Clarissa said smoothly, "We chanced to meet up with my

cousins on their way to Bath, Miss Bouldeston." And to the gentleman, "How does your mother, Cousin?"

"She is recovering, thank you, and I know she would wish me to convey her greetings," Mr. Devereaux replied.

Lucretia turned to Mr. Devereaux. "Your sister is well, pray? I take leave to present to you my own sister, Miss Lucasta Bouldeston. She met Miss Bess while staying with some cousins in Hampshire."

Lucasta spoke up. "Bess is as beautiful as an angel, and the sweetest girl in the world. We were *instant* friends. I should love her direction."

Mr. Devereaux bowed politely, then said, "You have only to direct your letter to Miss Battersea's Academy in Bath, Miss Lucasta."

His horse sidled a little, and touched his hat to the group, murmuring a polite farewell that encompassed them all. Then he rode away.

Kitty breathed in relief. A horrid scrape — averted. Later, when she was safe, she would reflect on the unfairness of fate that the gentleman Lucretia had described as the handsomest in London should be the very one to witness Kitty's *faux pas*. Why was he not safely on the way to Italy?

"...and you must write as soon as we reach Mount Street," Lucretia was saying to Lucasta. Miss Bess will want to know that her brother is arrived in Town."

"I know what to write," Lucasta said in a slightly peevish tone, for she hated being treated as if she knew nothing.

Lucretia ignored her as she turned her widest smile on Kitty. "And so, Catherine, how long is to be your stay? A good while, it is to be hoped."

"For the season," Kitty said.

Lucretia's eyes rounded. She flushed, then, if possible, her smile widened the more. "How very charming for you! I trust you will be able to turn this felicitous event to good account, for of course you will be looking for a good marriage."

"I should like to help my brother," Kitty said with heartfelt sincerity.

Lucretia's smile turned to a smirk that Clarissa found puzzling.

"And that is just like you! I shall be able to tell Mama the good news. I know she will wish to call." Lucretia pinched her sister's arm, causing a muffled gasp, and then smiled at the group. "That puts me in mind of the time. Mama will be looking for us. Good afternoon!" The sisters walked off, Lucretia's low scolding punctuated by Lucasta's higher voice in protest.

James then declared a wish to walk on to White's, to which he had recently been elected, and as his friends offered to accompany him, the party separated with polite words on both sides.

As soon as she and Clarissa were at a distance, Kitty said guiltily, "I know I ought to have written to Lucretia on our arrival."

"It is understandable," Clarissa said. "I am afraid I have kept you very busy."

"Which I have enjoyed beyond anything," Kitty said wistfully.

They waited for a fast-moving carriage to roll by, during which Clarissa gazed thoughtfully at the hats in a milliner's shop. On becoming aware of Kitty's regard, Clarissa said, "Do but look, pray. Is there anyone who would not appear ill in that puce bonnet?"

Kitty's eyes narrowed. "You think I have done wrong, then, in neglecting to write to Lucretia?"

"That is not at all what I think."

Kitty sighed. "The truth is, I have been a little afraid." Then she straightened her shoulders and said, "Did I never tell you about my one fateful visit to Tunbridge Wells?"

Before Clarissa could answer, they were hailed by a familiar voice, "Clarissa! Lady Kitty!" Amelia came down the other side of the street, accompanied by Mrs. Latchmore, who began scolding Amelia in an undertone for the vulgarity of making a present of her sister's and guest's names to the street.

Amelia twitched impatiently, and as soon as the scold was ended, addressed the two who had drawn near, "Lady Sefton is to call upon Mama tomorrow, and she is bringing Lord Molyneux. Mama says that she is sure to promise vouchers for Almacks, so you must be there, too, Lady Kitty. Did you know about Almack's Assembly Rooms, and the weekly balls?"

"I am still not certain I approve of a gambling den giving itself over to dancing," Mrs. Latchmore scolded. "At all events, these matters are better discussed at home."

With Mrs. Latchmore ready to animadvert upon the doubtful respectability of Almack's (which Lucretia had told Kitty was become known as The Marriage Mart), the inclination for walking left the three young ladies, and they soon reached the Chadwick house, where Clarissa found amid the early invitations a long letter.

She opened it, and discovered a closely written, crossed and recrossed screed from Lady Wilburfolde, outlining the reasons why the future Lady Wilburfolde need only spend a week or at most two in the metropolis, before returning into Hampshire to prepare for her wedding. She wished to set a date for their first conference on the matter.

Clarissa thrust the letter into her escritoire to deal with later, and went out to consult Kitty about bonnets.

Fourteen

THE NEXT DAY THE ladies sat in the front parlor, hosting a constant stream of callers. Between visitors, Amelia could not be got to sit long. She kept flying to the window to peer out for sight of anyone she knew, or to count the fine equipages. When she recognized Lucasta Bouldeston walking up the street with her mother and sisters, she scowled and flounced to her chair, but behaved politely enough when the three were announced.

Lady Chadwick welcomed them as Kitty's acquaintance. After a strict fifteen minutes of polite utterances, they took their leave as more visitors arrived, Lucretia looking back to promise in languishing accents that she would see her *sweet Catherine* again soon.

There was a lull at last, causing Amelia to wail that Lady Sefton would *never* come.

Undercover of Mrs. Latchmore's stream of fretful remonstrances, Kitty observed to Clarissa, "If only I were not so aware of the crushing importance of this meeting. What if Lady Sefton discovers that I have no accomplishments, besides a small talent for watercolors?"

Amelia shot her a sympathetic glance, then reluctantly sat down on the sofa yet again.

Clarissa could not help a small laugh. "Unless you offer this information, she will not ask. She is not known for being inquisitive. Really, she is the kindest of women. Here is my suggestion." She lowered her voice conspiratorially. "You must think of yourself as Andromeda. Here you are, ready to take the town by storm. Three dukes will lay their lives and worldly goods at your feet, swearing they will expire if you do not choose them. But you will spurn them because your heart is given to a mysterious highwayman whom you glimpsed only once, on Finchley Common at midnight when he single-handedly saved you and your carriage from being overcome by a set of mysterious ruffians sent by Bonaparte."

Amelia had stopped fidgeting. Tired of ignoring her aunt, she had caught some of this, then she looked at Clarissa in astonishment. "When have you been on Finchley Common at midnight?"

Clarissa and Kitty could not help but laugh. Then Clarissa said, "Here is another recollection. Lady Sefton and my grandmamma Norcaster have been friends any time these past thirty years."

"The Duchess of Norcaster?" Kitty asked.

"Indeed. So she is well disposed toward my family."

It was true. Lady Sefton proved to be a kindly woman who, aside from a rather odd way of speaking, reminded Kitty of Mrs. Finn, the Tarval Hall housekeeper. Consequently, Kitty was able to converse with the easy, pretty-behaved poise that was her habit when she was not self-conscious, and she pleased the lady very well.

Tildy had joined them, chattering to young Lord Molyneux, stiff in his proper blue jacket and knee breeches. The little boy was polite enough, only brightening when at last Lady Sefton rose to leave.

She promised the vouchers, which sent Amelia shrieking upstairs the moment the street door was heard closed.

The next morning, Amelia was cast into agonies of vexation when her mother calmly informed her that they must spend the morning returning certain calls. Not all, as she was not Out, but their near relations and young ladies their own age must certainly receive their due. Amelia, who had planned to lie in wait upon the deliveries of the post, muttered that she hoped no one would be at home so they could leave cards and return to Brook Street.

Some were home, and others weren't. They called in Mount Street, and found the Bouldestons at home.

Here, Lady Chadwick observed the stiff care with which her guest behaved, which surprised her enough to pay more attention to her hostess and family than she otherwise would have.

Lady Chadwick preferred to believe the best of people. Life was too fatiguing otherwise. Everybody had smiled and been kind when she was growing up, and after she'd had a wonderful year on the town exactly as she'd expected, her parents told her that marrying a widower with a child gave her two persons to love, and she would gain great credit thereby, which again had proved true.

Clarissa had written that she would find Lady Kitty charming and diverting, which was true, so she was ready to love whomever Lady Kitty loved. But Lady Kitty gave no evidence of loving these Bouldestons, in spite of the elder one's gushing compliments.

Lady Chadwick said nothing when they came away after their quarter hour, but noted the great breath of relief that Lady Kitty drew as soon as they stepped into the street.

The next day, the highly anticipated vouchers arrived as promised. Among the stream of invitations there also arrived the following note:

My Sweetest Catherine:

How Transported I was when you and the Harlowes called. I meant to Speak of this then, but it was Driven out of my Head by my Delight at seeing you looking so well, and in company with the charming Miss Harlowe and Miss Amelia, and the beauteous Lady Chadwick, whose hat Mama declared the most beautiful hat she has seen in fifty ages.

Since you are no Schoolroom Miss, I am Certain that you are not expecting poor lady Chadwick to Present you Formally along with her Daughter. Therefore I take it you are going to begin attending Society Functions at once.

I am in transports at the notion of one who is to be my most cherished Sister (as soon as my papa can be Brought to name the Date to my marriage with your dear Brother) attending Lucasta's ball. Mama has writ to Lady Chadwick and the Harlowes, but I felt I must send your invitation myself. If you come, I will take it upon myself to Present you to the most eligible Men we know.

With all my love—
L. Bouldeston

Kitty read it through twice, then said to Clarissa, "May I trouble you upon a point of etiquette?"

Clarissa signed assent, and Kitty handed her the note, which Clarissa also read through twice, her face unreadable. At length, she said, "Do you wish to attend this ball?"

"Not this one in particular, but I do wish to attend any ball. However, only when it is proper."

"Well, then, that is simple enough: you decline, with thanks. There is already a conflict for the rest of us, for one of my step-mother's connections has already secured us for a soiree that evening. As for..." Clarissa frowned down at the note, then up. "As for these assertions, I must beg pardon, but Miss Bouldeston labors under a misunderstanding, I believe. My step-mother intends to introduce you at Amelia's ball, I thought you understood that. It is what she meant when talking earlier about making certain your gowns complement. And it is only four days after Miss Lucasta's, so it is not long to wait."

At that moment, Lady Chadwick herself appeared. Clarissa said to Kitty, "May I?"

On Kitty's nod, she held out Lucretia's note. Lady Chadwick read it, and then looked up. For once, she was almost animated. "Yes, I just received an invitation for us. I will have to decline on our behalf, for my cousin's soiree is that evening, and we are already expected. But I must say, I am somewhat surprised this assumption that I would be so remiss as to introduce you into the town without as much as a by-your-leave." Lady Chadwick laid Lucretia's note down. "I must say..."

Without vouchsafing any actual utterance, in spite of that curious beginning, she walked out again.

Kitty looked after her in puzzlement, but Lady Chadwick's daughters were too used to their mother to be surprised.

----◆◆◆----

The days sped by, each filled with activity. There were last-minute touches to arrange for their toilette. There was the dancing master to make certain Amelia and Kitty were ready for the intricacies of the ballroom floor.

The day of Lucretia's ball came and went. Kitty encountered Lucretia the next day in the park, and was favored with a description of how successful it had been: the girls had danced every dance, a thousand gentlemen had darted penetrating glances their way, but Lucretia was ever faithful to her dear Carlisle.

However, she also knew that he would not wish her to languish away any more than he would want her to be rude to those who desired her company, and so she was forced to accept the invitations flooding in, and it was to be hoped that her dearest Catherine would have as much luck, but even if she had not, Lucretia would make it a rule to look out eligible gentlemen for her. "I am quite laughed at for my fidelity to my sex," she said, "but *you*, of course, must be held above them all."

The day of Amelia's ball dawned at last, and after two days of rain, it was even clear, promising a night of signal success.

From early in the morning the house was rendered chaotic by an army of hired servants bent on transforming the entire ground floor into a bower of flowers. The younger girls were hugely entertained by watching everything, and getting in the way. The older members of the family heartily wished the day over. Only Amelia and Kitty were delighted by every detail.

Lady Chadwick bestirred herself when her eldest daughter Hortensia, now Lady Badgerwood, arrived with her dandy of a husband, and a full coach of baggage plus half-a-dozen supernumerary servants, all for a two-day stay. This arrival could not have been worse timed for the laboring servants, Kitty noticed, a fact of which the embracing ladies remained sublimely unaware.

Kitty also noticed that Clarissa seemed quiet, even subdued. She attributed it to headache caused by the noise, until Mrs. Latchmore came into the small back room, where the girls sat to be out of the way, exclaiming, "Oh, Clarissa, have you heard anything from Lord Wilburfolde? Was he not to arrive today? I so looked forward to introducing your intended to the world."

Clarissa looked up from her book of poems. "I believe he was intending so, yes."

Kitty kept her gaze on the letter she had begun to her brother, not daring to comment.

At a quarter to eight, the family gathered in the dining room, which had been set up with card tables. Lord Wilburfolde had still not arrived, and Mrs. Latchmore was fretting about that as she bustled about, shifting a candlestick here, a pack of cards there, and twitching a tablecloth that was already straight.

"We shall be quite out of the ordinary, tonight," Hetty exclaimed. "What a handsome family we make!"

She smiled at her mother, who had changed her choice of dress three times in the past two weeks. This new dress had arrived that morning. It was the very latest fashion from Paris, brought by the Duchess of Devonshire, who had taken advantage of the Peace of Amiens to go to France, where she visited the Tuileries to be introduced to the First Consul and his charming wife. Lady Chadwick had been among the ladies invited to view the duchess's new clothes, sending them all to their dressmakers.

This gown was not made of diaphanous muslin, carefully dampened, for Lady Chadwick had decided notions about what was glorious and what was notorious. But the Grecian tunic over white, with the embroidered bunches of grapes, and the graceful headdress of laurel leaves and rubies to resemble grape clusters binding up her hair, was graceful and smart.

Hetty was lovely in blue sarcenet, her husband a Pink of the Pinks in evening attire with the added glitter of fobs and seals and an ornate quizzing glass on a chain. He stood with Lord Chadwick against the far wall, enjoying a fortifying glass of sherry, joined by James, looking tall and lanky in his evening-rig, as he termed it.

Hetty turned her step-sister's way. "And you, Clarissa, I do not recall you ever looking better. Is it being engaged? I hear it adds to everyone's beauty, for the worry is over. And you, Lady Kitty — you will set hearts afire tonight, I think!"

Clarissa colored. She looked elegant in jonquil crape with lace at the neck and hem, but privately she took pride in Hetty's heartfelt compliment aimed at Kitty, for it was very true that Kitty was splendid in a spider-gauze gown of white with a satin under-slip of palest green, and pale green velvet ribbon at the waist. Simple, demure, yet devastatingly elegant. Her headdress was as simple, merely two bunches of white roses threaded by green ribbon that matched the spring green of her eyes.

Amelia twirled around, hands out-held. "And I?" She looked ethereal in pure white, with two white roses in her hair. The only color was the rose of her sash, the blue of her eyes, and the guinea-gold of her hair.

She touched her neck, where her first grownup necklet of pearls lay.

Hetty kissed her sister. "I think you will be even more popular than I was last year."

"Do not twitch at that lace, you will make sad work of it before your first guest," Mrs. Latchmore scolded.

Amelia dropped her hands, but then raised them again. "I hope I do not look like I am trying to copy Lucasta Bouldeston, for I hear she wore white, too, and Mary Yallonde wrote me a note yesterday, saying that Lucasta called on her, and hoped I would not be all in white, for I'd look such a figure after she—"

"You know very well that girls always wear white," Lady Chadwick said calmly. "I do not know how Miss Lucasta got such a silly notion."

"And hers was trimmed with floss, and spangles," Mrs. Latchmore added. "For I had it myself from Mrs. Somerset."

Amelia then went on nervously, "I do not want to dance the first dance with anyone *old*. I want to fall in love, just like Hetty did at her ball—"

"If his grace attends, the honor must go to him, dear," Lady Chadwick said. "And be sure it will get out that your first dance was with a duke. After that, you may accept whom you please, but it would look better if you honor..."

She lowered her voice, talking quietly until Amelia whimpered, "But he's fat!"

"Oh lord," James said, rolling his eyes. "When Tildy comes out, I shall be in another country, see if I'm not."

Just then the door knocker rapped, and the family moved to the landing to form the greeting line.

Some time later, Kitty's face ached from smiling, and her knees from curtseying over and over. Scores of people had passed by as Lady Chadwick repeated her name what seemed a thousandfold.

But at last the stream of arrivals slowed to a trickle, at which time Lady Chadwick, usually so vague, tipped her head as the clock chimed sweetly eleven times. "It is time to open the ball," she said.

Kitty followed the family into an anteroom. The brilliance of the candles, the hot air, the murmur of voices seemed to be drowned by the curious rushing in her head. She moved without being conscious of it to a chair, and sat down abruptly.

"Lady Kitty." A voice broke into the fog.

Kitty looked up, and blinked until she recognized James's face. "Here," he said, and pushed something into her hands.

She sipped, and her mouth took fire, spreading coals down as she swallowed. "What is that?" she gasped.

"Brandy." James grinned. "Drink it off."

"No. Please, take it away. That is, thank you. But it tastes horrid, and I should very much not like to smell of spirits. I am much better, thank you."

"What happened?"

"Nothing. That is, I was standing, watching your Mama talk to that last group of people, and then, I don't know."

"Eat anything today?"

"Of course. That is," Kitty amended as she recollected the picked-at dinner, then the tea swallowed at breakfast. "What a goose I am."

"Hetty did the same thing last year. But she fainted right on the landing. Badgerwood was there to help—but they'd been making eyes at one another for two weeks. He lived with his family across the street, you know. Thing is, Clarissa sent me, for they are making up the first set. I'm to lead you out."

"I thought you despised dancing." Kitty laughed up at him.

"Not with you, I don't. For one thing, we've practiced together, and I know you will not tread on my toes. And for another, I know you won't bullock me into a second one."

Together they walked into the ballroom, where Kitty spotted Lord Wilburfolde next to a pale Clarissa. "Oh, he's here," Kitty said under her breath.

James muttered, "Just arrived."

Kitty turned his way. "You don't like him?"

James evinced surprise. "He's not a bad fellow, just a slow-top."

"I am convinced Clarissa does not want to marry him," Kitty murmured. "Can you help me think of a way to save her?"

James's eyes rounded. "Nothing to be done. Puffed off in the papers, family wants it—Lady Wilburfolde. Lord!" He made a warding motion. "No gainsaying *her*. If Boney ever met her, he'd mend his ways. Besides, it's Mama's and my aunt's business. If I were to go poking my nose in, they might take it into their heads to try foisting a wife onto *me*."

Kitty thought that Ned and Carlisle would not be so poor-spirited, not to mention selfish, but she liked James, so she kept that to herself.

And so at last the dancers begin the dance, each pair appearing to be in perfect amity, led off by Amelia and the stout, middle-aged Duke of Norcaster, with Kitty and James after. Clarissa and Lord Wilburfolde followed Hetty and her husband. The music began, everybody smiled, and they were in motion. Once Amelia trusted that she would not falter, she enjoyed the exhilaration of being the center of attention.

Kitty and James probably had the most fun, exchanging joking comments all the way through. Kitty was completely unaware of how very well she looked on a ballroom floor, more graceful than the self-conscious Amelia, her eyes and cheeks glowing.

Clarissa's cheeks also glowed, but from suppressed irritation when her betrothed, after their first exchange of greetings, inquired, "Have you written in response to my mother's letter yet?"

"I have not, Lord Wilburfolde." And because he waited for an explanation, she felt obliged to utter a social nothing, "I have been so very busy."

"Miss Harlowe, I feel it my duty to point out that my mother is strict about the rules of etiquette." And when Clarissa nodded acknowledgment, "Then you must realize she will regard herself bound by the rules of civil discourse not to write again until she has received an answer."

Clarissa was surprised, and not pleased, to discover a petty retort rising to her lips. He was thoroughly in the right, and she had erred, and yet she was not sorry. She was surprised at her own spitefulness. To scold herself, she said, "I beg pardon. I will amend my error."

He thanked her with painstaking courtesy, and went on to enumerate the sacrifices his mother was making in staying alone at The Castle while Edmund attended his betrothed in the metropolis.

By the end of the dance, Kitty and Amelia were surrounded, the young bucks gravitating to Amelia and the more sophisticated to Kitty, so that neither robbed the other of attention.

"My dance, I believe, Worthington?" A tall gentleman, his hair worn short in a Bedford crop, appeared at Kitty's side as the orchestra struck up for the fourth time.

Mr. Worthington, fair-haired and smiling, said, "But this was my dance, was it not, Lady Catherine?"

"How am I to answer?" she replied, looking from one to the other. "I confess I do not remember where we are at."

The new gentleman said, "Bare-faced piracy. I am convinced that it was my dance."

Kitty sent an appealing glance up at Mr. Worthington. "Is it permitted to request of you to return for the next?"

Mr. Worthington bowed, then sent an ironic glance at his rival. "I find I must surrender to *force majeure*, but only to spare the lady, otherwise I should call you to account, sir."

"Name your time and place, sir. I expire happily if I might dare to request a single rose before I die."

There was a little more banter like this, nothing that hadn't been heard on countless ballroom floors, but it was all new and dazzling to Kitty. She glowed with pleasure, bestowed the rose, then moved happily enough out onto the floor with her new partner, thinking, *Now what was his name?*

"Dare I asked, Lady Catherine, whether you are tolerably pleased by tonight's festivities?"

"I've been told it is fashionable to protest an *ennui*, but truly, everything is so fine, the musicians excellent, and in short, boredom for me is to sit in the countryside with little to do."

"An idea the most criminal, such beauty sequestered in the country unseen," her partner said gallantly.

There was a lot more like it. Kitty enjoyed it all, did not believe a word, and danced happily as the hours chimed away. People were all so kind! For where gentlemen took an interest, the wiser young ladies exerted themselves to strike up a conversation with the fascinating new beauty who was said to be sister to a marquess.

And so it was thus that the last arrival of the evening found them: Mr. Philip Devereaux.

Fifteen

ARRIVING SO LATE, DEVEREAUX did not expect to be greeted. It was his responsibility to locate his hostess and make his bow. Just discernible within the card room were Lord Chadwick and his son playing least-in-sight. Immediately before Mr. Devereaux was Amelia, her roses drooping as she romped in a circle dance with a number of other very young ladies and gentlemen, the latter whose wilting shirt-collars evidenced the warmth of the room as well as the exercise.

Standing side by side in the line were Clarissa and Lady Catherine, the former looking more animated than he remembered ever seeing her. But her smile faded into politeness when the hands-across brought Clarissa in contact with her partner. Wilburfolde was concentrating on his steps, his lips moving...yes, he was counting aloud, with brow-furrowed concentration.

Lady Chadwick was seated against the wall with the more dashing dowagers, shining down half the younger generation in her Grecian robe that managed to be flattering and yet not revealing. Emily Cowper studied the embroidery through her quizzing glass, cooing compliments.

"Ah, Devereaux." The Duke of Rutland appeared out of the crowd. "We had about given you up."

"I could not get away before this," Mr. Devereaux responded. "Permit me to make my bow and my pardons to our hostess."

"'Tis the nature of spring." His grace lifted his hand in an airy wave. "Some will say it's not a successful evening unless they arrive late at no fewer than six balls before morning."

Lady Cowper laughed, and Mr. Devereaux bowed over the hand of his hostess.

As always, the sight of a handsome man animated this lady, and so it was not at all with her customary languor that she welcomed him, adding with simple maternal pride, "Amelia opened the ball with your uncle. It is Hetty all over again. And my guest no less. You may call it a double success."

Lady Chadwick had a fondness for this cousin-by-marriage, who was only ten years younger than she was. His being unmarried made her feel young again. She kept him by her side for a few minutes as the dance wound to its end, then said, "Go and dance with my daughter and my guest, and give them *éclat.*"

"I scarcely think either of them need it," he rejoined with a smile and a bow, but he politely obeyed.

Kitty had not been aware of the newcomer. She only saw the crowd of Amelia's swains part in a little disorder, through which walked Mr. Devereaux with Amelia on his arm.

They took up their places at the head of the next line. Amelia had calmed a little, as if she were on her best behavior, her uncertain glances at her partner amusing Kitty very much. Kitty could almost imagine the thoughts going through Amelia's head — oh no, the man who hates women — Clarissa's cousin — oh, was her hair tumbling down? For you can be certain that Mr. Devereaux was not flushed from the heat, and his shirt points were not limp.

"My dance, I believe, Lady Catherine?"

Kitty turned, and found her next partner waiting with a quizzical expression on his face. Her cheeks burned as she begged his pardon, and they took their place in the middle of the line. She was thus in an ideal position to catch murmurs of conversation — killingly correct on both parts — between Amelia and her partner, and the observations, given in a manner that did not permit of discussion, much less agreement, on the part of Lord Wilburfolde, who had unaccountably risen to dance with Clarissa again.

His occasional puzzled glances toward Mr. Devereaux made Kitty wonder if he had suspected some attachment between the cousins, and Kitty mentally gave Lord Wilburfolde credit for his interest, as she gave him credit for attempting a conversation. Judging from the little she had seen of his mother, she did not fault him for uttering observations in the declarative, as if issuing a *fiat*. She wondered if he had ever dared a question in his life.

If only he did not make Clarissa so unhappy!

She was deep in thought as the dance ended, so much so that she performed her thanks and her curtsy automatically. Who was next?

"Lady Catherine, would you do me the honor?"

Kitty turned around—and stared wordlessly up into Mr. Devereaux's face. Mr. Canby deferred, as this was his second dance; he gave her a sign and mouthed the words 'next', leaving her confronted by the gentleman she'd hoped never to see again.

"So hesitant, Lady Catherine?' And in the softest of voices, "Am I still unforgiven for abducting my sister?"

It was said on impulse, the intent humor, but if he could have retracted it, he would have. He braced for coy bridling, or the assumption of moral superiority—any of the arts assumed by young ladies who tried to gain interest by investing trifling situations with the passions better left to the stage. He did not blame them—it was what most of them were taught—but he'd endured so many such scenes.

Kitty, however, was suffused with embarrassment and regret. She put out her hand automatically, an unconscious gesture almost of appeal, and said, low-voiced, "Though I am to blame for suggesting it, she did agree with me. How was I to know it for an untruth?"

"A fair question," he responded, as the music started up, and they moved into line. "Yet I still wonder. If I were such a villain, would it not have been more expedient to have called for the innkeeper to come to your aid?"

"No, for of course he would be in your pay," Kitty responded.

The unexpected answer surprised a laugh out of him.

She gave him a startled glance, and, finding no scorn or judgment, she said reflectively, "Which would require much advance planning, would it not? One would have to select the right inn to avoid having to bribe half the innkeepers in the county. Either that, or know ahead which were knavish enough to accept bribes, which raises the question... no." She had gone unawares into Andromeda's story, and caught herself up, blushing uncomfortably.

They walked down the dance, and then took their places at the bottom of the line, whence Mr. Devereaux prompted, "Question, Lady Catherine?"

Her brow wrinkled in perplexity. This conversation was not at all like the proper responses she had been so carefully taught by the dancing master. Nor was it like anything in the romances she had so eagerly read in order to divine how people got on in Society.

And yet she saw no evidence of satire, or disgust, and so she said, "Well, it is just that I cannot help but wonder what inspires a gentleman to wish to abduct an unwilling female, for among other things, would it not require a vast amount of work? Then there are the disagreeable aspects of one another's company, he having to utter a string of threats, and she responding like a watering-pot. I must suppose that is one of those mysteries that delicacy forbids ladies from inquiring further into," she added hastily.

But he ignored the platitude. "Can it be that successful abductions require a certain amount of cooperation, perhaps covert, from the female in question? There is historical precedent, you know."

"Are you referring to my mother, sir?"

It was the gentleman's turn to blush, though she did not utter the question with accusation. "I did not remember the circumstances of your parents' marriage, though I was probably told. Forgive me."

"Oh, but it was quite true. Mother told my brothers that she arranged everything," was the surprising answer. "She told them she had historical precedent in Lady Mary Wortley Montague. My grandmother St. Tarval was used to offer her as an example of ill behavior, yet my brother once pointed out that Lady Mary could not have been all evil, for she was the one who brought the smallpox cure to England. At any rate, I think there may be a disagreement in terms, for a willing female elopes." She chanced to glance up, and caught his profile, which was severe; she did not know him well enough to perceive that he was schooling himself strictly against laughing out loud.

"But there," she said in politely colorless accents. "I suspect that this topic is not proper in the circumstance, and so, if I may shift it, how does Miss Elizabeth in Bath?"

"She is heartily bored, of course, and quite counts upon her visit to this household. How do you find London?"

She gave him a properly polite answer, making an effort to confine herself to the topics—and the language—that the dancing master had taught them were the most acceptable, and in this way, they came to the end of the dance.

They parted most correctly. He, having done his duty by his hostess, went off to dance with a dashing widow newly returned to society after her mourning period, and she to Mr. Canby, relieved that the man who hated women had been... *interesting.* She did not expect to see him ever again, but at least she had the comfort of knowing that her *faux pas* was not regarded by him as significant.

Then it was time to go down to supper. James reappeared, conscientiously offering his arm to Kitty, who was relieved to have his unexceptional and undemanding company.

Mr. Devereaux bowed to his hostess, and skillfully disappeared without raising any notice.

◆◆◆

After waking up late the following morning, Kitty descended to find all four sisters at the breakfast table, but as yet no one else.

On side-tables surrounding them stood vases of flowers of every imaginable variety. Amelia looked a trifle bleary-eyed, and Clarissa was calm and pale as always, but everyone seemed to be in a good humor, if tired.

"Look, Lady Kitty," Amelia exclaimed. "It is more than Hetty had last year, is it not, Hetty?"

"Of course, as there are two taken together," Hetty said.

Eliza waved her hands. "So many of them are for you," she said to Kitty. "Shall we help you open the cards?"

"Oh, pray do."

Eliza and Matilda began tearing through the cards attached to the bouquets, comparing and giggling. Two gentlemen had sent bouquets to both young ladies; several had attached verses to the floral offerings. Kitty recognized about half the names. Most of the evening seemed a blur, in retrospect. The only conversation she remembered was the one with Mr. Devereaux. He had seemed almost friendly—but of course his being cousins with Clarissa would account for it.

Amelia cast a loud sigh. "Did you form an eternal passion for anyone, Lady Kitty?"

"Do you know, I had so fine a time dancing, I quite forgot that I was to fall in love?"

Amelia giggled, then began telling them of the extravagant things her swains had been saying, until their aunt entered. At once everyone confined themselves to tea and toast.

Mrs. Latchmore, however, appeared to be in an excellent mood. "A successful evening all around, was it not, girls? And Lord Wilburfolde arrived, dear fellow, exactly as one would wish. Every exertion made—so attentive to Clarissa, it bodes well, does it not?"

No one had anything to say to this, but it had the general effect of hastening breakfast.

The hour had just struck noon when Pobrick entered the room to announce that the Miss Bouldestons were waiting in the drawing room.

The young ladies found Lucretia and Lucasta standing over one of the many little tables that Lady Chadwick had placed throughout the house, examining and commenting on some miniatures of the family.

On the entrance of the young ladies, greetings having been exchanged, Lucretia said, "We are come to introduce you to Hookham's Lending Library, Catherine, knowing you are excessively fond of books."

Kitty turned to Clarissa, saying, "Do come with us."

At once the Bouldeston sisters reinforced this invitation, each claiming that only the addition of Miss Harlowe could make it the most complete walk—the sweetest day ever.

Clarissa was taken aback. She was used to being left out,

except when the family was invited — or when some young man wished to plead his case for her pretty sister — or when her fortune was being sought. She did not know what motivated the Misses Bouldeston (for she had heard about the *completest, sweetest thing ever* too many times to count such superlatives) but she read appeal in Kitty's countenance.

There was nothing to keep her home, save the nod and smile she had given Lord Wilburfolde when, on parting the night before, he had informed her that she was tired and required rest, and that he would be reporting to his mama that he had extracted her promise to do so.

Amelia, of course, had no interest in a lending library, still less in the Bouldestons, whom she abused as encroaching mushrooms with their *sweetest Catherine* as soon as the four young ladies were out the door.

"You can see how much Lady Kitty detests that," Amelia said to Eliza as the door closed below.

"Bess Devereaux had it from some girl at Miss Battersea's that Lucasta Bouldeston hides in the chimney closet to spy on her sister and her callers if she thinks they are talking secrets," Eliza declared, and with a toss of her head. "I should despise lowering myself to such tactics. I hate secrets and gossip!"

The sound of a heavy tread on the stair broke up this conversation, sending Eliza to the door. She peeked out, then looked back, her eyes round with horror. "It's he," she whispered. "Run, or we will be stuck listening to him prose for*ever*."

They fled out the side door before the butler could open the double doors.

Lord Wilburfolde was left alone in the parlor, to soon be joined by Mrs. Latchmore, who was always glad to see him. "The young ladies are still recuperating their beauty upstairs, I may suppose?" he asked with a ponderous attempt at levity.

"The young ladies are hardier than we old ones," she said coyly. "The girls are somewhere about, and Clarissa is out walking with Lady Catherine and the Misses Bouldeston."

"I do not credit what I am hearing," he said, aghast.

Mrs. Latchmore gasped. "I assure you, the Misses Bouldeston are quite unexceptionable. Sir Henry, I understand, has —"

Lord Wilburfolde was too overset to be aware of his inter-ruption. "It is not their identity that distresses me, it is my concern for Clarissa, if I may be permitted to use her Christian name. She promised me she would rest, and then attend to my mother's missive, so that my mother might write to her again. I do not know what is to be done. Perhaps I may catch them up if I hasten."

He punctiliously took his leave.

───────── ✦ ─────────

The walk to Hookham's was conducted in apparent amity. Clarissa politely asked Lucasta about her ball, and as the latter launched into a detailed account, well-wreathed with superlatives, Lucretia quizzed Kitty on who had attended Amelia's ball, what they had worn, and with whom she had danced.

Kitty retailed all those she could remember, adding with a spurt of self-consciousness left over from memory of her ghastly error at the inn, "And the last arrival was Mr. Devereaux."

"Of course he did not dance. He never does," Lucretia stated.

Kitty remained silent, and Lucretia turned her head and eyed her. "You do not mean to say that he did?"

Kitty nodded, and Lucretia's eyes narrowed. "With you?" Her affected lisp came out rather sharp.

"Yes, but he danced with Amelia first. And then a widow, I forget her name, but the way they talked, it seems they are either connections or old friends."

"Oh, I know, it must have been Lady Silverdale, who just came out of mourning. Lord Silverdale was a friend of Mr. Devereaux, but he was a diplomat, and died in that horrid battle on the Nile River. It was quite four years ago, but she stayed on her estate with the two children until recently. Everyone says it is so romantical and tragic! Perhaps they mean to make a match of it."

As Kitty had nothing to say about persons not known to her, Lucretia went on, "It was certainly in compliment to Lady Chadwick, but you may mention that he danced with you, and watch the green eyes at Almack's. I have told you that he is a great catch, though he is known to regard our poor sex with scorn, in the generality. Here we are."

Kitty was relieved to discover the discreet windows of the shop before them, with lampoons posted in the front window. A small crowd had gathered around one of Gilroy's latest; from the coarse laughter and commentary of the onlookers, it was something vulgar about the wife of Napoleon Bonaparte.

Kitty walked inside, and here her emotions underwent a vast change. So many books! So many imaginations and voices! Perchance her own might be added to those shelves, handsomely bound and with gilt lettering. As she examined the newest publications laid out on a table, she wondered if any were written by a young lady waiting at home in hopes of earning a fortune to rescue her family.

Clarissa's voice recalled her attention. She knew several of the people already in the shop. Kitty had met Miss Pennington at Amelia's ball, and so there was a gathering, and mutual compliments offered.

When the fashionably dressed Miss Pennington finished praising Kitty's and Amelia's gowns, Lucretia said, "But you have not finished telling us how you enjoyed your *very first* ball, Catherine."

Her voice seemed curiously penetrating. It certainly caused a silence. Kitty said, "It was very fine," and then, belatedly, "Are you acquainted with Miss Pennington, Lucretia? May I make you known to one another?"

Lucretia touched her fingertips to her lips. "My dear, you forget that *I* am not newly arrived from the country. But of course you mean well by us, so I will pretend that Miss Pennington and I were not introduced at Lady Sefton's ball last year. How do you do, Miss Pennington?"

Miss Pennington bowed, and said, "I believe we have met, and apologize for not remembering."

Lucretia bridled. "Oh, you are forgiven. It is the curse of those of us so modest and shy, never to be noticed. You have no idea how lucky you are, Catherine! Come Lucasta, let us not be dawdling in front of the books forever, it is quite unfair to the others here."

Lucretia drew her protesting sister aside: Lucasta wanted to look at a book she had been dying to read, if only Lucretia wouldn't maul her about. Whispering fiercely, the sisters walked down an aisle, leaving Kitty looking in worry at Miss Pennington's pursed mouth and stiff posture, wondering how she'd managed to step wrong.

But hard on that thought Miss Pennington smiled, saying in a friendly tone, "Pray give Miss Amelia my regards, Lady Catherine, and tell her that my sister is quite counting upon her company at her own come-out three days hence..."

Sixteen

AND SO SEVERAL DAYS sped by, each with its walks, rides, and parties. Twice Lady Chadwick entertained. Once she invited the Bouldestons, and the favor was returned. Kitty found herself involved in a constant round of select concerts, soirees, dinners, and impromptu dances as well as balls. She began to notice that though occasionally she saw Lucretia at the larger parties, the Bouldestons rarely seemed to count among the guests at the smaller affairs.

Rain set in. On the fourth morning after three very wet days, the young ladies were longing to get out. Kitty had been invited by Miss Melissa Atherton, sister of Lord Badgerwood, to join a party of friends bent on hunting for bargains in the shops.

Clarissa had long known Melissa, whose house lay directly across the street. It was not the sort of outing she sought, but she had been gratified by the way Kitty turned to her with hope widening her expressive eyes, clearly wanting her to accept the invitation as well. But Clarissa had been engaged to visit the British Museum with her betrothed.

Clarissa would have preferred the relative space and air of the park, but was not going to get it while in his company, for Lord Wilburfolde was convinced by his mother that the source of all illness lurked outdoors. Clarissa longed to lose herself in the verdure just coming into bloom.

She had agreed Lord Wilburfolde's proposed outing in a spirit of anger, of self-punishment, partly for not having yet answered that officious letter of his mother's, but also for permitting her mind to stray to Kitty's brother after Kitty received letters from home. Speculation, she had discovered too late, hurts just as much as hope.

The hurt was still there, but the anger had cooled, leaving her aware that no one had put her into this position but herself. By night she worried at mad schemes — throwing Lord Wilburfolde over, weathering the storm of comment and shame — by day she would brace herself, thinking, *I cannot expose my family to the inevitable talk. Surely marriage will not be so very terrible. The Wilburfoldes are a respected family in our parish...* But an hour in her betrothed's company never failed to give her a headache, because every word he spoke, every action, was a reminder of what life with Lady Wilburfolde would be like.

A good woman would liberate him from his mother's control, a strong woman. Clarissa knew herself to be neither, but even if she had been, should one liberate someone who gives every appearance of contentment within his cage?

At the end of a long day, the young ladies met again in the front parlor. Kitty was sharing her finds with Amelia and Eliza.

Clarissa, taking off her bonnet, said, "Did you find anything of interest?"

"Only some fresh ribbons, some new feathers, and these pearl rosettes that look quite real, don't you think? I thought I might put them on my old traveling bonnet, which I cannot bear to part with, but which I know looks sadly shabby. I was very careful with my purchases, which is boring, I know. The fun came in watching Miss Atherton, who bought all manner of things."

"Melissa will buy anything if she is convinced it is a bargain," Clarissa said, pressing her fingertips to her temples. "I expect most of her purchases will be judged hideous once she got them home, and will handed off to the maids."

Kitty laughed. "I hope they might find a use for strings of red beads, and Egyptian scarabs." Her manner altered to polite concern. "Did you find the Museum interesting?"

Clarissa dropped her hands, lest her headache be noticed,

exclaimed upon, and unwanted nostrums offered. She knew the cause.

So what to say? She had found it interesting, or would have, had not Edmund considered it necessary to read aloud to her the cards labeling each exhibit, as if she could not read them herself, after which he would inform her what his mother would expect her to think. Lady Wilburfolde had opinions on everything, quite remarkable for a woman who kept to her room most days, never opening a window. The sights had reawakened the desire to board a ship for distant vistas, but all Clarissa said was, "Very instructive."

The next morning, accompanied by Amelia, they went out for a ride, Kitty taking Lady Chadwick's well-mannered hack. The ground was still too muddy for walking, but everywhere they encountered other riders, and a variety of carriages. Everyone in town had been taken by the same wish for the fresh air — or for the sight of others in want of air.

When they reached the park, Clarissa experienced a strong impulse to gallop. She knew it for a wish to escape to the countryside. As it was, they scarcely went ten feet before encountering acquaintances who all seemed to have something to say to Kitty, Amelia, or both.

From the opposite direction came a dashing curricle drawn by a magnificent pair of matched bays. Clarissa recognized the equipage — and there was Cousin Philip driving, with the elegant young Colonel Lord Petersham riding beside him.

Kitty had begun by noticing the fine horses, then the phaeton. Her attention was drawn to the driver who handled the high-bred horses with such apparent ease, and she experienced a rush of interest, a flurry of heartbeats when she recognized Mr. Devereaux's broad-shouldered silhouette in the many-caped driving coat.

Looked at from the safety of a distance, he really was as handsome as everyone said. She could not look away, she had to take in every detail of the beaver worn at the correct angle on his dark hair, the way it somehow emphasized the strength of the bones in his face, the smooth gloves so assured on the reins, and the hint of a flawlessly fitted riding coat within the greatcoat when he lifted his arm to check a start from the leader. When her gaze shifted to his face, it was to encounter his own gaze, and she quickly looked down at her own hand on the reins, embarrassed at the hot tide of color she could not prevent flooding her face.

She hoped her bonnet hid it. He was handsome, that was true, but her foremost emotion now was a sharp bond of sympathy with all the females said to be languishing over him.

She did *not* wish to be one of them.

Amelia, however, was more forthright. Not that she desired to marry Mr. Devereaux. He was too intimidating for that, besides being nearly ten years older than she was—an eternity—but she knew how important he was in the social world, and so she beckoned to him imperiously with her whip. She knew he would not snub her, being family; her objective was to not only to be seen talking to him, but to secure an introduction to Lord Petersham, who was rarely known to show interest in debutantes.

The curricle was obligingly pulled up, the introductions made. Amelia then exerted every nerve to keep the gentleman in conversation.

While that was going on, Mr. Devereaux asked after the family, and when Clarissa had given a slight, polite reply, he said, "I trust you still find amusement in town, Lady Catherine?"

Kitty glanced at Amelia, who was just now affecting fashionable *ennui*, which accorded oddly with her flushed face and triumphant glances. She hid the impulse to laugh, and said, "I do indeed, sir."

"... and tomorrow we are to make our debut at Almack's," Amelia was saying to Captain Lord Petersham, with a languishing sigh. "Everyone says it is the greatest bore."

"Then you are greatly to be pitied," Lord Petersham murmured so dulcetly that Amelia was not aware of satire. Besides, she had caught sight of that odious Lucasta Bouldeston, whom she already detested, and so she went on to illustrate just how bored she expected to be.

When she paused for breath, Mr. Devereaux ventured a question. "You will be making your debut there as well, Lady Catherine?"

"Yes," Kitty said.

"I trust you will not find it too taxing."

"How could anyone find dancing—" Kitty began, then remembered that Lucretia had called Almack's *The Marriage Mart*. What bachelor who has been pursued for years would want to go there if he did not deem it his duty?

Kitty broke off in confusion and Amelia, who had been impatiently waiting to take over the conversation again, began a castigation of the poor refreshments to be expected at Almack's, ending with what she hoped was the assurance of town-bronze, "Oh, Lady Kitty, *he* is never seen there."

Mr. Devereaux bowed to Amelia. "I am only there when I may be assured a dance with three charming young ladies."

Kitty merely nodded, accepting the words as polite nothings, but Amelia was more forthright. "Then you may be certain I shall save a dance for you, sir."

The horses were restive; the gentlemen excused themselves with polite tips of their hats, and the two parties separated.

"Mama must have prevailed upon him," Amelia said triumphantly. "Capital! If he does appear and dance with us, then it will make Lucasta look no-how—" She caught a look of embarrassment in Clarissa's face before she glanced away, and recollected herself. "Well. I apologize, Lady Kitty, for I know she is a friend of yours. If she would not say such *horrid* things—yes, Clarissa, I will be silent."

"Oh, my dear Clarissa," Mrs. Latchmore said as their coach jostled in the long line toward the plain Palladian-style front of Almack's. "It is a pity our dear Lord Wilburfolde was claimed by relations this very night. You are so good to be dedicating yourself to your sister and guest when you must wish to be at his side."

Clarissa was puzzled to know how to answer that, and the other two were looking at their hands as if their futures lay written on their gloves. She was saved by another jolt, and the rattle of the door.

"You could alight here, Miss," Thomas the footman declared when Clarissa peeked out. "The flagway is swept."

Before Mrs. Latchmore could protest about their gowns, Clarissa said, "We are capable of walking another ten feet. It is a fine night."

Amelia was as eager as Kitty to see the inside of the famous assembly at last, and was far more forthright about being first to walk inside, once they had left their wraps. She raised her fan and plied it nervously as she scanned the knots of early arrivals for anyone she might know.

Kitty looked around more slowly, and when Clarissa whispered, "Are you impressed?" Kitty glanced into her face, detected the hint of satire, and smothered a smile behind her hand.

"I thought it would be grander," she admitted.

"It is not termed the Marriage Mart for the excellence of the architecture," Clarissa observed dryly as Mrs. Latchmore fussed and fretted about the best place to sit.

Kitty's scrutiny shifted to the crowd, which seemed so far to comprise young ladies in light-colored gowns, dotted here and there by a blue coat.

'The Marriage Mart.' It was a vulgar notion, but not inapt because of the quick, darted looks, the sudden smiles and trilling laughs, voices in sharp tones, or languishing, raised slightly to catch and hold the attention. Kitty could not prevent her mind from offering the comparison of peaches and apples and pears on display for sale. She knew that such a thought was as vulgar as the appellation, and further, here she was adding to their number, her own gaze having swept the room in expectation of partners.

But that is to dance, she thought. She loved dancing, loved the easy talk. She had formed the notion of finding a wealthy gentleman when she first accepted Clarissa's invitation to come to London, knowing that marriage was the business of young ladies, especially if one wished to help one's brother. Nor were those of her sex to be faulted for doing what they must to catch the attention of eligible gentlemen.

But the reality was so very daunting. She could not bring herself to make up to some fellow in whom she held no genuine interest, in hopes of one day spending his money. The idea seemed... horrid.

Kitty took her seat, lost in reverie as she considered all that had been hidden hitherto. She loved her brothers, and must expect to live with them always. Of course if Carlisle were to marry Lucretia, that would change things, but surely, as a marchioness, Lucretia would have something better to occupy her time than require Kitty to listen to her singing, or even her brag. And Tarval Hall, say what you like about its shabbiness, was large. Kitty could find plenty to do in her own rooms, and they might only meet at mealtimes.

Her thoughts splintered when the musicians made noises preparatory to starting up, and Lady Sefton approached to perform the introduction that would permit Amelia and Kitty to dance.

Kitty was so self-conscious that all her attention was reserved for her curtsy as she regarded the fine stockings before her, below satin knee breeches and a gala coat. Her gaze flicked upward to meet a humorous pair of brown eyes.

Lady Sefton, having done her duty, turned her attention to Lady Chadwick, leaving Kitty staring incomprehensibly.

Clarissa had begun to understand her friend fairly well by now, and so she said gently, "Kitty, this is a trifle awkward, but I think you will understand, and forbear. Perhaps you were unaware that Lord Arden is one of your maternal relations? And here is Mr. Fleming, who is also a kind of family connection, I believe?"

"Very distant," Mr. Fleming said with a bow. "But I've run tame at Carlisle Hall since we were boys, as we are also neighbors."

"I hope you will forgive me for begging Lady Sefton to introduce us," Lord Arden said. "I cry craven, hiding behind a lady, but you have to know it was entirely motivated by pure feelings. Well, that and a wish to pass myself off as respectable."

Kitty smiled at Lord Arden's sally, causing his expression of polite inquiry warm to an answering smile, and she wondered if gentlemen might feel on display, too? For what would one feel like if a young lady turned down his offer to dance — to marry?

Was *that* why Clarissa accepted Lord Wilburfolde? To spare his feelings?

"Now that our bona fides are established, may I have the

honor, Cousin?" Lord Arden asked.

Kitty happily accepted, Mr. Fleming asked Clarissa, who bowed acquiescence, and they joined the line forming for the Cotillion.

"Who is Amelia's partner?" Kitty said to Clarissa.

"Henry Brocklehurst, a friend to the Seftons."

Amelia was farther down the line, next to a young lady who was dressed in a light muslin gown, simple in form, but stylish, edged with Grecian motifs.

The dance claimed them, and Lord Arden said, "I am relieved to see you smile, I have to confess, Cousin. When I took courage in hand to approach you, I perceived a formidable countenance."

"I?" Kitty couldn't suppress a laugh. "I was merely thinking."

"May one inquire the topic?"

"'The Marriage Mart.' I was wondering if gentlemen think about coming here to look over the display in a quest for wives."

Lord Arden glanced at her in surprise, then they were separated by the movement of the dance. He saw her catch her lower lip between her teeth, and when they came together again for the hands across, she said, "I beg your pardon. That was assuredly indelicate. I've only had the company of brothers, you see, and I know very well that what they say *about* us, when among themselves, can be different than what they say *to* us."

Lord Arden, who had sisters, could not help but laugh. "And is it not the same for ladies?"

"Yes," she acknowledged. "Though perhaps not *quite* the same?"

Her glance was full of fun, her smile both sweet and mischievous. Lord Arden had come as a result of a wager, for the older generation had fired the younger generation's interest by their vehement declaration: *The Carlisle family does not acknowledge the Decourceys.*

Of course anyone with spirit must take that as a challenge, and besides, the rumor that had flown about that one of the mysterious Decourceys was actually in town had been accompanied by the assurance that she was a diamond just as her mother had been. And so, in a spirit of fun he'd accepted Fleming's wager and begged Lady Sefton for the introduction.

By the end of the dance they had come to such a high degree of friendly understanding that he went away to extol her charms as he collected his winnings.

The ladies having sat down again, Kitty caught the high, restless laughter of the very young lady in the daring gown, and asked, "Who is that, pray?"

Mrs. Latchmore sniffed. "That would be Lady Caroline Ponsonby, part of the Devonshire House ménage. The duchess brought that horrid style back from Paris, but no unmarried girl ought to wear such a thing here."

"Except that one is," Amelia pointed out, quite reasonably, Kitty thought.

Mrs. Latchmore observed in an angry undertone that if Miss Pert had any more to offer on such a topic, she could speak it in Brook Street, and they would depart at once.

Providentially, the shy young Sir Oliver Standish approached Amelia just then. And as the baronet had not only recently inherited his title but a vast fortune, Mrs. Latchmore's manner altered remarkably.

A stir went through the company, heads turning sharply enough for feathers in headdresses to twitch and bob. Kitty leaned out to see what attracted the eye. In the center of a party of gentlemen was the now-recognizable figure of Mr. Brummel, not very tall, his hair rather more sandy than brown, but his evening dress was faultless. Equally faultless, and a hand taller, was Mr. Philip Devereaux. Kitty looked away so that she would not be caught staring twice.

Clarissa caught her cousin's eye and they nodded at one another across the room. A familiar high titter drew Kitty's attention to the pair of young ladies entering the ballroom arm in arm, followed by a third. Lucretia Bouldeston stood next to a tall, thin young woman whose gown of cream figured muslin was even more lavishly trimmed than Lucretia's. Clarissa recognized Miss Fordham. Lucasta trailed them, her chin elevated as her gaze darted this way and that.

The three young ladies expertly crossed in front of the gentlemen just entered, forcing them to give way. Clarissa observed how Miss Fordham, who had the habit of speaking with the assurance of one who is very well aware of her large dowry, addressed the gentlemen in such a way as to cause five bows.

Lucretia then laid her fan on Mr. Devereaux' arm. Kitty and Clarissa could not hear her words, only the high titter that accompanied them, but they saw the gentleman bow again most politely.

A string of newly arrived ladies passed between the little group and Clarissa, who had made a private wager within herself that Lucretia had been hinting for an invitation to dance, a hint to which she was almost certain her cousin would be blind. A peculiar sense of having been there before assailed her, and she recovered the exact circumstances of her first observation of Lucretia Bouldeston, in this very room four or five years ago.

Miss Bouldeston had laid her fan on the arm of Cousin Philip in exactly the same manner as she threw out a broad hint about whether it was possible for such a tall gentleman to accommodate his steps to one who Nature had sadly given delicate form. Was that before or after this secret engagement with Kitty's brother?

A shift in the colorful gowns and fine blue coats, and there was Cousin Philip himself, bowing politely to Mrs. Latchmore, Kitty, and Amelia as he held out his hand to Clarissa. "Will you venture to take a turn before it's impossible to move?" he asked her, smiling.

"Thank you," she said, and rose.

They had just joined the forming dance when Lucretia confronted Kitty. "Well, my sweetest Catherine," Lucretia said. "Good evening, Miss Amelia! Catherine, do you find pleasure in your first visit to Almack's?"

"Good evening, Lucretia. I do."

"Catherine, may I make you known to my dear friend, Miss Fordham? Lady Catherine Decourcey. You look positively ravishing, Catherine," Lucretia went on as she helped herself to Clarissa's chair, and Miss Fordham took Amelia's as the latter jumped up in response to a partner approaching to dance. "You must be permitting Miss Harlowe to guide you in your choice in gowns," Lucretia said to Kitty. "A wise decision, as you look delightfully."

"Miss Harlowe has excellent taste," Kitty said warmly.

The conversation flowed along, Lucretia wreathing with compliments a great many questions about the Harlowes, until here was Clarissa again, with Mr. Devereaux.

Lucretia flicked out her fan and applied it prettily, saying, "Miss Harlowe, I relinquish your seat. You look refreshed for the exercise, and one does get tired of forever sitting, I was just saying to Miss Fordham and dearest Catherine. To move about just now would be the most welcome thing in the world, would it not, Mr. Devereaux?"

He bowed, then said to Kitty, "If you are tired of sitting, perhaps I may claim that promised dance?"

Seventeen

KITTY WAS SO SURPRISED she scarcely remembered to speak the proper thanks as they walked out to join the nearest line. Because of the crowd, the lines must of necessity form closer together. Though no one likes a crowd, at least this way partners could converse while waiting to move.

"Does Almack's meet your expectations, Lady Catherine?"

"The rooms are not precisely *distinqué*, as my father used to say, but we are here to dance, not to admire the wainscoting. Or perhaps everyone is here to admire one another," she amended.

A movement of the dance revealed the beautiful Mrs. Bouversie, who was living out of wedlock with Lord Robert Spencer.

When Philip Devereaux saw the direction of her glance, he was aware of sharp disappointment. But so far, Lady Catherine had not uttered the same threadbare comments or allusions that he had been hearing all his life. And so he said, "Are you acquainted?"

"With whom?" she asked, looking surprised. He was surprised by the sense of relief that he had misjudged. She went on, "I beg pardon for being inattentive. I was just thinking..."

"Will you share your thoughts?" he asked. Now would be the time to conform to the expected—for which no one should be faulted. Human nature was predictable. That was a part of order. It was no one's fault but his own that he found himself so easily bored.

She said, "I wonder if it is in our natures to be always thinking something other than what one is doing? For example, my brothers and I were used to play a game when we were small, called Guess."

This was nothing he had expected, after all. "Guess?"

"Perhaps we will sound ill-behaved," she said as they paced in a sedate circle, then performed their turn. "I am from the country, so I am still learning what people in London society talk about and what they do not." A quick glance, full of mischief, but also question.

"Go on. You played a game called 'Guess.'"

"We played it when the homily in church was exceptionally long and dull, or when my grandmother expected us to sit in the parlor in our best clothes, in expectation of some friend of hers who dared to darken our unhallowed door. Though that was less exciting, because we had only the family portraits on which to exercise our imaginations, which, you know, do not change themselves, whereas at church, there were many people to choose from. But however, shall I demonstrate, rather than explain the rules?"

The line had clumped up again. "Please do," he said, grateful to discover himself mildly entertained.

He was not entertaining to her, but she knew he never had to be. No one, gentleman or lady, who was much sought needed to be. He listened, he tried to be agreeable. That was all she hoped for.

"At first we used to guess at their lives, but we found it more fun to make up new lives entirely for them. For example, see that gentleman with the old-fashioned tie-wig, and the hair powder?" Mr. Devereaux glanced at the gentleman in question, and recognized the retired Col. Parkinson, who was pontificating lengthily to his partner, no doubt on his favorite subject, the superiority of army over navy.

"He is contemplating challenging *him*." Kitty's laughing glance pegged the shy young Sir Oliver, two couples down the line. "To a duel over the fine eyes of that lady." Her glance picked out the Duchess of Gordon, whose arrogance had made her infamous. She, too, wore the new French fashion, having recently returned from Paris—rumor having it she had attempted unsuccessfully to secure Eugène de Beauharnais for one of her daughters.

He laughed aloud at the unexpectedness of the contrast. "Are you acquainted with the lady?" he asked.

Kitty's eyes flashed up in surprise. "I am not. It would be horrid if I were. I mean to say, I shouldn't make up things if I knew her at all, or even knew *of* her. That was the fun of it, we had no notion of the true lives of the persons in question. Sometimes I play the game inside my own head when I have to sit very quietly somewhere, or I plan my... Perhaps it was very ill-bred," she finished contritely.

He thought this game much less ill-bred than listening to gossip, but he forbore saying so aloud. At best he might sound satiric, but at worst, he suspected he would merely sound insufferable.

So he changed the subject to an unexceptionable topic. "Your brother is the present marquess," he observed, and on her assent, "I take it he prefers to remain in the country? I do not think I have ever met him in town."

"He was here briefly. At least, I know he was in London when he sat before the Admiralty board to pass for lieutenant, but I do not know if he was introduced into society," Kitty answered. "He does prefer the country, though he confesses a weakness for the sea." Her fondness warmed her voice, and her smile flashed, quick and merry. "He could not comprehend my wish to see London."

As the orchestra moved into the coda, he asked easy questions about the marquess, and she answered them happily enough—Carlisle's cutter—his fondness for horses—his brief career in the navy, as around them, those in the habit of watching Mr. Devereaux noticed that though the young lady seemed to chatter quite a bit, he did not look bored. At least one mother of young ladies whose lures he had been blind to wondered aloud if Lady Catherine was as desperate a flirt as her mother had been.

When they returned to Mrs. Latchmore, the lady was deep in conversation with a pair of hopeful mamas. Lucretia had lingered to talk to Clarissa, her sister at her side, Miss Fordham having walked out with an aspiring partner to join the next set.

Lucretia rose immediately from Kitty's chair, her fan fluttering, but before she could speak, Amelia jumped up in expectation. "Is it my dance, now, Mr. Devereaux?" she asked.

He bowed. "If you are ready?"

They moved to the forming square as a short, round fellow came up to Lucasta and bowed deeply. He had curling tufts of butter-colored hair, shirt points high as his jug ears, and at least three fobs evident between the plate-like buttons of his coat.

Lucretia smothered a titter as her sister blushed and walked out with that quiz as if he were Prince Charming.

Lucretia turned back to Kitty. Wreathed in smiles and "dearest Catherines," she proceeded to interrogate Kitty about the conversation during her dance with Mr. Devereaux.

Clarissa, seeing the slight answers Kitty made—"We spoke of knowing no one in society, and my brother's sailing, a little"—attempted to turn the subject at least three times.

Lucretia gave up after receiving no exact answer to her satisfaction, but at least by then Amelia's dance was over. She turned her attention outward in expectation, but unaccountably Mr. Devereaux and Amelia chose to stroll the length of the room. While they were obtaining a glass of lemonade for Amelia, they chanced upon several young gentlemen, with the result that Amelia was led out again by one triumphant young man, with his friends looking on in disappointment.

Mr. Devereaux strolled on to greet acquaintances until he found Lady Buckley, the pretty wife of his friend Sir George. Lady Buckley regarded him with an expectant eye and a smile of expectation. So he offered his hand.

As soon as they were on the floor, she lowered her voice. "George says they are laying wagers about you at White's."

"About?"

"Which of the two will snare you at last, the second Golden Guinea, or the Decourcey beauty."

"I have known the first since she was a schoolroom miss bent on escaping her governess, and the second I scarcely know anything of beyond she possesses two brothers, and has never been to town before now. But I promised Lady Chadwick I would dance with the pair."

"Should I congratulate you or commiserate?" she asked archly.

"Neither. The one is a schoolgirl, the other a friend of my cousin Clarissa Harlowe, whom I believe you know."

Lady Buckley had made her own attempt on his heart before hers was given to Sir George. Tender feelings had long cooled to friendship, though she could not resist the mildest flirtation from time to time. And she loved being in the know.

"Amelia Harlowe is so young it is difficult to determine if she's a ninny, and I do not know Lady Catherine, but my mother does go on about how both her parents set the town by the ears during the days of Fox and Pitt and enormous hats. And that was before they eloped—in spite of her being destined for a duke, and he was betrothed to that horrid Philomena Bouldeston, who snubbed me unmercifully one year, when I...but I digress. Lady Bouldeston had it from her daughter, who seems to know Lady Catherine well, that she foisted herself on the Harlowes in order to gain a husband."

Mr. Devereaux had no intention of exhibiting the least interest in Lady Catherine. She was a beautiful girl, and she seemed possessed of a good heart and some wit, but he was very well aware that the least sign of interest would be carried from lip to ear over teacups by Lady Buckley who, though never intentionally cruel, was known to practice her own wit upon the foibles of their peers. And what she said so wittily tended to be repeated. "If you believe that Lady Catherine had an eye to inveigling James Harlowe into marriage," he said, "then you are more credulous than I thought possible."

She let out a peal of laughter. "People say that Lady Chadwick has more hair than wit, but I believe her obliviousness a defense against Lady Bouldeston's clack. I have never liked that woman, who was even less pleasant than her sister Philomena, back when we were first introduced into the *beau monde*."

Mr. Devereaux did not intend to demonstrate how annoying he found Lady Buckley's persistence, for it was clear that her inquiries were not idle. But then she had admitted as much in her comment about wagers. That, he could take as a warning.

She was watching him closely. The slight narrowing of his eyes, the pause that threatened to stretch into a silence, caused her to say winsomely, "They all come to me, you know. Wouldn't you rather I repeat what you want them to hear?"

He had to smile. "The truth of the matter is that my grandmother Norcaster asked me to single out Amelia, and I cannot do that without including Lady Catherine. My grandmother is fond of the Chadwicks for being good to my cousin, when so frequently a second marriage, a second family, goes the other way."

"Ah," she said, "that is quite true." If she was disappointed at so phlegmatic an answer, she hid it, and turned the talk to other matters until the dance ended.

He danced three more times — a girl just out of the schoolroom, a short-sighted elder sister five years his senior, who was often passed over — a widow of a friend, all chosen at random. Then a bow here, a smile there, and he regained his freedom.

Lucretia Bouldeston left Kitty and Clarissa the moment Mr. Devereaux approached Lady Buckley.

Amelia and Lucasta were both dancing, Lucasta for the second time with that same little fellow; Mrs. Latchmore was busy gossiping. Under the protection of that, Clarissa said to Kitty, "You made Cousin Philip laugh out loud. I cannot remember the last time he did that in company."

Kitty opened her fan, then surprised Clarissa by saying, low-voiced, "I have been informed that he despises women."

"Who in the world was spiteful enough to tell you that?" Clarissa asked.

Kitty colored to the hairline, and Clarissa gave her head a quick shake. "The fault is not yours. You only asked to be told the truth. The worst I can say of my cousin is that people have administered to his vanity all his life. He knows it is for all the wrong reasons. He has been sought for his position, his wealth, everything but his heart — I have sometimes blushed for my sex, the tricks ladies will get up to. Not just the young, but sometimes their mothers. And so he is wont to be very careful. The moreso as he is responsible for his sister's upbringing, their mother being... delicate in health."

Kitty took all this in, then said, "So in effect, fortune hunters are not confined to men."

"Not at all."

"And yet there is a difference," Kitty said slowly.

"I see none, if trickery and falsity are used to hide the motivation of greed."

"But I do perceive a difference, for it is said that it is the business of a young lady to find a husband, but a man can do quite well without a wife."

"I had not considered it from that perspective, but you are very right."

The current dance ended, there was a stir, and Kitty was approached by Mr. Canby. She agreed with a ready smile, but while she danced, she was thinking hard. Kitty was very sure that Clarissa had not agreed to Lord Wilburfolde's proposal out of love. It had to be duty, then. If so, would it not be acting the part of a true friend to find her a better? Did not Mr. Philip Devereaux say that he liked his cousin Clarissa best? Kitty had seen at first hand that his reputed attractions were, for once, not exaggerated. Surely Clarissa felt the same, if "every other female" did.

If. *If* it could be contrived, he would be a better match for Clarissa than Lord Wilburfolde, would he not? She examined this idea from every angle, and liked it. Except the question remained, how to detach Clarissa from the latter, and prompt the former?

That night, a last load of spirits was landed in Kent, and Innkeeper Dobbs himself obsequiously oversaw the transfer. The pay was prompt. The brothers pretended not to see the anger in his eyes, the calculation in his voice as he asked about their plans.

Ned happily spun out a farrago as the marquess counted over the coins with deliberate care.

Two hours later, the brothers celebrated with their hand-picked crew in a friendly tavern some miles away. Toasts were offered to success, to the brothers' help, to the foiling of Dobbs's wiles, and (because it was habit) the confusion of Boney.

Then the party broke up into several conversations, as liquor poured freely, and food was passed from hand to hand.

Through the party St. Tarval sat smiling, face flushed, eyes bright. Though he was not regarded by the older folk to be as handsome a devil as his late father, the local girls clearly found him attractive, especially at times like this, sitting back in his riding clothes, his silky black hair a little disheveled, his long hands loose on the table. But though he was ever polite, he never responded to those whose boldness was matched by their ambitions, and he kept his livelier brother from the sort of dalliances that had required Carlisle to find work for several country sprigs a few years his senior who bore more than a chance resemblance to their father.

For this, he was far more popular among the more respectable local merchants and farmers than his parent had been, though the rougher element still mourned the bad old days.

Ned joined him at his table, glass in hand. "I might have to find business in the countryside next month, just to enjoy the spectacle of Dobbs's men lying up in the brambles above Wrecker's Cove. D'you think he will have to refund his blood money to the excise men if they don't turn us up?"

"I am most certain he will," St. Tarval replied.

"So, what is next, now we're officially gone respectable? The roof repairs, of course. And, what, pay off Sir Henry?"

"I thought I might write to him in London, and propose sending him half, and in trade for the remainder, I would dig the canal we've talked of for ages to drain off Wardle Marsh. Bring it down past Home Farm, to the benefit of us both."

"And if he agrees? What of what's left, for it ought not to cost that much, if we put the men to it after harvest, before the frost sets in hard."

"Which is my plan. I've set aside a sum that I believe will meet the case. You and I may split what is left."

"Then I shall buy that hunter off Maitland, before John Cozen gets it. And you?"

"First, a tailor," the marquess said, and to his brother's round-eyed face, he added, "and with what's left, a visit to town to see how Kit is doing."

"By Jove," Ned exclaimed. "I'd almost think you planned it all along."

Eighteen

"I DO NOT WANT to go to another soiree," Amelia said, pouting. "Not if it is all talk, and worse, poetry."

"The least attractive quality in a girl is to be choosing among her invitations as if she were a fine lady," Mrs. Latchmore began in a scolding voice.

Lady Chadwick said calmly, "Lady Badgerwood would like to see you there, Amelia. Hetty told me that her mother-in-law invited Charles DuLac in especial to meet you, at the encouragement of his cousins. He is recently come down from Oxford, before he goes to York to take up his living."

"The girls have mentioned their Cousin Charles." Amelia wrinkled her nose. "He's the clergyman, isn't he? I remember him, I think. He was come down from Eton for the holidays, and he was horrid to us. He called us simpletons and lackwits for not knowing Latin."

Mrs. Latchmore made a scandalized noise. "I take leave to remind you that the DuLacs are as wealthy as the Athertons, if not very likely *more*."

Lady Chadwick's tranquil voice did not change tone. "In any case, you are not going across the street to get married, only to listen to a few poems, and meet this fellow now you are all grown up."

"But I don't like Charlie DuLac," Amelia muttered, when her

aunt was out of the room. "He has a head like a hayrick on fire, as well as a horrid tongue. This soiree is probably his idea. I trust they do not expect me to know a poem." She turned to Kitty. "You have better things to do than read horrid poetry, do you not, Lady Kitty?"

Kitty gave Amelia a sympathetic smile, but shook her head. "I must confess I like poetry very much, but you must remember I live in the country, and there is not much to do besides read." She opened her hands in a plea. "Besides, the poetry I like is funny, or full of love and adventure. The horrid stuff we had to copy out as children is not what I think of as poetry, even if it did scan and rhyme."

"Love?" Amelia stated, askance.

"Oh, some of the poems from before our grandmothers' day were quite scandalous. They had a different taste then, and they were not so nice. If you look in some of the older books in any library, you might be surprised," Kitty said.

Amelia did not want to scoff, or retort that she would never look into *any* book, especially an old one — not to Lady Kitty, who was so pretty, and always friendly, ready to accompany one on a walk even when one's own sisters were being selfish. So she abandoned the subject as Kitty went on to sift through the invitations at her plate.

"Look, two balls... and a masquerade! I have always wanted to go to a masquerade."

"A masquerade ball?" Amelia started up.

"You are invited, too," Clarissa said, smiling. "My grandmother is holding it. Your name is included in the family's invitation."

When Amelia's transports had subsided, and she and Eliza began considering wild ideas for costumes, Kitty reached the last of her letters, then sighed. "Nothing from my brother. I am almost certain it's been a week."

Ten days, Clarissa thought.

"...but there might be a problem with the post, or he might have too much to do than be forever writing letters. I will not repine. Do you go to return books, Clarissa, or are you busy?"

As the ladies got up from the breakfast table, Amelia gradually lost interest in the masquerade, which seemed impossibly far into the future. First she must get through another horrid soiree.

Her mood stayed sour through a long, rainy day. She did not want to go out just to get splashed, but no one of the least interest thought to call. Horrid people, selfish every one! She remained sufficiently disgruntled when evening arrived without an excuse to throw over the soiree. She put on her most hated gown, rather than waste a favorite, and scowled at the paving as the family walked across the street.

Melissa Atherton was there to do hostess duty for her mother, who could not rise from the Bath chair that she had been confined to ever since the carriage accident that had occasioned the present Lord Badgerwood's inheriting while still at Eton.

The arrival of the Chadwick party coincided with the delivery of another large party, causing a crowd to be ascending the stairs to the parlor. Into the confusion Mrs. Latchmore must insert herself, offering to move chairs about, to shift candles or push Lady Badgerwood to a better spot— in short, to get in everyone's way, while exclaiming that she lived to help.

Amelia, pressed against a wall by her aunt's unnecessary bustle, found herself next to a tall, striking young man. He had a high brow from which waving auburn hair swept back above a pair of gray eyes that were vaguely familiar.

His gaze met hers. The corners of his mouth deepened as she muttered, "Never was there anyone who could make such a piece of work out of a trifle. And all to be thanked."

"She wants to be of value. Is that not a human trait?" the fellow responded.

"I wish she *were* of value, instead of pestering us about it," Amelia grumbled, and when he did not agree, she said in haste, "Oh, I know she cares about us in her own way. My eldest sister always reminds us of that. But she goes about it all wrong."

"She never had children of her own, I collect?"

"No," Amelia acknowledged, then came a new thought, as people began to move at last. "So what you are saying is, she never was put in the way of it?"

"I would scarcely go that far." He laughed ruefully as he stretched out a hand, and invited her to take a chair. When she did, she was glad when he took the one next to hers. "There are many with a quiverful of children who ought not have been parents at all, strictly speaking. But we were speaking of your aunt. I don't suppose you heard Dr. Ross's homily on that head in church Sunday-last?" He peered into her face and said with amusement, "Of course you didn't. Half the congregation was asleep, and the other half looking at their watches, or one another's new hats. I found myself nodding, though his topic was compassion, a quality perhaps scarcer than we could wish."

"If only Dr. Ross were not so boring," Amelia said, astonished that so handsome a fellow would ever bring up church.

"It is the style," he admitted. "But I am afraid that our attempts to employ an elevated style sail above the heads of the congregation, for our human feet are firmly set on the ground. I am learning that a little levity—nothing inappropriate—catches the attention better than well-rehearsed and complicated periods."

Amelia studied him in amazement as a new idea occurred. *This* was Charlie DuLac! He was not the horrid redhead she remembered, skinny as a broom, his clothes always dusty. He was dressed like a man of fashion, and his eyelashes were the longest she had ever seen.

And he had recognized *her*.

She fought the tide of heat flooding her face, and ventured a remark. "I forgot you are a clergyman." Now he flushed, and looked away, and she said in haste, "I hope I did not misspeak. I meant it as a compliment."

"I know. And I thank you for it, Amelia—no, it's rightly Miss Harlowe, now. I think..." He hesitated.

"What is it?" she asked, aware of Lucasta Bouldeston on the other side of the room. But *for once* Lucasta was not poking into others' conversations.

"Will I be a bore if I say anything more about clergymen?" Charlie—no, Mr. DuLac—asked.

She knew she had been rude, though not by intent. She said very quickly, "Please enlighten me," and couldn't help but think that Aunt Sophia would not fault her for that platitude.

"Very well, then, thank you. We are taught to be above mere human concerns, but I wonder if that merely leads to others

176

forgetting that within the bands and the shovel hat is a man like any other. Dr. Ross has asked me to give the homily one Sunday before I go up to York. I promise that it will not be boring, if I can contrive it."

"I'm sure it won't be," Amelia said, thinking, How can a man have eyelashes *that long?*

A tinkle of a silver bell, and Melissa Atherton stood up. "I believe everyone is here? Shall we proceed in a circle, then?"

In Mount Street the next morning, the Bouldeston ladies met alone at breakfast. This was too regular an occurrence to cause remark. The indolent Sir Henry was rarely seen at this hour, as he often was just returned from Watier's not long before his wife and daughters rose. But even when he had not gone to his clubs, he had definite opinions about peace and quiet.

Consequently the ladies felt his presence as a constraint, and in his absence, enjoyed the freedom to give vent to their thoughts.

Lady Bouldeston's entire business was not only to get her daughters wed, but to make certain that the marriages were better than those her sister might arrange for her girls. All this on an extremely stingy budget. She had definite ideas about how Lucretia and Lucasta ought to attain this laudable goal, but as her elder daughter in particular had inherited her combative nature, the instructive discourses she lay awake planning at night were too frequently met with argument and complaint.

An unlooked-for gain had occurred with Lucasta's having apparently attracted an eligible suitor, Mr. Bartholomew Aston, the second son of a wealthy baron. Mr. Aston regarded himself as a poet and a patron of the arts, in particular music. Introduced at Almack's, Lucasta and Mr. Aston had formed an interest in discussing German airs.

Mr. Aston was distantly related to Lady Badgerwood. Subsequently it was through his offices that Lucasta (and her mother) had been invited to the soiree the previous evening, an event that Lucretia had regarded herself well out of.

It being the first time Lucasta had ever been invited without her sister, she relished furnishing a detailed description as she buttered her third muffin.

Lucretia tolerated this for exactly as long as it took to finish her own muffin, then said, "Must you bore on forever, Lucasta? I can scarcely conceive anything duller than a soiree, unless it is hearing about one."

Lucasta eyed her sister, then shrugged. "Well, I had hoped there would be music, for Mr. Aston thought there might. But Lady Badgerwood got them onto poems, and required everyone to recite some lines. Mama did quite well. I did not know you had any such things by heart, Mama."

Lady Bouldeston's thin brows lifted ironically. "I do not," she drawled. "As girls, my sister and I were required to know one piece, precisely against these occasions, and our hands were slapped with a ruler if we faltered. I have never forgotten those wretched lines from Milton."

"You never did that to us," Lucretia was surprised into observing, for she'd meant to pretend her sister was not speaking. She frequently felt her sister was getting above herself, and consequently administered well-deserved snubs.

"Because I believe my daughters can get husbands just as well without muddling their heads with a lot of dull poetry."

"Of course you had to excuse yourself," Lucretia declared, eyeing her sister.

Lucasta shrugged. "I did, but I was not the only one. Amelia Harlowe mumbled a line or two out of Cowper, helped along by Miss Harlowe, and she sounded stupider than a block. Even Lady Chadwick knew a few lines of Pope, I believe she said it was."

Lucretia glanced sharply up. "Amelia Harlowe? I suppose of course Catherine Decourcey was there?"

Lucasta spread jam over her muffin. "Of course. And Miss Harlowe, and coming late was that horrid prose-wind she's betrothed to. He bored on forever with something or other —"

"Milton," her mother interpolated, sipping chocolate.

Lucretia had no interest in either Milton or Lord Wilburfolde. "Catherine certainly is shooting up in the world on the Harlowes' coattails."

"Yes," Lucasta said, knowing how much her sister would hate

hearing it. "I understand she is invited everywhere."

"I suppose she fascinated them all with something too marvelous?"

Lady Bouldeston regarded her daughter, and chose to administer her own snub. "She delivered Jonathan Swift's 'An Echo' to general approbation." And she turned languidly to the correspondence on the silver salver at her plate.

The conversation faltered there, each busy with her own thoughts. Lady Bouldeston frowned suddenly over a piece of mail, and without a word to her daughters rose and left the room.

Lucretia eyed her sister, who was pushing a muffin around on her plate, smiling dreamily, and said, "You look like a sapskull, mooning like that. After all you've prosed and prated you will look all no-how if your *Mister* Aston takes up spouting bad poetry to some other miss."

Lucasta's unheated "You don't know anything about him" was so unlike her usual tearful or shrill self that Lucretia wondered if there was some danger that her younger sister—just turned eighteen—would marry before she did. Even if to a silly fellow like Aston.

"Who else was there?" Lucretia went on.

"All people of the first rank, for you know that Lord Badgerwood is related to one earl, and distantly to two dukes—"

Lucretia stirred milk into her teacup. "Was Mr. Devereaux there?" On her sister's nod, "Did he show any interest in the Harlowe party? Miss Fordham tells me that it is whispered all over town that he has a weakness for Amelia Harlowe."

Lucasta snorted. "If he does, he has an odd way of showing it. He did not sit near them, and scarcely exchanged two words with any of them outside of Miss Harlowe and the prose-wind."

"He did not speak to... anyone else of the party?"

"Just good-evening to the others, and he only spoke to Catherine the once, after his turn, when he faltered on the last line of his poem, and she finished it for him."

"I trust he gave her a set-down for thrusting herself forward."

"Not at all. She whispered it, meaning to jog his memory, I think. He only looked surprised, then leaned forward, and uttered the first line of another poem in this toplofty voice, by some fellow

Mama said was quite horrid in his day. Rochester? Anyway, she capped his line, and they traded off, these old-fashioned words in this odiously polite tone, which set everyone to laughing. That ended the poetry, as it happens."

"I suppose it was to be expected that she would throw herself in his way. I wonder if he knows she hasn't two pennies to bless herself with."

Lucasta said with evident enjoyment, "He sought her out, when the tea came, but only to thank her for the line, whereupon he sat down next to Miss Atherton with his tea. And when Lord Wilburfolde insisted that Miss Harlowe ought to leave, as it was past midnight, and not healthy for anybody, Mr. Devereaux asked Lady Chadwick if he could call today, for he had a piece of business to execute, and what time might be convenient, well, Catherine was not even listening."

"Oh," Lucretia affected carelessness. "What time does Lady Chadwick consider convenient? I confess myself interested in what great ladies consider fashionable times for calls."

Lucasta grinned knowingly. "Not before noon."

Their mother returned, and Lucasta said quickly, "Mama, may I go out walking with Mr. Aston this morning? *Without* Poggon?"

"No," Lady Bouldeston said. "You must take Poggon, but I will drop a hint in her ear that she may lag behind. I would like it better if there were no older brother, but the family is respectable. See that you do nothing to drive him away."

"Then I may go?"

"Lucasta, do not bounce so. You know my nerves are unequal to it in the morning."

"Yes, Lucasta, pray *try* for a little self-control," Lucretia added.

Lucasta rounded on her, ready with a retort, but then she shrugged, and walked out.

"At least she won't be listening at doors if she's out walking with that fop," Lucretia stated.

Lady Bouldeston said, "I really did not think to see your sister married before you, Lucretia."

Lucretia tossed her curls. "If I were to settle for the likes of a Mister Aston, I could have been married these four years. I am going out to make some necessary purchases. I will have to put new trim to my second-best bonnet, as Papa keeps us on such a horrid budget. I will be laughed at everywhere, wearing the same two bonnets. But I will need something to buy trim with."

"Do you not have trim upstairs? I know you do. I laid out far too much when you were in Widegate Street last Wednesday week. Lucretia, you had better understand that we are not made of money. Yes, St. Tarval did make another trifling payment, which will hold us for a time—if your father does not gamble it all away—but I discovered only last night that he and St. Tarval are agreed to sink the remainder of the debt. Something or other about canals, and borders, and other disagreeable articles too fatiguing to enumerate. My point is, we are going to be more straitened than usual as a result."

"How *selfish* men are," Lucretia declared with feeling.

Lady Bouldeston did not disagree. "You will find a few coins in my reticule. You may take half only, mind. I will count it when I come upstairs."

Lucretia ran upstairs and put on her walking dress, spencer, and bonnet. She fetched the money, walked outside and down the street, but instead of turning toward the stores, she hailed a hackney, feeling greatly daring. "Brook Street," she said.

Nineteen

ON FINDING HERSELF ALONE after breakfast, Kitty added to her latest letter to her brother. That did not take long. Then she eyed the stack of papers on her desk.

There was no profit in avoiding Andromeda. This glorious London visit would not last forever. Too soon Kitty would be back at Tarval Hall, surrounded by all the familiar problems. Since she had decided against trying for a wealthy husband, then she must square herself to the task of readying her book for publication. It was selfish to waste all her time on her own pleasures, when she had been given the opportunity she had never expected: to learn about fashionable London.

The problem was, there were so *very* many errors in what she had written so far. She had done her best to discover facts about London, but all she had had to rely on were her grandmother's memories, and Lucretia's anecdotes. Grandmother's fashionable recollections were hideously out of date, but Lucretia's anecdotes were hideously distorted in other ways. For example, Kitty had discovered her first day in town that Mount Street was not the very center of London. Nor were Almack's Wednesday balls as glorious as Lucretia had claimed. Sumptuous parties were reserved for select sets, and even there, Lucretia had exaggerated in odd ways, making Kitty suspect that Lucretia was invited to few of those.

She glared at the manuscript. It was going to have to be entirely rewritten.

She turned over a page or two, sighed, and decided that she could as well begin on a rainy day. Right now she ought to be a good guest and walk down to the parlor. If the girls were there, she could talk to them, which amused her mightily, and also had the advantage of affording Lady Chadwick some peace. Oh, to have had sisters like Eliza and Tildy, as well as Amelia and Clarissa!

As she started down the stairs, she heard the knocker far below. From the voices echoing up the stairwell, she determined that the caller was a gentleman, and a heartbeat later she thought she recognized that voice: Mr. Devereaux. A hot blush suffused her.

She dared a peek over the banister as Mr. Devereaux handed Pobrick his hat. She backed away in haste lest the gentleman lift his eyes and catch her spying. The dearth of female chatter from the parlor meant that Lady Chadwick was probably alone.

Kitty recalled herself to her plan. It was a good plan. She knew that Clarissa would be much happier with someone like her cousin than with Lord Wilburfolde, well-meaning as he might be.

She took a cautious step forward for a quick look as the gentleman was let into the parlor. His wavy dark hair and the tops of his broad shoulders re-animated the vexing blush. Even his ears were attractive.

Katie patted her cheeks, willing them to cool. She knew what this was. Perhaps, one day, she could look back and enjoy the experience, but right now she wished she did not have such common taste that she was attracted to the gentleman who seemed to cause a similar response in every other young lady.

Not that he was common. That was the problem. She had since her arrival become acquainted with many men, from young to old, tall to short, fair to dark. Some had beautiful eyes. Others a flashing smile. Most of them dressed very well, and were well spoken. But no one was quite like him.

She drew in a slow breath. She could school herself. It was only an attraction. Though she might give Andromeda an eternal passion that darted simultaneously into the breast of each of her deserving lovers at first glance, that was the hyperbole of a story. One expected to read such. The fun of the novel came in how many adventures contrived to keep the two apart before the reward of wealth and marriage on the last page.

Kitty had seen attraction come and go. She looked back in memory to her sixteenth year, when she entered into the garden to fetch roses for the table and discovered Lucretia weeping and clutching Carlisle's jacket. As Kitty stared in astonishment, his arms had circled Lucretia, and they kissed.

Kitty had instantly run away, of course, but Lucretia soon found her out and described the kiss in detail. She had even used that very same language that Kitty had borrowed for Andromeda: Cupid's bow darting an arrow into their hearts at the same moment, inspiring eternal love — two souls eternally entwined — tender passion.

Kitty had believed it. And she'd done her best to regard Lucretia as a sister after Carlisle confessed his part of that *rencontre*. But as time passed, she had seen less ardency and more question in Carlisle, and as for Lucretia, Kitty sometimes wondered if Cupid's darts had shot right through her and out into the world.

Kitty had learned to put no especial trust in Cupid or his darts, especially when she herself had had occasion to feel that delicious but untrustworthy warmth. First, John-coachman's son Bob, when he tossed Kitty up on her first pony. Then the new vicar's younger brother when he visited from Oxford. For two days, Kitty had thought herself singled out, until Lucasta had spied him flirting (and using the same exact phrases) with the squire's eldest daughter at the glove-maker's shop. Lucretia, perhaps stung that he had taken her at her word when she had said her heart was given, spread it all over the village that he was a desperate flirt.

Kitty had to smile when she remembered those two very intense days at the ripe old age of seventeen, when she had gone from eternal love to her heart being buried forever.

So here she was. She could acknowledge this attraction to Mr. Devereaux, but she must simply regard it as an ephemeral thing, as fragile as the blooms Lady Chadwick put in vases each day. By next week they would be withered.

Kitty must put her rational mind to work, and find a way for Clarissa to find a better chance at happiness with her cousin, because there was little chance of that happening with Lord Wilburfolde. And Kitty owed Clarissa her best effort for her generous invitation to London.

She descended the rest of the stairs, and was able to enter the parlor with a polite composure.

Mr. Devereaux rose to greet her, aware of the quickening of his interest—the sharp thorn of ambivalence. He should not have come—he had had no intention of calling at this house while Lady Catherine still visited. Until he had seen the laughter in her eyes, and heard the enjoyment in her voice as she capped his lines, and then ripped out that provocative poem by Rochester in that mock-missish manner, he fully intended to convey today's message to Lady Chadwick on his way out as the soiree ended.

Yet here he was, to see her in the sober light of day.

Lady Chadwick was speaking. "...and as I was saying, Chadwick is still abed, and the girls walked out with their aunt while the weather is fine. And did not Lord Wilburfolde take Clarissa out for a ride, dear Lady Kitty?"

"It was a planned excursion," Katie said conscientiously, as she gave the gentleman a curtsey in greeting. "He wished to give her a tour of the Houses of Parliament."

Kitty spied a faint pucker between Mr. Devereaux's dark brows. He was not angry, she felt certain. She had seen a like expression in Carlisle from time to time, when he was troubled by some question he could not answer. Mr. Devereaux said, "You did not accompany them, Lady Catherine?"

"I was not invited. I believe his lordship wished to spend the morning alone with his betrothed."

"At the Houses of Parliament?" Lady Chadwick asked blankly.

At that moment, Pobrick appeared at the door again. "Miss Bouldeston."

And here was Lucretia, dressed in glossy, frilly pink from top to toe. She took three tiny steps into the parlor then halted, her mouth rounded. She raised a forefinger to her bottom lip in a way that looked rehearsed as she exclaimed, "Oh! I did not know—" And in a meaning tone, her eyes blinking rapidly, "Do I intrude?"

Lady Chadwick greeted her from her corner chair. "Good morning, Miss Bouldeston. I trust Lady Bouldeston is well?"

"Oh, I did not see you there, Lady Chadwick! Forgive me. Very well, thank you," Lucretia lisped, choosing the chair nearest Mr. Devereaux as she turned to Kitty. "I happened to be walking in the area, and as the day is so fine, I bethought me of my sweetest Catherine, and stopped in hopes you might join me for an airing. But if you are otherwise engaged..."

"Not at all, Lucretia," Kitty hastened to assure her. "I just this moment walked into the parlor myself."

Mr. Devereaux then said, "Lady Chadwick, you behold in me my sister's envoy. If it would be acceptable for her to arrive for her proposed visit on the twelfth, instead of the thirteenth as settled, then I shall be able to bring her myself. I am required to be in the country on business the day previous."

Lady Chadwick waved a languid hand. "Pray bring dear little Bess whenever it is convenient. Eliza will be in transports."

Devereaux rose to shake her hand and take his departure. "Then I will go immediately and write to allay her anxiety."

Lucretia spoke up. "Oh, pray, Mr. Devereaux, is dear Miss Bess coming to London?" When the gentleman bowed assent, she went on with fervent enthusiasm, "I hope and pray we shall have the felicity of seeing her. Such a lovely, sweet girl, and so accomplished for her age. Pray, when does she arrive in Grosvenor Street? My sister Lucasta will be *aux anges* to see her again. Did you know they are acquainted?"

"My sister does not come to Grosvenor Street, but directly here," he said as he reached the door. "I fear I cannot stay. May I wish you ladies a good morning?"

"If you are walking, Mr. Devereaux, may we accompany you? As you just heard, dearest Catherine and I are to take the air."

"Unfortunately, I am driving today, Miss Bouldeston," he replied.

"Oh, I did not realize that was your curricle being walked up and down out front, though I suppose I ought to have recognized that handsome pair of matched bays that my father has pointed out at least fifty times."

Mr. Devereaux thanked her, bowed again, and departed.

Kitty could not help but stare at Lucretia. Maybe these were her company manners while in London, but the contrast between her trilling voice now and the sharp tones she often used to her sister nearly made her laugh. She got to the door, saying quickly, "Pray excuse me, Lucretia. I will make ready as swiftly as I can."

She gave vent to her laugh as she ran upstairs to change into a walking dress, wishing it would not be indelicate to share the absurdity with anyone else.

Lucretia was thus left alone with Lady Chadwick. That lady rose and said, "If I may be permitted to step out a moment, I will see if the girls are returned."

Lucretia was just as happy to pick up a number of the latest fashionable magazines, which lay on one of the smart little tables.

Within a minute or two, there was a commotion outside the door, Clarissa Harlowe's voice coming clearly, "...for a few minutes, until I rid myself of this headache."

The door then opened, and Lucretia stared in surprise at the unfamiliar gentleman who stepped in. He was dressed soberly and conservatively, his hair cut closer to his scalp than was fashionable, which gave his head rather the shape of a potato. His complexion was florid, his neck above his neckcloth damp, but his features were pleasing enough.

Lucretia, accurately pricing his clothing, exerted herself to politeness as she rose to her feet and made her curtsy. "Oh, sir," she said breathlessly, admiring the way she managed to sound aflutter. "Pray forgive me. It is so very awkward, finding myself here with a stranger."

He bowed. "It is for me to beg forgiveness," he said. "And yet I do not know how it comes about. I might have thought—but there, I do not wish to appear to be casting aspersions upon our good hostess. She must assume we are known to one another. My name is Wilburfolde, and you might have seen the interesting information inserted to the morning papers with respect to the..." He paused, looking a little confused, then went on in a determined voice, "...to the expected Hymeneal celebration between Miss Harlowe and myself."

"Congratulations," Lucretia exclaimed, shaking his hand. "My mother, Lady Bouldeston, would have accompanied me, but she suffers from delicate health." Lucretia had always thought her mother's title sounded well, for anyone might take her as a countess, if not higher. "I am ever so delighted for our good friend Miss Harlowe. I wish you very happy, and I apologize for this uncomfortable situation. I am laughed at everywhere for being so shy and modest that people forget I am in the room."

Lord Wilburfolde had no idea how to answer that, and so he bowed again.

"Pray be seated," Lucretia said winsomely. "If I may for this moment appropriate to myself the duties of hostess. Did I hear dear Miss Harlowe without?"

"Yes," he responded. "We are just returned from a tour of the Houses of Parliament."

"Oh, how very interesting," Lucretia exclaimed.

"So it might have been, but for Miss Harlowe being taken with a sudden headache. We had to return after only an hour and eighteen minutes." He consulted his pocket watch, then tucked it back into his waistcoat. "I believe it is these late nights that are to blame," he said. "I am concerned, I must confess, Miss Bouldeston. Is it Miss Bouldeston?"

Perforce a nod, though she had longed all her life for the empyrean heights of Lady Lucretia.

Lord Wilburfolde settled into his chair. "I do not remember her ever racketing about town so much in the past, when I visited the metropolis. But she is exerting herself beyond her strength. It must be her effort to entertain her visitor."

"Catherine?" Lucretia exclaimed, surprised.

"You are acquainted with the lady?" Lord Wilburfolde asked.

"Oh yes indeed. We are neighbors, that is, our estates share a common border in the country."

"Please forgive me," he said. "I do not intend any slight upon the lady in question, it is merely that I fear Miss Harlowe overtaxes herself."

Lucretia made a little business of smoothing her skirt over her knees, making certain that her flounces revealed no more than an inch of the toes of her little slippers. She had been meditating a comment about the prospective walk that she charitably had suggested for Catherine's enjoyment, for she did not like to miss an opportunity to imply close acquaintance with the sister of a marquess. It sounded well in company, and she could also laugh over the effort it would make for her little feet to keep up with her friend's great strides, for it was always important to draw a gentleman's attention away from the purely happenstance arrangement of features that was so tritely termed "beauty."

Men were such simple creatures! As well, for she knew they also valued the contrast of frailty and daintiness to their great selves. They only needed reminding of it.

But here was a new, more interesting prospect. Did this Lord Wilburfolde disapprove of Catherine's visit? Lucretia did not believe for one moment that Mr. Devereaux took the least interest in Catherine Decourcey, when he had half London at his feet. But it did not suit Lucretia at all to see Catherine invited everywhere instead of seeking Lucretia's advice and patronage. The sooner Catherine went home to St. Tarval, the sooner everything would go comfortably back to the way it ought to be.

"I am very, very sorry if Catherine's visit has occasioned distress for Miss Harlowe. I know she does not *intend* so." Lucretia kept her voice soft and sweet, and cast down her eyes in pretty bashfulness, hoping the gentleman would say more.

"It is just that I find them engaged every evening until far later than the rational being ought to be up, and too many days have been given over to frivolous concerns, such as shopping, when Miss Harlowe ought to be resting and husbanding her resources. Then, my mother and I had prepared, with no thought to the hours spent in doing so, a list of improving activities to make best use of our time in the metropolis. To this date, however, we have barely covered five of them, and Miss Harlowe, who I know has little liking for London, seems determined to remain here at the cost of her health."

Lucretia did not believe for a moment that Miss Harlowe was making herself sick while enjoying the Season, but here was a chance to curtail Catherine's unconscionably long visit. It would be foolish, even wasteful, to ignore what so clearly would be the best for everyone.

"Lady Catherine quite understandably wishes to make a wealthy marriage," Lucretia whispered. "It is not doing my duty by my sex if I were to cast aspersions on so proper an ambition. However, it seems a shame that someone as young as Miss Harlowe is called upon to serve in such a capacity. She is so kind and generous to overtax herself in this way, but it makes me hope that she will be able to rest once the visit of our mutual friend comes to a close."

"I find we are in complete agreement," Lord Wilburfolde said, eyeing the young lady complacently. This Miss Bouldeston was sympathetic as well as modest.

They were both thus very pleased with themselves, and their company, when Kitty rejoined them in her walking dress, bonnet and gloves in hand.

"There you are, Catherine," Lucretia greeted her in her sweetest tones. "I must say, you look prettier every time I see you. Good day, Lord Wilburfolde. I am delighted that we have met."

"As am I," he said, bowing the ladies out of the room.

Once they reached the street, Lucretia decided to capitalize on the success of the day. "I intended to simply enjoy the walk, but I would be failing my duty as a friend, not to mention perhaps one day a *closer* connection, if I did not venture to give you a little hint, Catherine," she said.

"Have I done something wrong?" Kitty asked, cold pouring through her nerves. This was too much like Tunbridge Wells all over again. "Miss Harlowe promised to let me know if I transgress against the rules of society."

"Miss Harlowe is very kind. One might say that she is kind almost to a fault, and of course the betrothed lady can be forgiven for having other cares to think about besides a guest who is not conversant, or as the French say, *au fait* with society. You must remember that I have been coming to London for four years, giving me experience with the niceties of etiquette. You might not remember why I am quite known everywhere for dressing in rose—"

Kitty suppressed an inward sigh, having heard this anecdote repeatedly.

"—but my very first year in London, when I was introduced to Mr. Brummel, he made a little observance about how someone as young and dainty as I should not wear white, as she might vanish altogether, and when he suggested a brighter shade, such as rose..."

Without any context, Kitty had accepted the anecdote at face value. Now, having heard Mr. Brummel's *mots* repeated—and overhearing from the distance of the next line over on Almack's ballroom floor the gentleman's tone of irony—she wondered if Lucretia had taken for admiration what had been intended as satirical.

Lucretia was enjoying this moment exceedingly—*this* was the treat that she had intended to give Catherine by inviting her before the season began. *Ton* was the idiom used by the *haut monde*. Now to give Catherine a reason to call her visit short.

"For example, someone not acquainted with you, and not as well-intentioned, might be forgiven for assuming when you so precipitously introduced yourself into a private conversation between Lady Chadwick and Mr. Devereaux, that you were attempting to introduce yourself to the gentleman's notice. You will forgive me for hinting that it does not show good *ton. Nothing* could be so fatal to your chances of attaching someone eligible than to gain a reputation for being forward."

Kitty looked at the ground to hide her hot face. So it *had* looked bad, then. No wonder Mr. Devereaux had taken himself off in such haste. "I must thank you for the hint, Lucretia," she said in a suffocated voice.

Lucretia reached out to touch Kitty's wrist with two fingers in a nicely judged gesture of sympathy. "There now. I *dreaded* saying anything, for you must know that anything unpleasant is foreign to my nature. We shall say no more about it. Pray, how is your dear brother? You must miss him quite as dreadfully as I do. When is he expecting to see you home? I know how happy that will make him. You will be able to tell him about Lady Taviscott's ball tonight, for of course you must be invited. Everyone of any importance will be there, and I know the Chadwicks are of the first consideration, which requires people to invite you as well..."

Clarissa lay upon her bed, pressing her fingertips over her

eyes, which were resolutely closed.

If only she could find the words to circumvent Lord Wilburfolde's well-meant attempts to guide her life into the direction laid out by his mother! He seemed incapable of understanding that Clarissa was not of a sickly nature, and she could never tell him that he was the cause of her headaches. Or, to be strictly honest, he contributed to the cause.

She knew her own shortcomings were to blame. If only he did not bring out the worst in her nature! Every mention of that wretched letter of his mother's strengthened her determination not to answer it, for she knew what her reward would be: more of the same. But she did not have the courage to tell him that. Again, a shortcoming.

She finally fell asleep, and woke much refreshed, to the news that Lord Wilburfolde had finally gone. Amelia bounced in to ask what she was wearing to Lady Taviscott's ball — she did not want to make them the jest of the room by appearing in exactly the same color.

Clarissa bethought herself that no one would notice one gown from another, but Amelia was that age when dress is all-conquering. "Which of your gowns did you favor?"

"The India muslin with the cameos at each shoulder," Amelia replied promptly. "And Lady Kitty is going to wear the white with the gold underskirt, which Mama and I are agreed goes capitally with her black hair."

"Then I will wear my sea-green gauze," Clarissa said. "Nothing could be simpler."

Her mood improved with the recollection that her betrothed had accepted an invitation from a cousin to hear a lecture on temperance. With a mild expectation of enjoyment, she climbed into the coach with the others.

Lady Taviscott had apparently invited the entire town. Her enormous ballroom was filled with people when the Chadwick party arrived.

Clarissa was surprised to see her cousin arriving just ahead of them. She did not remember seeing Cousin Philip at so many balls. Once she'd made her curtsey to their hostess, Clarissa started in his direction to greet him, but halted when she observed Miss

Bouldeston crossing the room to intercept him, Sophia Fordham at her elbow. The two determinedly engaged the gentleman in conversation, preventing his moving into the ballroom. Clarissa stayed with her family as they slowly navigated the press of new arrivals proceeding with excruciating slowness through the second door.

Lord Chadwick promptly departed for the card room, and James was lost in the crowd; Lady Chadwick sighed, and began to look about her for somewhere to sit, but then Cousin Philip stepped up to make his bow to Lady Chadwick and offer to conduct her to a chair. She agreed with obvious thanks, and he turned to pay his respects to the rest of the family, as Amelia gazed around in search of someone she knew.

Clarissa was surprised to see Kitty behaving with stiff rectitude, but then her cousin, Amelia, Kitty, and everything else including her wits flew out of her head when she looked across the ballroom at the new arrival framed in the doorway.

Tall, elegantly attired from his black hair to his new dancing shoes, was Carlisle Decourcey, the Marquess of St. Tarval.

Twenty

"DID YOU LIKE MY surprise?" James turned to his family to perform the introductions.

Clarissa was too stunned to speak. The world had begun to sparkle oddly.

A quiet voice came through it all, "Are you quite well, Miss Harlowe?"

It was *he*—Kitty's brother. Clarissa couldn't seem to find her knees to curtsey, or the words to utter a polite greeting. But he didn't seem to expect an answer as he guided her to the nearest chair.

She roused herself enough to say, "I will be well, a moment only. It is just the heat in here."

He did not pester her with questions, each prefaced by a *my mother says*. She knew it was unjust—that Lord Wilburfolde meant the best—yet the contrast could not have been more devastating, and her eyes stung.

But no one was watching, or bothering her. The gentleman had turned obligingly away, permitting her to recover her poise.

Meanwhile, Kitty was exclaiming happily, "Ned! You, too? What a wonderful surprise! How does this come about?"

"It was all my doing," James said modestly, and at a cough, he said hastily, "Well, actually, Arden, here, played a small hand in the affair." He tipped his chin as Lord Arden edged past a stout gentleman, who was attempting to speak across James to the people in the adjacent chairs.

James said jokingly, "I should make you all known to one another, if you promise not to challenge one another to a duel, at least not here, for I promised Lady Taviscott that there would be no pistols drawn on her ballroom floor."

"I will introduce myself, rattle." Lord Arden bowed, and said to Kitty, "A few days ago, we chanced to be in Grosvenor Street when your brothers were just going into your family's house. We knew it had been shut up these several years, so you can imagine our curiosity when a pair in overcoats shouldered the door open."

"I laid a wager it was thieves," James admitted. "But how were we to know?"

"So we walked over and introduced ourselves," Lord Arden went on.

St. Tarval turned to Kitty. "Though Arden will probably get a peal rung over him by the rest of the family, he told us how to go about getting the house opened up again."

"We even unearthed the old porter," James added. "And he brought his wife to turn the place out. Lord, the dust! Then I remembered this party, and thought it might be a capital joke to bring you here as a surprise. *There* you get no credit, Arden, for I braved the lioness's den myself in order to procure them an invitation." He finished in triumph.

Edward said, "Arden was the one who put us in the way of tailors and so forth. So here you have us."

"I am so happy!" Kitty exclaimed, hands pressed together, her face glowing. Then her brow puckered. "But I suppose I must leave Clarissa, then?"

The marquess said, "To tell you the truth, we've only opened a part of the house. It's a great barrack, the furnishings still in Holland covers. I don't know how long Ned and I will stay. If Miss Harlowe does not object, you may remain with her, for I don't know where I'd get hold of sufficient staff."

"Oh, then I have nothing else to wish for," Kitty exclaimed.

So great a party could not but be noticed by others in the room.

"Who is that newly arrived gentleman?" Miss Fordham inquired of Lucretia Bouldeston, who was frowning at her sister fawning all over that foolish dandy she had taken up with. Really, Lucasta would make herself a laughingstock if Mama did not intervene.

Miss Fordham recalled her attention by saying insistently, "I have never met him, and yet he seems familiar. But I would remember, surely. He certainly has an air."

Lucretia looked up impatiently, and stared, aghast.

Carlisle? This was worse than ever!

"He is—that is the marquess of St. Tarval," Lucretia stated, striving for an off-hand manner, which did not fool Miss Fordham at all.

Sophia Fordham, at five-and-twenty, prided herself on her taste and discernment. The gentleman lucky enough to win her hand and her fortune had not yet materialized, though she had given her choices plenty enough encouragement. Mr. Devereaux, heading this select list, also headed Miss Bouldeston's list, along with the lists of far too many single women in London. But Miss Bouldeston also displayed (in spite of her frequent claims to modesty and shyness) a taste for gossip. In short doses, she could be amusing, and there were few enough people with whom Miss Fordham could enjoy tearing apart every character of note.

Here was unexpected entertainment. Could this fine-looking man be the mysterious nobleman to whom Lucretia was all-but-engaged? Miss Fordham had come to regard this unnamed mystery man a fabrication.

She linked her arm through Lucretia's. "Since you appear to know the gentleman, pray introduce us."

Lucretia felt herself borne forward, her thoughts caught in a species of nightmare.

Kitty was just saying, "Ned, fie! And here I thought you would offer me a dance," as all the gentlemen laughed at the undisguised horror in the young viscount's face.

"Card room's this way," James said briskly, spotting the approach of Lucretia Bouldeston.

Ned followed him, delivering a parting shot over his shoulder, "All I can say is, if you cannot find yourself someone to caper with in this room, Kit, then... what a set of cork-brains in this town."

He sketched a hasty bow to Lucretia, muttered something that could be taken as a greeting, and hastened after James.

Lucretia never saw him. "Carlisle," she said in her sweetest tones. "Oh!" The fingertip rose to her lips as she batted her eyes rapidly in the expression her mirror had told her was bashful modesty. "Pray, forgive me. Miss Fordham, may I introduce you to the Marquess of St. Tarval? So you are come to Town, after *all* my begging. It must take the words of a sister to get you here, but Catherine failed to tell me you were expected."

"Kitty did not know, so you must excuse her." The marquess bowed, his smile having lessened to politeness.

Lucretia then chattered on, asking after everyone at St. Tarval, without listening to a word he spoke, as she waited desperately for him to remember his duty and ask her to dance.

St. Tarval could tell by the anger in Lucretia's eyes and the shrill note to her voice that she was waiting for something, probably to ring a peal over him.

He was going to have to talk to her, but he had no intention of holding this conversation in the middle of a room full of strangers, so he stood there politely, determined to wait her out.

Watching all this from the other side of the ballroom was Mr. Devereaux. He had witnessed the entire scene from the moment Lady Catherine had gazed across the ballroom with such genuine, unshadowed joy. Once again her beautiful face had glowed into something beyond mere beauty.

So here was the impecunious brother. Mr. Devereaux was aware of a sensation of rue, not unlike irony, that this fellow no older than he could inspire such a reaction in his sister. Mr. Devereaux would be making a wearisome journey all too soon on Bess's behalf, full knowing that his reward at the end of his road would be a scowl and a string of demands.

A friend appeared at his shoulder, and he turned away before the object of his attention could be descried.

The next morning, Clarissa gazed down in a bemused way at a card on heavy linen paper.

Seeing her expression, Lady Chadwick glanced at the envelope, and though she could not quite make out the broken seal, she recognized a part of the crest. "Good heavens," she murmured. "Is that from her grace?"

Clarissa smiled. "Yes. Grandmother writes to inform me that Kitty and I would be delighted to pay her a call this morning."

James gave a crack of laughter, and Lord Chadwick said, "Better you than me, my girl. Do give her our best, and all that." He flung down his napkin and made his escape as though the dowager duchess loomed outside the breakfast room.

Clarissa laughed, and turned her attention to Kitty's wide gaze of consternation. "You will like her. I promise."

Kitty changed her gown three times before settling on the newest of her morning dresses. It was with nervous apprehension that she climbed into the coach for the short drive to Cavendish Square—the girls did not dare walk as it looked like rain, and even if the weather held off, neither wished to arrive with soot on her gloves, or smudges on her shoes.

Kitty stared at the enormous house. "She lives alone here?"

"Yes, and very nip-farthing she considers it," Clarissa said with a quiet laugh. "Compared to the family place in Grosvenor Square, which she relinquished to my eldest uncle on his marriage."

The door was opened by a footman in old-fashioned livery, who greeted them with stately obsequiousness. Another footman conducted them up a wide, shallow marble staircase, and down an imposing hall with rococo gilding in festoons high on the cream-colored walls and around painted panels that depicted mythological creatures disporting in bright pastel colors.

Kitty recognized the style as belonging to the last century, but unlike Tarval Hall, this place seemed as if it had been painted and furnished a week ago.

They were brought to a double door and bowed into a saloon that glittered with gilding, heavy silver and porcelain ornaments, and lovely, fragile French chairs with embroidered seats. They crossed a carpet that rendered their steps completely soundless, and approached a tiny old lady who sat in state in a big carved chair piled around with cushions.

Kitty curtseyed low as she was introduced to the Duchess of

Norcaster, and Clarissa bent to kiss one withered cheek.

Her grace was dressed in a brocade court gown of forty years ago, in the Parisian style. The bodice was stiff, with bows down the front, the rich skirts falling in shining folds. The lace above the bodice almost made a ruff, covering the duchess's neck. A heavy gold necklace lay on the bodice, with an ivory cameo set around with diamonds that winked and gleamed when she breathed. Her blue-veined hands were adorned with several rings. Her hands had been fine in her youth, Kitty guessed, and the duchess was proud of them yet.

"Sit down, girls, sit down," she said, and called to the footman, "Bring the refreshments, Thomas." Then back to Kitty, "Now, tell me, does London please you?"

Her grace's face had once been fine, Kitty could see. The lineaments of her eyes were somehow familiar, her gaze sharp and intelligent.

"It is vastly amusing, your grace," Kitty said. "I am ever so grateful to Clarissa for bringing me."

The duchess smiled. "Lud! You are your grandmother come again, child. Ecod, she was a beauty. And you have her smile." She turned her gaze to Clarissa. "I understand I am to congratulate you on this alliance you appear to have contracted."

"Thank you, Grandmama," Clarissa said.

The duchess's eyes narrowed, but she said nothing more as the door opened and refreshments were wheeled in.

She waited until the footman had set things out, and indicated for Clarissa to pour out the tea. This Clarissa did, as they conversed a little about the delicious cakes and pastries.

When everyone had eaten a few bites and drunk some tea, the duchess said, "*Fi donc!* You're no more pleased than I am. Clarissa, did someone bullock you into this *mariage épatant?*"

Clarissa's rose and gold Worcester teacup clashed onto the saucer. "Grandmama," Clarissa said helplessly.

"Don't Grandmama me. Old I may be, but my eyes are still as good as they were. You ain't any happier than I am. Deny it if you dare."

Clarissa looked down unhappily.

The duchess sighed. "Clarissa. I know nothing against young

Wilburfolde—from all accounts he is a hapless muffin much like his father. What I cannot stick is the thought of you bowed under Susannah Wilburfolde's yoke. You may not have been bullied at home, but ecod, you shall know bullying when you are living under her roof. Why did you agree to it? I cannot believe that fool Chadwick gave you an ultimatum."

"No, Papa was all that is kind—but when he charged me with my age, and hinted that I would hang around James's neck one day..."

"So it's a demmed *faut de mieux*? But why? You can live with me! Or if you can't stick my temper, either of your uncles would take you in. Philip would take you as well, though he might put you in charge of that spoilt brat Bess. But you know these things."

Clarissa pulled out her handkerchief and pressed it to her eyes. "He offered, Grandmama. At my age, I was not likely to get another."

"*Nom d'un nom!* Your mother was four years older than you are now when she married. And last year, that clapper-jawed Sophia Latchmore crowed all over town about two offers."

"They were...not serious offers."

"Better them than Susannah Wilburfolde for a mother-in-law. Monstrous! As Susannah Millbrook she frightened half the men in town into decamping for Paris when she came out. Wilburfolde tripped over his own feet, and next thing he knew, she'd shackled him."

Kitty gazed raptly, her teacup suspended halfway between lip and saucer. Her emotions veered wildly between intense enjoyment at this plain speaking, which matched her own sentiments exactly, and sympathy for Clarissa's obvious distress.

"Nevertheless," Clarissa said unsteadily, "I have accepted. I cannot in good conscience cry off."

"Nonsense. These chits cry off all the time. Either someone bullied you into it, or..." The duchess smacked the arm of her chair, and leaned forward. "Clarissa, have you fallen in love with someone ineligible?"

To Kitty's surprise, Clarissa's face whitened, her chest heaved, and she leaped to her feet and ran. The duchess let her go.

As the door clicked shut behind her, the old woman sighed

unhappily. "I was afraid of that the moment she walked into the room. Just like her mother, who fell in love *à corps perdu* with that damned Winterdale, and her decline began the day he married that rabbiting Villiers chit."

"Clarissa's mama? But I thought—"

"*I* found Chadwick for her. He was kind. Cork-brained but kind, and prodigiously handsome, so she wouldn't shudder if he came near. Thought he could give her a brood to love instead of that *scélérat* Winterdale. But she was too worn down by childbirth when Clarissa came, that and low spirits. However, Clarissa ain't that weak. In fact, given time, I think she could route Susannah Wilburfolde, but that wouldn't make her happy, and I promised myself when my Therese died, that I would make her daughter happy."

Kitty said fervently, "She is not happy with him. He cannot help it, but he frets her. She comes back from every outing with the headache, but I know she will not cry off."

The duchess fortified herself with some tea, then crashed the fragile cup back onto its saucer. "She hates scandal, and crying off would kick up the sort of dust she mislikes. What I must do is discover whom she is in love with. I hope he is not married. Do *you* know?"

Kitty gave her head a shake. "She has never mentioned anyone. But..."

"But what? Speak up, girl! She will be back any moment."

"The subject has never come up."

"You mean she has been silent. Girls can find *any*place to talk, if they are of a mind."

Kitty looked up wonderingly. "That's true."

"How long has she been pokered up?"

"I could not say for certain, as she has always been quiet since we first became acquainted." Kitty thought of her plan, looked uncertainly at the formidable duchess, thought again of Clarissa bursting into tears, and stiffened her spine. "If she favored anyone, I would guess it must be her cousin."

"Which cousin? She's got dozens of 'em littering England and France, thanks to my busy daughters. Not France, anymore, but Holland. *Eh bien!* Which?"

"Mr. Philip Devereaux."

The duchess's brows shot up. "Philip? What makes you think that?"

"Well, she talks fondly of him. They get on so well together, and he apparently has been attending more parties."

The duchess nodded slowly. "It was the wish of my heart, five years ago, but they have always been like brother and sister — too much alike."

"Alike?"

"They are both bookish, sharing much the same tastes, for one thing. Quiet, for another."

"He is fond of reading?" Kitty could not help but exclaim. He did know some poetry, but anyone who had been schooled could recollect a poem if put to it, she had thought. And fashionable gentlemen were *not* bookish.

"He don't mention it in town, where ignorance is prized by these boobies nowadays," the duchess said bluntly. "The last book I remember anyone talking about was that maudlin nonsense Georgiana Devonshire wrote, and they only read far enough to see if they were in it. Them or their enemies," she added trenchantly.

Kitty choked on a laugh, and raised her hand to her lips to prevent the question she wanted to blurt.

"Yes, I was in it," the duchess said, giving a gust of a laugh. "But only a bit part, you might say. I never gave Georgiana trouble, she or that fool duke of hers. Whatever they and Bess Foster were up to was their business, and I liked what she did for young Fox. *Fi donc!* My eldest son has reached sixty without an heir, his twin will never marry, I expect, and I do not want to see the Devereaux line die out. Do you think you can find out if he's the one?"

"I shall do my best," Kitty promised fervently. "I owe her, oh, everything."

"*Bon!* That's where we'll rest it, then, since I know if I summoned him here he would sit like a stone and not tell me a thing. Now. You stay here and drink your tea, and don't blab about this conversation to anyone. She would be annihilated if gossip got around."

"I would never do that," Kitty said.

"Capital. And you'll send me word if there is anything I can do. Promise!"

Kitty nodded, and the duchess got to her feet and walked out with a great belling of skirts. Kitty was left staring up at a portrait of a sweet-faced girl in an enormous white wig. Upon the wig perched a hat that appeared to support half a garden. The girl was dressed as a shepherdess (if shepherdesses ever wore silk and lace), posed against a sylvan background. The wig and the clothing were absurd, but Kitty could not mistake the resemblance to Clarissa in that long face.

Clarissa in love! Kitty turned her mind to Andromeda, who was laboring under the same passion. Kitty thought of all the sighs, megrims, and fainting she'd filled the pages with, without ever thinking about how being in love might be *painful*.

Clarissa and the duchess soon returned, Clarissa pale except for pink-rimmed eyes. They drank tea, and the girls took their leave, the duchess muttering that she only wanted to see Clarissa happy.

When they were alone in the carriage, after a quick look at Clarissa's averted face, Kitty rushed into speech. "You know, I have not touched Andromeda since our arrival in London. I intended to finish it and copy it out fair so that I might find a publisher before I returned home. But first I will have to change the clothes..."

Clarissa's responses were mechanical, and Kitty chattered on until they reached the Harlowes' home. Then Clarissa leaned forward, pressed Kitty's hand gratefully, and then climbed out and went straight to her room.

Twenty-one

ON SUNDAY MORNING, AMELIA took the family considerably by surprise. "Hurry," she urged, "We shouldn't be late for church!"

She herself was dressed in her finest day gown, a fact that Eliza pointed out with sisterly curiosity.

Amelia flushed, but as she bade Eliza to leave off in a decidedly unsanctimonious voice, Lord Chadwick dismissed the hideous idea that his second daughter had suddenly turned Methodist — for in his mind, anyone who took a sudden hankering for what he considered a duty must have fallen under the pernicious influence of that fellow Wesley.

After divine service, Kitty remembered the young curate who gave a very good sermon as Mr. DuLac, the gentleman they'd met at the soiree across the street. She regarded Amelia with silent interest. Amelia was flushed, smiling in an odd way, and chattering rather less than usual.

The weather being fine, the young ladies chose to go out for an airing in the park that afternoon — that is, all the young ladies except Clarissa. Lord Wilburfolde carried Clarissa off to spend the afternoon with his Aunt Annadale.

Lord Wilburfolde had wavered about inviting Kitty, who he knew was Clarissa's guest. Mindful of what Miss Bouldeston had disclosed, he wrote to his mother on the subject and was enjoined by return mail to encourage the separation now. She would also instruct her sister to drop hints about the unsuitability of her guest, that Lady Catherine's visit might be brought to a close the sooner.

Kitty was left therefore to the company of Amelia and Eliza, Tildy having foregone the boredom of walking around the park in favor of visiting her friend Jane Atherton across the street, whose dog had just had puppies.

Almost the moment that Kitty, Amelia, and Eliza stepped outside they encountered the marquess, who was coming to pay his respects. After the exchange of politenesses and the disclosure that Ned had gone off with James Harlowe on some pursuit of their own, St. Tarval fell in step beside Kitty.

By the time they reached the park, all the polite subjects had been canvased, and they divided naturally into two parties, the Harlowe girls walking ahead to ogle a party of very young men who ogled them back.

Kitty remembered her manners. "You found the Bouldestons well, I trust?"

"I called before I came here, but Lucretia was away," Carlisle said. "You look as though London suits you."

Kitty clasped her hands. "You cannot conceive how happy I am. Everything is delightful. Clarissa and her family have been so kind and generous."

"You have written a great deal about them, but your letters have said little about your own affairs."

"Affairs?" she repeated.

He had to laugh. "I am to understand, then, you have not found your rich duke?"

"I did not suppose there *are* any, or if such a man exists, he has not come in my way. The closest I've encountered is the Marquess of Hartington, but everyone says he has eyes only for his cousin, Lady Caroline, and I can see why. Besides, I have been too busy to pay attention, I must admit." Kitty stole a guilty glance at her brother. "I suppose I am being very selfish, but I promise I have been thinking a great deal about my book, for I still hope and trust I can earn something thereby."

"That is absurd, Kit. You are to do precisely what you are doing, which is to enjoy yourself, and do not fret about St. Tarval.

As it happens, I have settled the last of Papa's debt with Sir Harry, and once we've dug the new canal, we will enter into a period of retrenchment. In ten years I think we will come about and find ourselves very comfortable. Perhaps the sooner, if we have good luck." He looked around. "So, to return to you. I trust that Miss Harlowe is well? I do not see her with her sisters."

"She is well, but that impossible man... No, I should not say such things." Kitty pressed her hands to her cheeks. "It is just that she is so unhappy, and though he means well, he vexes her. I would never say that much, except her grandmother agrees."

"I am very sorry to hear that," he said.

Kitty heard the conviction in his voice, and rushed on. "Her family will not make a push to help her. They do not seem to see her unhappiness. I am alone in my effort to, oh, I hardly know what to do. Carl, you must help me."

"Kitty, propriety forbids me to interfere here at all."

"Oh, Carl, I thought at least I could count upon you."

"What would you have me do, Kit? I cannot challenge this fellow to a duel! Especially as, from all accounts — for you must know that James had plenty to say on this head — the fellow is punctilious to a fault."

"We must help clear the way for her to be with the man she truly loves."

St. Tarval frowned ahead at the unoffending trees.

"Carl?"

"I do not know what to say," he responded finally.

"Carl, this concerns Clarissa's happiness, she who has been so kind and generous to me." Kitty's voice trembled.

The marquess stretched out his hand to his sister. "Then you may be sure I will do whatever I can. Who is this gentleman we are to encourage her to unite with?"

Kitty's cheeks tinged with color. "Her cousin, Mr. Philip Devereaux."

The marquess had to look about him before he could speak. "I do not know who he is."

"He is very handsome, and I am reliably told that he loves to read. I do know that he likes poetry," Kitty amended, then went on hastily, "at any rate, he is devoted to his family, as she is, and in short, he would be perfect in every way."

"Kitty, it sounds like you are acquainted enough with this fellow to do a better job of encouraging than I ever could."

"Oh, no, no, no. It seems I have already intruded myself too much on his notice. Lucretia told me that I am not—that is, I know that I have not the experience to—oh, I am tangling myself hideously. Carl, please say that you will help."

"I do not see how I can, but I promise you this. If there is anything I can do to aid your friend I will do everything in my power."

Kitty took his arm and hugged it. "How very comfortable it is, to have you here, Carl. I am so very glad you are come."

When Clarissa arrived home late that evening, her first impulse was to fling wide her bedroom windows so that she might breathe. Even the air of the street was better than the close, airless salon of Lady Annadale's home, and her stultifying lecture about precisely what was wrong with the nation, society, and her neighbors. What was it about that family and their predilection for overly warm, stale air?

Kitty scratched at her door. Clarissa let her in, relieved to be away from the endless round of her thoughts. Her head these days felt as stuffy and airless and inescapable as that horrid room.

Kitty stood on the threshold, her eyes wide and green, her expression solemn. Clarissa became aware of a thick stack of wrinkled pages clutched to her bosom.

"Here," Kitty said, holding out her burden to Clarissa. "I thought, that is, I hoped you might like to read it. I thought I could only benefit from your opinion, if you did not mind very much. I know that you do like books, and so I hoped you might read this one, even if it is only mine. And not finished."

Clarissa took in Kitty's lowered gaze and hazarded a guess at how difficult was this gesture. Clarissa was overwhelmed by her trust. "I would like to very much," she said, accepting the papers.

Clarissa added, "My grandmother is also fond of novels. She has always had a taste for romance, and I think might be excused for imagining things. I would be grateful if you would forget her surmises."

Kitty said, "I shall never mention it again unless you do."

"Thank you. Then we can go on comfortably again. And I will read this as soon as I may."

Kitty withdrew. Clarissa set the manuscript down on her desk and moved to the window. She must accustom herself to the fact that Kitty's brothers were here in London. She could even permit herself to be glad for Kitty's sake. No one could have mistaken Kitty's delight in seeing her older brother, a delight that had contrasted with Miss Bouldeston's reaction. Clarissa did not know Lucretia Bouldeston well enough to understand her thinking, but she could have sworn she had seen more dismay than delight.

However that may be, they must be left to conduct their lives as they saw fit. It was uncharitable to intrude where one was not asked or wanted. She must behave with politeness, and the distant friendliness of Kitty's friend.

She was called upon to exercise this determination much sooner than she expected.

Lady Chadwick had been put to considerable trouble trying to find a way to entertain Lord Wilburfolde that would not cause his mother's ire. She had finally hit upon the perfect solution: they would invite him to the Opera.

Unfortunately, she could not get her husband to agree. Lord Chadwick had commiserated with her and even praised her for hitting upon the perfect solution. But, as he put it, "I can stick the Opera, or I can stick that young blockhead. But I cannot stick both. You will have to get James to escort you."

She had turned to her son, without much hope of cooperation. James had scowled, then said reluctantly, "I will if you include Ned Decourcey and his brother in the party. Lady Kitty'll like it, and I'll have someone to talk to, which will lessen the torture."

And so it came to pass. They were gathered in an excellent box. James, with his own comfort in mind, made certain that there were plenty of refreshments at hand, and he pretended not to see Lord Wilburfolde's disapproval of wine being included among them.

Reactions to the first act were very much according to their several natures. Lady Chadwick dozed peacefully throughout, content with her achievement. She woke with a start when the curtain went down. Raising her looking glass expectantly to survey the other boxes, she began her evening's real entertainment.

Having fortified themselves during the caterwauling with most of the refreshments, James and Ned promptly escaped in search of more. The marquess sat back, prepared to take part in any conversation as expected of a guest, but he could not prevent the hope that Clarissa would participate. In a family party, in such a public place, he could enjoy her proximity with perfect safety.

As Kitty seemed to be in a reverie, and his hostess was busy surveying the other boxes, he turned slightly in order to observe Clarissa, who was looking particularly attractive in a gown of pale green with ivory lace, inclined her head politely as her betrothed painstakingly related to her what she had just seen.

Kitty turned to her brother. "How beautiful the music is, how excellent the singers! Now I understand why people praise Mozart. His piano airs are all very well, but *Cosi fan tutti* is extraordinary. Clarissa told me earlier that *The Magical Flute* is even better." She cast a glance around, and whispered, "How beautiful this theater is. I wonder if I ought to set a scene here. I could have Count Scorbini abduct Andromeda from one of these boxes."

St. Tarval said, "It would certainly liven up the evening."

Kitty continued in a whisper, "I hope while you are here you might take me to a play."

The marquess stared at her in surprise. "I thought you would have been to a dozen of them by now."

"The only person partial to plays is Clarissa," she whispered even lower. "But her betrothed disapproves, and the Chadwicks don't seem to attend plays. So we have never been." At that moment, Kitty, who had been looking around at the different boxes, spied Mr. Devereaux on the opposite side of the theater. His party included Mr. Brummel and several well-known leaders of society.

Happenstance brought his gaze across the sea of faces to meet Kitty's. Unconsciously she smiled, then consciously glanced toward Clarissa, hoping he would pick up the hint.

But hard on that she remembered Lucretia's warning and quickly dropped her gaze. She dared not look up again, but she said to her brother, "If you do buy tickets to the play, pray include

Clarissa. We needn't invite Lord Wilburfolde if he dislikes plays."

It was time for the second act, and Kitty settled back, preparing for enjoyment. James and Ned reappeared, smelling rather strongly of spirits.

On the other side of the theater, Devereaux listened to Brummel's sallies with only half an ear. "He might, were he inclined toward wit, term that style 'A Night at the Opera' for really it belongs on the stage," Brummel said in an undertone.

Everyone uttered a well-bred laugh at the expense of the Prince Regent and his lamentable taste in waistcoats as the curtain rose.

Mr. Devereaux had not missed the sudden smile followed by the equally sudden stiffening of self-consciousness on Lady Kitty's part (for so he found himself thinking of her, though he would never trespass out loud), that in its turn led to the quick glance at his cousin. Her behavior had all the air of second thoughts, as if someone had said something disobliging to her.

Clarissa? No, that was not in her nature. And yet...he recalled remarks he'd let fall over the years, in particular judgments both harsh and toplofty of rural misses, especially those who employed their wiles to entrap him. These words had been those of a young man who had grown up accustomed to privilege and praise. He had since repented of his callowness, but Clarissa might, in good conscience, have warned her friend off to protect her. He should be grateful. He should let be.

And yet he knew he couldn't permit Lady Kitty to return home believing him to be a coxcomb.

The remainder of the opera was as good as the beginning, for those who attended to it.

As soon as the final curtain came down, Lord Wilburfolde said, "I am informed by my parent, whose tastes can be relied upon for delicacy and moral rightness, that the farces that usually follow are unfit to be seen by young ladies. Shall we call for the coach?"

Lady Chadwick had been looking forward to this very thing. She said with more animation than she usually displayed, "I believe I may be trusted to determine what is unfit for my daughters and our guest."

Lord Wilburfolde looked disconcerted. "My apologies, Lady

Chadwick. I myself have never witnessed any of the entertainments in question, for my estimable parent has been very careful about my education. But if you have no objections, then I must, in politeness, abide by your decision." And he sat back, uncomfortably aware that he had failed in his duty—and yet he was curious.

The farce engendered gusts of laughter from the audience. Lord Wilburfolde was startled into mirth by an unexpected pun or two, followed instantly by guilt. His mother considered puns vulgar at any time, no matter how innocent. But then he had also never heard his mother laugh.

When the evening was over, he walked out in a brown study, partly resentful that he had been put into this position—for he knew what his mother would say—but partly bewildered, because he had never before heard Clarissa laugh until now. The oddest part of it was that she had laughed at jokes he considered indelicate, whereas the puns that had so entertained him had only raised a smile. He did not know what to make of it.

James had the coachman leave Lord Wilburfolde at his lodging first. Thus he soon sat down to his desk to report on the evening to his mother like a dutiful son.

The others began to talk the moment he left the coach. When Kitty and Amelia got involved in discussing the singers, the marquess turned to Clarissa to say quietly, "I wish to thank you on my sister's behalf. I have never seen her so happy, and she keeps telling me that it is all due to you."

Clarissa stammered a disjointed disclaimer.

"Lord Arden has been introducing us around," he continued, "and thus we have received an invitation to Lady Castlereagh's *rout al fresco* Tuesday next. If his lordship does not claim all your dances, may I ask for one?"

She knew that she should say no. But being angry with herself had resulted in her present position. She was not yet married. Dancing with her friend's brother was not only perfectly acceptable, some might regard it as a politeness.

Mostly (she was honest with herself) she was determined to make precious memories while she could, which must suffice for a lifetime.

"Yes, thank you," she said.

Twenty-two

THE MARQUESS HAD CALLED twice upon Lucretia, first to be told that she was elsewhere, and then that she was unwell.

Lady Bouldeston informed her eldest daughter that when the gentleman called again, she would neither be away nor unwell. "Take care what you are about," she warned Lucretia. "You have treated St. Tarval as if he were in your pocket, and while I applaud your desire to make a better marriage, you would do well not to drive him completely off."

"Of course I can do better." Lucretia tossed her head, thinking of Lucasta and her stupid Mr. Aston.

"I should hope you can do better, but Lucretia, the truth is that you have not done so. And though I had higher hopes for you, St. Tarval is a very good title. A marchioness is a marchioness."

"Except what is the use of being a marchioness if one is stuck forever in a ramshackle house? There would be no London—I am certain he's only here to see his sister. He is also dull. Has not a thing to say beyond his horses and pigs and canals, or worse, books."

Lady Bouldeston shrugged. "These airs and graces are all very well for those who can afford them. We cannot. If your sister gains her poet, this will be the last year we will spend in Mount Street. At least until your father's affairs come about. You have had four years of London. Perhaps you would do better in our own neighborhood, if you cannot find someone to suit. There is always the vicar's brother, and the squire's son."

Lucretia fled to her room, sobbing in fury. How selfish they all were — Lucasta most of all! What business did she have, throwing herself at the first fool who looked back at her? She was barely eighteen!

Lucretia scowled and dried her eyes. Since she had no allies, she must simply form better plans, and exert herself to carry them through. Titles! What use were they without beautiful town houses and wealth to match? Even better, when the man who offered all these things was counted among society's leaders?

Tears burned her eyes at the memory of Mr. Devereaux at the opera last night, sitting in the box surrounded by everyone who was important. Lucretia could see herself, ever so clearly, seated next to him, every eye in the place comparing his height and breadth of shoulder to herself all in the palest rose. For it must be rose; she could hear the admiring whispers, "Brummel himself told her she should wear nothing else. It is above all things romantical, but no more romantical than the circumstances of their marriage..." She would make the *perfect* future duchess, if that fat old heir could safely be kept from having brats.

She just had to arrange those circumstances.

Yes, and that brought to mind another troubling observation. He had smiled once, not at any of the important people in his box, but at someone in the boxes on the other side of the theater, above where the Bouldestons were sitting.

She'd had to resort to subterfuge in order to discover that the box directly above her contained none other than Lady Chadwick and her party.

Lucretia flung her fan down in anger. Perhaps Catherine was trying to draw attention to herself in a desperate attempt to catch his attention? But his smile had not been the mirth one exhibits at a vulgar or preposterous display.

She was brooding about that when the door knocker sounded below. Lucretia ran to the door and listened. When she heard Carlisle's voice asking for her, and her mother's pointed, "She is upstairs in the young ladies' parlor," she had time to arrange herself accordingly, her toes just peeping out from under her hem, a piece of delicate sewing that she kept for these occasions in her lap.

The fiction of the young ladies' parlor was an agreed-on thing: the upstairs room served them all as occasion warranted. She would not be interrupted, alas. Mama would see to that.

So she just had to see to it that Carlisle could not cry off.

St Tarval's heart sank when Lady Bouldeston sent him upstairs. He knew he had to end this pretence with Lucretia, but he had hoped to put it off. Or that she would be merciful and end it for him, preferably with an advertisement of her coming marriage to someone else, inserted into the newspaper.

Lucretia was alone. She gave a false little start of surprise, and he suppressed a spurt of irritation at this habit of hers, and wondered if he could bear a lifetime of that little round mouth and the girlish "Oh!"

He closed off that thought. These little tricks must be the way young ladies were trained to act. No doubt Kitty would gain similar habits. Though he'd never seen anything like that from Clarissa in those brief days at Tarval Hall...

"Lucretia," he said. "I hope I see you well."

"Vastly, I assure you. And you are looking so well that I need not ask. A new coat? May I ask, did you come into a legacy?"

"No, merely a piece of business ended better than expected, and so Ned and I thought to visit Kitty in town. I hoped to have a few moments of privacy with you."

She began, "You know Mama is very strict with us girls, and reposes the greatest trust in us..."

A satiric glance reminded her of that day in the garden, which it had taken her an entire summer to engineer. She blushed, turned her head, and daubed at her eyes with her handkerchief, giving her eyelids a surreptitious scrub or two to help them pinken.

Carlisle said, "Lucretia, we were sixteen, and can, I think, be forgiven the boy-and-girl gesture of affection. Nobody knows about it but us. The truth is, you do not really want to marry me, do you?"

Lucretia pressed the handkerchief to her eyes, and gave a shuddering sob.

"Lucretia..."

"How could you say that?" she demanded, and then, "Catherine has maligned me to you. Is that it?"

"What? Where did you get that idea?"

His genuine astonishment, followed by the tone of exasperation, made it clear that this tack, which had sounded so good in her head, was entirely wrong.

He went on, "You yourself said that you have so many interested suitors, I naturally thought—"

She quickly brought out her next line. "I have remained constant, but you wish to throw me over for Another?"

This was so near the truth that he was silenced.

She missed the regret tightening his face as her lacy handkerchief was still hiding her eyes, which remained stubbornly dry. So she let out a beautifully modulated wail of anguish, and fled from the room, leaving him to make his excuses as best he might, and depart with a choking sense of failure.

Kitty entered the parlor to discover Amelia bent over an old, dusty book.

"What is that, Amelia?"

"I can make neither heads nor tails of it." Amelia sighed. "Oh, why am I so stupid?"

"What are you trying to read, pray?"

"It is this play. Mr. DuLac said it is about Shylock, and toleration, but I can make no sense of these words. However, there is not a thing about the evils of liquor."

Kitty held her breath so she would not laugh, then said with care, "Did you mean temperance?"

"No, that is Lord Wilburfolde's word," Amelia declared in disgust. "I've heard it a thousand times. Toleration, Mr. DuLac was speaking of, and he said Shakespeare argued for it these two hundred years ago, and so I got down the plays, but I cannot understand a word."

"Here, let me help you. As it happens, I had to tutor Ned in this very one, when he was at Eton, and you know, I had nothing else to do, so I happen to be fairly versed in Shakespeare."

"And yet you are so very fashionable," Amelia said wonderingly.

Kitty smiled, and gave Amelia credit for the true intent of the compliment. "So let us begin with the story of the play..."

They were still at it when Lady Chadwick sent Eliza up to fetch them. "Remember, you are to go to the dressmaker's to be choose your fabrics for the duke's masquerade?" Eliza plopped on the sofa, scowling. "I should so love to attend a masquerade. Only who gives them anymore?"

"The Duchess of Norcaster, silly," Amelia said, setting the book aside. "Thank you, Lady Kitty. It is beginning to make sense, and you know, it isn't altogether horrid, in parts."

Lord Chadwick, happening to pass by on his way downstairs to take his leave for his club, overheard this remark, and was puzzled enough to put a question to his wife.

"What is Amelia doing that she expected to be horrid?"

"Nothing less than reading Shakespeare."

"What?"

"Lady Kitty is helping her to it. What's more, she seems to be taking some of it in. Which is more than I ever got her to do with that succession of governesses."

"Hey day," Lord Chadwick exclaimed in wonderment as he picked up his hat. Then he bethought himself of another extraordinary circumstance, and said, "Would this be owing to that young parson she was making eyes at in church the other day?"

"Mr. DuLac? I believe so."

"My daughter, chasing a parson?" He shook his head. "If she did not look like the rest of 'em..."

Lady Chadwick caught his meaning, and gave a scandalized laugh; though she dearly loved a flirtation, she had never ventured beyond, a fact of which he was well aware, and so his joke remained just that.

She sent a quick glance at the door to make certain the younger girls had not been by, and said, "Mr. DuLac comes of an excellent family, and as Clarissa said to me, anyone who can get Amelia to look inside a book cannot be discounted as a possible husband."

Lord Chadwick grabbed his gloves, shaking his head as he descended the steps.

Before long the ladies were on their way to the bazaar in order to get ideas for their masquerade costumes. "Only the dull will wear dominos," Amelia stated, not knowing that Lord Wilburfolde had faithfully relayed his mother's preferences for setting an example of taste and breeding with the wearing of dominos in a subdued color. "I think I will be beautiful and tragic as Mary Stuart, in white lace, with a red ribbon round my neck."

"You will be taken for Marie Antoinette," Clarissa said. "The poor thing having been guillotined scarce years ago, people are bound to think of her first."

"I do not want to be Marie Antoinette, for that requires a great wig, and one of those hideous gowns like in the pictures at your Grandmother Norcaster's, with the skirt wider than a door. And that horrid white powder, like the old people wear."

"What would you like to be?" Kitty asked Clarissa.

"I have not thought about it," Clarissa said untruthfully. She knew that she ought to do what Lord Wilburfolde asked. But she wanted to order an extravagant costume. Something beautiful and romantic... so that someone would see it.

She would not permit herself to name the Someone.

She was still trying not to think of Someone when the family departed for Lady Castlereagh's rout, and found Lord Wilburfolde awaiting them, full of anxious little worries for protecting Clarissa's health.

The Castlereaghs' gardens were lit by quantities of decorated lamps, and pretty fairy lights floating in the ponds. Guests drifted in and out of the large, golden-lit house, the soft air of late spring carrying the sounds of laughter, and of violins scraping.

Everyone of the first rank was there, and a great many who weren't.

Lady Bouldeston was not in Lady Castlereagh's circles, but Lucretia had foreseen that, begging and flattering her friend Sophia Fordham, who was connected to the hostess, for an invitation. Miss Fordham was sufficiently intrigued by the prospect of Lucretia's intentions to comply.

From the very first it appeared her expectations would be met, for Lucretia sought her out, then said, "Oh my dear Miss Fordham, I am in your debt forever. But to be in this company, it makes me so very shy, I must look out the quietest and most out-of-the-way corner."

Having said this, she proceeded to tiptoe through the entire house, scanning thoroughly. Miss Fordham had a silent wager going with herself that Mr. Devereaux was the target. Sure enough, she spotted him seated with the Earl of Chatham, Pitt's brother, and Lords Delamere, Apsley, and Malvers. The latter's brother, the elegant Mr. Pierrepont, was in the middle of retailing the latest anecdote of Mr. Brummel.

"Here is a good place, away from the hideous press," Lucretia declared, sitting down as near to them as she could get.

Miss Fordham hid her amusement. "Are you not afraid of drawing attention from that party of gentlemen?"

"I pay no heed to them. It is giving them too much notice," Lucretia declared with a toss of her head.

Miss Fordham wondered how Lucretia was going to gain the attention of the gentlemen. Even if she didn't capture that of Mr. Devereaux, there were several rich and single lords here. And she had no objection to Lucretia Bouldeston making a fool of herself. Would she not appear the better by comparison?

But before either of them could execute these amiable plans, Lady Castlereagh appeared from the other direction, and confronted the gentlemen. "It is too bad of you to hide here," she scolded, "when we are entirely in want of partners in the other room. Come! Do your duty, or I shall bring the dancers out here."

The gentlemen complied with a laugh and a compliment. Miss Fordham counted to herself, and had scarcely reached thirty before Miss Bouldeston began to quarrel with her place. It was too cold—too dark—there might be insects. She could not hear the music, and no one was more partial to excellent music than she.

They reached the ballroom as a dance was ending. Across the room, the Chadwick party had arrived, and Mr. Devereaux and his neighbor Lord Arden paused to talk to them. Miss Fordham was too busy watching Lucretia to notice Mr. Devereaux's manner as he greeted the newcomers. But Lucretia watched as the gentleman performed his bows. Was there a significant pause, a significant smile, for Catherine?

It couldn't be—and yet there was Catherine grinning up at him in the most vulgar manner, and dressed so ostentatiously in silver gauze with green trim. She probably thought it brought out the color of her eyes.

Lucretia was thoroughly disgusted. She could tell others that he laughed at Catherine — she could tell herself that — but she could not be certain it was true, and she *had* to be certain.

She walked in that direction, catching their voices as Amelia Harlowe was saying, "...already promised this dance."

"Then in that case, I will turn to your sister or her guest, whoever is not promised," Mr. Devereaux said.

"Come, Clarissa," Kitty said, holding out her hand to Lord Arden. "You know I promised my cousin. Come be in our set."

The four walked off, Lucretia staring after in astonishment.

That emotion was swiftly followed by rage. How selfish people were! And what hypocrites! The worst of all was Catherine Decourcey, thanking Lucretia so humbly for her truly excellent and selfless advice about not putting herself forward. What could be more brazen?

Lucretia looked around. Something had to be done, and this summer, as well, thanks to Lucretia's equally selfish parents. Lucretia remembered her promise to Catherine on their first meeting in town. If Catherine was that determined to catch a husband, then Lucretia must help her before she made the entire family into a laughing-stock.

"Let us take a turn about the room, Miss Fordham," she suggested. "The motion is so refreshing."

Now, which of the single gentlemen would be suitable for Catherine? Not anyone with tastes that would be called *nice*. Not for a country mouse with no dowry. Oh, here came Papa's friend Mr. Redding, who everyone said was on the lookout for a new wife. While Lucretia found him revolting in every sense — *she* could certainly do better — he was quite good enough for the likes of Catherine...

Twenty-three

KITTY HAD NOT SAT down once for three hours, but never had time passed so swiftly.

The best dance thus far was the first. She, Lord Arden, Clarissa, and Mr. Devereaux made up a square, which occasioned conversation as they waited to go down the dance. Lord Arden began by mocking a character from a play, begging them to guess which was meant. Clarissa knew the character, and responded in kind.

They began with comical plays, but when Mr. Devereaux quoted a line from the translation of *Sorrows of Young Werther*, and Clarissa promptly guessed it, somehow the moment devolved into a game of ladies against gentlemen. Kitty, put on her mettle, forgot her promise to hide her extensive knowledge of novels and plays. Consequently she came off best, but not by a large margin, for Mr. Devereaux and Clarissa were nearly as fast. Only Lord Arden was left out, castigating them good-naturedly as a parcel of bagwigs and blue-stockings.

When the dance ended, Kitty found her brothers there. Ned exclaimed, "Arden! I looked you out all over. We need a fourth for a hand," and bore him off.

Kitty turned to her elder brother, who was just bowing to Clarissa. "My dance?"

Clarissa curtseyed, and Kitty sighed. So much for leaving

Clarissa with Mr. Devereaux. At whom Kitty should not be looking, or *throwing herself* at as people said. What a very vulgar image,
and she would never do that to anyone!

But if people said it, then her conduct must be amiss. She had
already made one hideous mistake when she first went into
society and did not know the hidden rules—and it had been
Lucretia, that time, too, to set her straight.

So she walked randomly away, wondering if *throwing herself at*
meant others could somehow see her interest on her face, like
some sort of invisible sign. If only he weren't so handsome—if he
weren't so *funny* at such unexpected times, and always uttered in a
serious tone, which somehow made his wit the more humorous.

"Oh, there you are, Catherine." It was Lucretia. "Looking
about for a partner? Look no farther. I am delighted to introduce
you to Mr. Redding," Lucretia declared, and performed this office.

She stayed long enough to assure Mr. Redding that Lady
Catherine would be vastly entertained by so nimble a dancer, and
then excused herself, saying her sister must be looking for her.

This gentleman was very tall and thin, probably closer to fifty
than forty. Kitty made her curtsey, looking in surprise as he smirk-
ed down at her and said, "And so, will you honor me with a
dance?"

Kitty politely assented, and they joined the next set.

He was a fine enough dancer, but when they were together, his
questions were put in an odd tone that she could not define. "And
so you adore dancing? Ah, you young ladies are naughty little
pusses! Perhaps afterward you would adore a cool walk in the
garden even more?"

Kitty had no idea how to answer that. In truth, the ballroom
was very warm, but she had no desire to be walking about with a
strange man, however friendly; there was something about the
pressing of his hands on her arm, the fact that he stood so close,
that made her uneasy.

"I am comfortable here," Kitty began.

Mr. Redding stroked her hand. "It is so perfect an evening, and
I was promised that you are a friendly young lady."

"I beg pardon, sir, but I—"

"Evening, Redding."

Kitty flushed at the sound of Mr. Devereaux's familiar voice. Her heartbeat quickened, but she was not altogether glad to see the gentleman. There was that uncomfortable sense that she was missing something—or that something was amiss—that she had somehow done wrong. Though she could not have said what, or how. She was both embarrassed and relieved, though neither emotion she could quite account for.

"Devereaux," Mr. Redding replied, with as good a grace as he could muster.

"My lady, I believe the next dance was mine?" Mr. Devereaux asked, and his reward for breaking his strict rule was the unmistakable relief in Kitty's countenance.

He had been intending to leave. Now the price for this impulse would be to spend the rest of the evening dancing, so that those who minded such things would not be able to remember one of his partners from another.

And yet he could not be sorry, he decided as they began to thread through the crowd in the ballroom. His partner's countenance brightened. Mr. Devereaux glanced up. Who could revive the young lady like a garden of flowers? Here were her two brothers advancing.

"Did you seek me?" she asked. "Is everything—that is, are you enjoying yourselves?"

"Not in here," Edward began, rolling his eyes. "Card room's full as it can hold."

"It's a fine evening," St. Tarval said, bowing to the gentleman at Kitty's side. "I believe we've met at Lord Arden's?"

"Oh, hey, you haven't met?" Ned exclaimed, and he hastily performed the introductions. Then he indicated the crowd, and gave a crack of laughter. "Good luck getting out there on the floor. Why anyone would want to in this heat—well, Kit, I hope you can wedge in, is all I'm saying."

Kitty stood on tiptoe, dismayed to see that he had not exaggerated. From the number of nodding feathers extending up from ladies' headdresses, it looked as if the entire ballroom was filled.

"We can take a turn outside, if you like," Mr. Devereaux offered.

"It would be much cooler," Kitty said thankfully, so relieved that it did not occur to her to wonder why the prospect of a walk in the garden now did not discommode her. She was only aware that it didn't.

"I believe I saw your hostess outside," Mr. Devereaux said. "We can walk in her direction, and I'll restore you to her."

"Thank you, sir," Kitty said. She was aware of a small feeling of constraint, and decided to apply her brother's advice about jumping fences: best to get over as quick as one could. "I understand that your sister, Miss Elizabeth, is to visit the Chadwicks."

"I believe, from the missives I have been honored to receive, that she is counting the hours. I trust the Harlowes are prepared to endure the household being turned upside down."

"With four lively girls," Kitty said, "they are surely ready for anything."

"They have not yet spent time with my sister," Mr. Devereaux said with a wry smile.

Kitty remembered the headlong conversation of that young lady, and could not help a spurt of sympathy for the brother who had to act as guardian. "She is very romantical."

"A generous observation," Mr. Devereaux said. "I only hope that when she does marry, she will find a gentleman possessed of both a sense of humor and a vast wealth of patience."

Kitty chuckled at that. "I have to admit, I was enamored of the idea of assisting to foil an abduction."

"Who could resist?" he countered. "Though I will admit that my part, being the desperate duelist, either as villain or as hero — we will not inquire too closely into which — has less appeal. In particular considering the weather, which did not cooperate at all with the romantical aspects of the case."

"Nothing did," Kitty admitted. "It was a farce. Until that day, I read them and laughed, but now I have only to think of similar situations and my sympathies are entirely with the victims."

"I have had occasion to note," he said as they walked over a little bridge that spanned an artfully designed stream, "that the individuals in novels and plays very seldom behave in any way one recognizes from the course of life."

"I have noticed the same," Kitty declared, thinking of Andromeda, and how very many changes she was going to have to make. "And yet I still read them."

"So do I. Do you think we're drawn back by the comfortable feelings of superiority over the benighted characters caught in the plots, or is it the comfort of calling up the range of sensibilities from horror to laughter for people who don't exist?"

"My brother once said much the same," she said, glancing down at the stream as fairly lights bobbed and twinkled in the quiet waters. "He said the proclivities for indulging in gossip stems from the same impulse as the reading of novels, only gossip touches on real people. Therein lies the harm. But I think there can be much to learn from a novel, if it depicts how people *ought* to behave when they have no idea, especially young ladies who as everyone knows *have* to marry, whereas young gentlemen might *want* to marry..."

She paused, looking upward, unaware of her entrancing profile contrasted against the golden lights of the house.

"I beg pardon," she said suddenly, turning to face him.

"You have it, of course. But may I ask what I am pardoning?"

"I have been taking more than my share of the conversation," she said contritely.

"Not that I was aware. Rather than argue over who talked most, tell me this. Which novels demonstrate how we ought to behave? I trust you're not about to name Goethe's hapless young hero."

"No," Kitty said. "How *very* selfish Werther is. I can only think of one of my brothers being found dead, by his own hand, and, well, no."

"Then you will suggest that pattern of perfection, Sir Charles Grandison?"

"Oh, so perfect, and so dull," she said, giggling.

"Dull? And here I thought he was the epitome of nobility..."

"Not dull, precisely. But so very *perfect*. He never makes a mistake, or changes a whit..." Self-consciousness forgotten, Kitty launched into opinions about literature, revealing how widely she was read, which led to talk about the doings of real people. She didn't pretend to experience she didn't have, but offered evidence from country life.

He was surprised to discover that he was not bored. He should have been bored. If anyone else had talked on about the doings of a set of persons he had never met, and would not travel an hour out of his way to encounter, he would have been bored. But she pressed no confidences on him as a way to presume an intimacy; she indulged no gossip. Her anecdotes touched on the vagaries of human nature without being cruel.

They had walked twice around the garden when he became aware of a speculative glance or two from other guests, recalling him to his desire to protect her from the sort of speculation he hated.

He guided their steps to Lady Chadwick's side. Kitty bowed and sat down, addressing herself to Clarissa without a single languishing look, and he turned dutifully to Amelia, and asked her to dance.

She agreed with alacrity, sparking amusement. She seemed determined to dance — or to be seen dancing — and so, as they worked their way into the press, she said, "Now, Mr. Devereaux, tell me about Shakespeare."

"Shakespeare," he repeated, astonished.

"Yes. I would like something to say, something with proper *éclat*. And I've used up all that Clarissa and Lady Kitty can think of. You're the only other person I know who has read such things."

"Very well," he said, very much amused. Was it the parson, inspiring these ventures into deep waters? "Which play shall we discuss?"

They had canvased three plays by the time the dance ended. Amelia was promptly claimed by a young sprig her own age. Devereaux relinquished her, satisfied that the idle eyes observing his actions would find him doing his duty by his relations.

He began walking in search of something to drink, smiling over Amelia's determined effort to master Shakespeare in a matter of days in order to impress her young parson. He was only a few paces from the tables where punch and glasses had been set out when Miss Bouldeston once again crossed his path.

He checked, out of habit, then became aware that he was not her target this time. St. Tarval and Lord Arden were fetching refreshments for their partners when Miss Bouldeston confronted them to make her curtsy.

Perhaps he had misjudged the young lady, who claimed to be Lady Kitty's friend. When he stepped up, Miss Bouldeston looked startled, a real expression rather than her customary affected manner. She was a pretty enough girl, and again he heard those sympathetic accents, *young ladies have to marry*. He said, "Would you care to dance?"

Lucretia turned away from St. Tarval, scarcely remembering her curtsey. She was positively giddy with triumph, and as she walked beside Mr. Devereaux through the crowd, she glanced about her, wanting to see envy in every pair of female eyes, especially those who had no partner.

She'd always known he could not resist forever; men were so very simple, after all. It had taken jealousy to get him to stir, for it could be no accident that this offer of a dance occurred when she was with Carlisle.

They took their place in line, and Mr. Devereaux's next words proved to her a similar train of thought. "You are friends with St. Tarval and Lady Catherine?"

Now to make certain that he understood her heart was perfectly free. "His lands border my father's. As you may expect, we grew up fond of one another, the old boy and girl interest. I grew out of that, of course, when I came to town, but he, I fear..."

She let her voice trail off, a nod to delicacy. Now to make certain that he quite understood about Catherine. Oh, who would've thought she would be given such a capital opportunity! "As for Catherine, I was her only friend as there are no other young females of birth within a day's ride."

"I observe that you use her given name, unlike the Chadwicks."

How to answer that? She must make their relative positions perfectly clear. "Such ill-chosen things, sometimes, childhood names that we ought to leave off when we leave behind our dolls and toys. I use her name as a reminder of the dignity to which she was born. Because she has no mother, my own parent, so careful in raising my sister and me, convinced me it is my duty to offer hints in the most delicate manner to guide Catherine's behavior as best I can. I think, to my sorrow, that the failure is mine when she errs."

"Surely your mother would be better equipped for such a duty? Or are you that much older?" the gentleman asked.

"Oh, no," Lucretia corrected emphatically. "Scarcely a year. My mother feels that Lady Chadwick's too-kind heart...well, in short, I have done my best to dissuade Catherine from being too obvious in her desperate search for a wealthy husband."

"I see," the gentleman said, his tone not quite the sympathetic understanding that she had expected.

She thought it best to leave the subject and get back to her own situation. They were nearly at the top of the dance so she must be quick. Casting her eyes down in a modest gesture, she said, "As for her brother, he has come to town to press me to the point."

He was silent. She dared a peek upwards. It would have been too much to expect an instantaneous effusion of love in this great crowd. Indeed, he seemed distracted by the press of people. She must be satisfied that she had carried her point. Both points, to be sure: the brother and sister were importunate in their separate ways.

When the dance ended, he walked her to her mother's side and bowed over her hand, exchanged a polite word with her mother, and then moved on.

"That is a connection I would like to see," Lady Bouldeston murmured.

Lucretia bridled as she busied herself with her fan. She watched him move to the horse-faced Miss Lasley. What was he about, paying attention to that dowd? Men—no one knew what they would be at!

She was noting critically every clumsy step performed by Miss Lasley as Lucasta appeared from her latest dance, damp and red-faced. But this time, when she bored on about her stupid poet, Lucretia could tolerate it, for she was cherishing her own vastly superior achievement. She decided against speaking of it, preferring to anticipate her mother's vast surprise, and Lucasta's discomfiture, when she declared to them that she would be the new Mrs. Devereaux, two deaths away from becoming a duchess.

Twenty-four

IT WAS DURING THAT evening that Clarissa at last discovered why her betrothed could not help but irritate her nerves even when he was not dutifully carrying out his mother's charges. He meant well, but he had no vestige of a sense of humor.

She had not thought about this subject before. Humor was like the air you breathed. It was there. When you've shared a moment of mirth, the laughter is soon gone, but not the memory of having shared it. Humor had not the importance of awe when one looked upon a painting of genius, or listened to a musical masterpiece. But during that very first dance, when she and Cousin Philip, Kitty, and Lord Arden had been laughing over their game, she had ended the dance with an inexplicable sense that they had shared something of great importance.

This seed of awareness had flowered when St. Tarval arrived to claim his dance. On the surface, everything had been scrupulously proper. They had talked about nothing but books. However, they had talked. He did not tell her what to think. He did not look at her with faint horror when she admitted to having laughed out loud when reading Mr. Fielding's *Adventures of Tom Jones*, or *Joseph Andrews*. He did not cite his mother's philosophy on the worthlessness of novels. Never had she enjoyed a dance as much. Never.

She could not dance twice with any man but her betrothed. She knew Lord Wilburfolde was willing to do his duty by her a second time, but that was part of the problem. He was only sure of himself when he was doing his duty, and if they were to dance again, he would enumerate all of the diseases that *might* occur as a result of this *al fresco* event.

She could not suppress the sting of tears, so she walked away to seek the cooler air of the terrace, where she might scold herself back into composure.

She had just reached the terrace when a familiar voice caught her up, "Would you like a stroll in the cool air, Clarissa?"

It was Cousin Philip. Though the terrace was in shadow compared to the brilliance of the ballroom, she understood from his quick look of concern that the light had still given her away.

He was a comfortable friend. He would not intrude upon her thoughts, either with impertinent questions or unwanted advice. She took his arm gratefully.

They walked over the little bridge and into the rose garden along the artificial stream. Many of the fairy lights had burned out, and ghostly paper bubbles bobbed on the water. She felt that those represented her soul, and then scolded herself for her fancy.

He said, "May I compliment you on your new style?"

"Oh, do not," she implored, then caught herself. "I beg your pardon. It is merely the headache causing foolish megrims."

He guided her to one of the stone benches and they sat down. The only sounds were the croaking of frogs nearby, and in the distance the scrape and flourish of violins, and the buzz of merriment.

She took a gulp of air and squared her shoulders. "I will only say that whatever is pleasing in my appearance is not due to any incipient change of state. It is entirely due to Lady Kitty. You know that I have never been passionate about dress. It was easier to permit my aunt to have her way, but this year, when I went shopping with my guest, it was an unlooked for felicity that she has a natural eye for style." She gave a watery chuckle. "You probably think me boring."

"I hope that we have been friends too long for that. We agree that our real interests lie in different directions than dress, and as always, I value your honesty. Speaking of which, there are times when I am conversing with your guest that I perceive a sudden restraint. If she has taken a dislike to me, it would be better to let me know now, rather than permit me to behave like a coxcomb in pressing upon her an unwanted friendship."

"That is not at all the case, I believe. If there is a restraint, I suspect she has been influenced from another quarter. At least, I have become aware that visits from the person in question invariably result in a mood of anxious worry." She stopped there, uncomfortably aware of having strayed into the area of gossip.

To her relief, he said only, "I believe I understand. Perhaps, then, on my return to London, if I were to invite you and your guest for a drive...say to Hampstead Heath? I am very much persuaded that you will need an outing after enduring the high spirits of our respective younger sisters for days."

"It would be a delight on my part, and I'll speak to Kitty." She rose. "Thank you for your kindness. I believe my head is the better for the fresh air, and I would not trespass a moment more on your time."

Kitty and St. Tarval observed the two from across the terrace. Kitty said, "Clarissa has just returned from walking with her cousin. See how much happier she is?"

Her brother patted her hand as they walked on, but he did not speak.

They were not the only ones who noticed; Lucretia, who wished to be available for a second dance, saw them as well, and smiled benignly. Miss Harlowe was safely betrothed, and indeed, there had been no signs of any special regard these past four years. She and her cousin Devereaux were merely friends.

Lucretia then realized that she had been remiss in that regard. A friendship with Miss Harlowe would enable Lucretia to call in Brook Street more frequently. Her reward would be evidence of her devotion to Mr. Devereaux's relations, should he find her there.

And so, after Clarissa took a seat with her family, Lucretia sat down beside her and exerted herself to be friendly.

Clarissa knew that this year she really did look better than she ever had, but what could motivate Miss Bouldeston to suddenly declare that Clarissa's gown was the sweetest thing she could conceive, and wasn't it lucky that she was betrothed, or else all the men in the room would fall in love with the way she had done her hair?

Clarissa was disconcerted by the increasingly lavish stream of compliments, returning ever shorter answers — which prompted Lucretia to greater efforts.

Kitty kept walking with her brother, hoping that Lucretia would go away soon so she could sit next to Clarissa and encourage her to talk about her cousin. St. Tarval wanted Lucretia to move on so that he could ask Clarissa for another dance.

Kitty said, "You have been invited to the Duchess of Norcaster's masquerade ball, have you not?"

"Yes. Arden saw to that. Why?"

"Did you bring Kirby to town, or anyone else?"

"Just Kirby, and he's not always with us. Perforce I rely on him to carry messages back and forth to Tarval Hall. Why do you ask, Kit?"

She smiled mysteriously. "I hoped that that was the case. It has to do with a costume for the masquerade. I will give you a letter for Kirby to carry to Mrs. Finn."

Everyone was surprised when Edward presented himself before Clarissa. Kitty and St. Tarval could not hear whatever it was he said, but the import was soon clear when she rose, and took his hand to follow him toward the dance floor.

"This is the first time I've ever seen Ned do that," Kitty whispered. "I didn't even know that he could dance."

"I saw to it he had lessons his last year at Eton," St. Tarval admitted, "but I never thought it took."

Ned brought Clarissa toward them; neither Kitty nor St. Tarval were aware of stopping until Mr. Worthington appeared, and asked Kitty to dance.

Ned seemed to be looking through the crowd ringing the dance floor for an opening to get through. But then he stumbled against one of the little spindle-legged chairs, and winced, exclaiming, "Ow, ow!"

Clarissa was quick to concern, as was St. Tarval, their voices colliding, "Oh, sir, are you all right?" "Ned, have you hurt yourself?"

"A spanking bruise is all," Ned said, shaking one foot. "Here,

Carlisle, will you mind dancing with Miss Harlowe? I'm going to sit right here until the pain goes off. It will in a trice. It was the merest glancing blow."

St. Tarval flushed at this obvious ploy, risking a glance at Miss Harlowe, whose expression of concern made it clear that such ploys had hitherto played no part in her life.

The marquess stretched out his hand. "I hope you will not mind, though it's our second?"

She glanced at his hand, instinctively responding to that gesture of appeal. She was distracted by a small gap between the edge of his glove and his sleeve. The skin was marred by a purplish scar.

"Were you hurt?" she asked, for the scar did not look very old.

He flushed becomingly. "An accident. A matter of a splinter, and my own unwariness."

The ballroom was if anything significantly hotter than it had been, the crowd thicker. The noise greater, so great there was little chance of being heard without shouting. But she was content to stand near him, content to enjoy the press of his fingers on her gloved hand, however brief, the sound of his breathing as he stepped near and then away. The sight of his face, as she memorized every feature, the quiver of his lashes, the slight curve of his mobile mouth. How could she ever have thought him ordinary? He was the handsomest man in the world.

He, too, enjoyed the moment, though he knew he ought not. He'd promised Kit to forward the cousin's chances, and Devereaux seemed an excellent man. But the marquess could not force the first words past his lips.

And so they danced in silence, each in a reverie of glory, the sharper for the awareness of how transient it must be. Each beat of the music carried them inexorably toward the moment when they must part.

That parting was brought home when the dance ended, and there was Lucretia, bridling and simpering as she made a play with lowered lashes. "I believe you spoke of the supper dance, Carlisle," she said—for she'd just seen Mr. Devereaux go off with one of his married cousins, whose husband had been posted to Spain.

St. Tarval bowed, held out his arm, and Clarissa parted with a polite word to both. She would not presume to know the gentleman's mind. But that countenance *seemed* as far from a man in love as was possible.

* * *

Later that evening, when the two young ladies went upstairs to bed, Clarissa paused on the landing. "Kitty, may I speak to you, or are you too tired?"

"Not at all," Kitty stifled a sudden yawn, and grinned at being caught, but she joined Clarissa in her chamber.

Kitty sat on the hassock, paying no attention to her ball gown, which was already sadly crushed. "Oh, my novel," she exclaimed, spying the papers on the escritoire. "Have you looked at it?"

"I am nearly finished reading it. Would you like an opinion now, or when I am done?"

"Oh, not now. Is that all? I know we're engaged to go riding in a few hours."

"Before they escape my mind I wished to put to you a pair of questions."

"Ask," Kitty said fervently. "You have been so good to me—"

"Please, no more of that. The pleasure has been entirely mine own. But, I confess a concern for your brother. I could not but help notice a healing wound on his arm, and having seen it, noticed that he favored the other. I trust there is nothing seriously amiss?"

Kitty laughed in relief. "Oh, that! Ned told me the other day, I forget, I think when we were walking. Carlisle makes nothing of it, but he and Ned carried out one last landing, and though it was a success, the landing was very rough, and Carlisle's hand was pinned between a barrel and the rail of the boat, where a splinter scored it. He is not materially hurt, and they will never go out smuggling again, but Ned said that this is why they were able to come to town."

"I see," Clarissa said. She found that she approved of this sign of sibling loyalty far more than she cared for a strict adherence to an unpopular law.

"Your second question?"

"Have you taken a dislike to my cousin Devereaux?"

Kitty stared blankly, her cheeks flaming. "Not at all! How did you—what made you think *that*?"

"I noticed a... a restraint in his presence, and hoped that he had done nothing to make you uncomfortable."

"Oh, not at all. It's just that I received a hint—advice—that I have been appearing forward, and that gentleman has been given a disgust for such behavior—"

"Nonsense," Clarissa said so sharply that Kitty blinked. "I beg your pardon. Your behavior is a very model of restraint. And if anything had been at fault, you may be sure that my mother, or I, would have long since shown you how to go on. Conversing with my cousin is hardly seen as forward behavior."

"Thank you," Kitty said, looking away.

Clarissa saw with surprise that betraying flush, and a new idea occurred to her.

Kitty was also thinking rapidly. So *this* explained why he had made no motions toward Clarissa. Having brothers, she had gained a different perspective on young men, and she said, "Though a great deal is said about female delicacy, the truth that I have discovered is that men are not born knowing how to court any more than women are. Perhaps, having been pursued so long, Mr. Devereaux actually does not know how to go about pursuing? If someone were to not care about his looks, and wealth, and so forth?"

"I think he would proceed with extreme caution, having spent most of his life as a topic for idle talk," Clarissa said. "So, if my cousin were to invite us both out for a drive to Hampstead, would you accept?"

"Gladly," Kitty said, and the young ladies parted, both with a better understanding—even if they did not quite understand the same things.

Twenty-five

"WHAT WAS THAT, KINGSTON?" Lord Wilburfolde sat up in bed and stared at his man, aghast.

"Your lordship, I said, if it pleases you, I should like leave to marry."

Lord Wilburfolde's first reaction was betrayal, and hard on that, the irritation of frustration. His mother had been correct in her warning that London only encouraged servants to gad about. If they were home, such goings-on never would occur.

"Why do you put me to this trouble?" Lord Wilburfolde muttered fretfully.

Of late he had wondered if his mother might be misinformed upon some points. For example, Clarissa never once turned up at death's door after any of Mother's dire warnings about sitting near open windows, or mixing among the lower orders in such dirty emporia as she liked to visit with her sisters.

He ran his fingers up and down the neat stitching that edged the sheet, as if the bumps would guide him toward what he ought to do. Here was Kingston, and Lord Wilburfolde knew what his mother would do. Any servant so presumptuous was instantly turned off without a character. Yet Kingston was so quiet, so perfect in every way. He knew how Lord Wilburfolde liked everything. He never had to *say* anything. Especially here in this noisy city, where disorder reigned over order, it was so comforting to return to his lodging and find everything waiting just so.

Kingston saw the ambivalence in his master's face and assumed his most deferential air. A fusspot Lord W. might be — and his mother a dragon — but the son could be managed, if one knew how to get over rough ground. "If I may be so bold, your lordship..."

Lord Wilburfolde, desperate for a way out, said, "Yes, Kingston?"

"My Bridget is under-maid to a milliner, but she's got a way with linens. Her mistress at the shop has even said no one has such deedy fingers. That very sheet, there, your lordship, she repaired it for me, when the laundry-maid brought it back with a rend, for it must be said, the linens are somewhat old."

"Her ladyship says they have years of use left in them," Lord Wilburfolde stated.

Kingston bowed. "Her ladyship's wisdom is a watchword among us, and we know her excellent, saving ways. But think of it this way, if I may be so bold, your lordship. You would be gaining another servant, not losing one. Surely, her ladyship would see the benefit in such a saving."

"Losing?" Lord Wilburfolde repeated, pouncing on the word that most concerned him.

Kingston bowed his head and assumed his most apologetic air. "I would very much regret having to give notice, your lordship. But I stood up in church and plighted my troth. There's no going against *that*."

"No indeed." Lord Wilburfolde gave a reluctant nod. Even his mother must acknowledge the greater claims of promises made before Providence.

He looked down at the edge of the sheet, and for the first time in his life, thought about the hands that had put in those even stitches. His imagination could not quite extend beyond those hands, except in the sense of convenience, and very convenient it would be to have someone so clever in the household. Surely his mother would think so. Would she not? He fretted under a renewal of that sense of betrayal. He anticipated his mother's extreme disapprobation, because she did not like servants marrying without her having been consulted, everything proper and with due attention to their betters.

Lord Wilburfolde plucked at the coverlet and sighed. He liked the notion of being married, once he'd become accustomed to it. Besides the obvious comforts, it would only improve matters if Clarissa and Mother would deal directly.

"I shall put the question to her ladyship," Lord Wilburfolde said.

"Pardon me, your lordship, but did you mean the *future* Lady Wilburfolde?"

Lord Wilburfolde stared, and the valet went smoothly on. "As head of your household—your future household—you of course must be the first consulted, but the new Lady Wilburfolde might welcome a thrifty, clever seamstress before she is put to the trouble of finding her own servants if you were wishful of establishing a separate household."

Lord Wilburfolde's first reaction was to deny being head of the household, as if his mother were listening from the next room, but then he bethought of the fact that legally, he *was* the head. The idea of a separate household was interesting, but he did not like to think about what his mother would say.

Kingston began straightening things about the room, and walked noiselessly out, leaving the question in the air.

Lord Wilburfolde was relieved. Tentatively, he tried out the idea of being head of a household. Perhaps he might begin as he would like to go on, with Clarissa. What would happen if he tried to tell her what he would like as head of their future household?

It was past time to return home, for he'd had enough of the metropolis. They could travel to Hampshire together. The presence of her maid and Kingston would make it perfectly respectable.

He moved to his desk to pen a note asking after her health. If she were well, he said, they might consult about important matters.

The light of day brought unsettling reflections to Clarissa's head, forming around the disclosure Kitty had made light of the night before. Why should the marquess and his brother risk their lives to gain the wherewithal to come to town, unless they had a purpose?

Impatient lovers would be understandable. But the reserve in St. Tarval's face when Lucretia Bouldeston had appeared could not have differed more from the expression Clarissa had met with when she accepted his offer to dance.

Was it possible that in some wise *she* had a part in his motive?

The first thought was of her fortune. Last year she had been pursued by fortune-hunters. The horror of such an idea seemed to argue for its being convincing. Clarissa reached for reason. First of all, how could St. Tarval know anything about her fortune? Who would have told him? She was fairly certain that Kitty did not have any idea.

She owed it to him and to Kitty not to leap to hasty conclusions. That (she realized with a sense of regret) would be to follow the somewhat absurd example of poor Andromeda in Kitty's novel, a thought Clarissa would never share out loud.

She began her day with determination to be rational and useful, but the first challenge to it came in the form of a note from her betrothed, saying that he wished to consult her about her departure from London for Hampshire.

She had always behaved with strict attention to delicacy and decorum, having been taught that the world would treat her with the same respect. Alas, it was not always so. Furthermore, the visit to Cavendish Square had served as a reminder that Grandmama had no scruples about speaking her mind. But no one could say she was not a lady.

Clarissa sat down and wrote to thank her betrothed for his solicitude, begged off because of an engagement that evening, and invited him to join their party on a ride the next morning, weather permitting. She folded the note and sent a footman to dispatch it so that it would arrive with the afternoon post.

Her mood did not lighten when Rosina pulled back the curtains to reveal a beautiful morning, the next day.

Rosina could see at a glance that something was disturbing her mistress. She knew that she would not hear the cause. Miss Harlowe never complained, though some felt she had reason a-plenty. So she talked cheerfully about the cake now baking, and

Pobrick's nephew, newly promoted in the stable, who had a way with horses."... and Becky has helped Alice ever so," Rosina added as she finished laying out Clarissa's morning dress.

Clarissa had not heard one word in ten, until her maid mentioned Alice, the Tarval Hall girl of all work who had been summarily promoted to lady's maid. Here was a chance to do some possible good at very little cost to anyone.

"Do you think Becky would like to work for Lady Kitty?" Clarissa asked.

Rosina clasped her hands. "I think she would like it above all things. At least while Lady Kitty is in town, for you know there is a deal more work to be got through in the season. We have all taken a hand, for poor Alice was in a state and did not know where to turn next."

"I will speak to Becky in the course of the morning, Rosina. Thank you for bringing it to my attention."

Clarissa threw back the covers and got out of bed. It was a strange thing, how the prospect of doing something for others could motivate one. Was there anyone who would put *her* first?

No, she could not let herself think like that. There could be no good in it. All the same, her mood remained uncertain as she shut out her sisters' high-spirited chatter at breakfast. Great was the anticipation of the younger two at the prospect of a visit from Bess Devereaux. She wondered how Kitty could express delight so sincerely, though she doubtless knew how the noise would increase with the addition of another volatile girl. But it was strange. Kitty never seemed to mind the girls, the noise, the high spirits.

Kitty admitted as much on the ride to Hyde Park. "Now that I know how I am to understand Elizabeth Devereaux, I have a great deal of sympathy. I expect it is because I was not so very different when I was fifteen."

"You could not have been so loud," Clarissa said, trusting in the safety of the crowded street not to be overheard.

Kitty chuckled. "True. But I might very well have been, had I sisters instead of a sickly grandmother who cherished her quiet."

It was then that Lord Wilburfolde appeared on his borrowed cob. He joined the ladies, scrupulous in his greetings and his queries after their health. It was very soon evident to both Kitty and Clarissa that he was wishing to speak to his betrothed. Kitty saw her brothers riding side by side, and hailed them with relief.

She turned her horse to joined them, before she became aware that the two riders behind them were Lord Arden and Mr. Devereaux, the latter of whom looked so very well on horseback. She could not define how, for the others were equally excellent riders, and one might say that a riding coat was a riding coat, but the fit of Mr. Devereaux's over his shoulders, the angle of his hat on his waving dark hair, even (she knew she must never utter such words aloud, but she felt it all the same) the line of his leg in the fawn-colored breeches, with the shiny boots coming up just so under the knee, his *tout ensemble* was altogether...

She mentally searched for a word to express how the sight of him made her feel as if her entire body had been turned into a fairy lamp, and someone had set a candle inside her. And when she glanced one more time, met his gaze, and he touched his hat before she quickly looked away, the candle brightened to sunlight.

He would make an excellent companion for Clarissa, she firmly reminded herself.

She urged her horse between her brothers as the parties combined. Mr. Devereaux dropped back to ride with Lord Arden, who was eyeing the pretty young ladies who passed by. This left Mr. Devereaux at leisure to observe Lady Kitty and her brothers, the three making so handsome a group they caught many an eye in passing. As usual, Lady Kitty appeared to be blithely unaware of the stir that she caused.

"London has agreed with my cousins, I apprehend," Lord Arden said to Mr. Devereaux, who bowed his agreement. He added thoughtfully, "Especially the distaff."

Mr. Devereaux sent an inquiring glance. "Would it be too inquisitive to ask if you've an interest there?"

Lord Arden looked startled. "Oh, no. That is, one wouldn't mind trying, if one weren't rung a peal over at any mention of their names. And," he lowered his voice, "if one were not sadly aware that one must look for a fortune."

Each gentleman took in Kitty's glowing complexion, the curl of her lips, the stylish habit that suited her charms. Lord Arden cast a sigh and contemplated the unfairness of a universe that seemed determined to place only the plainest and most awkward heiresses in his way.

The Decourceys were a startling contrast to the pair riding directly behind them, Clarissa riding stiffly, with heightened complexion, Lord Wilburfolde talking volubly. Occasional words floated back: "esteemed parent," "metropolis," "nuptials."

Mr. Devereaux was not certain, but he thought he caught a reference to *Hymen's saffron robes*. Clarissa interpolated each time the man paused to draw breath, "Ah, there is my grandmother's friend Lady Wimbourne," and "I beg pardon, but I must make my salute to General Bligh, who is connected to Hetty's new family," and once, "Oh, do but look at that delightful hound. I so admire that particular breed." All to no avail, it seemed.

The party reached the end of Rotten Row. The marquess and his siblings wheeled their horses, pulling to one side so that Lord Wilburfolde and Clarissa might have space to turn. In that moment Clarissa looked St. Tarval's way, her face expressive of longing — an expression Mr. Devereaux would have sworn was foreign to her quiet nature.

He drew his horse back, wondering what exactly happened at Tarval Hall?

He was not the only one aware of Clarissa's unhappy expression. Kitty sighed to herself, wondering how Lord Wilburfolde could be so oblivious to the effect he caused. She could not think of a way to rescue Clarissa without causing a stir.

But Mr. Devereaux did know. With such excellent address that none of the others were aware of how it came about, he contrived at a turning in the path to cause an interruption in the party.

Lord Arden instantly secured Lady Kitty's company to himself for a pleasant interval of flirtation, leaving the brothers and Lord Wilburfolde riding together, St. Tarval posing questions in order to get a better sense of this man Clarissa was expected to marry, and Lord Wilburfolde expatiating happily. In his own family, it was not often that he was the principal talker.

Mr. Devereaux did not like intrusions into his private life any more than his cousin did, but he now understood a great deal more about his cousin's inexplicable behavior this spring.

Riding next to Clarissa, under the protection of the others' conversations, he murmured, "I have often observed that marriage being used as a cure for the might-have-been is seldom successful. There are fewer errors in motivation more conducive to unhappiness than that." He then shifted to the masquerade ball their grandmother was planning, which kept her from having to reply.

Lord Wilburfolde talked of the extent of his property, enumerating exact numbers of acreage, cows, bushels, and parishioners. Carlisle sympathized with the pride of place; had he been asked, he would have provided similar facts, but he was not.

Edward privately wagered with himself how many times he would hear the words *my honored parent says*.

Lord Wilburfolde liked being the principal talker but his mood did not improve. Clarissa had *not* given him the expected assent to his insistence that she terminate her visit to the metropolis.

He was determined to carry his point, and this very day, so he was on the lookout for an opportunity to change places with her cousin. However, when the party did change, and he secured the place by Clarissa's side, he was frustrated in his intentions by presence of Clarissa's guest riding at her other side.

He was not witness to the look of anguish Clarissa threw at Kitty, and her voiceless plea, "Stay."

Kitty courageously embarked on a long conversation about hats. Mr. Devereaux observed all this with private amusement, and an increase in admiration for Lady Kitty's loyalty, while keeping a prudent distance.

So Lucretia, riding by in her mother's barouche, did not see him paying any attention to that country-mouse *Lady* Catherine Decourcey. But scarcely had she acknowledged her sense of justice when she glanced at St. Tarval, to discover him gazing steadily at...

At whom?

She turned all the way round in the carriage in an effort to see.

Her mother smartly rapped Lucretia's knuckles with her fan "What will people think, Lucretia, when you gawk like the veriest country bumpkin? You owe your father and me more than that..."

Lucretia ignored her, too amazed to retort. Why would St. Tarval be staring at that dowd Clarissa Harlowe like that?

She scarcely heard one word in twenty of her mother's scoldings all the way home.

Twenty-six

THE LORD WILBURFOLDE FOUND HIMSELF unequal to the task of hinting away the persistent Lady Catherine. Determined to establish himself as the head of his future household, he stayed at his post all the way to the stable, where he obliged the Chadwick stable hands to accommodate his cob. "I shall accompany you to the house," he stated to Clarissa, "as we have not finished our conversation." As he spoke, he glanced at Clarissa's guest.

Even that failed to divide the young ladies, and so the three of them walked in silence to Brook Street, no one speaking unless required to as the ladies paused in the vestibule to put off bonnets and gloves. Lord Wilburfolde relinquished his hat, his mood sorely vexed.

Clarissa led the way to the drawing room to discover it in the possession of Tildy, Eliza, and two schoolgirl friends who had been permitted to make a morning call. They were in the middle of a noisy game of Speculation, overseen by Miss Gill, the younger girls' governess.

Ordinarily Clarissa would have been amused by the startling change of smiles for sobriety when the girls first hailed Kitty then became aware of Lord Wilburfolde, who had politely permitted the ladies precede him into the room.

The girls scrambled to their feet to make their curtseys. "Good morning," the girls chorused, hastily echoed by their friends.

"Your lordship, Miss Clarissa," Miss Gill said in her nervous twitter. "Shall I remove the children to the schoolroom?"

Tildy proclaimed, "But Clarissa, Mama promised we could entertain Celeste and Margaret, and we are to have apple-tartlets to tea!" She indicated their best morning gowns, evidence that indeed, Lady Chadwick had sanctioned the girls' use of the parlor.

"Child," Lord Wilburfolde said heavily, venting his mounting frustration on Tildy. "What kind of example do you set to thus address your elders without your opinion having been sought?" Ordinarily he did not mind young persons, as long as they were presentable and quiet, but every moment he was in this house seemed to surround him with noise and disorder.

Tildy flushed, and muttered an apology.

Clarissa said, "We shall use the back parlor, Tildy. You and Eliza and your guests may bide here."

Lord Wilburfolde was left with nothing to say. Kitty observed the back of his neck reddening, and stepped out of the way. The last time she had witnessed Clarissa in this mood was when the latter had flung her cloak around Kitty and bade her to sit in the coach, the night the yacht sank. She followed the betrothed pair, wondering if she should stay or go.

The back parlor proved to be occupied by Lady Chadwick and Mrs. Latchmore. The latter immediately entreated her favorite to join them, enabling the gentleman to say, with a glower at Kitty, "Thank you Ma'am, for your kind invitation, but I entered this premises with the intention of begging a moment's private conversation with Miss Harlowe."

Kitty flushed, apologetically meeting Clarissa's gaze.

"In that case," Clarissa said, still using that crisp voice, "we shall repair to the schoolroom. Thank you, Kitty, for your company."

Kitty nodded, flicked a polite curtsey to Lord Wilburfolde, and retreated to her room.

Up one more flight of stairs Clarissa trod, her lips tightened against an exclamation. Her head throbbed; rudeness to Kitty was the last straw.

They entered a sunny room redolent of apple juice and chalk dust, the sturdy, much-used tables and chairs too small for a grown man. Clarissa moved to the window to open it she said,

"Would you care to sit?"

He frowned at the battered furniture. "I am comfortable standing, for I only intend to remain a moment." And he delivered himself of the much-interrupted speech that he had been formulating, and practicing, all through the morning.

She listened without speaking.

He reached the end, and as she was still silent, he said, "Pray inform me when it will be convenient for our departure from the metropolis? I should like to give orders as soon as I may."

"When my father desires us to leave, of course."

Lord Wilburfolde stared. "But I just represented to you the reasons why, with my great respect for your family, you ought to bring your visit to a close. We could save considerable money traveling together. With your maid along, no one would question an affianced pair—"

"I beg your pardon for interrupting, but I feel I ought to assure you that you were most clear, Lord Wilburfolde. But I intend to remain with my family until our customary time of departure."

"I do not understand why," he exclaimed.

"If we exclude my duty to my guest, there is also my family who have a claim on my time."

He fidgeted with his gloves, angry and frustrated. "I believe," he said, "that an affianced man should not have to remind his betrothed that his claims ought to be put before anyone else's."

"And what about her claims?" Clarissa asked so softly he almost did not hear the words.

"Her claims? Lady Catherine may return home, or stay as your mother's guest. I see no claims here," he said.

"I meant the claims of the bride."

"The bride?" he repeated, hands out. "What claims? A lady brings to her marriage her good name and her dowry, and the gentleman endows her with his good name, his family, and all his worldly goods. What claims can she make?"

"Put that way," she said slowly, "it places the blame squarely on the woman who is not grateful for the bestowing of your family and worldly goods. But there is no gratitude in my heart. No more can I relinquish my soul in taking your good name, sir, and so..." Her heart beat in her ears. "... And so I must inform you that I find that I cannot consent to wear that name."

Exhilaration thrilled through her, coupled with a sense of recklessness that she usually only felt on horseback; yet she was not flying on the back of a galloping horse, she stood right here in this dusty room. She went on more firmly. "If you believe that your claims ought to be put before my family's, and I believe my duty requires me to put my family before all else, then we have reached an impasse that might be insurmountable."

"Insurmountable," he repeated, wondering how he could state his case the more strongly.

"By that I mean that we had better put an end to this engagement."

"Miss Harlowe! You can't do that," he exclaimed, thoroughly appalled. "The papers — the neighbors — my mother — "

She had said the words and the sky had not fallen. But she had never feared the malice of the stars. "Surely your mother will find you a more biddable wife, Lord Wilburfolde. I am very sorry if I have given you pain, but on reflection, I believe that we do not suit."

"I — I — "

"You have only to send a notice to the papers that our engagement it at an end, and then you may ride home as soon as may be, and you will be comfortable again," she said kindly. Oh, how good it felt to be free!

Lord Wilburfolde felt himself to be caught in a nightmare. First his valet wanting to marry, and now this! He managed a bow, and put his hand to the door.

She did not call him back.

As soon as he was gone, Kitty entered the room, her eyes widening when she took in Clarissa's flushed face, her odd smile. "Clarissa?" she ventured.

"I did it. I jilted him," Clarissa said, and sat down on a battered chair meant for a ten year old, and laughed breathlessly. "I should write his mother and thank her for reconciling me to the life of single blessedness, for she claims she lives to be useful. But, however, it is all too likely that she would write back." She laughed unsteadily. "I had better talk to my father."

"I believe I heard him in the breakfast room," Kitty said.

Clarissa went straightaway downstairs, her heart still beating fast. There she found her father just finishing breakfast. He gave a great yawn as the butler took away the coffee things. "You down here to escape those girls, too?"

"Papa, I must speak to you." Clarissa said.

A thumping overhead, and the faint sound of shrill voices caused him to say, "Let us repair to the book room."

She followed him to his own chamber, about which the odor of cigars hung. The room was dark, and backward-facing, not that Lord Chadwick cared for that. Against one wall stood a bookshelf of untouched volumes, and the other walls were decorated with sporting prints. Dominating the room was a green baize-topped table with four deep chairs set around it.

Lord Chadwick sank into one and Clarissa took a stance before him. "Papa, I have just parted with Lord Wilburfolde."

"In the schoolroom? Where's he gone?" Lord Chadwick swiveled his entire body around so as not to crease his shirt points.

"I am no longer to be married."

Lord Chadwick gave what in a lesser man would be termed a vulgar whistle. "Not just a tiff, eh?"

"I'm sorry, Papa, but I do not believe we would suit."

He stared at her for a long moment, then grunted. "I'd begun to wonder if it would be a good thing, after all."

"What, Papa?"

"T'other day, at luncheon. Young Wilburfolde said he wasn't used to the chatter of girls, and I thought, of what use is it to have one of you married, if you can't fire off the rest of your sisters? I'd thought Hetty would do that, but she's already increasing, and sicker than your step-mother was. And a fortnight past I invited him to a snug little card-party, thought I'd do the fatherly, and he mouthed out long periods about how iniquitous card playing is."

Clarissa found her emotions in that uncertain balance between amusement and exasperation. "Why did you not speak up, Papa?"

He blinked in honest surprise. "Thought you might've approved. Never seen you gambling."

"I have no interest in such things, but I've no objection to others who do."

"Well, you've always known your own mind. Fact is, the more

I saw of him, the more I wondered how it would be. But there's also the fact," he added, "that a girl your age don't hand a fellow his hat without some reason. Nobody'll offer now, so I expect you're back on my hands for good. Which is as well for the younger girls. Try as she might, your aunt seems to have no influence over them."

Clarissa then took her leave, and with a great sense of lightness, turned her mind to enjoying the afternoon before readying herself for Almack's that night.

Those sensations of lightness resolved into gratitude and determination. So she was destined for a life of single blessedness. She was aware of a qualitative difference between isolation and connection to others. Cousin Philip's concern, her grandmother's rough sympathy, and above all Kitty's steady friendship, all had contributed to bolstering her courage.

With the idea of repaying Kitty in mind, Clarissa sat down and determinedly read through the rest of the manuscript pages while Kitty was out walking with the younger girls in the park.

On her return, they sat down to dinner, and Clarissa was able to say to Kitty, "I have finished reading."

Kitty's eyelids flashed up. She said nothing before the family, but Clarissa perceived her strictly controlled excitement.

Directly following dinner, the two repaired to Clarissa's bedchamber, where she returned the pages to their author. Kitty clasped the manuscript to her bosom and said breathlessly, "What did you think?"

"I think it is as good as any I have read, and in some ways I like it better, because there are some things which made me laugh," Clarissa said slowly.

"Are there too many dramatic scenes? Carlisle once said he feared that I might have too many abductions, but I did not know how else is she to get about!"

"These sorts of stories always employ such devices as abductions. There must be excitement, I perceive, and I do not know how else to get it in except by such methods. I have only two suggestions, and I offer them without confidence. I am no writer."

Kitty ducked her head, her eyes wide in mute appeal.

"The first you have acknowledged yourself. The clothing and

some of the expressions need alteration to make them more modish. But I also think you might consider a bit more description of the mysterious Duke whom I gather is to be Andromeda's savior and lover. The text repeats many times that he is the handsomest of men, and the best at whatever he does, but I get no sense of him. What kind of a man is he, besides the best? What does he look like, other than the most striking of men?"

Kitty's hands had tightened on the pages until she became aware she was crushing them. She was so afraid Clarissa would tell her it was impossible. Kitty could see no other way to a fortune, and *somehow* she must help her brothers. She set no store by Carlisle's promise not to smuggle anymore. She was afraid he would take any risk if it were to benefit St. Tarval.

Clarissa went on to praise many of the scenes, but Kitty heard the kindness in her voice, the effort to please, and her thought stayed with the criticisms, which she had to acknowledge were just.

This went on until a scratch on the door was followed by Rosina reminding them it was time to dress. Kitty thanked Clarissa profusely, and returned to her room to ready herself for Almack's.

They departed soon after, and so deep was the need for reflection that the only person talking was Amelia, who surprised everyone by twice pointing out the historical significance of the street they were riding along. "It is such a strange thing to think of," she commented. "It seems as if London has always been the way we see it. But even our grandmothers saw a different London, when there was no Almack's, or rather, it was different. No one would go to Ranelagh now, but not so long ago it was all the crack."

"Amelia!" Mrs. Latchmore scolded. "Where have you been hearing such language? You do us no credit by employing vulgar expressions."

That effectively silenced conversation, as the coachman jogged the carriage into the long line. Each of the young ladies fell into reverie, and Mrs. Latchmore sat back in triumph, feeling that she had carried her point.

Ahead of them in the long line was the Bouldestons' carriage. After some conversation with the baronet, Lady Bouldeston had sent an invitation to St. Tarval and his brother as well as to Mr. Aston, inviting them all to a family dinner, and to ride with them to the Wednesday ball at Almack's as neither Mr. Aston nor the Decourceys kept a carriage.

This invitation had been settled upon by Sir Henry and Lady Bouldeston as the surest means of indicating their approbation of the prospective connections. Mr. Aston's tendency to interrupt the dinner conversation with somewhat ponderous effusions of his poetic afflatus were disconcerting, but a reflection upon his family's wealth enabled the elder Bouldestons — neither of whom had the least interest in poesy — to look upon his efforts with complacency.

As for the marquess, though they would rather see their daughter married to a man of wealth and influence, there was no doubting his rank, the extent of his lands, nor the fact that he looked well at their table.

Lucretia was cognizant of the fact that a marquess joining their party at Almack's would appear well. Carlisle himself was prepossessing enough, though he hadn't the modish elegance or the chiseled features of Mr. Devereaux.

And that was the trouble, she thought as they entered the establishment, trading the odors of horse and coal smoke from the street for the scents of beeswax candles, perfumes, and pomade. What was the use in being married to a marquess if you were consigned to a tumbledown barrack in which you could not afford to entertain properly, so there was no one to give way before you but a pack of servants?

Her mother, as always, had brought them early that they might secure the best place from which to observe the arrivals. Lucretia took care to keep a little distance from Carlisle, so that when Mr. Devereaux arrived — and last year she would not have expected him to look in at Almack's but once — he might see them near one another, but not too near. She wanted to inspire jealousy, not hopelessness.

There was another reason to station herself at an advantageous position, to witness Carlisle's expression when Miss Harlowe arrived, for *that* family *always* attended the balls.

Catherine's obviousness in her desperation to throw herself at any man could be understood and pitied. Less understandable was Mr. Devereaux's tolerance, for he was known to be a high stickler, but of course he would be forbearing to his cousin's friend. However, what could possibly inspire Carlisle to study Miss Harlowe so intently? Men were such simpletons, they did not know where they would be at.

Selfish simpletons, Lucretia thought as she spied Miss Fordham, and ascertained that she was not wearing that hideous lilac gown that clashed so with her own delicate pinks. It was always better to walk about with a friend.

She greeted Miss Fordham, and had just suggested a stroll about the room when the Chadwick party arrived. Lucretia, on the pretence of adjusting her hem, turned so that Miss Fordham's curious eyes would be safely otherwise, and glanced past her shoulder at Carlisle, whose head came up. He stilled.

Lucretia sought Miss Harlowe, whose sallow cheeks flew two spots of color as she met his gaze and then looked away.

What could *that* possibly portend? Nothing good.

And not five minutes after, Mr. Devereaux appeared. Miss Fordham said insinuatingly, "I trust the gentlemen at Watier's have not wagered on his making an appearance so many times this season. In what quarter sits the wind that draws him hither, do you suppose?" Her tone was decidedly mocking. Insufferable girl!

Lucretia put down her spleen to jealousy, for Mr. Devereaux had never asked *Sophia Fordham* to dance. He could be harboring no secret inclination for so sour a female. Safe in the recollection of that never-to-be-forgotten dance at Lady Castlereagh's, Lucretia cast down her eyes modestly, and said, "I have no idea."

As she continued to walk arm in arm with Miss Fordham, she was busy turning over plans. Not only did she need to help along the gossip about Catherine's desperation to insure a disgust in high sticklers such as Mr. Devereaux, but an end must be put to Carlisle's disloyal propensities. Could she tie the two together, and perhaps prompt Mr. Devereaux to action at last?

Twenty-seven

IN THE HARLOWE HOUSEHOLD, the only persons who habitually read the newspapers were Lord Chadwick, who never paid any attention to personal announcements, and Lady Chadwick, who occasionally did, when there were no letters to be read. That usually meant during winter.

Clarissa seldom read newspapers, especially while in town. She did search the morning paper following the breaking of her engagement, noting with satisfaction that Lord Wilburfolde had indeed inserted the notice. She went about her day feeling as if she had woken from deep winter and here it was, spring. She and Kitty went to exchange books at the lending library, returning scarce moments before the rain moved in.

Two days of heavy rain followed, preventing many from going out. Miss Gill had caught a cold, and so Clarissa supervised the younger girls, with Kitty's willing aid.

They were confined inside, but our heroes were not. Mr. Devereaux had gone to Bath, and St. Tarval had to ride home to see to pressing estate matters.

The marquess arrived back in Grosvenor Street late at night. The next day the weather began to show signs of clearing, but the rain was sufficient to keep many at home. St Tarval and his brother used the opportunity to go over the entire house with the elderly butler who escorted them from room to room, reminiscing about past events.

The marquess had begun this tour with an idea of seeing what must be done in order to sell the place, but as old Mathews related stories about doings of past Decourceys back in Queen Anne's time, and even during the time of Charles, when the house was first built—St. Tarval discovered in himself a regret, even the stirrings of family-feeling. What might it be like to live in London for a time each year, if he had his own family? If he was side by side with someone like Clarissa Harlowe, with whom he had only to exchange a private smile to discover a shared sensibility?

How would it be to attend the theater with her, and to voice their opinions without the constraint of bored relatives, or the earnest lectures of...

He must not permit that direction to his thoughts.

"Phew, the dust," Edward said when the tour was ended. He brushed his arms vigorously. "There's a deal of work to be done, first, or we won't get twopence. Should we look into that while we're here?"

"Let us wait," St. Tarval said.

Edward observed his elder brother's thoughtful brow, and hoped he wasn't thinking of Miss Harlowe. Edward could see no good ending there. That Wilburfolde fellow was not likely to throw Clarissa over for anyone else. He was far more likely to stick like a burr.

What a sorry world, Edward thought as he went down to the dining room, where had been laid a cold collation for the midday meal.

On the sideboard the newspapers had stacked up unread, along with a pile of bills and invitations. Not being a reading man, Edward left the latter to his brother to deal with, and picked up the first of the newspapers. As always, he glanced at the political news—Mr. Fox, Pitt, more about Boney and something or other having to do with the West Indies—and went straight to the personal announcements. The first thing that met his eye sent him straight upstairs again.

"Carl!" He burst in on his brother, who sat at his desk, frowning over accounts. Edward stabbed his finger at the news item. "There's some sorry news about how Lord W— and Miss H—are no longer to be entered in the Hymeneal rolls. What does that *mean*, Hymeneal? No, don't tell me."

St. Tarval had thrown down his pen. "Let me see that." He turned his eye to the print below his brother's pointing finger, and indeed, the words he had never let himself hope to see were there for all the world.

"What are you waiting for?" Ned declared.

"Ned. I cannot possibly force myself on her a day after this notice appeared."

Ned glanced at the top of the paper, then tossed it aside. "Actually two days. This one came out the day you rode down to Tarval Hall. But I take your point. You ought to go to Brook Street and spy out the territory."

"Spy out," St. Tarval said, laughing. "There is still Lucretia, with whom I am honor-bound to reach agreement, even if it were proper to address another lady first. Which it isn't. However, one of my tasks was at Kitty's direction. I was going to send her parcel around, but why not deliver it ourselves, and see how she does?"

He could not prevent the exhilaration of hope, which brightened even the age-dulled hangings and outmoded furnishings of the room. Surely Lucretia could be brought round? She couldn't possibly still want to marry him—she'd stayed busy on the other side of the room the entire night they attended Almack's.

"Good," Ned said. And then, with a burst of generosity, "I'll come along with you. Keep Kit busy, so you may talk to Miss Harlowe without interruption. You don't have to bring up marriage."

With this laudable intention, the two changed their clothes, picked up the parcel, and hailed a hackney.

Mr. Devereaux and his sister appeared in Brook Street as the family sat down to a late breakfast. Mr. Devereaux and his sister had arrived in London late the previous evening, and that morning she had awoken bright and early, insisting she would expire if she must wait a moment longer to see her dear friend Eliza.

She was Bess again, having declared that it would be *too trying* to be Elizabeth in a household with an Eliza, and anyway, Arabella Campbell had made such a piece of work about "Queen Elizabeth" and "fine ladies."

And so, with a maximum of noise, Bess descended upon the Harlowes, amid bandboxes, trunks, and transports of felicity as only young girls can express them. The girls raced upstairs, everyone talking at once — Bess, being accustomed to making herself heard among the other girls at her seminary, the most indefatigable talker.

Clarissa and Kitty quietly withdrew to the back parlor, Kitty to write more of her novel, and Clarissa to face the task of responding to the small spate of consolatory letters that had arrived consequent to the news of her broken engagement.

Most of the letters filled out the space with conventional expressions and unasked-for advice, but her grandmother's made her smile ruefully: *I am well Pleas'd that you recover'd your Wits. Do not lose them again!*

The marquess and Ned found them so employed when they arrived. No one was about to notice the addition of a large parcel to the numerous bags and trunks already waiting to be carried upstairs. One of the footmen was dispatched with the parcel upstairs, under Rosina's direction, to deposit it safely in Kitty's bedchamber, as Pobrick opened the door to the back parlor to call out the names of the visitors.

Kitty and Clarissa looked up with warm smiles of welcome.

The world regarded Kitty as the prettier of the two but St. Tarval could see nothing past Clarissa's quick, heartfelt smile.

Edward saw that smile as well. He professed not to know anything about romance (and his venture into the mysteries of romance was confined to some kisses exchanged with an enterprising milk maid who ambushed him when he turned sixteen, and a joking, uncertain flirtation with the squire's horse-riding daughter after church of a Sunday) but he would have laid down a thousand pounds on Clarissa Harlowe returning Carlisle's regard.

He liked Miss Harlowe almost as strongly as he disliked Lucretia Bouldeston. How to get two reticent people to declare themselves? As the others exchanged the polite nothings of a morning call, Edward looked about for a subject to keep his sister occupied. When he spied Kitty's book, he said, "Ah! Still scribbling away?"

Kitty flushed, but was not averse to talking about a subject Ned had shown no interest in before. Edward drew his chair closer, and said bravely, "What is it about?"

Kitty would admit to no one that the work of rewriting had become more drudgery than inspiration. But she was determined not to be a charge upon her brother. Why, if she were successful, not only might she help discharge the debts of the estate, but she could come to London again!

So she launched into a detailed summary of her novel, as Clarissa and St. Tarval established that the weather was excellent, and each other's health was good. Then they reached a slight impasse, for neither felt it right to reveal what lay in their hearts.

And so he said, "One of the tasks I had to accomplish was to execute a commission for Kitty, in preparation for her grace's masquerade ball. To which we are also invited. Have we you to thank for the distinction of our invitation?"

"If it is a distinction," she said, smiling. "But you need not thank me. I believe my grandmother discovered by some other means that you and Lord Edward were arrived in town. Kitty and I called on her not too long ago, and she took a liking to your sister. So you may credit Kitty with such distinction as exists."

The marquess glanced Kitty's way, and overheard enough to cause him to exclaim, "I would not interrupt her for the world."

He was such a good brother, Clarissa thought, her eyes stinging. Her heart was so full, another moment and she feared she would betray herself.

He was struggling under similar sensations. He hitched his chair a little closer, reaching for words that would be acceptable, yet still express what he felt, when a shriek from downstairs startled them all.

A moment later the door banged open, and Amelia raced in, waving a folded newspaper under Kitty's nose. Then she saw who had arrived, and whirled to face the surprised St. Tarval.

"Why did you not tell us? You might have — we could have hosted a party!"

Amelia stammered out her felicitations to the stunned marquess as Kitty's astonished gaze and Clarissa's stricken one took in the words:

A marriage has been arranged between Carlisle Claudius Stephen Decourcey, Marquess of St. Tarval, and Miss Lucretia Augusta, elder daughter of Sir Henry Bouldeston, Bart.

Twenty-eight

ST. TARVAL HAD TO MAKE his way past the entire Bouldeston
family before he could speak to Lucretia.

Lady Bouldeston was in the parlor. She greeted him pleasantly
enough, but he had begun their acquaintance years ago being
made to feel as if he were a grubby schoolboy. On reaching adult-
hood, he had come to see that she regarded the entire world with
that air of cynical disappointment.

"Ah, St. Tarval, you are finally here. You will wish to speak to
Sir Henry, I know," she said with a languid wave of her hand. "He
will be downstairs anon. You'll find the girls in the young ladies'
parlor."

St. Tarval passed Sir Henry on the narrow stairs. Sir Henry
blinked rapidly, his gaze red and bleary. "Lucretia tells me you're
impatient to get it done. Well, well, my boy. All my life I've wished that I could break the entail, but never more so than now. You
two might not have a penny to bless yourselves with, but at least
you come together with no surprises."

With a friendly clap on St. Tarval's shoulder, and a gust of
whiskey-laden breath that made the marquess's eyes water, he
passed on by.

St. Tarval heard shrill voices coming through the door of the
young ladies' parlor. Lucasta's rose higher. "...think yourself so
superior, Lucretia, when you have not managed to attach anyone

beyond Carlisle Decourcey. Yes, he has a very grand title, but as for *your ladyship*, and your entering any room before Mama and me when I am Mrs. Aston, very grand indeed will you be in your ramshackle dining room, served three peas apiece on that horrid plate that was out of fashion at the time of Queen Anne!"

The door was wrenched violently open and Lucasta nearly ran St. Tarval down. She brought herself up short, hiccupped tearily, and said in a quick rush, "I feel sorry for you, Carlisle, even if you wear a shabby coat. *You* have always been kind."

She did not wait for an answer, but pushed on past and all he saw was a flurry of skirts as she bolted upstairs.

St. Tarval entered the parlor to discover his betrothed sitting in a chair, arms crossed. She wore as always a pretty pink gown covered in ribbons and furbelows, but as he looked across the room it struck him that in ten years Lucretia would resemble her mother.

"The notice in the paper. How could you do that, Lucretia?" he asked, closing the door behind him.

Her chin jerked up, and her mouth tightened. The resemblance to her mother was pronounced. "I have been faithful to our under-standing, sir," she declared breathlessly, and daubed at her dry eyes with a handkerchief. "Are you here to confess that you dare to trifle with my affections?"

"Trifle with *what?*" The marquess said with asperity, "Lucretia, we're alone. If you know nothing else about me, you do know that I tell the truth. When I told you that summer that I could not marry until I had settled my father's debts, I meant it."

Lucretia tossed her head. "So that's why I saw you making eyes at Miss Harlowe? You would throw me over to gain her fortune?"

St. Tarval was so stunned and infuriated that he could not speak for a long moment. Lucretia glared at him in angry triumph. So there *had been* something in those looks.

"We will leave the lady's name out of this," he said softly.

She tossed her head again, enraged at the very idea that he could actually prefer that dowd. "Or what? You'll challenge me to a duel?"

"Or I will send a notice to the papers that the announcement of our betrothal was in error," he said.

Fear chilled her rage. "You cannot do that."

"I can."

"The world will condemn you..." She hesitated, knowing who would really be the target of scorn.

"I do not care what the world says about me," he stated. "As I am unlikely ever to return to the world of London." Guilt assailed him at her blanched expression of fear. He would willfully hurt no creature weaker than he, and at one time he truly had been fond of Lucretia. He asked more quietly, "Why did you cause your father to insert that notice into the paper?"

"I sent you a note asking you to call," she said, some of the heat returning to her voice. "These three days at least."

"I had to ride down to Kent," he said. "There was business that could not wait. You know that I am my own steward, and there are some matters that Kirby cannot compass, but we'll leave that. You could not wait three days?"

Lucretia tightened her arms across her chest. "That selfish, *stupid* sister of mine is likely to contract a marriage with that blockhead Aston. I could not *bear* the thought that my sister would marry before me. The entire world will be laughing behind their fans."

"I am sorry for it, if that is true. But you must see that you owed it to us both to talk to me first."

"Just to be put off for another half-dozen years?"

"It might take that long to recover. You yourself know what it is to live under the weight of a father's debt."

Lucretia made play with the handkerchief again, mostly to gain time. Her anger had been cooled by fear, which was tempered by relief. It appeared that she had carried her point. Carlisle was not repudiating the engagement outright. The six years before they could marry could only be considered beneficial. It gave her time, for she was determined to encourage Mr. Devereaux. She closed her eyes, reveling in the image of herself a duchess.

She just needed time.

She opened her eyes, and gave Carlisle her sweetest smile. She must say something conciliatory and send him away in a better frame of mind.

He noted the subsiding of anger, and her smile. If she were Kitty, that attempted smile would be her way of putting a brave face on disappointment. Surely Lucretia could not be so very different. She was a female, and close to the same age. They must share some emotions, even if they differed in point of personality.

The hard truth that he must face was that Lucretia's remark about Clarissa must also be shared by the world. If Lucretia could leap to such a conclusion from afar, what must Clarissa's relations think were he to make his wishes known?

He was very certain that Clarissa herself did not feel the same. Though he was not coxcomb enough to assume that she was in love with him without the lady speaking for herself, he was certain he could not have been mistaken in the warmth of her smile, her readiness to dance with him. This accursed notice could not have come at a worse time!

Yet even if it had not, he must face the fact that the world must think him mercenary. Lord Chadwick seemed a genial fellow, but that might change if he saw in Kitty's brother a fortune hunter.

"There is much in what you say," Lucretia observed in a coaxing voice. "It seems a wise decision to wait upon events. I know I cannot bring a respectable dowry to any marriage, and so I believe it is my duty to bide until affairs are more propitious. I cannot pretend to understand such things."

The marquess perceived this much: she agreed to give him time.

She had been watching him carefully. Seeing the signs that he was relenting, she lisped in her sweetest voice, "I told Mama that, given the circumstances, a betrothal party might not be the thing, and so we might make it a musical party instead, a general party. You will find the invitation among those notes that you did not see. The party is for three days hence. That will enable Lucasta and Mr. Aston to shine their particular lights."

He hesitated, the desire to speak the truth nearly over-whelming. Fortune hunter—Sir Henry as neighbor—that stupid promise he'd made six years ago—he forced himself to say what was expected, and took his leave.

Lucretia's chief motivation for talking her parents into hosting a musical party was ostensibly to show off Lucasta's accomplishments, but in truth it was to be a family party, which would enable them to include along with the older Harlowe girls their guest, Bess Devereaux. Lucretia had learnt through Lucasta that Mr. Devereaux's sister had musical pretensions. And from thence it was quite natural to send an invitation to *him*.

Once this schoolgirl had been visiting in Mount Street, even if her brother did not accompany her, it would be quite natural to include him in subsequent invitations, and as an engaged woman, Lucretia would not be perceived to be on the catch, as the vulgar termed it. She simply had to make certain that it was evident her intended marriage was not a love match—that a jealous admirer might with impunity sweep her off her feet.

Already there were unexpected benefits to the engagement with St. Tarval. First of all, Papa must quit himself of recommending his daughters to particular cronies, like that horrid Mr. Redding, or old Lord Penwick. While both were wealthy, there their recommendations ended, the one having an unsavory reputation, and the other his advanced age.

Then there was the invitation to the Duchess of Norcaster's masquerade ball. The duchess herself wrote, begging pardon for the lateness of the invitation. In her old-fashioned handwriting that made f into s in the middle of words, she praised the Decourcey family, and wished to extend her welcome to their prospective connections.

The Bouldestons had never before attained such select company, and their mother was in a fit of temper over how to contrive suitably sumptuous masquerade costume. No dowdy dominos for them, Lucasta exulted, dancing the invitation round the room.

Lucretia agreed fervently, for Mr. Devereaux was sure to be there.

Lucretia wore one of her finest gowns the night of the musical party, and when St. Tarval arrived, she acted the fond part of the future wife so that when the Harlowe party arrived with Bess

Devereaux, she quite naturally crossed to the other side of the room. Bess must not see them together, and report it to her brother, whose name was not announced.

Lucretia had no interest in music at any time. She sang when it was her turn, but she had long since discovered that no one but her mother enjoyed her singing, an observation that simpleton Lucasta had yet to make. Two songs only she sang, and then she made a little business of modestly retiring. As always, only her mother called for more.

Then Lucasta took over, Mr. Aston leaping up to turn pages for her, though his shirt points were so high that Lucretia wondered if he could even see the music for the blinkers at either side of his foolish face. But Lucasta was so busy rolling her eyes and striking absurd attitudes that she neither observed her ridiculous swain nor the boredom of her audience.

Lucretia occupied herself with that tiresome brat Bess Devereaux, offering her the most favorable place in the room, and constantly pressing refreshments on her, then seeing to it she took her turn at the instrument, turning the pages for her, and leading the applause. So why did the chit sit there like a stuffed owl?

Lucretia's third piece of business was to introduce Catherine to Lord Penwick, just as the singing began. But when Catherine, after rising to get a glass of lemonade between songs, chose another seat, Mr. Redding took the one next to her, and exerted himself to win her smiles with the sorts of compliments ladies liked. He cared too little for what might go on inside the heads of beauties to notice that Kitty's flush was not one of pleasure. His interest was not in their heads.

It can safely be said that no one enjoyed the music other than Lucasta, Mr. Aston, and Lady Bouldeston, who liked seeing her girls the center of attention. Bess only enjoyed playing, but not with Lucasta's horrid sister standing so close.

A convenient clap of thunder brought the evening to a close, everyone claiming they must get home before the impending storm broke.

Kitty's complaint about that horrid Mr. Redding, ready to be aired the moment they got outside, died when she saw the familiar tension in Clarissa's brow. "Headache?" she asked, reflecting that

Clarissa had not betrayed that faint wince once in the days since her break with Lord Wilburfolde.

"A little," Clarissa admitted, and then, as she always did, "It will pass off presently. Fresh air is beneficial," she added as they stepped into the street.

Kitty loved London, but she had to smile at the idea of the sooty air being fresh, so still and warm it was, not to mention the odor left by the horses passing up Mount Street. Lightning flared somewhere to the south; the air was heavy with that peculiar stillness before a storm, but as yet no rain fell.

As they walked down to where their carriages waited, Clarissa murmured, "You did not appear to be pleased with your place."

"I don't know why, but I do *not* like that Mr. Redding. He smiles too much, he sat too close, and even though the music was indifferent, I would rather have listened than to be whispered to, and to have to thank the man again and again for compliments I would as lief not have received. There! Scold me for being impossible to please."

Clarissa shook her head slowly. "I would not do so." The only good thing she had heard about Mr. Redding was that he was not a fortune hunter, but as everything else was gossip, she did not say more.

When everyone reached Brook Street and rejoined in the Parlor, Amelia greeted Kitty with a scowl. "I do not blame you a bit, Lady Kitty, for changing your seat, but it was a hard thing to have that horrid Lord Penwick patting my hand through Lucasta's caterwauling. Why, his son is older than Papa!"

Mrs. Latchmore exclaimed against that, then added, "Lord Penwick is extremely well-to-live, I will remind you."

"With nine children to provide for?"

"Even so," Mrs. Latchmore said. "And a new Lady Penwick would never have to see them. The elder two are married, and the younger ones can be left in the country. Lord Penwick has a very fine house in Grosvenor Square, and it is said that he is looking in particular for a young wife."

"He's *old*," Amelia stated in disgust.

"It is said that an older man makes an excellent husband," Mrs. Latchmore chided.

"Then *you* marry him, Aunt."

This unfortunate remark caused a spurt of laughter, which sufficed to bring down a scold upon all their heads. Mrs. Latchmore left, adjuring them to improve their thinking, or they would never find husbands.

As soon as the door was shut, Amelia heaved a loud sigh. "Was not Lucasta's singing hideous, Bess?"

"Oh, I am well enough accustomed to Lucasta's airs, always rolling her eyes in that die-away manner, and pretending to faint as she squeaks those high notes, but my brother said not to blame her for she's probably tone deaf, and though I think him tiresome all the time, there are moments when he's right, for she can*not* seem to hit any note true. What frightened *me* was the way Miss Lucretia danced about piling my plate with food, and asking if I should like another cushion, or a better chair, and then breathing down my headdress when I played. After all of Lucasta's stories about the mean things her sister does to her, I kept expecting a frog to jump out of a pastry, or a goldfish to be swimming in that punch, or her to drop a spider down my dress while I played."

"That was very odd," Amelia said. "I noticed it as well."

"At least it is over," Bess said with an air of casting off a great burden. "Now we may be comfortable."

As Kitty and Clarissa walked upstairs toward their bedchambers, Kitty looked with worry at her friend, who had not spoken a single word since their arrival home. She said tentatively, "I do so hope your headache is gone by tomorrow."

Clarissa looked up in an absent manner. "Tomorrow?"

Kitty stared. "We are to accompany your cousin to Hampstead."

Clarissa's indifference astounded Kitty when she said, "Is that tomorrow, already? I had forgotten."

Kitty wished her a good night and passed into her bedchamber, not knowing what to think. She had fully intended, now that Clarissa was free, to encourage Clarissa and her cousin. For days she had thought out every aspect of this prospective outing, but always with the idea of self-sacrifice so that the other two might be alone to speak.

She knew that Clarissa would be hurt if she suspected they

shared, besides friendship, a...Kitty dared not call it love. Outside of the impassioned words of romance, she was not quite certain what love truly *was*. Call it a shared *regard* for Mr. Devereaux.

I am going to enjoy this outing, she decided as she climbed into bed. *But I will not put on my new carriage dress, in preference to the old. I do not want to be noticed.*

The next morning, Clarissa appeared to have woken in a better frame of mind. She had put on her new royal blue carriage dress, the one Kitty had talked her into buying. It looked well with her pale complexion and brought out the warm tones in her hair under the pretty ribboned hat. A pair of tan gloves completed a modish toilette.

For Clarissa had remembered the idea that had once occurred to her, to be forgotten in the wake of other events. A little guilt had attended the realization that Kitty demonstrated more interest in a mere carriage ride than one might warrant, but then Clarissa had never set herself up for penetration into secrets and motives after the sometimes cruel, and often vulgar, manner she often heard around her.

There had been no dramatic awakening here, no vows to perish under violent passions, but Clarissa had learnt on her own part that love could warm one's life as gradually and as softly as the sun appearing over the horizon. When she thought back, she suspected that Kitty's interest in Cousin Philip had kindled into a genuine regard, and what's more, Clarissa suspected that it was in some wise returned. Why else would he break his invariable rule, and attend so many events where he was sure to meet them?

She sent a covert glance at Kitty as she helped herself to eggs. Kitty wore her favorite green carriage dress, instead of the new one that Amelia and Clarissa had insisted she could carry off. However, the green brought out the shade of her eyes, and contrasted with her dark curls. Though it was not the dashing dress of blue and white stripes with the caped lapel a la Menèrve, the green one was if anything more flattering to Kitty's charming figure.

The younger girls were chattering away. Eliza said presently, "Lady Kitty. You have got on your carriage dress. Are we going out for an airing?"

Clarissa watched Kitty blush as she said, "We were invited on an expedition to Hampstead."

"Dull!" Eliza stated.

Any more conversation was forestalled when the knocker resounded, and Mr. Devereaux was announced,

"Oh, *Philip*," Bess Devereaux exclaimed in accents of disapprobation the moment the gentleman appeared. "What are *you* doing here? Why are you come? Is all well with Mama?"

"She was when last I heard. I am not here to see you at all, but to give your cousin and her guest a respite from a household that must by now resemble Bedlam."

Bess bridled. "Wretch! And I have been so *very* good, have I not, Cousin Clarissa? Lady Kitty?" She gave the latter a look of patent admiration, and said, "For you must know that Lady Kitty has played Charades with us, and asked her own maid to put up my hair when we attended Lucasta's soiree, but do not think I've pestered her, for she said she enjoyed it, and I have not got myself into any scrapes, either, for I've been *much* too busy."

"Permit me to depart, then, and you may return to your dissipations," Mr. Devereaux said to his sister. "Are you ready, ladies? Or shall I have the horses walked?"

"Our hats are by the door," Clarissa said, as Kitty's cheeks bloomed yet again.

Clarissa was thinking, as Pobrick's nephew Kelson handed her up into the curricle, that life had become interesting again.

Kitty found herself on one side of the gentleman, Clarissa on the far side. She was so surprised at the new sensations caused by such proximity to a gentleman that at first she was scarcely aware of the city streets they drove through.

But gradually her awareness extended outward. James's style was the heedless speed called neck-or-nothing, putting pedestrians, carts, and animals at risk if they did not get out of the way. Ned probably would have driven much the same, if their older brother had not trained it out of him.

Kitty would have disliked it very much if Mr. Devereaux had endangered the population of London in order to show off the speed of his matched pair of bays. But he did not. If anything, he demonstrated greater skill by the way he managed to conduct the curricle smoothly through all the hazards of traffic, endangering no one.

Mr. Devereaux could not see Kitty's face, only the edge of her bonnet as she gazed straight forward. But he found himself distracted by the entrancing curve of shoulder to waist, the line of her neck above the lace-edged collar, and he noted the subtle tightening and twitches of her gloved hands, which suggested unconscious responses to handling reins.

There was little conversation until they reached the outskirts of the city, and a gradual cessation of traffic. Once he had a clear view of the road, Mr. Devereaux dropped his hands, and permitted the horses to spring.

A chuckle of enjoyment from under the bonnet at his right inspired him to give the animals a good gallop, pulling them up to keep them from becoming overheated in the warm day. They preceded sedately up the pleasant valley between Clerkenwell and Holborn, slowing when the Fleet River, so unpleasant in its proximity to the city, ran clear in pretty streams.

As always, Clarissa's spirits rose when they reached the countryside. Problems seemed to fall behind with the noise of the city.

Kitty diligently tried to pay attention to the wildflowers and bubbling brooks, but she was distracted by Mr. Devereaux's strong hands on the reins and the outline of a fine legs in their buckskins — all that was visible at the edge of her bonnet. She dared not lift her head.

The horses slowed to a walk to cool down, then Mr. Devereaux guided them to a stream whence they could drink safely. After that, he pulled up under an oak, saying, "We might give the animals some time in the shade before returning. If anyone wishes to walk down this path to inspect the river — for this is the origin of the Fleet — I can tend to the horses."

"There is no need," Clarissa said. "I would prefer to sit right here in the shade. I even came equipped." She pulled from her reticule the slim volume of Wordsworth's poetry. "If you will entrust me with the reins, I would consider myself well occupied, sitting here reading, and watching the butterflies, so you two may refresh yourselves by walking about."

Kitty gazed at her helplessly. This was not what she had planned!

Clarissa turned her way. "I've been here before. It would be a great pity not to see the stream, which is exceptionally pretty, while you have the chance."

Mr. Devereaux turned a smile up at Kitty, and held out a hand. She placed her hand on his to be helped from the curricle, her heart beating unaccountably fast.

One last glance toward Clarissa, but she was already reading her book.

That was *not* the countenance of a woman in love.

Mr. Devereaux led the way down the path, Kitty nearly giddy as she tried to properly admire the delicate white flowering cherry, bell-shaped lavender foxglove, and sun-yellow celandine, but mostly aware of the crunch of footsteps at her side.

Mr. Devereaux said, "I was in the habit of driving two of my cousins up here frequently, when I was still a schoolboy: Clarissa and a mutual cousin who now lives in Surrey. Both came from noisy households and craved verdure. I, being an arrogant school-boy, favored any excuse to be showing off my horses and driving."

He went on in this manner, in an ordinary voice, about ordinary matters, gradually winning from Kitty more responses, until it occurred to her that she must be a trying companion. How could Lucretia accuse her of throwing herself at someone who had to do all the work to make polite conversation?

She responded more naturally, and the conversation flowed along. The countryside—wildflowers—"Are you fond of gardening, Lady Catherine?"

"Well, no," she said a little guiltily. "That is, I like to pick fresh flowers for the table when they're in bloom, but I do not much care for tending shrubs."

"What do you do to fill the time, then?"

Her tried to see her face, but only caught the edge of a blushing cheek. "There are myriad chores that must be done in aid to my brother, who acts as his own steward. That fills the day."

"Do you find it tedious, then?"

"Oh, not at all. But it can be time-consuming. It is not only the household. In truth, Mrs. Finn is a most admirable housekeeper, leaving me little to do in that regard. I spend more time visiting the tenants on our land, when my brother is otherwise occupied. One cannot just stop, but must go in, and drink some cowslip wine, and listen to tidings of the parish as if it were all new, but I rather like it more than not. Each person sees things differently, and it's rather like living in a story, which is good for writing—"

"Writing?"

"Letters—and things," she said hastily.

"May I inquire how you get about on these parish visits? Do you drive?"

"I do. My brother taught me to handle our gig when I turned twelve. Later, he entrusted me with his team when I had to go farther than was comfortable for our old pony. But of course a female can drive about alone in the countryside," she added hastily, "in one's own land."

"Should you like to take the reins, then, for a time on our return?"

Extremely gratified, Kitty closed at once with his offer, and that thawed the remainder of her shyness. Once again they talked as they had at Almack's that first night, cementing his conviction that her constraint was not natural to her.

When they wandered back up the path toward the spreading oak, he made a reference to Clarissa's favorite, Wordsworth, and ventured a question on the topic of reading. He had already suspected that Lady Kitty was at least as well-read as Cousin Clarissa.

"My brothers and I often read plays together at home, during the winter. When we can agree on one," she said.

"You all have different tastes?"

"Vastly. My younger brother has two tastes, either horrific ones, with ghosts, and madmen, and duels, or comic plays. My elder brother prefers the tragedies, the more high-flown the better, and I must confess a preference for the more romantical comedies."

"I have a fondness for Congreve myself," he said. "Though I'm assured by many that his plays are thought outmoded."

"My favorite of his is *Love for Love.*"

"Mine is *The Way of the World.*"

"That was Papa's favorite. I quite like the valet Jeremy, in particular the way my brother Edward reads him. He, Ned, that is, makes the most famous Jeremy, and his Sir Sampson is as pompous and as nasty as you can stare."

"It sounds a pleasant pastime, reading plays aloud," he said. "I've not participated in such an activity since I was a schoolboy, and then of course one holds the wisdom and vision of the poets cheaply."

"It's entertaining only if everyone in company is a good reader," she said. "It can be otherwise if someone is slow, or reads in a dead tone."

Though the conversation was quite ordinary—nothing the poets would acclaim—they found one another's utterances bewitching, perhaps the more because they were true. Neither made extravagant claims, nor changed their opinion to flatter the other; they even argued in a friendly manner, Kitty insisting that Mrs. Haywood's works were superior to those by either Fielding or Richardson, and he holding to a preference for Richardson.

They quite agreed that nothing was to be made of Sterne's *Sir Tristram Shandy*, Kitty offering her brother's theory that the printers had dropped the pages upon the floor and picked them up anyhow. When Devereaux suggested that the author had made up a novel from one of his dreams, mixed up with a lot of Burton, Bacon, and Rabelais, Kitty admitted that she had read nothing by any of these three gentlemen.

They had to turn back, and here too soon was the carriage once again. But it was time to return.

He kept his promise, handing her the reins for the first stretch of road. Kitty proved to be an excellent driver, with a care to the horses as well as to the comfort of her fellow passengers. Mr. Devereaux was almost sorry when they began to see other people on the road, and they must trade places, Kitty feeling as if she moved in a dream.

Mr. Devereaux acknowledged he must abandon his pretence of indifference. It was done by the time they reached Camden.

He was still not entirely certain of the lady's heart, which only bewitched him the more. He, sought for most of his life, had discovered the enchantment of courtship.

Twenty-nine

THOUGH COURTSHIP WAS NOT to be without its obstacles. The first he saw as the curricle drew up in Brook Street. A glance upward at the parlor window disclosed faces pressed to the glass, foremost the avid gaze of Miss Lucretia Bouldeston.

A quick glance at Kitty revealed a stricken, even guilty expression. That convinced him he had found the source of Kitty's earlier stiffness.

"Would you care to come inside, Cousin?" Clarissa asked as the porter helped her down.

"I had better return the horses to the stable," he said, and thanked her.

After Kitty and Clarissa thanked him for the outing, he took his departure, deep in thought.

The young ladies put off their bonnets and gloves, and went up to find the Bouldeston sisters still in the parlor.

Lucasta had been in the middle of a long, exacting account of Mr. Aston's recent excursions into poesy. Lucretia interrupted her sister to bestow compliments on the new arrivals and ask about their outing.

Clarissa undertook to answer, and draw Lucretia's attention away from the silent Kitty to herself. After three or four uninformative, polite exchanges, Lucasta tried to resume her recitation of the new poem, but Lucretia cut her off, saying sweetly, "Lucasta, we must not overstay our welcome."

Lucretia could scarcely wait to get outside. What was that stupid dowd Clarissa Harlowe about, parading all over town with Mr. Devereaux? She, who could have any man she wanted—who could *buy* any man she wanted, if the whispers were even half true about her immense dowry. But now that she'd thrown over Lord Wilburfolde, she must have her eye to her cousin's fortune. Rounding out the family properties, perhaps? And what was Catherine doing there? Lending her countenance, of course.

It was past time to bring Catherine's long visit to a close. Then Lucretia must turn her mind to the problem of Miss Harlowe. How could anyone so plain be so arrogant? It was probably due to her constant awareness of that immense dowry, and her grandmother being a duchess, Lucretia thought in disgust as she prodded her sister to walk faster.

"I'm walking as fast as I can."

"You always dawdle. And that puts me in mind of another thing, the way you were going on about that tiresome poet of yours, I scarcely knew where to look. Could you not see how very bored they were? Bess Devereaux will be pouring a long tale into her brother's ears by tomorrow..."

* * *

While that was going on, Bess Devereaux, Amelia, and Tildy vented their feelings about Mr. Aston's poetry, much as Lucretia had foreseen, but not nearly as long as Lucretia spent in scolding her sister. They soon shifted to other matters.

Bess Devereaux had developed a schoolgirl's passion for Lady Kitty. In such cases, the earnest desire to emulate the object of one's affections caused questions that could in any other circumstances be regarded as impertinent. "How much do you spend on gowns?" "Have you ever been kissed?" "How many offers of marriage have you had?"

Kitty dealt with these and more questions kindly, if a trifle absently, relieved when they were called to dress for dinner.

Afterward, the younger ladies went across the street to join the younger Atherton girls in a schoolroom party of round games and

Speculation. Clarissa retired to answer a letter to her grandmother, and Kitty repaired to her bedchamber, feeling restless.

Her gaze fell first upon her costume for the masquerade ball, which she and Alice had been secretly working on since Carlisle had brought it to her from Tarval Hall. She had not shown it to the girls, for she wanted it to be a surprise.

But she had no taste for sewing at this moment. A resurgence of determination caused her to sit down, mend her pen, and light a second candle that her hand might not cast a shadow across her page.

Remembering Clarissa's suggestion, she began going through her manuscript from the beginning, altering and sharpening descriptions. When she came to Andromeda's first encounter with the mysterious Duke, she began to write feverishly. Intent upon making the Duke less indistinct, and to convert some of the same sort of high-flown figurative language that the girls had been mocking in Mr. Aston to more realistic detail, she found her pen dashing along.

Her candles had burned down halfway when she laid her pen down and wrung her aching fingers. She was tired, and yet her mind seemed clearer than it had for days. She got up and took a turn about the room to refresh herself, then she sat down again and took up the page that she had just written.

She read over with increasing satisfaction the vivid description of the Duke as he drove up in his high perch phaeton. This description was so vivid that it caused the flicker of memory: Mr. Philip Devereaux as he took the reins from her on the road alongside the River Fleet.

She looked down again at the words she had written. She blushed and blushed again when she recognized what she had done. The mysterious Duke had become Mr. Devereaux.

She flung her pen down, gathered up her manuscript, and flung it into the bottom of her trunk. Then she whirled around and sat upon the trunk as if the papers might grow arms and legs and climb out to tell their tale to the world.

Was this what 'particularity' meant? She had only had time to acknowledge that the day's outing, so quiet — so absent of anything like the dashing romance of Andromeda's life, the floods of tears *con amore* or precipitously dramatic actions—had somehow been the best day of all her stay in London.

Was this how all those other females felt? If only she had real experience, and not just that of books! For in real life the women around her did not get abducted before they were married, nor did they faint away at the sight of their beloved, or indulge in such wild bouts of weeping that the faculty despaired of their lives.

Why *this* man? Why not Lord Arden, who made it plain in so many little ways that he admired her? She could not explain it, except that she regarded him in the nature of a brother. Why not Mr. Canby? He was kind, even wealthy, and sought her out at every party or ball. But though she liked him, she did not find herself looking at his hands, his eyes, his *tout ensemble*. She did not listen for his voice when she arrived at a gathering. Or why not Beau Brummel, who was easily the most popular man in London? Yet she did not care if she never exchanged a word with him, handsome as he was.

If she had to sum up Mr. Devereaux in a word, that word would be kindness, and yet there was nothing kind about the way he looked in those flawless coats, or the line of his leg so near to her own in that curricle...

She got up from the trunk, and crossed the room. She knew two things: that Clarissa had no interest in her cousin, or she would not have sat reading poetry when she might have been the one to walk down to the water. And second, Kitty wanted very much to see him again, and again, and again. To see him every day, if only that were possible.

Wednesday morning, Kitty stayed in her room to work on her costume while Clarissa called upon her grandmother alone. Kitty was a little surprised not to be asked to go along, but she knew she should not expect to be tied to Clarissa in all things.

Kitty came downstairs for afternoon tea, to discover Amelia returned from an outing with the elder Atherton girls, and Eliza, Bess, and Tildy entering after their visit to the park. "We were at a reading party hosted by Isabel DuLac," Amelia reported.

"You, reading?" Tildy exclaimed.

"It makes a great difference, when someone *explains* things," Amelia said. "But that is not what I wanted to tell you." She leaned forward, after a glance at the door. "You would never guess who we saw riding by—none other than Lord Wilburfolde!"

"I thought he was safely gone back to The Castle," Kitty exclaimed.

"He must be hiding out from the dragon," Eliza declared, her china-blue eyes round with mischief.

Amelia giggled, and lowered her voice. "Not what I heard. Miss DuLac knows Edmund's aunt, Lady Annadale, who is just such another dragon, and apparently, Lady Wilburfolde is quite determined to gain an heir to The Castle, and so Lord Wilburfolde has been forming a list of eligible ladies."

"I pity the daughters of Methodists and Temperance Society leaders," Eliza said.

Amelia shook her head. "You forget what Lady Wilburfolde feels is due their name and position in society. His list will only be well-born girls of whom the dragons approve."

"I hope and trust any female who meets all those qualifications meets his mother before sealing her fate," Kitty exclaimed with heart-felt sympathy.

Amelia giggled again. "From what Miss DuLac said, that is exactly what has happened, only it is Lady Annadale who scares them off."

Bess looked from one to the other. "Who is this man?"

The girls tumbled over one another telling her the history of Clarissa's short-lived betrothal, offering examples of Lady Wilburfolde's choicest remarks, and her son's least admirable characteristics.

During it all, Kitty remained silent, until the girls turned her way, and Amelia said, "What say you, Lady Kitty? I recollect he dropped many hints about how you ought to go home."

Kitty said, "As every remark of his that we found most offensive was almost always prefaced by a reference to his mother, I wonder if, were he to gain independence of her, he would not be quite so objectionable. A wife—*not* Clarissa—might be just the thing for his happiness."

Amelia's eyes narrowed. "A wife to hide behind, that she might take the brunt of Lady W.'s dragonish tongue," she said shrewdly.

"*Not* Clarissa," Tildy declared. "She hates brangles. She hates it when *we* brangle," she added cheerfully. "Come, Bess. Miss Gill has decreed I must master that Bach piece. Will you show me how you managed not to make it sound like a pianoforte falling down a flight of stairs, tinkle-tankle-tink?"

Amelia took out her Shakespeare, which caused Eliza to flee incontinently. Kitty stayed to hear her, and was surprised to discover that Amelia had begun to gain an understanding of what she was reading, and furthermore, not every observation was prefaced by *Charles says*. The two thus passed a pleasant hour with *The Tempest*, Amelia listening closely to everything Kitty said, and Kitty gratified by her attention.

Clarissa returned from Cavendish Square, her mood thoughtful. Since she had gone to visit her grandmother with the purpose disclosing, not only the entire history of her unfortunate betrothal, but also her intuitions about Cousin Philip and Lady Catherine, preparatory to asking her grandmother's advice, she had little to say on her arrival home.

The duchess had listened with evident satisfaction, but she had vouchsafed only this: "I'm demmed glad you told me, my girl. Very glad. Much is now clear. But you know how Philip hates interference. He is worse than you."

"That is why I came to you, Grandmama," Clarissa sighed.

The duchess had patted her hand. "That does not mean that we are at a stand. We shall speak again. Go home, dance, and see to your own happiness. You are past due," she added gruffly.

Clarissa left in a sober mood, not wishing to admit that her happiness was as out of reach as ever. But one thing she had learnt during her prospective engagement: there were definitely worse things than living with one's family as a spinster, especially when facing the prospect of inheriting, as she would at twenty-five, her fortune, which surely must be large enough to support her in her own household.

She arrived to hear the end of Amelia's bout with Shakespeare, which surprised her. Who knew where *that* might end?

Dinner was served, after which the ladies dressed for the weekly ball at Almack's.

They were not the only ones getting ready. Mr. Devereaux, with a mind to protecting his lady from speculative gossip, had determined to be seen squiring a dozen partners on the dance floor before the Harlowes' arrival.

St. Tarval and his brother were also on hand, the former determined to gain one dance with Clarissa, even if he could have nothing else, and the latter to try and find out some way to get his brother out of this damned tangle. He cared about Carlisle's happiness, but as strong was his determination to avoid sharing a house with Lucretia, if he possibly could.

The Bouldeston ladies also arrived early. Lady Bouldeston liked to find the best seat from which to watch the room. Lucasta waited for her swain, that they might dance as many times as was allowed, and Lucretia was surprised to discover Mr. Devereaux already there. She began to count his partners, despising each for her shortcomings, and kept well away from St. Tarval so that she could contrive to be available when Mr. Devereaux was free.

Thus it was when the Harlowes and Kitty arrived, and once again all our dancers were gathered.

In a single glance, Clarissa distinguished St. Tarval talking to Lord Arden and some other gentlemen. She schooled herself to look otherwhere, though she was always aware of his movements in the crowded ballroom.

Kitty was promptly beset with partners. She smiled, said yes readily, and was so distracted that afterward she was hard put to name a one of them, until at last she looked up, and there was Mr. Devereaux. Her nerves fired as she smiled at him, and they moved out onto the floor.

After trying half a dozen unsuccessful attempts to place herself in reach of Mr. Devereaux when he finished a dance, just to see him escort his last partner somewhere across the room, Lucretia began to wonder if she had made a mistake in contriving to stay away from St. Tarval. She had forgotten the motivation of jealousy.

She went up to her betrothed, dropping a hint that she had not danced with him this age, and he promptly held out his hand, his expression of irony missed by her, because she was searching the room to see if Mr. Devereaux was watching.

She did not find him on the periphery. She scanned again during the second hands across, and discovered him dancing with Catherine!

At that moment, Mr. Devereaux was saying to Kitty, "Would you do me the honor of favoring me with your opinion on a matter concerning my sister?"

"If it is within my power," she said, not hiding her surprise. "I have lived so secluded myself, and having not had any sisters..."

"Your situation has been much like hers, I believe, until I contrived to send her to school. And having spent as much time with her as these past days as you have, you must have formed a tolerable estimation of her character. Do you think she should be presented next year, as she so desires, or should we wait until she is eighteen, as her mother wishes?"

Kitty's brow knit thoughtfully for a long moment as they moved toward the top of the dance. When she saw him waiting for her answer, she said, "I would be tempted to bring her out as soon as you can. You might wait until she is eighteen to present her to the Queen, but going into society appears to be a different matter."

"Has she recounted some of the scrapes she has contrived to get herself into?"

"Yes. She has been very forthcoming. I really believe most of them stem from an excess of high spirits, and from being confined to a dull place with too little to occupy her. I know what that's like, for winters at home are very much the same," she said with feeling. "But when there are things to do, she is very good. And I believe she does understand the necessity of not setting up the back of those in importance. As for scrapes, it is so easy to fall into them, much easier than one would think, even when one has the best of intentions. I think you know what I mean."

She cast a doubtful look at Mr. Devereaux, and when he smiled and said, "I quite understand. But there was more than one person in that scrape."

Kitty smiled back. "I've used my own experience to try to convince her that gainsaying one's brothers can be fatal."

"Capital," he said with appreciation. "I hope she listened. No doubt I will discover on the ride to Grosvenor Street on the day after the masquerade ball. My mother will be in town, and she has made it plain that Bess must come home at that time."

The remainder of the dance passed in pleasant nothing-talk, and when it was over, Mr. Worthington was waiting for the next.

Kitty did not look back to see who Mr. Devereaux danced with, for she would never be so impolite to her partner, but she was thinking about the conversation, and about how wonderful an evening could become when the right pair of eyes smiled back at one.

And so she did not perceive the calculation in Lucretia's long gaze, as she tripped lightly down the dance.

Lucretia was tired of waiting in proper female delicacy. It was time to matters into her own hands.

Thirty

TWO DAYS LATER, ON the eve of the masquerade ball, Kitty and Clarissa were both surprised to receive an invitation from Lucretia Bouldeston for an impromptu picnic to Richmond Park. They were especially invited to meet Lucretia's cousin Cassandra Kittredge, newly returned from France.

"I'm glad it doesn't include me," Amelia declared. "Every day has seen a thunderstorm by sunset, and I know not why today ought to be any different."

"That's my thinking as well," Clarissa said.

Kitty sighed, feeling duty-bound to go, now that the betrothal with Carlisle had been announced. She ran to the window and gazed in disappointment at the pure blue sky. "There's not a cloud in sight. If I cry off, it might look particular."

Particularity. Clarissa had no inclination to see Lucretia in proximity with the marquess, parading her engagement, but felt she must go for that very reason. She must behave as normal. So they dressed for the weather, choosing bonnets that would ward the glaring sun, and as an afterthought, Clarissa fetched her umbrella. Shortly thereafter they found themselves in the parlor awaiting the arrival of the Bouldeston barouche, which was prompt arriving in Brook Street.

The ladies climbed in, and Lucretia introduced Clarissa to Miss Kittredge, who looked very much like Lucretia with her honey-colored hair and round face. Kitty had met her briefly when they were all much younger, during Miss Kittredge's visit to her cousins. The Kittredges, Lucretia informer her and Clarissa, were stopping only for a day or two in London before continuing on home.

The barouche was joined by a gig driven by Sir Henry's friend, Mr. Redding, and a curricle containing Mr. Aston and his particular friend, Mr. Nolan.

Kitty said, "Where's my brother, Lucretia? Is he not coming?"

"He had other plans," Lucretia said and added with a simper, "I would not make myself a jest by always confining him to my elbow." She then turned to point out to her cousin all the famous sights and people she knew, until the traffic began to thin.

Kitty sat back, struggling to contain her irritation. She consciously tried to give Lucretia credit for arranging an outing for her cousin. Of course she would invite the sister of her betrothed.

While she struggled to excuse Lucretia, Clarissa asked Miss Kittredge about Paris, and as this young lady was quite ready to talk, the rest of the ride passed agreeably. They slowed when they reached Richmond Gate, and then turned upward to King Henry's Mound. Here the horses halted, drivers tending to the heated animals as the Bouldeston maid-of-all-work began the task of unloading the promising hampers from Gunter's.

Everything had been thought of for an elegant repast, save the weather was hot and breathless, as it had been these several days. The magnificent view over the Thames Valley in one direction showed a threatening line of cloud on the horizon, but when Lucasta pointed it out to her sister, they all heard the "Pho! Pho! It means nothing—we are quite safe—look above us!"

Everyone glanced up at the bright blue sky to reassure themselves, then wandered to the Mound to exclaim over the view, those who had been there previously pointing out Saint Paul's some ten miles to the east, a hazy thumb jutting upward from the uneven horizon. When all had talked themselves out about the skyline of London, they separated into smaller parties to wander along the paths, seek shade under the spreading oaks, and to talk and laugh.

Mr. Redding had come with a specific purpose. Lady

Catherine's beauty was everything he wanted in a wife, and, having been encouraged by Lucretia, he sought out Kitty, who remained by Clarissa's side. When he demonstrated a wish to take Kitty's arm, the latter's expression of alarm prompted Clarissa to open her umbrella, with a claim that the sun was too bright for comfort. She invited Kitty to get out of the sun, and the edge of the umbrella perforce kept the ardent gentleman at a distance.

Lucasta's voice rang through the glades as she wandered with her swain, the two exclaiming snatches of Mr. Aston's poetry (for he did not willingly suffer comparison with other poets), and Mr. Nolan—who had also ventured over the water earlier in spring— walked with Miss Kittredge, exclaiming with comfortable horror over her descriptions of the destruction of the French countryside by the revolutionary rabble.

It was hunger and thirst that drew them to the cloths spread under a tree, with the hampers all unpacked by the maid who had ridden with the barouche's driver. The repast was hailed with general delight: there was wine for the gentlemen, lemonade for the ladies, ham-shavings aplenty, with cakes, trifle, cheese, and grapes.

As they sat down, some looked upward, discovering that the line of clouds was much nearer.

"Pooh! Nonsense," Lucretia declared. "We know how it is. A few clouds, maybe some distant lightning, and no more than a drop or two. I hope we are not to be afraid of a cloud, after I went to all this trouble."

The ladies' apprehension was satisfied, at least outwardly, though a silent testament to the oppressive heat was in how quickly the lemonade was drunk. Clarissa pitied the gentlemen, for Lucretia was pouring wine into their cups as fast as they could down it. From what she had learnt from her father, wine only succeeded in assuaging thirst for a short time, whereupon the thirst would come back the stronger.

The approaching clouds stole up from the east, not interfering with the golden slants of late afternoon sunlight until, quite suddenly, the light vanished behind the clouds. The company felt on wrist or face the first drops of rain.

Lucretia struck one of her affected poses, glancing skyward as she thumbed a drop of rain from her cheek. "Oh, no, I was wrong," she declared. "Oh, you will forever hate me—I am so very sorry—I was quite wrong—the storm is coming after all—let us hurry!"

"What about the lodge?" someone asked.

"It is locked up—I already ascertained when you were walking about," Lucretia declared. "We must go. Raise the hood on the barouche, Williams, at once!"

Her sudden alarm had the effect of infusing everyone with fright, the moreso as the storm smothered the twilight and darkness appeared to be descending with sinister alacrity.

Clarissa opened her umbrella as Lucretia darted about, thrusting people this way and that.

Kitty started toward the barouche, intending to catch up with Clarissa, but Lucretia took her by the shoulders, exclaiming, "Not yet—not yet—the hampers—Mother paid down a horrid amount of money for those hampers, we dare not lose them—" as the poor maid-of-all work labored to gather the remains of the picnic and thrust it into the barouche without any thought to neatness.

Kitty obligingly stepped out of the maid's way, as Miss Kittredge exclaimed in fright at a branch of lightning.

"Quick! Quick! Get in!" Lucretia appeared in front of Clarissa, pushing her toward the barouche. Because of the umbrella, Clarissa lost sight of the others as she was propelled toward the vehicle.

Kitty felt a strong hand under her elbow. She experienced a moment of gratitude, as everyone around her seemed to be in a panic, and lightning flared in the distance.

A breeze had kicked up, causing her to clutch at her skirt with one hand and her bonnet with the other. She found herself not at the barouche, but beside a gig. "This is not my place," she protested to Mr. Redding, who had guided her.

"T'other appears to be full," Mr. Redding observed, his words slurring. "The servant's flung the hampers on the benches. You will have a much finer ride with me," he added in a meaning voice, remembering Lucretia's whispered, *She wants encouragement!*

Kitty was going to pull away, then thought of Lucretia

scolding and the seats in the barouche all tumbled with hampers. Though she did not like Mr. Redding, he was a friend to Sir Henry. What harm could come to her in the gig, following directly behind Lucretia's carriage? And Mr. Aston trotting right behind.

So she consented to be handed up. Mr. Redding climbed to the seat next to her and released the brake on the gig, which enabled his restless horse to put the vehicle in motion. Turning her head, Kitty was startled to discover Mr. Aston's curricle, being drawn by a restive pair, vanished into the gathering darkness.

The barouche pulled ahead, its four horses given the office to gallop, and for a few moments Kitty thought with heartfelt pity of Clarissa inside being tumbled about with the serving maid, the Bouldestons, and their cousin.

But the gig did not pick up speed. The horse walked sedately, and Kitty watched in growing indignation as the barouche gradually vanished down the tree-shrouded lane.

As the barouche vanished, an unfamiliar weight settled around her shoulders. It was Mr. Redding's arm!

"Sir!" she protested.

"I'll protect you from the rain." Mr. Redding's hot breath was redolent of wine-fumes.

Revulsion flashed through her with every bit as much electricity as the lightning flaring overhead. She tried to shake off Mr. Redding's arm, but there was nowhere to go—the gig was designed for a single person.

The hand squeezed again. "Give us a kiss, now."

"Mr. Redding! I must request you to unhand me at once!"

She attempted to pry his fingers off her arm, her efforts causing the gig to swing. The horse jobbed at the bit, and Mr. Redding perforce must use two hands to subdue the beast. He said, his words slurred, "Save the fight for th' wedding night, my beauty. I like it fine then, but right now, you must sit still."

"*Wedding* night?" Kitty repeated in horror.

"Sir Henry's girl said you was looking out for a wealthy marriage, and I'll give you a *gen-rouss* allowance, the more if you look out ways to please me."

Kitty's throat closed. Tears stung her eyes as she tried to speak steadily. "I'm sorry, sir, but you misunderstood, that is, Lucretia must have misstated my wishes."

"Seems to me you stepped into th' gig readily enough."

"Because I thought you would follow the barouche," Kitty retorted. "Pray let me be clear: I do not want to be married to you."

Mr. Redding laughed again, a sound she was beginning to
hate. "I am content with that, and you will find me generous, but I
must say, I did not foresee your wishing to come on the town. I
would have spoken before."

Kitty gasped, then said in strong accents, "I do not wish to be
with you at all!"

"But here you are, my pretty. Just save the tussle for when
we—"

"Oh!" Kitty seethed with rage. And then, remembering what
had happened the last time she thought she assisted at an
abduction, she gathered her skirts in one hand, and with the other,
she balanced against the side of the gig.

And then she sprang out.

The gig was not moving very fast, for the horse had already
traveled from London on a hot day, and Mr. Redding had other
things in mind besides the drive, but even so, the movement of the
gig was enough to send her tumbling into the dirt.

She rolled to her knees and then stood dizzily as Mr. Redding
uttered an oath and pulled up the horse.

"Lady Catherine," he enunciated. "This display pleases neither
of us. Get in the gig."

"I will not," she said. "Unless you promise not to touch me."

The sound of the brake engaging darted fear through her
nerves. So *this* was an abduction. A real one! There was nothing
romantical about it, she thought desolately, as lightning flared, this
time accompanied by a clap of thunder.

Mr. Redding jumped down and started toward her. She ran to
the other side of the gig, crying, "Stay away from me."

"What is this play-acting?" he retorted, fury replacing the wine
fumes as the wind kicked up. "It pleases me not. Sir Henry's girl
promised you liked me fine, and here we are, miles from anyone. I
play fair—if you are the maiden you pretend to be, I'm willing to
stand up in church, but if you like—"

"How *dare* you offer me violence," Kitty cried, edging around the side of the gig. If she could get her hands on the reins...

But Mr. Redding gripped them tight, the horse plunging and jobbing as its head twisted. "Do you see a pistol in my hand?"

"Dastard. Coxcomb!"

"Upon my word, you are a prosy one. What is it you want to hear, *I love you* and *adore* you? I will say anything you like, only get in the gig!"

At that moment, the storm reached them, a sudden downpour battering Kitty, Mr. Redding, and the restive horse.

"I just want to go home," Kitty stated between shut teeth.

Mr. Redding lunged around the wheel, then swayed, catching himself against the tracings. Kitty sprang away — and tripped over her hem.

Mr. Redding uttered a hiccoughing laugh, then cursed. From the sound of his impatience, the rain was beginning to sober him a little. "Where are you, gel?"

"Just go away," Kitty said as she rolled to her feet. "I do *not* wish to be abducted by you *or* married to you!"

"Then you shall not be," came a calm voice out of the darkness.

Thirty-one

"CLARISSA!" KITTY CRIED WITH heartfelt gratitude.

"Who is that?" Mr. Redding cried, as rain hissed all around them.

"Miss Harlowe," Clarissa stated calmly.

"*Chadwick's* girl?" Mr. Redding said, in accents of dismay. His expectations had been confounded. Foremost in his emotions were disappointment and anger, but under those, the sickening suspicion that he had been made game of.

He leaped back into the gig, which would not have seated three even if he wished to tax his horse so abominably. "That is very well," he said angrily. "If you will have none of me, then I'll none of you."

With that he clucked to the horse, and the gig swiftly vanished down the road, leaving the two ladies standing in the rain.

"Poltroon," Clarissa called in clear accents.

Kitty began to laugh uncertainly, which nearly turned to tears. She wiped rain off her face repeatedly, her fingers trembling.

"Oh, Kitty, I am so sorry," Clarissa said.

"I'm fine," Kitty stated rather grittily. "That man does not deserve tears."

"Quite so. I wish I had my umbrella," Clarissa responded. "I could have used it to thump him over the head. As well as to ward the rain."

Kitty lost control then, and gave vent to wild laughter, which caused Clarissa to laugh as well. For a time they stood there in the rain, laughing and laughing, in spite of sodden gowns and ruined hats.

When the gusts died away, Clarissa said, "We had better begin walking."

Kitty fell in step beside her, but observed, "It's quite ten miles. It will take us all night, if highwaymen do not get us first."

"No," Clarissa said, practical as always. "I fully expect a respectable house or cottage to appear before long, or perhaps another carriage, to which we may apply. Visitors go to Richmond Park every day, and surely we are not the only ones who missed their party."

"Is that what we will say?" Kitty asked.

"Yes," Clarissa stated firmly.

"Is that how you came to be alone on the road, did you miss the others?"

There was a long pause, then Clarissa said, "No. Miss Bouldeston was a little too quick to jumble us all into the barouche without you. So I let myself out the other side. I do not know if she noticed or not, and I don't care. Especially as she promptly gave the driver the signal to go. I was on the other side of the gig, which prevented me from gaining Mr. Redding's attention. Or perhaps he ignored me, but I got left behind." Clarissa smiled Kitty's way. "So I started walking. I thought I might catch you up before long."

Kitty said, "Mr. Redding gained a false impression of me."

"I think," Clarissa said, enjoyed the relief of speaking her mind, "Miss Bouldeston deliberately misled Mr. Redding about you. That is not to excuse his behavior."

"He was certainly in liquor, which may explain the *things* he said. But *she* was not. Why would she do that?"

Clarissa pressed her lips together, then said, "As I am not in the lady's confidence, her motives can only be guessed at."

Kitty said aggrievedly, "I'm a simpleton. I set myself up for understanding, yet I have *never* understood Lucretia."

"That is because there are so many inconsistencies in her words as well as her conduct."

Kitty sighed. "I was going to tell you once, about my single entry into society, when I was eighteen. Lucretia had been to Town for the first time, and, well, it was before Papa died, while Grand-mama was ill."

"Go on," Clarissa said as they tramped down the rutted road.

"The Bouldestons always went to Tunbridge Wells for the assemblies. They invited me. I think my brother asked Lucretia to, but at all events, I *know* I told Lucretia that I was making over one of my mother's gowns. It was a very pretty yellow silk, with a long sash with a fringe, and when we met outside the Assembly, she had nothing but compliments to speak, though I did have my cloak on, but I am certain it did not cover my gown entirely. But once we were inside, someone came up to be introduced, to ask me to dance, and she came up, and made a show of looking at me all over, and she said how pretty I was, but then she said in very loud accents, *Catherine, I am desolated, but if I do not do my duty, who will? Only married ladies wear yellow silk, or is there an Interesting Event I did not know about?* Everyone laughed — or at least, my memory insists everyone laughed, though they may not have done. They may not have noticed at all. But I was so ashamed, I made an excuse, and went to the cloak room, and cried until it was time to leave, and then I had to lie to Papa and tell him I was ill. And I did not want to go into company for ages after, for I was convinced I had become infamous. Why could she have not told me before? I never understood that."

"Spite," Clarissa said.

Kitty looked her way, but she could make out nothing except the barest outline of Clarissa's form in the emerging starlight, as the clouds above began to disperse. "Spite? But what could I have done to deserve it?"

"Again, I cannot penetrate her motivations, but I would assert that if your conduct was then as it is now, the problem has never lain with you."

"Spite," Kitty repeated, then said in a rush, "I have tried and tried to like her, to be glad for Carlisle, but I never could. Every summer when she returned from London and talked about how many men were secretly in love with her, I kept hoping she would jilt my brother and marry someone else. Well, I shall take great pleasure in telling my brother about *this*."

Clarissa said, "I quite understand the impulse, but I believe it would be better not to do so."

"Why not?"

"Think it through with me, Kitty. First of all, your brother must naturally go to Lucretia for an explanation, and what will she say? That you were not missed in the bustle—a bustle that she carefully planned, but I cannot prove that. That she thought to help you find a husband. She will even insist that you encouraged Mr. Redding."

"But Mr. Redding said that *she* put that idea into his head. I must send Carlisle to him."

"Then what must be the result of that?"

Kitty raised hands to her hot cheeks. "Oh, then Carlisle must call him out, or insist we be married, either of which would be horrid."

"At the very least your name would end up on everyone's lips, and that, I may venture to say, was probably her intention."

"But Mr. Redding *can* ruin me," Kitty said, as the possible consequences began to harrow her. "He has only to say that we were alone in that gig..."

"I do not think he will," Clarissa said.

"You do not?"

"No. First of all, as you observed, he was in liquor. Lucretia, I saw, kept his glass well poured. In that heat, and all that wine—I feel fairly safe in venturing that he will be fit for nothing by to-morrow. And when he does regain his intellects, a moment's reflection will show that he would appear a sorry, even laughable figure. My appearance would do nothing to help his case, and then, you know, his going off and abandoning two ladies in a storm... no."

Clarissa ran her hands up her arms, then wrung her fingers. "The more I consider, the likelier I think it that the gentleman might prefer to retire to his estate in case *you* tell a tale that does not redound to his credit. He may also fear my father," she added. "He does not know your brother except whatever tales Miss Bouldeston might have told of him, but he is old enough to know that my father fought a couple of duels when he was younger. He had rather a reputation."

In spite of the rain, her clammy, sodden clothing, and her

vexation, Kitty could not help being diverted by this unexpected disclosure. The indolent Lord Chadwick, fighting duels? "Very well. If it is as you say, then I must suppose my reputation will not be smirched, but it seems hard not to tell Carlisle what happened. And to think he will take her to wife!"

The longest silence yet grew between them as they walked steadily, Clarissa saying finally, "I believe we must leave it to your brother to question his intended wife, or not, as he sees fit. But I think it would be a great mistake to force him to choose between the two of you. For I would be surprised if Lucretia has not a tale ready to explain both our absences by now."

They had reached Richmond Gate, which still stood open, as the last of the visitors had not departed. The ladies walked out, and twice carriages dashed by, splashing both sides high with muddy water. They leaped back to avoid the splash, which perhaps prevented them from being seen, but in any case, neither carriage halted.

They resumed their trek, their shoes ruined, not that they noticed. Each was too burdened by conflicting thoughts.

At least the rain had become intermittent, as the moon shone bright and silvery-blue in between the silently sailing clouds.

The girls began to talk determinedly of other things as they walked along the road. No more carriages passed. The moon had moved higher in the sky when the rhythmic thud of horse hooves once again reached their ears. Only this time, they were coming from the direction of town.

The two looked at once another, each seeing no more than a pale blob of a face, before Clarissa said, "This will not be a party leaving the Park. Perhaps we ought to take a place beyond the safety of that hedge."

Kitty ducked her head, and scrambled off the muddy road, Clarissa on her heels. They peered out. Visible at first were the carriage lamps, two eyes of winking gold, and between them a uniform darkness.

The sound grew, the darkness resolved into the silhouette of a team of horses, and behind them, seated high, the shape of a man in a caped driving coat.

The equipage neared, began to pass. The driver turned his

gaze from one side as to the other, and as his moonlit profile was briefly outlined against the darkened countryside, Kitty gasped.

Clarissa's nerves turned to snow as Kitty cried frantically, "Carlisle!"

St. Tarval pulled up the curricle. Kitty pelted down the road, Clarissa running after. Kitty leaped up onto the floorboard of the vehicle to fling her arms around her brother, but the horses, thoroughly unsettled, jobbed and pitched, causing the curricle to sidle, and Kitty fell backward, once more landing in the mud.

Clarissa bent to offer a hand, but Kitty said breathlessly, "I'm fine, truly. It's not as if I have not taken a tumble times out of mind." She stood up, trying to brush the worst of the mud from her gown as she exclaimed, "Carlisle, what brings *you* here! Did you come to rescue us?"

As she spoke she looked up, to discover her brother was not listening to her at all. His hands were busy with the reins, but his countenance was turned away from her, his hat throwing all but his chin in shadow.

Looking from him to Clarissa, upon whose uplifted face the moonlight shone in full, Kitty made a stunning discovery.

Thirty-two

THE MARQUESS HAD NOT begun the day in a good temper.

He had been in a reflective mood ever since the night at Almack's, at which he had witnessed his betrothed's determined efforts to catch the attention of Mr. Devereaux.

In part he hoped that she could succeed in catching the gentleman's eye, for that would solve his own problem so neatly. At any rate, he was convinced that in spite of her getting her father to insert that notice into the newspaper, she had no regard for him whatsoever.

After a couple of days of thought, he came to the conclusion that he had better have a frank talk with his betrothed. This prospect he regarded with dread, for he had seen her temper when she pinched at her sister. But temper or not, he was determined to come to an understanding with Lucretia before he left London.

The morning he made his decision, it seemed impossible to extricate himself, for he came downstairs to discover Lord Arden having joined Ned at breakfast, full of reminders of their plan to go off to a shooting parlor. Ned did not want to forego, and the marquess could not think of a sufficient excuse to avoid something he'd agreed to.

What with that and the luncheon afterward, it was later in the afternoon when St. Tarval at last was able to extricate himself and take a hackney coach to Mount Street.

However, when he arrived there, it was to the surprising discovery that the sisters had taken a party of friends to Richmond Park. He thought nothing of that until he went on to Brook Street to call on Kitty, to discover that she and Miss Harlowe were absent—that they, Eliza Harlowe informed him, were gone with Lucretia and Lucasta.

Why had he not been invited? St. Tarval was walking back down the steps to the street, wondering if Devereaux had been invited, when the gentleman himself arrived.

The porter called one of the footmen out to walk the beautifully matched bays as Mr. Devereaux touched his hat to the marquess. They greeted one another politely as they passed on the stairs. St. Tarval heard the butler saying "Miss Devereaux is in the parlor with Miss Matilda and Miss Eliza," before the door shut.

Obviously this expedition to the Park was not a ruse aimed at Mr. Devereaux. What could possible lie behind it?

A glance skyward showed a distant line of cloud that promised the usual late-afternoon storm. Surely the picnic would have been finished by now. He determined to get the talk over with.

As Mount Street was not quite a mile away, he decided to stretch his legs in a walk. The city was confining enough as it was; he needed air, even city air, and to be moving. Perhaps it would clear his head. At least he could rehearse what to say.

He was halfway to his destination when the storm broke. He stepped into a public house and drank a tankard of cool ale while the violent downpour got rid of the worst of the heat, then he set out again the moment it began to break.

When he reached Mount Street, the children in the parish workhouse were poking their heads out an upper window, watching the lightning as the storm moved away. St. Tarval had almost reached the Bouldestons' house when the familiar barouche rolled up, disclosing a parcel of angry females. Lucasta tumbled out, twitching her bonnet straight. "See if I *ever* go with you again, Lucretia," she declared, and ran up the stairs into the house.

Lucretia began to follow after, leading Cassandra Kittredge, whom St. Tarval had not seen for several years. The cousins started up the steps as the maid labored to unload the sodden barouche. He ran, catching up before the two young ladies could vanish into the house.

When she heard his step, Lucretia whirled around, her mouth popping open. Was she dismayed to see him? But she smiled and simpered, saying, "Cassie, dear, I believe you have been introduced to my—"

He could not bear to hear the word spoken, and interrupted. "I beg pardon, but I just came from Brook Street. I gather you left my sister there?"

Lucretia's gaze flickered, and once again St. Tarval detected dismay. Then Lucretia said airily, "I believe she is there, yes." As her cousin shot her a surprised look, Lucretia pushed her inside the door, saying, "Come, Cassie, let us shift our clothing. Carlisle, you will perceive that the rain caught us. You would not wish us to catch our deaths, would you?" she asked sweetly, and before he could answer, she whisked herself in and shut the door in his face.

He was tempted to rap the knocker, except what would he say? This was clearly the wrong time to demand a conversation.

So he made his way back to Brook Street, his pace far quicker than previously. He ignored the intermittent rain, for the more he considered Lucretia's response, the more definite he was that something was amiss.

When he reached Brook Street, it was to discover Mr. Devereaux on the point of departure, his sister following with a mutinous expression. She stood squarely in the doorway, hands on her hips, as she declared, "I think Mama is horrid, not letting me attend the ball in my own grandmother's house..." she began.

St. Tarval interrupted a lady for the second time that day. Touching his hat, he said, "I beg pardon, but if I could see my sister..."

Miss Bess stared at him, her complaint forgotten. "She has been gone this age, to Richmond Park!" A glance upward, and her expression changed. "I hope they're not caught in the downpour. Amelia and I were agreed that we would not go out today for a million pounds..."

Mr. Devereaux now interrupted his sister, coming quickly into the light shining from the doorway, his expression one of concern. "They might still be on the road."

"Except that I have just come from Mount Street, and I was told they were here." St. Tarval took a few hasty steps toward the corner, his intent to look for a hackney.

Mr. Devereaux caught up, and said, "Take mine."

St. Tarval turned around. "I beg pardon?"

Mr. Devereaux had been thinking rapidly. If he went in search of the missing ladies, it would cause exactly the sort of talk everyone would wish to avoid. But a brother? "Take my curricle, St. Tarval. The horses are ready for a run. You will have moonlight to drive by, I believe." He pointed. "There is a coat in the trunk, in case it rains again."

The marquess did not know Devereaux except as the apparent target of Lucretia's attentions, and as one of his sister's many dancing partners. He had once hazarded a guess that this was the one Kit preferred, not from anything she said, it was more the way she smiled when they were dancing. But then Kit was friendly to everybody.

This was not the time to sort out the intricacies of these connections. Relief — gratitude — St. Tarval did not waste time on a protest, but closed with the offer, and was soon off.

He was a good driver, but he was not used to this type of sporting vehicle, nor the sort of high-bred, high-fed pair that only very wealthy men could afford. For a time it was all he could do to hold them in hand, especially as it was by then full dark. However, he soon attained the road, and the full moon was enough to give him light.

He dropped his hands, and the pair sprang into a gallop.

They had slowed to a more sedate pace as he scanned continually; he was beginning to wonder if he had come on a fool's errand when he heard Kitty's voice cry out his name.

And there they were, standing by the side of the road, both soaked to the skin. Clarissa looked up at him with such mute appeal, and gratitude, that for a time he could not look away.

"Here, you get in first," Kitty said in a breathless voice, breaking the spell. "I have the greatest dislike of being in the middle."

"What happened?" he asked, when both had climbed into the curricle.

He already suspected some mystery here, but he was sure of it in the way Kitty stole a look at Clarissa, who said in her calmest voice, "The storm struck, and it seemed we were missed in the haste of the departure."

"We shall be back in a trice," he said as he carefully guided the pair in a turn. "I hope you will not catch a chill."

"In summer?" Kitty scoffed. "We are not such poor creatures as that!"

"Nevertheless, I do not believe Devereaux will object if you two share this greatcoat," he said, shrugging it off. "It is capacious, as you see, and warm as well."

Clarissa and Kitty had climbed in side by side. They shrugged the coat around them, and the curricle began moving again.

Kitty was still struggling to come to terms with the long glance she had seen between her brother and Clarissa. A blinding new idea came to her, for it was clear even in the moonlight that Cupid's darts had gone in both directions, and furthermore, if she hazarded a guess, this was not Cupid's first visit.

What could she do?

Nothing. They were both proud, and private, and though Clarissa had rid herself of her entanglement, her brother was still bound to Lucretia. *Do not force him to choose between you*, Clarissa had said. Kitty wondered if this statement was also true for the both of *them*. She wanted to speak — oh, how badly! — but she could see that it would be a mistake.

And so she gazed determinedly out at the countryside, over which the moonlight cast a mysterious silvery glow.

Clarissa was, for once, too stunned to think. She clutched at her side of the greatcoat, the fabric under her hand heavy and a little rough. It was a thick garment, but not too thick to entirely mask the sensations of the marquess wedged against her side. She had huddled into the warmth that the marquess had made, and fancied that his warmth, and not her own, enveloped her still; she wished they might never reach London, that they could travel like this, on and on, forever.

She was aware of the deep fremitus of his voice before she heard the words, and when she recognized them, her nerves thrilled.

"...and I have felt
A presence that disturbs me with joy
Of elevated thoughts; a sense sublime
Of something far more deeply interfused,
Whose dwelling is in the light of setting suns..."

He spoke so softly one might not have heard it over the thunder of hooves, or the creak and swing of the curricle. But she did hear it, and so she responded,

"...Therefore I am still
A Lover of the meadows and the woods,
And mountains, and of all that we behold
From this green earth..."

They traded verses, sometimes groping for words, for neither had set out to memorize it, but each had read it so many times they remembered most.

The forgotten words caused laughter, for there was no competition, no striving to impress. Kitty sat silently, smiling at the pleasure she heard in their two voices, so dear. *Why did I not see it?* she thought. And with less satisfaction, *What can be done?*

The conversation might have been taking place during a spring day's picnic, so full of hilarity and pleasure it was. Kitty took part enough so that the other two might not feel self-conscious, but by the time they reached Brook Street at last, she was troubled indeed. She had desired justice before, but now she had added reason.

The door opened as they drove up, light spilling out as Mr. Devereaux leaped down the steps to help the ladies descend. Clarissa he let go with only a polite word, but Kitty, who hesitated without being aware, her smile a little shy, her gaze full of question, he detained long enough to say, "Are you much chilled?"

"I am perfectly well. It is only rain," she said a little breathlessly, blushing as she gazed up into his face. She was only aware of her sodden hat and her hair straggling down, and not of the fine glow in her cheeks, or the sweet expression of her eyes;

she looked into his face, and did not see handsomeness, but the concern in his steady gaze, the softened mouth. Her nerves tingled.

"Then I'll wish you good night," he said, breaking the spell. "And I will also, if I may, request the honor of a dance at the masquerade ball in Cavendish Square?"

Kitty curtseyed, oblivious to the gown plastered to her form, then she sped inside, her soft "Good night," floating behind.

As St. Tarval held out the reins to Mr. Devereaux, the latter asked where he'd found them.

St. Tarval said evenly, "I found them a mile or so from the Gate. Walking, quite alone."

"I will drop you in Grosvenor Street," Mr. Devereaux offered, as St. Tarval shifted, and laid the damp driving cape over the trunk.

As soon as they reached the end of the street, Mr. Devereaux said, "By rights I should wait upon you in form, but if you will permit me a liberty—"

"By all means," the marquess said, tipping his hat, and ignoring the water that dripped off the brim.

"My request is simple: that you honor me with your permission to court your sister."

St. Tarval had not had much experience with young ladies, but he had seen that exchange on the doorstep. Remembering the happiness he had seen so plainly in his sister's face, he said everything that was proper, adding only, "If I'm not mistaken, you will not have long to wait for your answer."

Mr. Devereaux smiled and thanked him, and there the conversation ended. The marquess's own situation was too vexatious to permit him as much joy as he wished to be feeling; he found himself hoping that Kit's path would be less torturous than his own.

They turned into Grosvenor Street, and Mr. Devereaux let the marquess down before his house. He then drove around to his stable, appreciating the fact that his horses were no worse for wear. The marquess was indeed an excellent driver.

Mr. Devereaux had, in the course of waiting, gleaned some odd details from his sister's chatter, determining him upon a course of action by the time the marquess returned with the missing ladies.

He was methodical in his actions, and he had had plenty of time to reflect. He was invited to most events in town, few of which he chose to attend. But that night he surprised his hostess by arriving at a soiree at which poetry was read.

Almost immediately he spotted a familiar blond head framed by absurdly high shirt-points. Mr. Devereaux took a seat, and gave every evidence of enjoying the poetic offerings, clapping idly after each. When all had taken their turn, the party broke up for refreshments. Mr. Devereaux contrived to fall into conversation with Mr. Aston, guiding the conversation through the storm to the day's outing.

He discovered two things: that Mr. Aston had indeed been at the picnic, but he and his friend Mr. Nolan had driven away when the rain hit, there only being room for two in his curricle. As they were first to depart, he had not seen the others, but he drew a vivid picture of a mass exodus as the storm struck.

"Redding only had a gig, though anyone could have told him we'd run into weather," Mr. Aston said.

"Redding," Mr. Devereaux repeated, remembering what he had witnessed at the Castlereaghs' ball.

"Old friend of Sir Henry's, I understand. 't any rate, Miss Bouldeston had invited him especially."

"I trust the gentleman did not take a chill," Mr. Devereaux said only, departing soon after.

Thirty-three

THE NEXT MORNING, MR. DEVEREAUX strolled around to visit his old friend Sir George Buckley, whose breakfasts were justly famed. There he found a number of old friends, for people had the habit of dropping in to share pastry and gossip.

Lady Buckley, as always, practiced her wit upon the foibles of their fellows, to the appreciation of all gathered there. Many names were mentioned as recent gossip was told over, but Mr. Redding's was not among them, nor were those of Miss Clarissa Harlowe or Lady Catherine Decourcey.

Mr. Devereaux departed, satisfied that whatever had occurred — or to put it with a higher probability — *did not occur* was not going to be noised about, and so his wish to drive himself to Redding's lodging and choke the life out of him must give way.

In Brook Street, there was far less satisfaction. While Bess Devereaux wrote indignant letters to her particular friends, dispatching them by the footmen in relay, the disastrous picnic was forgotten by the Harlowes in the face of Amelia's storm of tears. She refused to come down to breakfast — refused to come out of her room — was threatening to stay there forever.

When Clarissa and Kitty came down at last and asked what

was amiss, Eliza rolled her eyes skyward. "She and *Charlie-says* disagreed."

Clarissa exchanged a startled look with her step-mother, who sighed. "I had better go speak to Lady Badgerwood," she murmured. "I thought those two were making a match of it."

"Never believed Amelia would make a parson's wife," Lord Chadwick said as he walked to the sideboard to load his plate.

"Let me speak to her," Clarissa said.

"I'm afraid if she does not attend the masquerade it will cause talk," Lady Chadwick said. "This is going to be the event of the season."

Clarissa went upstairs, and scratched on the door.

"Go away!" came the tearful voice.

"It is I," Clarissa said.

There was no answer, but a few moments later the key turned in the lock.

Clarissa walked in as Amelia flung herself back into her bed, her tear-streaked face distraught.

"What happened, dear?" Clarissa said, sitting down on the side of the bed.

"It was last night. We were at the Athertons' for dinner, and after, Melissa wanted to read from *Delphine*, which had arrived that morning, straight from France. But no one wanted to listen to her reading in French, and you know I don't really understand but a few words, so I suggested we read *Tempest*, for I had more good things to say, from Lady Kitty. We began, and it was all very fine, but then Charlie asked me what *I* thought."

"He was not listening before? I don't understand."

Amelia stirred, plucking at the sheets. "He asked what I thought, instead of what you thought, or Lady Catherine thought, or Miss Gill thought. I said I told him what I thought, and he took the seat next to mine, and said, *Amelia, it seems you are bringing clever things to say from everyone's minds but your own. What am I to make of that? What did I say or do that caused you to think I want to hear this wealth of literary insight from your friends?* Amelia sniffed. "He sounded so sad, too, as if I had done something wrong!"

"You had not," Clarissa said. "Unless you were presenting everyone's ideas as yours."

"But they *were* mine! That is, when you — Lady Kitty — even Mr. Devereaux, once, when you all explained, I agreed! And so those thoughts were now mine." She choked on a sob, and reached for her handkerchief.

Clarissa picked it up from the bedside table and handed it to her.

Amelia wiped her eyes. "I told him I did it all for him — and I do — and he said... Charlie, that is, *Mr. DuLac*, the evil beast, said that he would do anything for me, and I said, then you may offer me a ring. I said I would love nothing more than to announce our impending marriage to my friends at the masquerade ball. For we were alone in the room right then, the others having gone off somewhere else. He *dared* to say he liked me very well, but he had no thought of marriage right away, he thought I understood that, and if I truly liked him as much as he liked me, then he hoped I might consider waiting until I am twenty, but he would quite understand if I did not wish to consider myself bound so young. *Twenty!*"

She wailed the last word, then collapsed on her pillow, sobbing. Clarissa rubbed her back, trying not to smile; the urge was more bitter than sweet.

Amelia gasped and turned over, glaring. "I told him he was a heartless, selfish coxcomb, and I never wanted to see him again, and I ran back home. You were already asleep by then," she added tearfully. Then she scowled. "And so I do *not* want to go to this masquerade though maybe I *should*, because Mary Yallonde thought my Queen of Hearts gown was Marie Antoinette on the way to the tumbril, and I would very much like to be Marie Antoinette, I might even tie a red ribbon round my neck. Except even if I do, what will that avail if I see Charlie — *Mr. DuLac* — making up to Mary Yallonde, or Jane Pembroke, or anyone else? And what avail if everyone I know, including that stupid Lucasta Bouldeston, will be announcing their engagement before we all go home for summer?"

Clarissa had shuddered at the idea of the red ribbon, but she forbore to speak about it. "You must do what you think best," she said. "For you are a grown lady now."

Amelia made a gesture of repudiation, but the words, simple

as they were, did have an effect. She sat up, sniffing. "What would you do?"

Clarissa's smile was rueful. "I would go on as if nothing happened. I would permit no man to see how much I suffered. If he is truly a coxcomb, he would enjoy seeing how much power he has over you, but if he is not, he would be hurt."

"I *want* him to be hurt."

"Do you really?"

"It is so horrid, Clarissa, you *cannot* conceive. Waiting until I am twenty? Why so *old?* Mama was scarcely eighteen when she married Papa, and Hetty was exactly my age!"

"But Hetty had known Lord Badgerwood forever, and Mama was luckier than many. In truth, I think two years of waiting a very good thing, for it gives you time to think it over."

"I *did* think it over. For weeks!"

"Here is another thing that you might not have considered. A woman must be absolutely certain she wishes to become wife to a clergyman. The wrong wife—an unhappy wife—can ruin his life in a way that the wife of a general, or admiral, or a lawyer cannot. She also leads the parish, in a way that the general's wife cannot lead the army, or a lawyer's wife cannot go into court. Think of Mrs. Matthews at home in Hampshire, always the first in sick-rooms, and teaching school to the orphans, and carrying baskets of food when one of the village wives lies in childbed."

Amelia's face changed. "But she's old."

"She began those very tasks as a young wife, I can promise you." Clarissa leaned down and kissed Amelia's hot forehead. "I'll send your maid in with a tray, shall I?"

Amelia agreed in a muted voice, and Clarissa whisked herself out.

Lucasta Bouldeston dropped her gaze to her hands, pretending a modesty she didn't feel as Mr. Aston shook his head—or tried to, for his ridiculous shirt points kept his head from moving very far. "I know it doesn't do to laugh, but really, Lucasta, how could your sister be so remiss as to leave a couple of ladies standing in the rain? Not one, but two?"

Mr. Aston ventured a glance at Lucasta, whose scowl surprised him. Hitherto she was all smiles and complaisance, whatever he said, and he had consequently formed the impression of a young lady as biddable as she was devoted to the arts.

He said hastily, "Not that I think it at all humorous, your part in the rumor. Well am I aware of the particulars of domestic intercourse in this household, that you seldom get the ordering of things, that your tender heart and sweet sensibilities are not as regarded as should be their due."

Lucasta smiled again, for she agreed most heartily.

"And so I exerted myself, with your image foremost in mind, to express my disapprobation to Nolan. I encouraged him to defend *your* good name, as Mrs. Aston to be, if he heard people talking."

Lucasta bit her under-lip. Mrs. Aston to be! *There* were words to cause reflection. As a wife, she would be free of forever following in Lucretia's shadow. She would even take the precedence of her, at least until Lucretia married Carlisle. As a wife she would have better things to do than sit there smiling with her fine sewing as she listened to long, boring poems. She would have her own carriage, and perhaps even her own house in town.

And so she returned a soft answer, pressed Mr. Aston's hand, thanked him for waiting upon them, and fondly returned his adieu when he said he would see her that evening at the masquerade.

But the moment he was gone, she stalked into the breakfast room, and looked around. "We're not going out calling anymore, are we?"

"No one is at home, it seems," said Lady Bouldeston, who had gone to fetch the card tray from the hall. From the looks of it, only a single caller had come while they were out, besides Mr. Aston, who had been waiting for their return. Lady Bouldeston tapped the card on her other palm as she said, "Either everyone is getting ready for the masquerade, or pretending they are, no doubt, if they were not invited."

"Has your poet got you in a pucker?" Lucretia tittered.

Lucasta stuck her hands on her hips. "He informed me that my sister has now made us a laughingstock all over the city."

"Oh, Lucasta, it is too early for your dramatics," Lady Bouldeston said wearily, until she observed Lucretia's scarlet face. Irritation caused her to fling the pasteboard card down onto the tray. "What's this?" she demanded. "Has this something to do with our being denied at three houses this morning?"

"I *told* you that Lucretia flung us into the barouche on top of one another, so that I was choking with half a chicken tumbled all over my gown, and a hamper knocking Cassie unmercifully. And I *told* you that I did not see Catherine, or for that matter, Miss Harlowe, but Lucretia said that everything was fine — that she thought Miss Harlowe was on the box with Williams, with her umbrella."

"I thought she *was*," Lucretia said, daubing at her eyes with her handkerchief. "She got out of the barouche, and what else would she do but climb up on the box with us all willy-nilly inside?"

"I cannot believe," Lady Bouldeston stated, her eyes narrowing as she gazed at her eldest daughter, "that Miss Harlowe would ever climb atop a carriage. Where are your wits gone begging, my girl?"

"And the consequence is," Lucasta stated triumphantly, "we left *both* Catherine and Miss Harlowe standing in the rain, and Mr. Aston says it has got all over town, and we are now become the jest of the city. And it is all *her fault!*" She pointed at her sister.

Lady Bouldeston glared. "Lucretia, is this true?"

"I thought—"

"It does not matter what you thought. You did not have the wit to turn back the moment you were uncertain you had everyone safe? Who else was to do it? You insisted that you must do everything — that this was to be your treat, in honor of your cousin. What must Cassandra be saying this very moment to my sister, I shudder to contemplate. This is very ill done, very. We had better go, *all* of us, to Brook Street at once, to inquire after the young ladies, and to offer our apologies."

"But of course they got home perfectly safe, or we would have heard something," Lucretia said, bitterly disappointed. Mr. Redding must have failed to take her hints and drove home alone, or Mr. Aston would have brought the delicious gossip that she had been waiting for. Men were such blockheads!

"That may be," her mother answered, "but the fact remains that you are in the wrong. I would not have had this happen for the world. We are going to call in Brook Street."

An hour later, they arrived, dressed in their best town gowns.

At that moment Clarissa was upstairs with Amelia, or she would have felt it her duty to take the call. Kitty, upon seeing the callers through the parlor window, fled to her room, saying she felt unwell. She could not bear to face Lucretia, not after that horrid experience with Mr. Redding. Bess remained with the younger girls, who wondered why the Bouldestons would be calling. Only Bess smiled grimly to herself.

Lady Chadwick said to Pobrick, "Tell them that we are not at home."

Pobrick carried the message to the doorstep, and repeated it.

Lady Bouldeston flushed, knowing very well what must be the truth. She left her card, spoke her compliments and apology, and bundled the girls back into the barouche.

As soon as they were in motion, she said, "We cannot help what is said in town, but we can at least mitigate the rumor. You are going to write letters of apology, and we will see them dispatched before we do anything else. And I think you had better stay home from the masquerade ball."

"Oh no I will *not*," Lucretia declared. That would be a disaster! Her beautiful gown—all her plans! At her mother's angry look, she said, "It is high exaggeration on Lucasta's part to say that we are the jest of the town, merely because a couple of ladies were left in the rain. Clearly they obtained a ride with one of the many carriages we saw going in and out, and are nothing the worse for wear, or as you say, there would have been messages. No one cares a whit about a bit of rain. We have all been caught, and nothing is made of it."

"Mr. Aston said—"

"Mr. Aston, Mr. Aston," Lucretia mimicked. "I am sick of the name. He makes a great dust out of nothing, you know he does. He thinks it poesy."

Lady Bouldeston's lip curled, and Lucasta flushed.

Lucretia said coaxingly, "This masquerade ball is important. It means we have made our entry into the best circles. You know it is true, Mama. We are invited where we have not gained entry for four years, and we have spent a great deal on our gowns."

Lady Bouldeston considered the justice of this remark, and so she gave in, saying only, "Then tonight you will be a model of good-breeding, so that everyone will forget whatever they have heard, or at most will regard it as exaggeration."

Lucretia rolled her eyes, but agreed.

Lady Bouldeston said musingly, "This might explain why St. Tarval has called twice since yesterday. Perhaps it is just as well that we were away from home both times. You had better send him a letter of apology before he calls again. I'm convinced that even his good-nature will not tolerate what appears to be an insult to his sister in your carelessness."

Lucretia writhed with impatience, but she had no intention of losing one prospective husband until she had secured to herself a better. "I will do that the moment we get home," Lucretia said submissively.

Thirty-four

DEAREST MISS HARLOWE:

I must write to Apologize with all my Heart for being so remiss yesterday. I can assure you I Believed that you were safely upon the box with your umbrella, as the Exigencies of the Weather forced us into haste and discomfort.

I assure you that I was most Grieved to discover your umbrella brought in by the maid, which caused us great wonder, but such was the uproar over my Cousin's arriving wet and unhappy, and my Sister making a great Noise and Bustle over the rain, and then we must prepare to go to Fenton's Hotel to meet my Cousin's family, that it quite went out of my poor head to inquire until this morning.

Chill, I am forced to Confess, is my greatest Enemy, as my health is sadly delicate. We were forced to remain for ages at Fenton's Hotel, and this morning we were also out, and such was our own distress that we quite forgot Your's. I beg your pardon most earnestly, and throw myself on the Mercy of that Nearer Connection I live every day in Anticipation of claiming, once I am married,

and have made our own dear Catherine my most beloved
of Sisters.

Your fondest admirer, Lucretia Bouldeston.

Clarissa forced herself to read it through. So vexatious did she
find the patent falsity in these words that she took the note to the
parlor and handed it to her step-mother, saying, "Need I answer?"

Lady Chadwick ran her eyes down the note, then handed it
back. "You needn't unless you wish to continue the acquaintance.
A curtsey and a polite word next time you see them will suffice."

Clarissa took the letter back upstairs, threw it onto the hearth,
and burned it. She did not ask what Kitty did with hers.

Several hours later, when the family began gathering below in
all their finery, Amelia was seen on the stair, her demeanor far
more like Marie Antoinette than the Queen of Hearts, but at least
there was no ribbon around her neck.

The entire family joined in praise of her costume, a pretty
wide-skirted *robe à la française* in green and peach, with silver lace
sleeves *engageantes*. Her bright golden hair was piled high, with a
headdress of lace.

Clarissa smiled as she complimented her. She had chosen to go
as Diana, in a pearl gray tunic over a gown of soft blue, her
sandals silver. James was costumed as a silk-and-lace dressed Dick
Turpin, complete to jeweled mask. Lady Chadwick followed the
daring fashion brought over by the Duchess of Devonshire,
favoring a filmy gown clasped by cameos at the shoulders, a
Grecian outline that had never actually been seen in Greece, but
made all the rage by Josephine Bonaparte. Lord Chadwick had
resorted to a black domino, but this poor-spirited effort was at
least lined in red, to his children's satisfaction.

Eliza and Bess exchanged longing comments about how much
they wished they could attend—the next season could not come
too soon—but then everyone fell silent as Kitty came down the
stairs, a vision all in white.

Lord Chadwick forgot himself long enough to give a low
whistle as Kitty descended with floating step. Her under dress of
white satin was revealed under a brocade over dress draped *à la*

polonaise, with rich white lace at neck, sleeves, and along the edges of the over dress. The stiff bodice glittered with diamante insets in the brocade flourishes. The pure white drew attention to her green eyes, vivid complexion, and her high-piled curling black hair, with two curls coaxed down to a sloping shoulder. The headdress was made up of pearls and lace, with high-standing two white plumes, and a single diamante set over one ear.

The crowning touch was a glittering necklace with three great pendants sparkling at every flicker of the candles overhead.

"I am going as my mother," Kitty said shyly, self-conscious before all those staring eyes. "It was her gown, when she was presented to the Queen of France."

"Upon my word," Lady Chadwick exclaimed. "They said your mother was a Diamond, but she cannot have been more beautiful than you, Lady Catherine."

"That will be one in old Carlisle's eye," Lord Chadwick exclaimed.

Kitty blushed. "Oh, but they will not know. See? I have a silk mask, and I mean to be announced as the mysterious marquise."

"That is very thoughtfully done, my dear," Lady Chadwick said. "Come, the carriage is waiting."

Bess Devereaux backed away, her hands clasped. "Oh, now I *truly* wish I were going," she said. "It is so *unfair* that I cannot!"

"Next year will be here all too soon," Lady Chadwick murmured.

Clarissa fell in step with Kitty, saying, "Do you have panniers under that skirt? It is so very wide, yet it falls gracefully, and my grandmother said that panniers had a tendency to swing like a bell if you did not walk carefully."

"I have on *four* petticoats," Kitty whispered. "You should see the stitchwork on them. I could almost wear them into the street."

"Are those real diamonds?" Clarissa asked.

"Paste," Kitty admitted cheerfully. "Papa sold off the true diamonds before I was born. But these paste ones were made exactly like the necklace. I thought they would do for this masquerade."

"They're splendid. Precisely the right touch."

As they followed the rest into the carriage, Kitty's fan shimmered, and she whispered in a lower voice, "I hope and trust that Mr. Redding has said nothing. It would be so very horrid to arrive and discover that I am become a disgrace."

"I very much doubt it will happen," Clarissa returned. "But even if he did, my grandmother would have something to say to any gossip, you may be certain. There will be no scenes of public spurning, like your villainous Count Scorbini contrived for poor Andromeda."

Kitty smiled, but it was a politeness. She was not ready to admit that the night before, after facing the realization that there was not a single word of truth in the whole of it, she had consigned Andromeda and her many abductions to the fire.

Conversation was minimal as the carriage joined the long line leading to Cavendish Square.

Even Amelia, sunk in gloom hitherto, was become impatient by the time they were finally let out, link boys and postilions calling to one another like hoarsened crows as the stream of traffic was routed past. Kitty and the Harlowes slipped on their masks and then followed the stream of guests into the brilliantly lit house.

Kitty had to blink several times before she could take in the dazzle of the great chandeliers, all lit, and the wings of the grand staircase made of peach marble, that framed the great carved doors leading to the ballroom.

Inside was a blaze of color as people in fantastical clothing admired and guessed one another's identities. Kitty nervously touched her own mask, discovering that others' masks did little to disguise those people she knew. They merely rendered it nearly impossible to distinguish strangers from acquaintance.

A Prince Florizel in blue satin appeared, and Lord Arden's voice was heard as he bowed grandly over Kitty's hand. "Your majesty," he declared.

"Her majesty is here," Kitty said, indicating the Queen of Hearts.

Prince Florizel promptly saluted this lady's hand, but he returned to Kitty's side, murmuring, "If a cousin is permitted a personal observation, you are the belle of the evening."

Kitty laughed, thanked him, and passed on by, well knowing that the masquerade was in honor of one of Clarissa's many cousins, visiting from Holland. This young lady, a serious person who thought mainly of her horses, was apparently destined to marry a German prince. She wore an expensive gown of tiered silk as Queen Titania, leading the first dance with one of the royal dukes. Clarissa's uncle the Duke of Norcaster followed, a stout figure stately in his Faustian robes, leading out Lady Castlereagh.

Many of the most famous beauties of London were there, in more or less guise—Ladies Ann Lambton, William Russell, Elizabeth Lambert—but among them Kitty could take her place as the partner of Lord Robert Manners, whom the duchess brought forth for an introduction. Mr. Devereaux, instantly recognizable in a satin, full-skirted coat and white wig, to please his grandmother, partnered Lady Louisa Stuart, dressed as the poet Sappho, with whom he conversed about literature with the ease of long acquaintance.

Such was the sight that met St. Tarval's eyes when he arrived at last. He had intended to wear a simple domino, but this his brother refused to countenance. Though Ned sustained little interest in flirtation, he loved an excuse for fancy dress, and therefore he had extended Kitty's idea of using her mother's clothing to that of their father. But looking over clothing in a dim attic turned out to be a different matter when said clothing was brought out of its trunk that morning, and examined in the light of day. Consequently poor Kirby, who of necessity waited upon both brothers, had spent the main of the day brushing and repairing the fine brocade.

St. Tarval had used that time to call twice upon Lucretia, to be denied both times. When he'd returned home he found a silly letter from Lucretia, full of excuses—the rain, her sister, her cousin—that sufficed to increase his ire.

So his mood was uncertain when he arrived in Cavendish Square. He longed to go home to St. Tarval. He fretted under the constraints of an engagement that was predicated upon entirely false circumstances, and he found the lace and satin irksome, though he did admit that he and Ned made a dashing pair. His mood improved slightly when he saw Kitty looking so beautiful, dancing among the leading lights of society.

As the crowd shifted, they found themselves before their

hostess, an elderly lady dressed in the same French fashion that they wore.

The duchess had been waiting impatiently for days to meet this elusive marquess at last. She knew it was foolish to be pleased with his taste in dress—that he appeared in the fashions of her day could only be accident—but eyes were eyes, and he looked as handsome as his father, perhaps the moreso because his hazel gaze was not roving, but steady, as he flourished the lace at his wrist and made an excellent leg.

She shook his hand, nodded at the younger brother, and said, "The card room is that way, my boy." She then tapped her quizzing glass on the arm of her chair, and said, "Bide with me a moment, St. Tarval. You have a look of your father."

He bowed again.

"And your maternal grandmother."

"My grandmother?" He betrayed a little surprise at this unusual form of address, but responded readily enough. "Yes, I'd heard that from my paternal grandmother, but only in the form of a judgment."

"Lady St. Tarval was almost as big a fool as old Carlisle," the duchess stated. "Your maternal grandmother was an exceptional woman, as beautiful as she was witty. She should never have been made to marry a man more than twice her age. But that is not what I wanted to say to you. Have you a *tendre* for my granddaughter?"

The abrupt address considerably startled St. Tarval. He stood very still, not certain what to say. Politeness would require a lie, and he could not bring himself to utter it.

The duchess said, "That is answer enough. I wanted to see for myself if it was a *tendre*, or an interest in her dowry."

St. Tarval flushed. "I am not free to—"

"Tchah," the duchess stated.

The marquess reddened a little, but resumed steadily. "Even if I were free, as far as I am concerned, anything of that sort would be tied up for future generations."

"High-and-mighty, sir. High-and-mighty. So you do not know the extent of it?"

"I do not. I never have thought of inquiring."

"I would have known if you had," she retorted, patting his

hand. "But I'll tell you, for she does not actually know the extent of it herself. When she turns five-and-twenty later this year, she will inherit twenty thousand a year."

Two hundred thousand pounds. The shock was like ice through his nerves.

The duchess was watching closely. She saw the impact, and the quick revulsion after, then forestalled him by saying, "*Besides* what I may leave her. Just so you know. But we will converse again, once you have cleared up your affairs."

She nodded an unmistakable dismissal, and he walked away very much at random, needing time to reflect, to master himself.

But he was not to get it.

Lucretia and her family had arrived two carriages ahead of the marquess and his brother.

Lucretia's mirror had flattered her that she looked her best in a gown of pink gauze, decorated with silk roses, with real roses fitted into her headdress. Her guise was Cendrillon, the headdress fitted like a fairy crown.

They made their bows to their hostess, then Lady Bouldeston went in search of a good seat from which to see and be seen, and Sir Henry sought liquid reinforcement.

Lucretia shook off her sister and her swain, and plied her fan as she studied the guests. First to catch Mr. Devereaux's eye, and then, she simply must use her wits. If nothing else, she could contrive to get him alone, for if they were discovered together...well, gossip could sometimes reward one, if one were sharp. Carlisle could do her a fine turn at last, if he could be got to discover them. But first she had better made certain that her letter had had its intended effect. Why not do that and spark Mr. Devereaux to jealousy both?

Ah. There was St. Tarval, walking away from that ugly old dowager.

Lucretia glided up to him, took his arm and said in languishing accents, "Oh, Carlisle, I trust you are not still angry with me — my poor head —"

St. Tarval looked at her. The speciousness of those downward cast eyes, the little pout, only served to inflame his emotions to recklessness.

He knew what was due Sir Henry, his neighbor. He knew that one must not hold conversations such as these in a ballroom, but as the first dance was ending, and Lucretia had the audacity to tug him in the direction of the ballroom floor, he started abruptly the other way. Perforce she must come after.

The gallery above was supported by marble columns, between which arches disclosed little alcoves. Drawing her into the first of these, he said, "Now we can hear one another speak. You will oblige me, I trust, with an explanation, Lucretia? I refer to the fact that I had to drive out last night in search of my sister, whom I found with her friend alone in the road, very much unprotected."

Lucretia's jaw dropped. "It was *you* who..." She could not imagine how that had come about. Nor did she care beyond the necessity of retrieving the situation.

But her wits were offering no solution, and so she must take refuge in delicacy. She brought her wrist to her forehead, and swayed, saying, "I fear I am going to swoon."

Still too irritated to wait, he said, "If that is all you have to say, then I take leave to inform you, before you swoon, that I will be calling upon your father to put an end to an engagement that we never should have made."

This was a disaster! Wild with desperation, she caught the sound of approaching footsteps, and cast herself onto Carlisle's bosom. If she were seen thus, he would *have* to marry her, for she could claim that he could not rule his passions—

Then a familiar voice drawled, "Miss Bouldeston? I had come to offer you a dance, but if I intrude—"

Her eyes flew open. "*Mr. Devereaux*," she exclaimed breathlessly, pushing St. Tarval away. To make certain that Mr. Devereaux did not misunderstand, she said to the marquess, "If you must end our betrothal so cruelly, then I cannot stop you."

She turned her back on him, and cast upward her most pleading, modest countenance, the one most often practiced before her mirror. "Oh, *please* take me away from this place. Mr. Devereaux, I scarcely know how to thank you—what you must think—"

"We shall have to hurry," was all he said. What a relief! No awkward questions! "We do not want to miss the set forming now."

"Of course," Lucretia said, to demonstrate how biddable she could be, and obligingly increased her pace. She had just enough time to cast a triumphant look at her mother—and to smirk pityingly at Miss Harlowe, sitting at the wall like the dowd she was—before they joined the set.

St. Tarval stood in the alcove for a minute or two, almost dizzy with relief and question. Devereaux had appeared out of nowhere, and reacted to what anyone would have taken as a disgraceful scene as if nothing had occurred. St. Tarval was no longer certain of anything except that he had regained his freedom. Lucretia had said it herself, before a witness.

And so his steps carried him toward Miss Harlowe the way the tide carries the ship into home port. He sat down beside her, and said, "I am free."

Clarissa had seen his arrival, and how Lucretia promptly carried him off, as was her right. The fresh pain of that had barely begun to numb when she saw Lucretia reappear on the arm of Cousin Philip. She had just enough time to wonder how that had happened when here was the marquess himself, his dear face still distraught, but his lips forming into a smile of heartfelt warmth. "I'm free," he said again. And he held out his hand.

Clarissa did not care who saw, though she doubted anyone had the least interest in them. She slid her fingers into his, and gripped them tight. There would be time and more for all the explanations necessary, the *who-saids* and *who-thoughts* and *I-nevers* and then, oh, and then the *will-you*, followed by *yes-I-will*.

For now, she would sit here in this brilliant light, music pouring all around, and hold tight to the man she loved.

She was wrong about no one looking. Kitty noticed her from the ballroom floor, where she was dancing with another new acquaintance, a Lord Buckley, whose adroit comments kept her in smiles. Clarissa and the marquess were also spotted by Edward from the safety of the card room, who gloated to himself and rubbed his hands. Maybe Carlisle's good luck would bring him good luck!

Kitty got a closer look when the dance brought her near, and this time she glimpsed their clasped hands, which could only mean one thing.

Lucretia saw her pass by, and pitied Catherine being desperate enough to dance with a married man. She was disgusted to see Catherine staring at her brother, and willed her to turn around so that she might be slain by jealousy: *See who my partner is!*

"I see you are watching Lady Catherine," Mr. Devereaux observed.

An automatic answer rose to Lucretia's lips, then she remembered with an inward smile that she no longer needed to pretend anything for her *future sweet sister.* "I was looking at her mother's gown," she said. "I am certain it was very fine, thirty years ago."

"Permit me to observe," he said, "that it is very fine now."

The dance separated them, relieving her of the necessity of any politenesses on Catherine's behalf. When they came together, he said, "I desired to dance with you for it is you I have to thank."

The dance separated them again, vexing Lucretia extremely, but it gave her time to recollect the modest, graceful words she had practiced in assenting to his proposal.

But he had not quite got there yet. "Thank me?" she said, giving him a cue.

"For drawing my notice to Lady Catherine," he said, as they performed the hands across.

"To *Catherine?*" she repeated as they reversed, and stepped the other way.

"Lady Kitty, I should say," he amended. "No, I believe she will shortly give me leave to call her Kitty, a name eminently suited to her."

Coldness flooded through Lucretia.

He went on as they paced down the dance, "If it was not for your notice, I might not have discovered as early as I did how beautiful she is, how kind. How witty, and generous."

Every word was worse than the last!

"And so I wished to thank you, with all my heart, and to inform you first of all her friends, that I intend this very night to ask her to be my wife."

First was numbness, then came fury, hot and bright, but then the numbness again. It could not be real—it must be a joke. But when the dance brought them together for the last time, he said, "I trust I have your blessing?"

She forced herself to utter something—she later could not recollect what—and then the nightmare dance ended *at last,* and she made it across the ballroom to her mother's side. And for the very first time, she did not watch him to see where he went next.

Kitty thanked Lord Buckley, turned away, and there was Mr. Devereaux. Why did the sight of him instantly fill her with light?

Mr. Devereaux in his guise as a gentleman of their grandfathers' day made an old-fashioned leg. "My dance?"

"La, sir," she said, putting out her hand.

They joined the set, each smiling at the other, until they were close enough for him to say, "This is not the time or the place, but I spoke to your brother..."

The dance drew them apart. She gave him such a smile that he had to laugh when they came together again. "Who had bestowed on me his blessing."

"His blessing for?" she prompted, when they met again. She knew—for she could see it in his countenance, but she wanted to hear the words, and to say her own.

"Shall I call tomorrow, when we are not in the middle of a great crowd, me laboring under this hot wig, and you... ah, there I must end, for you are always beautiful. The more I see of you, the more impatient I am to be alone with you."

"That you may be any time you like," she said, her heart beating fast. "And as often as you like! Since my brother has given you his blessing." And because she saw the curl of smile in his lips, she knew that he had more to say, and she would always want to hear it. "You will call tomorrow for?"

He leaned forward a little as they gripped one another in the hands across, and he whispered in an intimate tone, "*Guess.*"

Her delighted crow of laughter drifted across the polished marble floor to the marquess and Clarissa, who had joined the dance.

The four smiled at one another as they hopped, twirled, and stepped in the pattern of the quadrille, watched with deep pleasure by the Duchess of Norcaster, who began to contemplate weddings.

Les Changements
de Danse

SIR HENRY THREW DOWN the letter in disgust. He supposed he could not blame the marquess, but the marriage would have been convenient. Better than convenient, for not only would he have got Lucretia off his hands, but he could have driven a hard bargain in settlements with her swain in order to make up his increasing debts.

It was time to send his wife and the girls home. The one it seemed he would never get rid of, and the other was in a fair way to being out the door. There was no necessity to keep them in London wasting money on furbelows and picnic lunches.

Greatly disgruntled, he rose, ready to issue orders to his family, when the butler knocked at his door to say that he had a caller.

While that was going on, the ladies sat in the breakfast room in silence. Lady Bouldeston was disgusted with Lucretia, who, she was convinced, was the reason their reception had been polite but distant at the brilliant affair the night previous. She was quite certain there would be no further invitations from any of those people.

Very well. It was time to go home; Lucretia had ruined her chances, and she should not be permitted to somehow ruin Lucasta's.

The latter sat mumchance over her hot chocolate, fighting yawn after yawn. Masquerade balls were all very fine, except what a crowd! Scarcely anyone had seen her gown, and as for select company, in spite of all the masks, she had danced with precisely the same people she always saw, Mr. Aston foremost. Well, at least she could write to Cassie that she had been to the Duchess of Norcaster's masquerade. That would look very fine in a letter, and in the future, she could let it fall to anyone she spoke with that she had made up one of the company.

Lucretia sat in stony silence, hating everyone, but that selfish simpleton Catherine Decourcey the most. It was her fault. *Everything* was her fault. But could Mother see that? No. All the way home from the ball they had quarreled, Mother declaring they would go home to Riverside Abbey by week's end. Not that Lucretia cared. There was nothing to stay in London for...

The ladies looked up when Sir Henry appeared. Lucretia braced for more quarreling, having recognized Carlisle's handwriting on the letter that had been waiting by his plate at breakfast.

But Father was smiling as he shut the breakfast room door. "Lucretia," he said, his voice increasing in irony on each word. "I never thought I should say this, but it seems that a young man of excellent connections and worth has called to ask permission to court you. He appreciates your birth, and appears furthermore to be laboring under the impression that you are a well-bred, modest young lady."

Crash! went Lady Bouldeston's coffee cup to the saucer. "What?"

"Who?" Lucasta asked, hoping only that he did not have a title, that she still might have precedence of her sister, for at least Mr. Aston was an Honorable.

"I gave him permission," Sir Henry added. "Unless you want to end up a spinster living on your sister's bounty, you will say 'Yes sir,' and 'When can we be wed?' Now go in there and make him the happiest of men."

Lucretia made her way to her father's book room, where she was considerably startled to recognize Lord Wilburfolde, who rose from his chair, hat in hand. Disappointment was so sharp she sank into a chair, her father's words echoing in her ears.

As the visitor reeled out his carefully prepared speech, she reflected on what she knew about him. He was not a prospective duke, but he had a title, a better one than her father's. Nor was he a leader of the *beau monde*, but that no longer mattered. Lucretia was fagged to death by those nodcocks and halfwits.

Lady Wilburfolde! Your ladyship. It sounded quite well. The worst she had ever heard concerned his mother. But if Lucretia became his wife, she was quite sure that that was a battle she could win.

When he finished his speech, she batted her eyes and gave his hopeful face her most practiced simper. "I believe you mentioned that your home is called The Castle, sir? I must confess, I have always been partial to castles..."

ABOUT BOOK VIEW CAFÉ

Book View Café Publishing Cooperative is an author-owned cooperative of over fifty professional writers, publishing in a variety of genres such as fantasy, romance, mystery, and science fiction.

BVC authors include *New York Times* and *USA Today* best-sellers; Nebula, Hugo, and Philip K. Dick Award winners; World Fantasy Award, Campbell Award, and RITA Award nominees; and winners and nominees of many other publishing awards.

Since its debut in 2008, BVC has gained a reputation for producing high-quality e-books, and is now bringing that same quality to its print editions.

Made in the USA
Las Vegas, NV
16 June 2024

91136225R00198